HEAVY LIES THE CROWN

A DAK HARPER THRILLER

RELIC RUNNER BOOK 4

ERNEST DEMPSEY

138 PUBLISHING

For all my Coffee Nation friends who show up every Sunday morning just to hang out with me for a little while. Love y'all. #coffeenation

JOIN THE ADVENTURE

Visit ernestdempsey.net to get a free copy of the not-sold-in-stores short story of *The Moldova Job,* plus six short stories that comprise *Dak Harper Origin Story*.

You'll also get access to exclusive content, private giveaways, and a chance to win signed copies.

While you're at it, swing by the official Ernest Dempsey fan page on Facebook at https://facebook.com/ErnestDempsey to join the community of travelers, adventurers, historians, and dreamers. There are exclusive contests, giveaways, and more!

Lastly, if you enjoy pictures of exotic locations, food, and travel adventures, check out my feed @ernestdempsey on the Instagram app.

What are you waiting for? Join the adventure today!

1

Dak Harper loathed being late. Especially for important meetings.

And this one was the most important of all.

He sat there in the corner of the bar; the faded paint on the walls around him seemed to crack a little more with every passing second. The uneven red clay tiles mirrored the splits and seams on the walls.

Miracle the place is still standing, he mused.

Colombia had faced its share of problems over the years. With rivers of cocaine flowing to the United States and other parts of the world for the better part of two decades, criminals and warlords had ravaged the nation. But the people of Colombia had endured, and pushed beyond all that.

The country was very different from the one Dak had visited long ago on a clandestine assignment. The drug lords that once ruled the land had been largely pushed back into the jungle shadows. He knew they still wielded most of the power, but their dominance was far from the absolute it had been. Tourism boomed, the cities had been rebuilt, and expats now occupied several key areas that had once thundered like war zones.

He checked his watch and noted the time with bitter irritation.

His contact was six minutes late. And every second that ticked by only spiked Dak's annoyance.

He'd already decided he would stick around for a total of twenty minutes before he got up and left.

Might as well have a good cup of coffee while I'm here, he thought. He picked up the white mug and took a sip of the java. Dak nodded in appreciation at the cup.

"That's good coffee," he muttered and raised the mug to the barista working the coffee maker next to rows of various liquors.

Out of habit, Dak checked his watch again and shook his head.

When he was in the military, being tardy hadn't been an option. And Dak couldn't imagine anyone from his Delta Force team ever showing up late for anything.

This ingrained sense of timing also worked in the reverse. When someone else was late for a meeting with him, it ground his nerves to their core.

He'd come to Colombia, on this occasion, in search of information—information that had been exceedingly hard to come by.

It had been over two years since the events in the Middle East had ripped away any fleeting chance he ever had at a normal life.

Those events were the reason he was here.

The last eighteen or so months had been a whirlwind. Dak had visited multiple countries in search of artifacts, or clues to find them. His employer, Boston McClaren, had been good to him, always rewarding Dak handsomely for all the trinkets he recovered.

Of course, they were more than mere trinkets. Dak had managed to locate and retrieve priceless artifacts from criminals across the world, including a pair of pistols that belonged in the National Civil War Museum in Harrisburg.

He thought back on the town of Dawsonville, North Carolina, and missed the simplicity of it. Though, here in Cartagena, things were much the same in terms of a slower pace of life. The language and customs were different, the entertainment options varied, and the food was nothing like back home in the South, but it was still the same.

People had to eat. They didn't want to be bored. They just wanted to live their lives.

With many of the conflicts of the past dying away in Colombia, Dak hoped the people here could continue to thrive and grow in what he considered a beautiful, fertile country.

He looked across the room at a couple of guys who'd been sitting there since before he arrived. They were drinking coffee but also had a few shot glasses of liquor sitting next to their mugs. The two guys looked mean, and Dak would have assumed they were part of a local gang if not for their clothes being more casual. One wore faded blue jeans. The other, brown trousers.

They weren't here on a work break, not from any job Dak knew of, and they were too old to be college students, though only by a couple of years at most. He wouldn't have thought much of the two if they hadn't been staring him down like a duck in a goose pond.

Two more men sat at the corner in the back to the left of the other two. They didn't appear to be together, but they were also looking at Dak in much the same way, as if keeping an eye on him.

He wanted to assume it was because he was an American, a foreigner hanging out in a local bar in Cartagena, but he had the feeling that wasn't the case.

And with every passing second, he worried more and more they weren't here for the coffee.

Dak swallowed another sip. As he set down his cup, the front door creaked open and a man in a dirty tank top and olive-green pants walked in. His dirty, brown leather boots clopped on the tile floor, and for a second, the bright light of day poured into the room, causing everyone inside to flinch.

Then the door closed itself, and the bar returned to the dim lighting it had enjoyed before.

The man looked over at Dak and grinned, tilting his head back.

He secured an army-green backpack against his left shoulder and walked over, moving with a goofy gait. "There you are," he said and sat down.

"Here I've been," Dak replied coolly but with a dash of petulance.

His contact set the backpack on the floor next to the chair across from Dak before sitting. "Hey, I got slowed down on the way here. Not my fault if traffic was heavier than usual."

Dak noted the men at the other tables paying close attention to their conversation. It seemed as if now they were even more interested than before.

"What traffic, Scully? There's no traffic here. Unless you count pedestrians. And we both know you drive a motorcycle, so even if there were a bunch of cars on the road, you'd get through it just fine."

Scully raised a skinny finger to make a counterpoint, then thought better of it. "Fine. I don't suppose you'd believe me if I said I stopped to get a cup of coffee?"

He peered hopefully at Dak with bright blue eyes. His short, dirty blond hair was tucked up under a trucker cap with a dark brown front and a lighter brown mesh portion on the back two-thirds.

"Because you don't like the coffee at this place?" Dak taunted.

"Maybe. Maybe I don't like it."

Dak raised his mug and looked at it for a second before taking a long swig. "Seems pretty good to me. Actually, this might be the best cup of joe I've had in a year."

"I feel bad for you. Coffee is religion here."

"I thought that was most places."

"I suppose." Scully looked around the room and nodded at the bartender to get her attention.

She acknowledged with a lazy smile and made her way over to the table to take his order.

"I'll have what he's drinking," Scully said in flawless Spanish.

The young woman smiled and walked back to the bar to pour a cup for him.

"Your Spanish has gotten pretty good," Dak noticed.

"Well, you live here long enough, you pick up a thing or two."

"I guess so." Dak looked across the room at the men in the corner. "Those guys friends of yours?"

Scully started to turn his head, but Dak stopped him. "Don't look right now," he warned.

Scully froze and then slowly returned his focus to Dak. "No. I don't know them."

"Well, they certainly seem interested in me. And got more interested when you showed up."

Dak's contact swallowed hard.

The barista-bartender brought Scully's coffee over and set it on the table. "Would you like anything else?" she asked.

"No, thank you. Not right now."

She gave another smile and returned to the bar to continue cleaning things that had probably been cleaned fifty times so far that day.

"Don't worry about them right now," Dak said, refocusing on the subject at hand, and the reason for his visit to Colombia. "Did you find him?"

Scully kept twisting his head back toward the men in the far corner at the rear of the room, almost like it was being pulled by a magnet.

"Stop. Looking. At them," Dak said. "They aren't your concern. They're mine."

"They're your concern?" Scully stuttered.

"Yes. If they want trouble, they can have it with me." Dak leaned forward. "I need you to focus on me. Not them. They aren't your concern."

Scully forced himself to stay locked on Dak.

"Good," Dak approved. "Now, tell me." He leaned forward, putting his weight on his elbows. He kept his voice low, conspiratorial. "Did you find him?"

Scully started to look back around the room again but resisted the urge. He licked his lips and tightened the cap down lower on his head.

"Look, he's not here. Okay? I asked around. And you know me. I know people."

Dak nodded. "That's why I'm sitting here with you and not someone else."

"Yeah, well, you're out of luck on this one. I heard he was here, but he ain't no more."

Scully's Brooklyn accent hadn't faded at all despite living here in Colombia for more than a decade. Dak had known him long enough to hate him but not long enough to cast Scully to the sharks just yet.

He'd never betrayed Dak, not that he knew of, and that went a long way in his book. *My how standards have fallen,* Dak thought.

"I hope I didn't come all this way just for you to tell me he isn't here. That could have been a text message."

Scully smiled wryly. "We both know you trust cell phones about as much as you do governments."

"Where is he, Scully?" Dak pressed, cutting through the bull. "Where is Colonel Tucker?"

The mere mention of the name seemed to suck the air out of the room. Dak had spoken quietly, so low that he didn't think anyone but Scully would hear, but perhaps he'd miscalculated the volume of his voice.

Scully looked around, concern covering his face in a pale veil. "He isn't here," Scully repeated. "Okay?"

"Where is he?"

"He skipped town two days ago. I heard he doesn't hang out in any one place for very long."

"Where did he go, Scully? I have to find him."

"Why not just let bygones be bygones? Huh? What's with this quest for revenge you're so hung up on? I heard about what happened to your team, by the way. Every one of them died or disappeared."

"Don't play your old NSA games with me," Dak warned.

Scully had worked for the NSA once upon a time. But he had run afoul of their protocols and systems when he discovered some documents he wasn't supposed to find.

Now he was living underground, just like Dak.

The big difference was, Scully was overly paranoid, and probably not under any dire threat. Dak, on the other hand, was a wanted man.

"This isn't about revenge," Dak said. And he meant it. Mostly. "As long as Tucker is out there, I'll never be safe. And neither will Nikki."

"Oh, you and her are still—"

"No. We're not. But I have to make sure she's safe."

"Where is she now?"

Dak replied with a look that could have killed an ox.

"Oh right. Somewhere safe and unknown, I assume. Smart. Keep her hidden."

"That's the plan. Now, where would a man like Tucker go? And why did he come here to Cartagena?"

Scully leaned forward, and Dak noticed the men in the corners stiffen.

"He came here to find a hitter."

Dak's eyebrows flicked up for a second. "He went to a nest?"

Scully nodded, the serious look on his face reinforcing what that meant.

Dak had suspected Tucker was using mercenaries in the worldwide network of guild houses called "nests."

They were places people with money and an agenda could go to hire some armed help. Most of the time, these nests were full of ex-military from all over the world—each one of them having their own demons and skeletons haunting them, pushing them to a life of murder for hire. If not killing, these types were game for babysitting jobs too, but everyone knew why they were really there.

You didn't go to a nest looking for work because you were going to babysit. You went because someone wanted someone else to die, and was willing to pay good money for it.

Dak had known about the mercenary nests since his time in the military. The guys from his team often joked about going into that world once they were done with the army. Dak had never seen the appeal. Once he was done working for Uncle Sam, he didn't plan on going right back into the fight for someone else.

"Yeah," Scully said. He sounded forlorn and looked down at the table. "He really wants you dead, huh?"

"You could say that. I ruined his long, distinguished military career."

"It wasn't that distinguished. And besides, based on what I heard, he got what he deserved. Tried to cover up everything that happened with you and your team over there. And he got caught. Serves him right."

"Except he didn't get served right. They let him off with a slap on the wrist. He'll get his full retirement package, commendations, medals, all of it. But I'm not trying to right a wrong by looking for him, Scully. This isn't about revenge."

Scully met Dak's gaze and saw the truth in his eyes. "Okay, Dak. I believe you. I'm sorry. I wish I had better news, but Tucker's gone. And I have no idea where he went."

"This nest. It's here in Cartagena?"

"Yes," Scully nodded. "But you know you can't—"

"I can get in," Dak interrupted. "That isn't a problem."

"You have to—"

"Have a referral from a known member in their database. Yes. I know. Or an invitation."

"And you don't have those things," Scully informed him.

"Actually, I do. Like I said, getting in isn't a problem. It's getting out."

The two men in the back corner stood up, their eyes fixed on Dak and his counterpart.

"How are you—"

"Don't look now. We have company," Dak said, cutting him off.

2

Scully disobeyed and turned around in time to find the four men from the corners now surrounding the table.

"Hello," he muttered in Spanish.

Dak rolled his eyes. "I said not to look." He directed his next words, in English, to the four men. "You boys need something?"

The biggest one, a guy who looked like a Colombian linebacker, nodded. "You must be Dak Harper," he said in a thick accent. His voice was the deepest baritone Dak had ever heard.

"No one must be anything. Except human," Dak countered.

The man's forehead tightened, and Dak could tell he didn't understand the retort.

"Sorry. Philosophical joke," Dak said. "Maybe this isn't the place."

"You shouldn't have come here," the grunt warned.

"Yeah?" Dak looked down at the coffee on the table and nodded. "I like this place." His eyes wandered around the room. "It has a good feel to it. You know? A chill vibe."

The leader didn't say anything. He merely stared down at Dak, ready to devour him.

"You know what . . . ?" Scully said, standing.

The man to the leader's right put one hand on Scully's bony shoulder and forced him back down into his seat.

"Never mind."

"You came looking for trouble," the leader went on.

"Actually," Dak said, standing up and flattening his gray button-up shirt. "I came looking for Tucker. Now, if you four boys know anything about where he might be, I'd be mighty obliged to you for sharing."

The four men chuckled derisively.

The leader looked at the one to his left and smiled, pointing at Dak as he spoke. "He's trying to make a deal so we don't kill him. Spineless Americans."

"No," Dak corrected. "I wasn't trying to make a deal with you. There was no offer on the table." His face darkened, and he felt battle energy ripping through his veins.

"Doesn't matter. We already made our deal. The man you're looking for paid us a lot of money to kill you. And we intend to see our end through."

"Ah," Dak said, nodding. "Probably one of those things where you get half the money up front then the other half upon receipt of proof?"

"Something like that."

"Was I part of this deal you guys made?" Scully injected. "Because I don't see how I have anything to—"

"Shut up," the leader barked.

Dak noticed the girl behind the counter slink back into the kitchen. *Good,* he thought. He didn't want her getting hurt, and he wasn't sure if this was going to turn to weapons, or if they were just going to beat the crap out of each other.

"Since you're into deals," Dak said, "I'll offer you one. Leave this place, and the two of us to our business, and be on your way."

The leader looked confused and ran meaty fingers over his nearly-shaved head. "Doesn't sound like much of a deal."

"The other one pays better," the guy to the right remarked.

"Oh, there's excellent pay," Dak argued. "You see, if you leave here, I let you keep breathing. You know, the air?" He looked around as if he could see it everywhere, mocking the four men before him.

"Doesn't sound like much of a—"

"I'm not finished," Dak said, being rude on purpose now. "If you leave right now, you may even be able to eat regular food for the foreseeable future. But if you stay, well"—he shrugged and tilted his head to the side—"no guarantees."

"My friend here doesn't necessarily represent me," Scully protested. "If it's just the same to you guys, I'd like to make my own arrangements."

"Shut up," the leader said to Scully, never taking his eyes off Dak. "Have it your way. We weren't getting paid to bring you in alive."

He took one step toward Dak, narrowing the distance between them to only three feet. The man didn't realize he'd just entered a very dangerous place.

Within arm's reach, Dak was a deadly fighter, and had won both himself and his buddies quite a bit of money over the years boxing in the barracks—when the COs didn't know about it. Then again, Dak figured they'd known about the fights. Heck, they'd probably encouraged them.

"This is about me and Tucker," Dak said, snapping back to the leader. "None of you has to get hurt today. Go back to the nest and find another job. Plenty of baddies out there who need to get their comeuppance."

"We've been well paid to kill you." The leader tilted his chin up, as if assessing Dak. "But if you can pay us more, maybe we let you live."

That wasn't the first time Dak had heard of his old superior spending reckless amounts of money. But it was the first time he'd heard of a merc from the network offering to let a mark live in exchange for more money than he'd already been paid.

Where was he getting all that scratch? That was a question for another time. Dak knew the colonel hadn't accumulated all that wealth in the military, not from his base salary anyway. He must have been skimming off the top somewhere else. Or he may have been running some kind of underground operation the entire time, accumulating huge amounts of money he kept hidden from the feds.

Either way, Dak knew these guys weren't cheap. If you were associated with the mercenary network, you were worth the price. The question about Tucker and his ill-gotten gains would have to wait.

"I don't suppose you'd let my friend here go?" Dak motioned to Scully. "He doesn't have anything to do with this."

The leader snorted. "Oh, he has plenty to do with this. How do you think we knew you would be here?"

Fear smacked Scully across the face, and he turned to Dak with wide, terrified eyes. "No. That's not true. I didn't tell them anything, Dak. I swear."

Dak glowered at his associate. "And here I thought we were friends, Scully." Dak sneered. "I thought I could trust you."

Disbelief veiled Scully's fear. "No. You know I wouldn't do that, Dak. How far back do we go? Years, man. Years. You know me."

"Do I?" Dak's eyes burned with rage, and he let Scully see it.

Dak reached down and grabbed Scully by the back of the neck and yanked him up. He pinned the trembling man against the wall, pressing his palm against Scully's throat.

"Please, Dak," Scully spat, barely able to get the words out through clenched teeth.

"I don't suppose you boys mind if I kill my friend here before we do our little dance," Dak said.

The leader laughed. "Be my guest."

"No. Don't," Scully protested.

Dak didn't listen. He delivered a blow to the ribs with his forearm.

Scully grimaced from the strike and his legs kicked up instinctively, like a marionette dangling from the puppeteer's fingers.

One of the goons behind Dak laughed at the blow.

The men were getting some entertainment before they went to work. Which was exactly what Dak wanted.

"This is what you get for betraying the people who trust you, Scully," Dak said, and delivered another forearm to the midsection.

Scully doubled over, his abdominal wall screaming in pain, but the only sound that escaped his lips was a gasp.

"Oh no you don't" Dak said, adjusting his grip on Scully's neck. "You don't get to pass out yet. Not until you die."

He leaned close and whispered in Scully's ear. "Keep your head down."

Scully frowned, the pain subsiding momentarily.

Dak reared back to deliver an even harder punch. He thrust his fist forward, slowing at the last second to soften the blow.

Scully still winced because he was weak. That's what weak people did.

This time, though, Dak reached to his acquaintance's right hip and in a single quick motion, drew the hunting knife hanging from Scully's belt. The leader of the group never saw it, not until Dak whipped around and flung the blade at him.

The long knife zipped through the air and struck the leader in the upper-right chest, sinking deep into tissue between his ribs.

The man scowled and stumbled back, his eyes immediately dropping to the knife handle sticking out of his shirt.

He touched it with his hand as he fell back onto his rear, scooting away toward the bar to recover.

"Kill them both!" he yelled in Spanish.

The second attacker, who had been to the leader's left, sprang into action before the words left the guy's mouth.

He stepped forward, raising his right arm to swing, but Dak jabbed him in the nose, breaking the appendage in one blow. Blood cascaded over the mercenary's lips as he shrieked like a little boy. Dak took a step to him and delivered a kick to his chest, knocking him backward.

The man stumbled over the leader, who sat on the floor, shock draining the color from his face as he continued to wrestle with what to do with the knife sticking out of his chest.

Scully slid to the floor against the wall, watching as he caught his breath.

The last two assassins came at Dak at the same time, flanking him on either side.

Their advantage in numbers was weakened by their lack of a cohesive plan. The one on Dak's right tried to get in close to grapple with him, probably in hopes of subduing him with a choke hold.

The other guy threw a jab at Dak's left cheek as he stepped toward the American.

Dak ducked under the punch, ramming his fist into the man's gut. The mercenary doubled over, the air leaving his lungs. Dak slipped around behind him in a deft move, grabbed the guy under the armpits, and laced his fingers behind the man's neck.

The killer yelped, still unable to breathe.

The fourth goon drew a pistol and aimed at Dak's head—or tried to. With the human shield in his way, he couldn't get off a clean shot.

"You want to kill your partner here?" Dak asked. "Drop the gun and fight me like a man."

The mercenary narrowed his eyes. Dak couldn't see his hostage's face, but he imagined the man wore the fear of the reaper in his eyes.

Dak saw Scully watching from the floor. To his credit, Scully was doing what Dak had asked. He was staying out of the way. The last thing he needed was his contact trying to get involved, thinking he could help.

Civilians usually made things worse in situations like this. Better to let the pros handle it. Still, that gave Dak an idea.

"Scully, no!" Dak shouted, letting the gunman see his eyes shift to his friend.

The gunman bought it, turning his head toward the wall and bringing the pistol's aim with it.

Dak sprang forward. Using the hostage for leverage, he vaulted toward the gunman, slinging both feet around.

His boots struck the assassin in the face before he could get his gun trained on Scully.

The pistol's suppressor muzzle erupted with a single muted shot. The bullet ricocheted harmlessly away.

The gunman staggered back but didn't lose his balance.

The kick to the face dazed him, though, and Dak wasted no time pressing the advantage. He jerked the hostage's right elbow backward, then twisted the hand down and back, instantly dislocating the man's shoulder.

The hostage yelled an obscenity as he dropped to his knees, the arm dangling awkwardly.

He kicked the guy in the back and sent him sprawling to the feet of the gunman, tripping him in the process.

While the gunman struggled to free himself from the tangle of his partner's arms, he raised the gun to fire again. His action was too slow.

Dak snatched the pistol while the muzzle was aimed at a window. He twisted it upward, bending the man's wrist awkwardly.

His trigger finger twitched and sent a round into the grimy white tile ceiling overhead. It was the only bullet he managed to fire before Dak broke his wrist, jerking the hand down and wrenching it back to the inside until Dak heard a pop.

He let out a howl. Dak forced him to his knees, then drove his knee into his chin.

The blow may have broken a few teeth. The guy fell over backward, unconscious before he hit the floor with the thud of dead weight.

Dak directed his attention to the one with the bloody nose. "Don't get up," he warned.

The guy slunk back, scooting away from Dak until he hit the façade of the bar next to the leader.

That one looked like he was about to faint, still undecided on whether or not he should take out the knife.

Dak heard Scully scramble to his feet behind him and turned around in time to see his contact kick one of the guys in the ribs.

"Hey," Dak said, holding out a hand to signal him to stop. "They've had enough."

"They were going to kill us," Scully whined.

"But they didn't. And they won't." He returned his gaze to the leader, who met it with newfound fear. The man who'd been so cocky before now looked like a whimpering child.

"Don't mess with that," Dak warned. "You could bleed out."

He wasn't sure if that was right or not. He'd seen enough wounds to know when someone was going to make it or not. Right now, this guy only had a little blood trickling down his shirt, but that could change the second the knife came out.

"Let a doctor tend to that," he offered. "Can you breathe?"

The guy grimaced but nodded weakly.

"Good."

The bartender poked her head back around the doorway behind the bar to see if the commotion was over.

"Get these guys a doctor. Can you do that?" Dak said to her.

She looked confused, then nodded. "Yes. I know someone."

"Good."

The leader looked up at Dak, disbelief filling his eyes.

"You're... not going to kill us?"

"No," Dak said. "I'm not."

"But—"

"Look, do you want to live, or you want me to off you right now?"

He swallowed and gave a short nod, lowering his eyes in shame.

"That's what I thought. She's going to call a doctor. I'm assuming it's probably someone unlicensed, so you won't have to worry about the cops snooping around, wondering what happened."

He returned his eyes to Dak. "I don't understand. Why would you let us live? You know how the network is. The second we're back on the street, we will hunt you down again."

Dak nodded. "Yeah. I know. But I've done my fair share of killing. More than I care to. But I've learned something along the way these last few years. If you kill an enemy, you rid your little world of a problem. Thing is, problems like you"—he jabbed a finger at the guy—"will always resurface. There is someone waiting in the wings to take your contract the second I kill you four."

The mercenary nodded again.

"But I'm placing a bet on letting you four go free. I know Tucker will send more men after me. More up-and-coming hit men will take the contract and hunt me down." Dak lowered to a crouch in front of the wounded assassin. "I need allies. And it's time I start accumulating them. If you could help me find Tucker, I would be much obliged."

The leader swallowed and shook his head. "I don't know where he went. He was here in Cartagena, like your friend over there said."

"See?" Scully added. "I told you he left town."

"I know, Scully. I believe you. But you said you don't know where he went."

Scully shrank back, nodding.

"I know where he went," the guy holding his nose chimed in.

Dak looked over at him. "Yeah? Where?"

"I heard he was going to England. That's all I know. I swear."

"London?" Dak twisted his head around and looked to Scully. "What's in London?"

Scully shrugged. "Big Ben? Parliament? Buckingham Palace?"

"You know you're really not helping," Dak groused.

"Yes. I know." Scully shut up again.

"Get yourselves patched up," Dak said to the leader. "And don't come looking for me again. Because next time, I won't be so forgiving."

"But you said you needed allies."

"I do. But I'll find you when I need you."

"How?"

"My friend here will be the go-between. If I ever need anything, he'll be in touch."

"Wait?" Scully protested. "What?"

"They won't hurt you, Scully." Dak said over his shoulder. "Ain't that right?" He directed the question at the leader.

The man shook his head gingerly, as if doing it too hard might aggravate the wound.

"Good." He patted the man on the head like a puppy, then stood up. "See you around."

Dak turned and started toward the door, then paused and looked back at the wounded man. He had a pistol in his hand, aiming it in Dak's general direction.

"Tucker paid us a lot of money to kill you," the guy said.

"Yeah. You mentioned that," Dak grumbled.

"But you paid us more to not kill you." He fired the pistol. The round zipped through the ceiling behind Dak's head. Scully's shoulders shrank for a second. "Have to make it look like I tried," the leader said with a fiendish grin.

Dak nodded. "Keep your eyes open." He turned to Scully. "He's to contact you if he learns any more details about Tucker or where he might be hiding."

Scully nodded, though he still looked bewildered. "Need me to do anything else?"

"No. Just keep your eyes and ears open. If Tucker is bouncing in and out of mercenary nests, he's bound to slip up at some point. When he does, I'll be waiting for him."

3

"Oh, you're going to London?" The boy's voice still sounded full of wonder and innocence, but he was thirteen now and he'd lost his childlike looks to the appearance of a teenager. His voice had also lost the higher pitch of boyhood, but had not fully transitioned.

"Yeah," Dak said. "There's some old business I need to take care of. You don't mind, do you?"

"Mind? Of course not. In fact, while you're there maybe you can check on something for me."

Dak had a feeling that might come with the phone call. His employer, Boston McClaren, was always hunting down historical artifacts on the internet, trying to find things that were lost or stolen long ago.

The kid made millions streaming video games online, but instead of spending his loot on frivolous things, he chose to spend a portion of it on what he referred to as historical preservation.

Dak's lifelong interest in history made him the perfect fit for the gig. Along with his particular set of skills. He grinned, looking out across the harbor from the café on the wharf. "What am I looking for this time?"

"This is a really cool one. The Welsh Crown."

Dak waited for more, but Boston didn't say anything else. "That's it?"

"That's it?" The kid sounded incredulous. "Seriously? That's it? Do you even know about the crown?"

"No. I must have missed that day in history class. And I made it a point not to miss history class. Outside of PE, it was one of my favorites."

"Well, I doubt they taught this stuff in basic world history courses. Although I haven't been to high school yet, so I have no point of reference."

No, but you're already talking like a twenty-seven-year-old.

"Tell me about this crown, bud. What's the story on it? And who has it?"

"I'll answer the easier question first. I have no idea who has it."

Dak swallowed, still peering out at the water. "You don't know who has it? I thought this was how our little agreement worked. You tell me where I'm supposed to go, who has what you want, and I get it for you."

"Sometimes things change," Boston said matter-of-factly. "We have to adapt."

"Wow. You sure you're only thirteen, kid?"

Boston laughed. "My mom says that. Then she also says I'm too big to complain like a baby sometimes."

Dak chuckled at the unexpected comment. "Yeah, well, you're never too old to complain. In fact, the best complainers I know are old guys."

"Like my grandpa," Boston offered. "He is always complaining about something with the government."

Dak laughed again. "The government is fertile ground for complaints. Tell me about this crown you're wanting me to look for."

"Right. Sorry, got distracted."

"No worries."

"The crown belonged to the Welsh prince, Llywelyn, in the thirteenth century."

"That's an interesting name," Dak quipped.

"Yeah. They have quite a few of those there in Wales, from what I understand."

"What happened to the crown? That was like eight hundred years ago."

"That's just it. No one knows for certain. Llywelyn," the boy struggled through the word, "left the crown in an abbey before heading out on his last campaign. He ended up dying later that year in 1282."

"Unfortunate."

"Yeah, and two years later it was taken from the castle ruins. That's where the story hits a dead end. No one knows what happened to it."

Dak waited, anticipating more.

"Eventually, the crown was taken to the shrine of Edward the Confessor by King Edward the First. I think it was meant to celebrate the destruction of the Welsh kingdom."

"And it just vanished?"

"Seems that way."

Dak's forehead tightened in a frown. "Doesn't sound like you have a lot of information to guide me on this little escapade."

"Oh, you know I wouldn't send you out into the wild without something, right?"

"I was wondering." Dak replied.

"The crown recently popped up on my radar. Someone on the web was looking for a buyer of a crown of unknown origin. And on top of that, the seller needed someone to validate the authenticity."

"Let me guess. You know the person who authenticated the crown?"

"There's a guy in Cambridge. He's a historian. Name is James Dyer. He might be able to help you out. He's an expert on missing artifacts, and one of the items he's been interested in for a long time is this crown."

"Does he have any intel on its whereabouts?"

"No clue," Boston said. "But I would start with him. If anyone has an idea about where to find it, it's that guy. I don't know much about the details, but I heard he was doing some work assessing artifacts. It's possible whoever has the crown now may have used him to analyze it for authenticity."

"James Dyer. Got it." Dak didn't bother writing it down. Even though his memory wasn't eidetic, it was still solid, and when he focused on something, he didn't let it go. "Anything else?"

"Not that I know of. I'll send you any other information if I can get my hands on it."

"I would appreciate that. Where can I find this guy? You said Cambridge. But what does he do?"

"He's retired now. Former professor there. Pretty sure all he does these days is play golf and watch soccer. Although, don't call it that when you get there. That annoys the Brits."

"Football. Understood." Dak had been a fan of the game most of his life, so he knew all about the subtle nuances regarding what the sport's proper name was. "When in Rome."

"Right. I'll forward the money to your account for the job."

"I do love how efficient you are."

"Just trying to make sure you have everything you need. Money isn't a problem for me. I don't want it to be for you either."

"Your mom and dad don't care about you spending it on wild expeditions like this?" Dak raised an eyebrow.

A beautiful woman with shimmering brown hair past her shoulders walked by. Her hair blew in the breeze, and as she passed, she looked up at Dak and smiled with full red lips over bright white teeth.

He simply nodded and returned her gesture with a shy version of his own smile.

Her faded orange sundress flapped behind her as she kept going. Dak didn't bother to watch her as she walked around the next corner and disappeared.

Seeing her forced his thoughts to Nicole, alone in Istanbul. At least he hoped she was alone.

He'd never been able to move on after they split. Then, when things in his life should have been less complex and more straightforward, everything went haywire.

The last time he'd seen her, things had been different. He sensed it. She didn't want to be alone. And she didn't want to be with anyone else. Dak saw it in her eyes.

But he also saw the regret of knowing it couldn't happen, that they couldn't be together. At least not at that moment.

He held on to that last part. It fueled the most dangerous thing for a person to cling to—hope.

It wasn't fair for him to hope they could be together again. But Dak rarely missed his read, and he saw it written all over her face. She wanted him back in her life. And that couldn't happen.

It pained her, and he hated it just as much as he loathed his own longing.

"You okay?" Boston asked, unaware of the thoughts racking Dak's mind.

"Yeah. I'm good. Just trying to figure out how to find this guy Dyer."

"Shouldn't be too difficult for a guy like you. I'm sure you'll figure it out."

"Thanks for the vote of confidence," Dak said dryly. He wished he at least had an address or something, but he knew it wouldn't be terribly difficult to locate the former professor. "I'll be in touch when I have something."

"Sounds good, Dak. Thanks for looking into it."

"You know, you don't have to pay me for something if I don't actually find it. That isn't really fair to you."

The kid had been overpaying for everything Dak brought him. At least Dak thought so. His efforts were probably being underpaid, if he were honest, but he felt weird about the money the kid paid him, and it had only increased since his first gig a few years before.

"Whether you find the relics or not, you're putting in the time, Dak. It wouldn't be fair of me to send you out there looking for all this stuff if I didn't pay you for your time. That's what you're being paid for, by the way. Your time. You can never get that back."

Again, the kid stunned Dak with his oddly mature piece of wisdom.

"You're an interesting kid, Boston. I'm glad I met you."

"Me too, Dak. Good luck. And be safe out there."

"Will do."

Dak ended the call and held the phone for a second, staring at the screen. "Shouldn't be too hard to find a retired history professor," he said, and looked up the number for his friend Will Collins.

Will could locate pretty much anyone. Well, anyone except Colonel Tucker, but the net was closing in around Dak's former commanding officer. It was only a matter of time until Dak caught him.

4

Mia Tanning watched the men from the corner in front of the Dancing Turtle—a pub with a black iron sign hanging in front of it over the sidewalk. The black sign featured a gilded tortoise waving its feet around in a dancing pose.

She stood there, leaning against the corner wall with her arms crossed, dark brown eyes locked on the men across the street as they walked to the intersection and waited with the other pedestrians for the light to change.

This wasn't her first assignment for the gang. The Savages had been making huge moves in their part of London for the better part of the last year, and today they were going to take their first steps toward an even bigger play.

Mia wasn't privy to what the leaders knew, or what their grander schemes were. She didn't have to be.

She was smarter than the average eighteen-year-old, and she'd grown up fast and hard. With only her father to raise her after her mother died at a young age, Mia had spent most of her time on the streets of London while her father worked two jobs to maintain their humble home.

It had been a hard life for her, and she didn't want to keep living that way.

School had promised her a better life at the other end of a bunch of years she could never get back, but she didn't buy into it.

She'd been recruited by the Savages when she was sixteen. Now she was one of the higher-up females in the crew, but the guys still didn't tell her what was going on or why they were so interested in the two men waiting across the street.

Then again, they didn't have to.

The men weren't members of one of the local gangs. They were part of something bigger—a mob organization that made what the Savages did look like child's play.

The fact she was ordered to observe their movements told her one thing: the leaders of the Savages wanted a seat at the big kids' table, and they were targeting some of the biggest kids.

The Houghton Mob controlled most of this part of London as far as protection rackets went. But people had gotten tired of paying their extortive fees, and the Savages had taken notice.

If Mia had to guess, her thought was that the leaders of her crew were planning some kind of a hit, a way to disturb the peace enough to hedge their way into making a counteroffer to the businesses who paid Houghton.

It was a dangerous play, though, and she had no way of knowing whether or not her leaders had really thought things through.

They made most of their money peddling drugs or fencing stolen items. But the mobsters; those guys were bigger operations. They moved drugs in much bigger quantities, along with other forbidden items.

Mia knew they operated human trafficking rings, too, usually in conjunction with Albanian connections who could transfer the "product" into France and then the rest of Europe. England was merely a landing spot for distribution to and from the West. Mia knew, though, that most of the poor souls who'd been caught in that trap usually came from the West. It was much more difficult to smuggle people into the United States than out, despite what she'd read about problems along their southern border.

The light changed, and the men started across the crosswalk. They both wore petulant looks on their smug faces under hoodies—one navy blue, the other gray.

Rain dribbled from the sky, splotching wet stains on their clothes as they stalked across the intersection. They reached the sidewalk fifteen feet away from Mia and turned left into the pub.

She watched for a second, grinning like a lion hiding in the weeds, then followed the two men in.

The heavy, dark green door closed behind her and snuffed the light from the gray slate of the sky outside, submerging her in the dim lighting of a proper English pub.

The two men made their way over to the bar and stopped at the drink station, where servers picked up beverages to deliver around the room.

Mia floated over to a booth along the far wall and eased into the seat. She picked up a laminated menu and started looking it over. She had no intention of eating. She was there to listen.

"Where's John?" one of the men asked.

Mia looked over as he spoke and saw it was the one closest to her. He had a cap on underneath the hood and faded, skinny blue jeans. The other guy's pants were black, but similarly slim.

Enforcers.

These two would have fit in better with a group like hers—younger, more with the times than the mobsters they worked for.

She figured one of them must be a son or a nephew of the Houghton boss, George Pickford.

The bartender looked confused for a second. "He's not here right now. He just stepped out."

The two guys looked at each other and laughed. Then the one in black pants and a gray hoodie reached across the bar and grabbed the guy by the apron straps. He jerked the barkeep forward until the man's midsection hit the edge of the counter.

"What did you say?" the goon pressed.

"I... I said he's not here right now. He just stepped out." The bartender stumbled through his answer.

"You hear that?" the guy turned to his partner with a mocking look of disbelief on his face. "He said John's not here right now."

"That's funny," the other guy said in a deep baritone. "He knows that we come in here on the first Monday of every month to get paid. And this is the first Monday of the month. Yet he's not here."

"So strange," Gray Hoodie concluded, then looked back to the bartender. "I don't suppose he left the money here for you, now did he?"

The bartender shook his head. The motion shook the loosely combed brown hair on his head.

"Imagine that, Reg," Gray Hoodie said. "This guy doesn't have our money."

"I swear. He didn't leave me any money," the bartender pleaded.

"You don't get it, son," the one named Reg said. "When you don't pay the boss, he gets mad."

"Yeah. Mr. Pickford don't like it when his clients don't pay," added the other.

"You see, son, when Mr. Pickford doesn't get his money, he can't pay his bills. When he can't pay his bills, he gets frustrated. He loses things. And Mr. Pickford doesn't like losing things."

"That's right. He don't like that at all."

"Nah," Reg agreed. "But you know what Mr. Pickford hates losing most of all?"

The barkeep shook his head rapidly.

"Respect, son. He hates losing respect. You see, when you don't pay him, other people think he's gone soft. That he's weak. You don't think Mr. Pickford is weak, do you?"

"No," the bartender blurted, his head still swishing left to right and back again.

"No? Then why don't you have his money?"

The goon shoved the barkeeper backward. He hit the back counter with his tailbone. The impact jarred several of the bottles sitting behind him on three shelves. One of the skinnier ones nearly toppled over.

Mia watched it wobble for three seconds before it settled on its base again.

"When is your boss coming back?" Reg demanded.

"I... I don't know. He said he had to run some errands. Maybe in a couple of hours?"

Gray Hoodie pulled out a switchblade from his left pocket and flicked the knife open. The shiny flat side of it glittered in the yellowish hue of the lamplight.

"Maybe we ought to make an example out of this one, hey, Reg?"

"Yeah," Reg said with a slow, sinister nod. "I think maybe we should. We can't have the other businesses on our turf thinking we've gone soft. But if we cut off a finger, that will send the right message."

The bartender shook his head more vigorously. Fear brimmed in his eyes. The one named Reg started to walk around the corner of the bar. He stopped and lifted the bridge that connected the two parts of the counter.

"No. Please. I don't have your money. John should be back in the next few hours. Please. If you'll just—"

Reg grabbed him by the back of the neck as the guy tried to retreat to the other end of the bar.

"Where do you think you're going, you little rat?" Reg asked, then shoved him to the front of the bar.

"Please. Don't. I'm just the bartender."

"Yeah. We know." Gray Hoodie stepped close to the bar and brandished the knife. "You can thank your boss for losing a finger. No hard feelings."

Reg grabbed the bartender's right hand and slammed it down on the counter. "There you go. Good lad. Mario, if you could be so kind. Let's show this whelp what happens when you don't pay Mr. Pickford on time."

"No. Please," the bartender begged.

The one apparently named Mario lowered the knife's edge to the index finger as the bartender squirmed and tried to wriggle free. Reg held him firm, though, and he could not escape the fate that rested against his skin.

"You know, Reggie," Mia said. "There are better ways to get what you want."

Reg turned to face her, fire burning in his eyes. "Keep your mouth shut, girl. This ain't none of your concern."

"Oh, I know it isn't. It's yours."

"What did you just say?" He let go of the bartender's wrist, and the man jerked his hand away from the blade.

Momentarily distracted, Mario didn't react fast enough to keep the barkeeper from darting out through the back hall. They heard the door in the rear slam shut as he escaped.

"You just cost us a little credibility, girl," Reg said, realizing the example they were about to make had just slipped out the back door. "If there's one thing Mr. Pickford hates losing more than money, it's cred."

"Maybe he shouldn't have sent a couple of buffoons like you two to collect his tithe."

"What did you say, girl?" Mario spat, taking a step toward her.

"Could you grab me a drink while you're over there?" she asked coolly. "Whiskey, preferably. Something in a bourbon. I like the way the Yanks make their hooch."

"Oh, she's a funny one. Hey, Reg?"

"You're out of your element, girl. What's your name?" Reg demanded.

"Mia. But I'm not the one you should be worried about."

Reg laughed. "We ain't worried about you," he sneered.

"It's the guys behind you. Them you need to worry about."

"Like we'd fall for that," Mario said.

"She must think we're—"

He didn't get the words out.

One of the two men standing behind Reg grabbed him by the back of the neck and spun him around. He gurgled, swinging both arms. The second guy went to work, sending a hard fist straight into the nose.

Mario turned to help in the fight, but felt his right arm suddenly restrained by a hand.

Two more men addressed him, one holding him while the other delivered blow after blow to the abdomen, ribs, and face.

Mia sat there in her booth, watching with disinterest as her Savage comrades beat the two enforcers to a pulp.

The hitters stopped when the men dropped to the floor, their eyes swollen shut. Blood oozed out of their lips.

They both groaned and writhed. That's when the men holding them started kicking. They drove the tops of their feet into ribs and abs and face until the two Pickford goons stopped moving.

Blood pooled on the wooden planks underneath them. Their backs and chests swelled with every pained breath.

"Don't kill 'em, boys," Mia said. "That's enough. The boss just wanted a warning sent. I'd say you did it."

One guy—a tall black man with thick hair delivered one more kick for good measure. "Message sent," he snarled.

Mia sighed. "Yes, good. Now, let's get out of here, shall we? I'd rather not get into the war with Houghton right this second."

She followed the four tattooed gang members out the back hallway to the rear exit. One of the guys held the green door open for the rest to leave and then hurried after them into the back alley.

As they retreated down the next street, Mia only had one thought on her mind. *I have to get out.*

5

Dak walked into the Flying Squirrel Pub and looked around. The place was just like most of the pubs he'd visited in this country: adorned with old, dark wooden panels and matching floors. Booths along the walls next to stained-glass windows and a row of taps behind the bar completed the iconic look of a proper pub.

All manner of beer signs hung from the walls, including many vintage ones made from metal.

The woman standing behind the counter with her arms crossed stared up at a flatscreen television. Her eyes remained glued to the football match as she waved a hand absently behind her back. "Help yourself to a seat," she said. "I'll be with you in a moment."

Dak smiled. He'd already seen his friend in the far back corner.

Will had spotted him, too, and showed it with an upward nod.

Dak sauntered over to the booth, taking note of the other eleven customers sitting around drinking pints of beer and watching the match. Some were more into it than others, shouting at the television whenever their team made a mistake, or even louder when the referee did.

"You should hear them when someone scores," Will said as Dak approached the table.

Dak's friend started to get up, but Dak shook his head. "I would tell you you're in my seat, but you're just as good there as me."

Will stuck out his lower lip and nodded as if impressed. "Well, well, well. Look who is getting less paranoid."

"More, actually. I just prefer your face be the first one a threat sees when they come through the door."

Will laughed and slapped his friend on the shoulder.

The two eased into the hard wooden bench seats and planted their elbows on the table. Will already had a half-empty pint of lager in front of him.

The crowd groaned, and Dak noticed on the television that the other customers were doing the same.

Dak heard the announcer say that Norwich scored, much to the chagrin of the Crystal Palace fans in the pub.

The bartender threw her right hand at the screen in disgust, then wobbled over to the end of the bar closest to Dak and Will.

Her light pink blouse fluttered behind her over black pants as she moved. Her silver, fluffy hair didn't budge.

"What can I get for you?" she asked, her voice grumpy but her eyes alight with a welcoming gleam.

Dak liked her immediately.

"I'll have what he's having," he answered.

She simply gave a curt nod, turned to the rows of glasses arranged on the rear counter, and picked one up. She filled it carefully to the brim until a white head of foam formed around the top. Then she pushed back on the tap, scraped the overflow off the top, and brought it over to the end of the bar.

She had no intention of walking all the way around to deliver the drink an extra few feet. Dak had already made that assumption and stood to meet her halfway.

"Thank you," he said.

"Sure, honey. Let me know if you want anything else."

She turned away before he could respond, returning to her standing place to watch the rest of the match.

Will held up his beer and clinked it against Dak's glass. "Good to see you again, my friend."

"Likewise," Dak agreed and took a swig.

Will chugged a few swallows of his and set the glass down. It was nearly empty. "I didn't think you were much of a drinker anymore," Will said.

"I'm not. Depends on the atmosphere and the crowd."

Will snorted. "You saying I turn you to drinking?"

"Nah." Dak shook his head. "But when in the jungle…" He looked around at the place, taking in the surroundings. Dim bulbs hung from lamps that might well have been original fixtures when this place was built. Dak had no idea how old it was, but it had to be early twentieth century, at the latest. "I also don't want to be rude. Plus, it's good to support local business."

Will assessed his guest with narrow, suspicious eyes. "How generous," he said with a cynical smirk.

"Yeah, yeah. What do you know about this guy I'm supposed to be looking for?"

"You just love to get right down to business, don't you? No chatting about for you. Just dive in."

"It's called being efficient," Dak replied. "But fine. We can do the pleasantries if you like. How's the family? Kids doing okay? Is little Billy starting college already?" Dak's dry tone got an eye roll from his friend.

"Okay. Okay."

"Please," Dak continued to antagonize. "Give the wife my love."

"Very funny. Fine," Will relented and produced a royal-blue folder from under the table.

"Was that here when you arrived?" Dak said, pretending to look surprised.

"You're on a roll today."

Dak shrugged and pulled the folder close. He opened it and began scanning the sheets inside.

"I just flew in from Colombia," Dak explained. "Sorry if I'm anxious to see what you have, get something to eat, and then go to the hotel for a sixteen-hour nap."

"Only sixteen?" Will huffed.

Dak laughed at the comment. "I figure that might be enough. Might."

"This guy wasn't too hard to find," Will said, diverting to the point of their meeting. "Doesn't seem like he's too dangerous."

"I would think not. He's a retired professor."

Will frowned. "If you know so much about him, what did you need me for?"

Dak lifted his eyes from the pages and stared at his friend. "I just like to keep you busy. Can't have you getting lazy on me."

"Seriously?" Will threw up his hands.

"No. Not at all." He watched Will's half-relieved reaction of shaking his head and giving another eye roll. "I needed more information. That was pretty much all I had." He returned his focus to one of the sheets and pressed his index finger to a line. "This says he's a gambler."

"Yeah. Big time."

Dak's brow furrowed. "How can a retired teacher be a big-time gambler? Was he embezzling money or something?"

Will chuckled at the question. "No. Nothing like that. I meant he loves it. The guy is always betting on soccer, baseball, basketball, NFL."

"No NBA?"

"Doesn't like basketball. And doesn't bet college football, either."

"Man after my own heart. Those college lines can be pretty crazy. Sixty-point spreads and whatnot."

"Yeah, fine. Anyway, word is Dyer is broke. Had to go into debt to some local loan sharks. Of course, you know what happened next."

"Same old?" Dak asked, meeting his friend's brown-eyed stare with his own emeralds. "Thought he had a lead-pipe lock on a line and went all in on it with the loan money. Lost it. Now the shark is in the water, and our friend the professor is trying to avoid him."

Will nodded, holding the glass loosely between finger and thumb. Then he took a drink, finishing the beverage. "You know it."

Dak sighed, shaking his head as he went over the dossier in greater detail. "Always the same with those types. Think they can win their way out of a pickle."

"Yeah, well, this pickle is way worse than most."

"I'm not a big fan of pickles. Unless they're fried. Then, a little ranch and boom." Dak looked over at the bartender, who remained fixated on the television. "You don't think they—"

"They don't have fried pickles here, Dak. So, don't even think about it."

"Fine. What do they have? I'm starving. Anything else fried? I mean, it's a bar, right?"

"I'm sure they do. I didn't have a look at the menu. Look, now you're the one getting distracted. And thanks. Now I'm thinking about fried pickles."

"Mmm, like the ones at Champy's back in Chattanooga."

"The fried pickle plate. So good." Will shook his head. "No. Stay focused."

Dak grinned from ear to ear, knowing he was pushing his friend's buttons just like he always did. Will was an easy target in conversation, though a tough one in a fight. He'd kept himself in good shape over the years after his service.

Part of that had been due to necessity. Running weapons to freedom fighters around the world was a tricky and dangerous business, with both criminals and governments after him.

Dak chuckled to himself at the thought. They were all criminals. That much was easy to see.

"I don't suppose this guy is at his home address right now," Dak said, hopeful.

"No. I already checked."

"That's why I love you. You're always so thorough, going above and beyond."

"It's called overdelivering. I gotta keep my best customer happy."

Dak laughed and took a swig of lager. "I'm hardly your best.

Unless things with some of those guerrilla groups have turned sour. They not pay you your money?"

"Everyone always pays," Will said. "Sooner or later."

"I like how you made it sound like you threaten people, but I know that's not how you operate."

"Yeah. I know." Will exhaled, as if disappointed with himself. "I wish I could be meaner, but it's just not me."

"That's a good thing. No one ever talks about someone glowingly by saying he's such a mean guy. They say nice guy. That's what you want."

"I'm a gunrunner, Dak. I need to present a tough exterior."

"And you do. I'm sure it really comes out when you are dealing with bureaucrats."

"Not really," Will argued. "I try to stay clear of those types. Once law enforcement or government starts snooping around, it's time for me to dip."

Dak turned the page to the last one in the folder. "I see there aren't any relatives in the area. Any friends?"

"Nope. The guy is a loner. He doesn't get out much, and when he does, it's by himself to a pub."

"You saw him?"

"Of course I saw him."

"So, you know where he is?"

Will rolled his eyes, shaking his head in disbelief. "It's right there on that last sheet of paper."

Dak read over the lines. "So, he has a place out in the countryside. I'm guessing the loan shark doesn't know about that."

"Correct. At least not yet. Only a matter of time."

"I've never been able to figure that out," Dak said. "If you have someone after you, why wouldn't you just leave the country?"

"Or at least the city. His cottage in the country is only about twenty minutes outside London city limits."

"Brilliant." Dak looked back to the page again. "You even have the address on here."

"Nothing is too good for my friend Dak."

"You going to take me out there?"

Will blurted out a laugh. "Nah, man. I got things to do. People to see."

"Yeah? Business booming?"

"You could say that. People are getting antsy about some of the stuff going on with governments around the world. They're afraid."

"People are always afraid," Dak said. "Heck, that's how the media makes all their money—on fear."

"Truer words have never been uttered, my friend. But no, I have some things I'm taking to a group up in Scotland. Farmers. They're harmless, but they're putting together a little militia. In case things heat up in the East."

"Worried about an invasion?" Dak sounded surprised.

"People are always worried about something, Dak. You know that."

"I do." His mind shifted to Nicole for a second. "So, this place isn't far from here," Dak said. "I'm going to head to the hotel and get some shuteye. I'll go find our friend the gambling professor tomorrow." Dak thought for a few seconds, rubbing his thumb around the rim of the pint glass.

"Yeah, that reminds me," Will said, cutting into Dak's thoughts. "You should probably be aware that the guy Dyer owes money to is bad news."

"I didn't know there were loan sharks out there that were good news."

"Yeah," Will huffed. "Well, this guy is worse than most. His name is George Pickford. He's a villain right out of a Guy Ritchie film."

"You think he keeps pigs at a nearby farm?" Dak raised his eyebrows.

"Good one. And it's entirely possible with this dude. He's bad news, Dak."

"Yeah?" Dak grunted. Will rarely repeated himself. "Seems like everyone I meet is bad news for me lately."

"Good thing you have me in your life, then." Will put on a stupid-looking grin. "I would avoid Pickford if possible."

"He doesn't even need to know I exist."

"Probably for the best. He runs a racketeering-and-extortion ring here in the city. His turf is one of the bigger areas. Has been for years from what I hear. And he has a pretty good contingent of guys working for him."

"Any former military?"

"Probably. So many of them end up looking for private security work when they leave the service. That seems to be a common thread around the globe."

He was right, Dak thought. More than likely, this George Pickford had hired a combination of security people to watch his back, from highly trained special operators to common street thugs. A street army needed troops at all levels, even as grunts.

Dak had seen this sort of thing before from afar. One of his friends in college, however, had lived it. Coming from Long Island, he was close to that sort of thing all the time. The mob forced people to pay them for protection, usually from other mobs or the street gangs that plagued certain areas. Where Dak's friend grew up, the gangs weren't as big of an issue, but the mob presence had hung over him his entire life until he moved to Tennessee.

He shook off the distracting thoughts. His plan entailed not meeting Pickford or any of his goons. Dak wasn't here to take down organized crime in London. He was just as happy to let the cops handle that.

The excitement built up in the pub as Crystal Palace drove the ball downfield, weaving passes through the defense with expert precision.

The crowd at the stadium grew louder as the attack gained momentum. Dak turned to see what all the fuss was about. He looked just in time to see the right winger bend a ball into the box, right onto the head of one of his attackers.

The center forward knocked the ball into the back of the net, sending the crowd into hysteria.

Inside the pub, the screaming was nearly enough to permanently damage Dak's hearing, but he only smiled at the reaction from the fans.

The bartender held up her hands, pumping them into the air over and over again before quickly returning behind the bar and filling four more glasses to distribute to her regulars.

She turned to Dak and Will. "Half-price beer every time Palace scores a goal. You boys want another?"

Will grinned. "Yes, ma'am," he said.

"I'm still working on this one," Dak explained with a polite smile.

She arched one eyebrow at him like he was nuts and then shook it off, filling a couple of additional glasses anyway. "He can drink yours, then," she barked, then set the two full glasses down on the end of the bar.

Dak looked to his friend and laughed again. "She's quite the salesperson."

"Never take no for an answer in sales," Will said.

"You can say that again."

Dak stood up and collected the folder, neatly stacking the contents back inside. He reached over and grabbed the beers, then placed them in front of Will. "You sure you can handle those two pints?" Dak asked.

"And the one you're not goin' to finish," Will said, indicating Dak's barely touched beer.

"Good. I'm not in the mood, and I need to get some rest. I'll just wake up later if I drink that now. Thanks for the intel, Will. You're the best."

Will raised one of the three glasses on the table, looking like a pauper who had just stumbled his way into a buried treasure. "That I am, my friend. That I am. See you soon. Let's catch a game or something."

"Sounds good," Dak said, and turned and walked out of the pub to the sound of the crowd celebrating their 2-1 victory.

6

George Pickford sat behind his desk with his elbows sticking out from arms crossed over his pot belly.

"Look at me," the sixty-one-year-old crime boss demanded, staring out from behind thick-rimmed glasses. His suspenders clung with all their strength to the black trousers he wore, and cut into the pink-striped, white button-up shirt covering his torso.

He breathed heavily even though he'd been sitting for the last hour or so. Pickford wasn't in the best shape, but his labored breaths had nothing to do with fatigue. At least not the physical kind.

He had, however, grown tired of incompetence.

"Look at me," he repeated.

The two men sitting across from him both raised their battered faces at the same time.

Two guards stood on either end of Pickford's unimpressive metal desk. The thing looked like it had come from a hospital yard sale. In the seventies.

A white clock ticked on the wall over the gray metal door. White walls and gray tile floors felt sterile under the cold fluorescent light above.

"Tell me again what happened," Pickford ordered.

The one to his right looked like he was chewing on his tongue. The one on the left simply lowered his eyes back to the floor.

"I didn't tell you to stop looking at me, son!" Pickford shouted, slamming his palm onto the desk.

The two younger men nearly jumped out of their seats. Both winced, probably from cracked ribs.

"I'm sorry, Uncle George," the one on the right said.

Pickford nodded. "I know you are, Reg. I know." He turned his focus to the other one. "And I'm sure you're sorry, too. Aren't you, Mario?"

"Yeah. I'm sorry."

"What was that?" Pickford pressed.

"I said yeah. I'm sorry." Mario threw up his hands and shrugged. "They ambushed us. We had no way to know."

"Ah. Well, then that changes everything. Tell me. How did they ambush you?"

Reg shifted uneasily in his chair.

Mario, however, tilted his disfigured head to the side, still full of false bravado. "We went in, just like you told us to. Collection day, yeah? We always collect on the first of the month. Like you told us to."

Pickford didn't need to be told the schedule. He had created the thing. "Thank you so much for laying that out for me. What happened when you went into the pub?"

"The bartender wasn't there," Mario said, shifting nervously. The cockiness he'd worn on his face drained away.

"Bartender? Who cares about the bartender?"

"Owner," Mario corrected. "Sorry. The owner wasn't there." His nerves gripped him now and wouldn't let go. Mario had seen what Pickford did to people who failed him. In some ways, he treated those poor souls worse than those who got in his way. Failure, to him, was another form of betrayal. "The owner wasn't there."

"Oh, I see. The owner wasn't there." Pickford bobbed his head like it was on a toothpick. He pounded the desk again with an angry fist. "Did he have the money?"

The two men in the chairs jumped again.

"No. No he didn't."

Pickford nodded as if understanding the situation now. "So, you go into the pub to collect our monthly dues, and the owner isn't there. Who *was* there?"

"The bartender, Uncle George," Reg offered.

"Shut up, Reginald," Pickford thundered. Within two seconds, he'd calmed his voice back down to a steady volume. "Now, Mario. You were saying?"

Mario's anxiety swelled. "Yeah, so—"

"Sir."

"What?"

"Sir. You call me sir, you impudent little urchin. You've been sitting here for fifteen minutes, and not one time have you called me sir."

"What?"

"Say what again, Mario." Pickford snapped his fingers, and the guard to his right drew a pistol. Pickford held out his right hand without so much as a sidelong glance. The guard placed the gun in Pickford's palm.

The boss lazily turned the gun toward Mario. "Say what again."

"Wh—I mean, yes, sir. No. I mean, no, sir."

Pickford's lips parted in a sinister grin, the way a wolf snarled at a wounded lamb. "Better. Now. You were saying?"

"Yeah." He caught Pickford's eyes as they narrowed for a split second, and quickly added, "Sir." He rubbed his thighs, pressing his fingers into the jeans with every pass. "The bartender said the owner wasn't there."

"We established that."

"Right. Sir. Anyway, they said they didn't have your money. That the owner wasn't there."

"And what did you do?"

"What we always do. We threatened him just like you told us. When someone doesn't pay, we take it out of them one way or the other."

"Yes. That's correct. Except something else happened. I want to know what."

Mario nodded.

Reg just sat there listening, his eyes firmly locked on his infamous uncle.

"I was going to cut off his finger," Mario said. "Like you told us, take fingers if they don't pay."

Pickford laughed. "Yeah. You start taking fingers when they don't pay; they start thinking about how much they would pay to get their digits back."

"Yeah, well, we did that. Or were about to do that, when someone else came into the bar."

"Who?" Pickford asked, leaning forward as far as the desk would allow.

"They snuck in, Uncle—"

"Shut up, Reggie!" Pickford boomed, turning the pistol's suppressor barrel toward him.

Reggie only nodded like a frightened puppy.

"I don't know who they were exactly," Mario explained. "But I know who they work for."

"Oh? And who might that be?"

"Savages." He said the word with disdain.

"Savages?" For a moment, Pickford almost looked like he had no clue who Mario was talking about. "Savages?" he repeated.

"Yes. Sir. Yes, sir." Mario couldn't cram the words together fast enough.

"Then what happened?"

"There... there were four of them. We were outnumbered, and they caught us by surprise. Before we knew it, they jumped us. You know the rest."

"Yes," Pickford demurred. "I can see what happened. Looks like you boys are lucky to be alive."

"They're the lucky ones," Mario snipped. "In a fair fight we—"

"We're criminals, son," Pickford snapped back, cutting Mario off like a yippy little dog. "We don't get to fight fair. Ever."

Mario swallowed and issued a single nod, licking his busted lip as he turned his head at an angle to avoid the angry boss's glare.

"You know what this means?" Pickford asked over his shoulder.

"Yes, sir," the guard to his right said. "It means a little fish thinks they want to be a big fish."

"That's right."

"Just tell us where to go and what to do, Mr. Pickford," Mario said, eager for a taste of vengeance. "I can't wait to teach those little—"

The pistol clicked in Pickford's hand. The muzzle spat a bullet through Mario's forehead.

Reg jumped out of his seat amid a hurricane of profanity.

"What the—" was a common pair of words with some of the expletives.

"Sit down, boy," Pickford ordered. He let the pistol wave toward his nephew.

Reg couldn't take his eyes off the dead body in the chair next to his. "You killed him. Why did you kill him?"

"I said… sit down!"

Reg saw the stern, cold look in his uncle's eyes. It was a look that meant he would kill his own family if that meant making the organization stronger. Gripped with fear and anger, Reg slumped back into the seat, but his eyes continued to wander to his dead associate to his right.

"Don't look at him. He can't help you now. He's dead. He don't know what's going on."

Reg trembled, his body gyrating involuntarily.

"Hey. Get ahold of yourself, boy. Jeez." Pickford shook his head in disgust. "If you weren't my sister's child."

All Reggie could do was sit there and whimper.

"Some enforcer you are."

Reg shook his head in defiance, finally getting a grip. "I won't let you down again, Uncle. I swear."

"Oh, I know you won't. Or you'll end up just like your partner over there." He wagged the pistol at the dead man. "Now, tell me about these Savages. Did you get a good look at them?"

Reg blinked and nodded after a second of thought. "Yes, sir. I saw them. I saw them all."

"What did they look like? Have you seen any of them before?"

"No," Reg said. Then he quickly backtracked. "Actually. I have seen one of them before."

"Which one?"

"The ones who beat us up. They were all guys. I didn't recognize any of them. But there was a girl, too."

"What about her?" Pickford leaned forward, pressing the pistol between his palms.

"Biracial. Curly brown hair. Medium height. Skinny but athletic build."

"Well, look at you, my nephew. You might be good for something after all." Pickford paused for a second and set the gun down. "Where have you seen her before?"

"One of the pubs in the area. Not that one. Winston's. I've seen her there before having drinks."

"Was she on a date?"

"No. I mean, I don't know. But I doubt it. There were a bunch of guys hanging around her; two girls, too."

"Savages?" Pickford asked, his intrigue building.

"Yes, sir. And I'm pretty sure they were there with the leader of the gang."

"Miles Tidmouth," Pickford said. "Are you sure?"

Reg nodded. "Yes, sir. Pretty sure."

"I don't want pretty sure. I need to be certain."

"It was him. They run in that part of town, usually working for us."

"Yes," Pickford agreed and leaned back in his chair. He steepled his fingers together and sighed. "We have used them in the past for a number of tasks. But now it would seem their leader has his eyes set on bigger ambitions."

"What you want us to do?"

Pickford thought about it, staring beyond his nephew to the wall behind him. "This is a very risky play by Miles. I'm not sure what's gotten him in the mood for a fight like this, but if that's what he wants, that's what he'll get."

The boss turned to the guy on his left. "Jerry. Take a couple of the boys and head over to Winston's. Send a message. We can't have our little underlings thinking they can revolt and change the pecking order of things."

"Yes, sir," Jerry said, and immediately headed for the door.

"Oh, and Jerry?" Pickford stopped him just as he neared the threshold.

Jerry looked back at his employer, waiting for the additional orders.

"Get a cleaner to come in here. They know what to do with the body."

Jerry glanced over at the corpse without affect. "Right away, sir."

When he was gone, Reg leaned forward, clasping his hands together. "I want in, Uncle. I want to go with Jerry and the guys."

"What you want is revenge, son. And that clouds your vision at a time like this. Vengeance has its place. Don't mistake that. But you must remember the reason for demanding payback. You must take out the emotional component. Once you do that, then you're ready to deal with the enemy."

"I'm ready."

Pickford snorted a derisive laugh. "You need to take it easy for a few days. Recover from the lesson you learned."

"What lesson is that?" Reg asked.

"Always watch your back."

7

Mia checked both directions along the sidewalk before she inserted the key into the door of her building.

The worn-down apartment building featured a red door and cracked white paint over old bricks.

Mia figured the owners of the building must have thrown the paint on to make it look renovated. They hadn't bothered touching the interiors of the flats, though.

She opened the door and walked into the lobby, passing the mailboxes on her way to the stairs.

No need to check their box. She'd paid the bills two weeks ago, barely.

They'd almost been late, but she managed to scrounge up a few hundred more pounds to take care of the rent.

Unfortunately, it would be due again in two weeks. She just needed to hang on a little longer.

She had a plan to get her family out of this mess, although it was unclear if her father would be a part of that escape strategy.

He was barely there anymore. He went to work, made money so he could drink, and continued the vicious cycle.

Mia knew what she was going to find in the flat when she opened the door. It was the same thing every night.

She climbed the stairs and stopped on the third floor, turning left into the dim corridor. Mia cringed. Dim was the right description. The walls painted in dark gray, the lights that barely illuminated the dingy navy-blue carpet, none of it projected a happy vibe.

This place was where dreams went to die.

The owner may as well have hung a sign out front of the manager's office that read, "Abandon All Hope, Ye Who Enter."

She walked down the corridor, moving her feet quickly to avoid lingering too long. She'd never been mugged in her building, but she knew it happened now and then. Even if she was assaulted or robbed, who was Mia going to tell? She was just a street rat, a gang member with a list of minor crimes attached to her name.

Soon, though, she hoped that wouldn't be the case.

Mia was over the gang life.

At first, she'd joined due to pressure from a few friends in the neighborhood. Without a real sense of belonging and a lack of interest in school, joining the Savages made sense. And it gave her purpose. She finally felt like she was a part of something, and that was a feeling Mia had never experienced before.

Only one person made her feel that way—her little brother.

For a while, things had been good after she joined the Savages. She started making a little money, even though she despised some of the activities she was conducting.

Mia had never been into drugs except a few times smoking pot at parties. She didn't care what people did with their own bodies as long as she could take care of hers. Now, though, being a part of the machine that was wrecking lives... Regret loomed over her like the clouds over London.

She still believed people could make decisions for themselves—to eat unhealthy food or not, to exercise or not, to use drugs or not. People could decide who they dated, who they married, what jobs they wanted in life.

Using all those rationales didn't strip away the guilt she felt.

And then there was the other component that gnawed at the foundations of her soul. She'd heard rumors, nothing more, and had never actually witnessed any evidence, but the whispers in the shadows sent chills through her.

Word on the street was that the leader of the Savages, Miles Tidmouth, was keen on cutting himself in on the human trafficking rings that operated in the United Kingdom, specifically the London underworld.

One of the other gang members told Mia he'd already started, picking up immigrants as they came in from North Africa and occasionally from Albania by way of France.

Mia stopped at her door. Number 221. She sighed, still aware of what she'd find on the other side.

She inserted the key and reluctantly turned the doorknob.

Disappointment filled her gut as she opened the door and saw inside.

As expected, her father slouched on a recliner in front of the television. A beer bottle sat on an end table next to him.

She closed the door quietly so as not to wake him and padded into the living room, setting her keys down on the kitchen counter to her left.

The little flat had two bedrooms down the hallway to her left, each room on opposite sides. She'd shared a room with her brother since he'd been two, only a few months before their mother passed.

Fortunately, the boy was asleep. Unfortunately, he'd passed out on the floor at the foot of the couch, she assumed while watching darts with their father—which was still on the television.

Mia tiptoed over to the entertainment unit—a cheap metal-and-glass job she was pretty sure her father found at a thrift store. Meanwhile, the flatscreen probably cost more than two months' rent in this dump.

She shook her head at the thought and turned the volume down slightly.

Then she stepped over to her brother and nudged him on the shoulder. "Adam. Wake up. Need to get you to bed."

She immediately worried about the contradiction in terms but continued to tug at his T-shirt until his eyes cracked open.

He rolled his head to the side and looked up at her puzzled. "Mia?"

She smiled down at him. "We need to get you to bed, little brother. Come on."

She helped him up off the floor and kept her arm around him, ushering him down the short hallway to their bedroom. Mia steered him over to his bed on the left side of the room and eased him onto the mattress.

He looked up at her with hope in his eyes as she tucked him in. "Do you think we'll ever have a house where I can have my own room?"

She smiled at him, doing her best not to show pity or pain. "Yes, Adam. I do."

He grinned back at her, pleased with the answer.

Part of her felt guilty for lying, even though it wasn't a real lie. Her dreams were to get out of here and find a place for her and her brother where they could live happily, peacefully, without concerns. Without a passed-out father in her living room who drank up all his money.

The reality was she'd joined the Savages. And once you were in that gang—like so many others—there was only one way out.

She reached down and tousled his brown hair, kissed him on the forehead, and told him goodnight.

Mia walked over to the door and was about to leave when Adam said, "I love you, Mia."

She looked back over her shoulder at him with kindness filling her eyes. "I love you, too."

After she stepped through the door, she closed it gently behind her and wiped a tear from her right eye.

He was such a good kid and didn't deserve to live a life like this. They'd had more than their share of bad luck. It was time for things to change.

She knew it could be worse. There were kids out there living in the street. At least she had a roof over her head, even if it had cracks running across it. Her bed wasn't fancy, and certainly wasn't the most comfortable, but it was a bed nonetheless.

The biggest struggle was to keep food on the table, and with things getting more expensive by the day, Mia knew it was going to only get harder to buy groceries.

She was lucky in that she usually ate with the gang. Food was one thing they always had plenty of, aside from stockpiles of drugs.

Usually it was fast food, but it was better than nothing, and Miles always paid the bill. Since Mia didn't really eat breakfast, that only left her with one meal a day to take care of for herself, and sometimes she had supper with the Savages too, depending on what they'd been up to that day. More often than not, pizza was the meal of choice.

She'd been able to sneak slices home for her little brother on several occasions. When asked where she was going with her food, Mia would always snap back with some witty comment that ended the conversation immediately.

Because Adam was in school, he always had breakfast and lunch provided by the cafeteria. Mia made sure he never went hungry when he got home, and only having to take care of one meal was easy enough for her.

She walked back down the hall and turned into the narrow kitchen. Instinctively, she opened the fridge and looked inside at the empty shelves.

Only a couple of bottles of beer, some cheese that she was certain would go bad any day, and a box of donuts her father had brought back from work—along with a warning that she and her brother were to stay out of them.

She closed the door, wishing she hadn't opened it to begin with. *No need to check the cupboards*, she thought. They would be just as barren as the refrigerator.

Her phone vibrated in her pocket, interrupting the growling in her stomach.

She took out the device and looked at the screen. It was a message from Miles. A twinge of apprehension shot through her gut.

"Aw, man. I just got home."

She shook her head, staring at the screen in disbelief. Then again, being a member of the Savages didn't afford banker's hours. There was no clock to check in and out of work. When Miles told you to do something, you did it without question.

The message on her phone had been simple. "Winston's Pub. Thirty minutes."

That was it.

She knew the place. They'd been there dozens of times, maybe more. It was one of Miles' regular joints, and the owner was more loyal to him than to the Houghton Mob, even though he paid George Pickford every week.

Miles Tidmouth had promised better rates, better protection, less invasiveness, and he'd bring in more customers—members of the organization, of course.

The owner had been keen on the idea of dumping Pickford, but he also knew that would come with a heavy price. He'd not agreed to the deal yet, but Mia knew that wasn't far off.

Miles had a way of convincing people to do things. That skill was, in no small part, how she'd become a member of the gang.

She slid her phone back into its pocket and walked to the door.

Mia looked back at her sleeping father on the recliner.

The man had never treated her with kindness, never told her he loved her. When she and Adam left this place, he might not even notice. Would he feel guilty?

She didn't know. And she didn't care.

There was a better life waiting out there for her and Adam. She wanted to attend university and eventually go into medicine, but she'd need some remedial schoolwork first—then a number of exams before she could even apply. That would take a tremendous amount of time and money.

Difficult? Absolutely.

Impossible? She didn't believe anything was impossible, not if you were willing to work hard enough.

Depending on how the meeting at Winston's went, Mia's timeline for getting out of London could move up or down.

As she closed the door and locked it behind her, she felt something in her chest that told her not to go, to skip the meeting.

But she couldn't do that. When Miles gave an order, you obeyed.

At least for now.

Soon, she hoped, no one would be bossing her around anymore.

8

Miles Tidmouth sat in the same corner booth he always occupied.

Winston's Pub featured burgundy upholstered seats with gold accents along the edges. The black bas-relief over the bar featured crests of famous English families from throughout history.

A man in is mid-sixties stood behind the counter, pouring beer from one of a dozen taps.

Miles watched the room from his position, always observing his surroundings. That mindset of always paying attention had probably both kept him alive and helped him climb through the ranks until he'd taken over.

Now, his vision was nearly achieved. Soon, his gang would run this side of London, and then it would be all about protecting what he'd won, and expanding deeper into the city.

He ran his fingers through his thick, curly hair. When he was done, he smoothed the thin black mustache above his lips and then rubbed the beard under his chin.

Having grown up on the streets, there wasn't much that scared Miles anymore. He'd seen it all, at least all that this city had to offer.

There were places a man like him might feel out of sorts—cities like Juarez or Mogadishu—but in London, where crime still had a sense of civility to it, he felt like it was his kind of briar patch.

He reached up and pulled his long black hair into a ponytail, then cinched it up with a scrunchy.

Happy with the hairdo, he reached for the lager sitting in front of him.

The bar was empty except for his people. He'd requested privacy from the owner, and even paid him for the loss of revenue.

While that would not always be the case, Miles was savvy enough to understand exactly how to ply a local business owner. Be generous in the early days, and they will eat out of your hand when it comes to asking for favors later on.

And they would ask. They always did.

Two of Miles' men stood at the door. One was outside acting as a bouncer who only allowed Savages into the building.

Three more members sat at the bar—two women and another guy.

Another man and woman sat at a nearby booth.

Most of them were Miles' guards, people he'd risen through the ranks with, and whom he trusted—as best a gang member could trust anyone.

That was especially true once you'd reached the top.

Once you were the king, that crown bore down with a crushing weight. He was constantly on alert, always paying attention to rumors, shadows twitching in the darkness.

Since he'd acquired an actual crown, however, he'd felt far more confident and way less worried.

The king always wore a target on his back. Assassins, would-be leaders, ambitious zealots all thought they could take his throne. They coveted it more than anything.

Those things had bothered him before.

Then a few months back, he'd taken the fabled Welsh Crown of Prince Llywelyn from a rival—after killing the man, of course.

The crown had disappeared centuries ago, from what he'd learned. And most had stopped searching for it, as Miles learned after taking the crown for himself.

Before executing his enemy, Miles had known nothing about the artifact. It was a pretty trinket, a trophy of war. He had no idea of its true value until one of his acolytes—a history hobbyist—told him it looked like it was authentic, and possibly quite old.

After conducting some research online for lost crowns in history, he discovered the one in his possession turned out to be pretty famous.

Once Miles realized how important and valuable the crown was, it imbued him with a sense of confidence unlike anything he'd ever felt before. He took it as a sign that he was meant to rule, meant to lead, and meant to sit on a pile of money.

Power. Miles had always craved it from an early age. Maybe it was because he hadn't had any in his home where his dad beat up him and his mom.

He'd felt utterly powerless.

Not anymore.

He thought about the crown, hidden in a vault back in his home—not dissimilar to the one he'd taken it from. No one knew about it except a trusted few, most of whom were in this bar right now—with one exception.

Miles checked the Breitling on his wrist. The watch said it was twenty minutes past midnight.

The timepiece was probably over the top for someone in his position, the leader of a lowly street gang full of thugs and common criminals. A watch like that was more fitting of someone running a powerful organization—legal or otherwise.

He'd always operated with a simple philosophy ever since he was high school age: If you act like you belong at the top, you will be at the top.

Once he began implementing that in his day-to-day life, things started to change.

School didn't really work out for him, but he found other ways to make a living beyond what the public education system could teach. He learned useful skills, survival tactics on the streets of London that not only made him stronger but also taught him the ways of the business world.

The door at the far end of the room burst open, and Mia stepped in. She looked mad as a raging volcano.

Miles regarded her casually before making a show of looking at his watch.

She strode over to him, ignoring the looks from the other gang members, and stopped at his booth.

"Don't act like I'm running late for something. You called me minutes ago, Miles."

He stopped glancing at his watch and turned his blue eyes to her. "Oh, I know," he said. His voice sounded seductive but also political. It was smooth and sultry, but with a hint of scripting to it, almost as though he was trying. "I'm just anxious to get started."

"Get started?" She put her hands on her hips and leaned her head to the side. "With what? It's after midnight. Most people are asleep."

"You know that nighttime is our time, Mia. Stop acting like a newbie."

She sighed and slid into the booth to his left. "What do you want, Miles? I just got done with the job over at the other pub."

"Yes, I know," he said. "And you did spectacularly, my dear. From what the guys told me, it was an excellent performance."

Mia remained unimpressed. "Don't try to flatter me, Miles. What do you want from me? Why am I here? I could be in bed."

Both his eyebrows shot up. "There's an image."

She rolled her eyes. "Don't even go there."

"I wouldn't think of it," he lied, grabbing the beer to take an interlude sip.

"Yeah, right. You gonna tell me what's so important that you dragged me out here in the middle of the night? Or you just want to keep getting shot down by a girl ten years younger than you?"

He shook his head once, impressed, and set the bottle back down.

"That's the thing I've always liked most about you, Mia. Always so...." He sucked in a long breath through his nose, looking up to the ceiling as if it knew the word he wanted. "Saucy. That's a good one. You're always so saucy."

"That's it. I'm out of here."

She started to scoot away, but he grabbed her arm and locked down on it with an iron grip.

"You leave when I say you can leave," he growled.

His eyes scanned the room, but no one paid attention. They knew better than to interrupt, even if they had been watching and listening to the conversation.

She looked back at him, incensed that he would lay a finger on her, but also afraid of what that might mean.

If Miles said the word, she'd be dragged out back and executed. Her body would wash up on the banks of the Thames later, or perhaps turn up in some farmer's field far from the city.

Knowing Miles, he'd opt for the river. It was closer, and she knew all too well that he enjoyed making examples of those who stepped out of line.

"Get your hand off of me," she cautioned. "You are never to touch me. You understand?"

He leaned toward her, vitriol dripping from his eyes. He was high, and the faded lines of blow on the table weren't the only clues giving that away.

His bloodshot eyes gave her a view into his total lack of humanity. This man, she knew, had no soul. Not anymore.

Now, his life was entirely about one thing—ambition.

"I will touch you if I want to. You understand?" He let his fingers slip down her arm, brushing against the bare skin along her forearm until he dragged them across her hand.

She felt a shiver ripple across her skin and shuddered.

"What do you want, Miles? Or are you just going to sit here trying to flirt with me?"

He leaned back, finally retreating from the failed attempt at subduing her. Miles knew she was untamable. As long as she remained on his side, he'd keep her around. But her attitude of late had been less than cordial.

"We're going to hit Houghton's next shipment," he said.

Her eyes widened. This wasn't just some ambush in a pub to send a message. Miles was talking about an outright declaration of war, if that hadn't already been done.

She was certain Pickford was putting together a retaliation plan at that very moment. If she were in charge, Mia certainly wouldn't be thinking offensively right now. She'd be planning for an attack by the Houghton Mob.

Her eyes wandered across the room, and she immediately felt a sense of dread. If the Houghton crew knew they were here, it would be easy pickings if not for the numbers Miles had brought with him.

Perhaps he was thinking *defensively*. As much as she hated to say it, he had a knack for leading. That came, in her estimation, purely from his relentless thirst for power. He'd learned by observation throughout the years during his climb to the top. Watching the people who ran the Savages, as well as taking mental notes of how other organizations operated, had been key in securing his claim to the throne.

"Their shipment of what?" Mia asked, suspicion brimming in her eyes.

He immediately understood her concern. "It isn't that," he said, pushing aside her fears for the moment.

"What then?"

"A little snow. Maybe a few other things. I don't know what they're bringing in. Only when and where."

"Is it tonight?" She wished he would hurry up and get to the point.

"No."

"Then it could have waited." She slid out of the booth, and this time when he tried to snatch her arm, she jerked it away before he could. "I'm tired, Miles."

"I thought you might want to hang out and have a drink."

She looked at him with a combination of loathing and pity. She and Miles had been through a lot together. At one point, she'd even wondered what it would be like to be in a relationship with him. But he wasn't the type for that sort of thing. Maybe she wasn't either.

So many who joined gangs lost sight of dreams or visions of a better future, a better life. Swallowed up in a world of the here and now, they only worried about a quick fix for whatever ailed them.

In most cases, just like with Miles, drugs were the salve of choice —especially cocaine.

"I'm going home, Miles. I need to rest. When is this shipment coming in? I suppose you have a plan for hitting it."

"I do. And it comes in tomorrow night. Should arrive between eleven p.m. and one in the morning. They'll be running it through one of their warehouses outside the city."

"Fine. Tell me the plan tomorrow."

"I'll walk you out. I was just about to leave anyway."

"I'm good, but thank you for the rare act of chivalry."

He scooted over to the edge of the cushion and planted his feet on the floor. "I insist."

She rolled her eyes. "Fine. But you're the one with the car out front. I walked."

"I can give you a ride home, if you like."

"No." She said it too quickly, then added, "but thank you. I'm fine."

"Not safe out there at this hour."

"I can take care of myself, Miles. But I appreciate your concern."

He stepped close to her and brushed her hair across her left ear, touching her skin gently. It made her cringe, and it took a herculean effort not to show that response.

"I know you can," Miles soothed. "Sooner or later, Mia, you're going to realize that it's okay to surrender now and then. Besides, every king needs a queen. You know?"

She assessed him in seconds, and when she'd finished, let her mouth drop open. "Oh. I see. Is that what this is all about? You want me to be on your arm while you run this side of London with your new crime syndicate or whatever it is you're trying to do?"

Her tone crippled him for a second, and he could only manage trembling lips in response. He wasn't sure what made him angrier—the fact that she was calling him out with such sarcasm or that it was clear she had no intentions of ever being his trophy.

"Because you should know by now that I am no man's prize, Miles. If someone wants to get with me, they're going to have to meet a higher standard."

"And I don't measure up?" He regained his playful expression.

"No. You don't." She turned and started for the door, but he grabbed her again.

This time, everyone in the room noticed, and none of them took their eyes from the scene.

"You will be mine," Miles said. "You might as well get used to that idea. It's not like you'd be treated poorly. Don't you want to be second-in-command of the empire I'm building for you."

Her head retreated, digging her chin into her neck as she feigned being impressed. "For me? Or do you mean for yourself? Because I have a hard time believing you'd do anything for anyone else that didn't benefit you."

He looked around, puzzled. "If it doesn't benefit me, why would I do it?"

She smiled and nodded. "Exactly." She slapped his hand away and stormed for the door.

Miles hurried after her, ignoring all the sympathetic and humored looks from the other members in the bar. They knew better than to laugh at his misfortune.

Mia stepped through the door before he could catch her again, and had to chase her outside.

He stopped next to his souped-up Impreza and threw up his hands. "You're going to come around sooner or later, Mia."

She waved over her shoulder without looking back.

Miles shook his head and fished the key fob out of his pocket. He'd rather not go back into the bar after the burn he'd just suffered at Mia's hands. Better to retreat and recover, fight another day.

He climbed in the car, started the engine, and sat there for a second as cars drove by sporadically. When there was room to maneuver, he whipped his car out onto the road, looped around in a J-turn, and drove away.

Less than thirty seconds later, four men in a black sedan parked in his spot and made their way toward the pub's entrance.

9

Mia had only made it fifty feet down the sidewalk before she realized she was missing her phone. She rolled her eyes and spun on her heels, doubling her pace to get back to the pub.

She didn't want to go back in there, but she'd heard Miles rev his engine, childishly, and then drive off. There was no mistaking the sound of that custom pipe he'd fitted onto his Impreza. It screamed like a mechanical banshee, though she didn't know whether it made the car any faster or just made it sound cool.

Knowing Miles, he likely only cared about the latter.

Mia reached the alley behind the pub and turned into it. The shadows didn't bother her. She'd spent enough time in darker, more disgusting places than this alley.

She kept moving until she reached the door. Then she stopped, grabbed the handle, and started to pull.

A loud thump against the surface startled her. She felt the door resist. Then she saw the hand and arm pushing against it.

The smell of overly expensive cologne drifted through her nostrils.

She spun around, fists raised, ready to fight off whoever was behind her. A hard backhand across her cheek knocked that intention from her mind.

"Yeah, that's right," Reg said, looking at her like she was a feral animal. "You remember me, don't ya?"

She winced and pushed her hands into her knees to keep from falling.

He punched her across the cheek, and her head snapped to the side. She stumbled deeper into the dark alley.

Reg spat on the ground at her feet, glowering over her. "You were the one there at the pub earlier tonight. Little distraction so your boys could ambush us."

"You like beating up girls, huh?" she spat back.

He huffed. "Not usually. But for you, I'll make an exception."

Reg raised his foot to kick her, but she blocked it to the side and punched him in the jaw.

He took a step back but grabbed her by the shirt at the same time, pulling her close.

Grimacing as he clenched his jaw, he drew her to him.

She tried to raise her knee into his groin, but he turned her aside and squeezed her neck.

"You're going to pay for that, girl," he sneered. "And for the ambush earlier."

Someone screamed inside the pub. Glass shattered. Loud thumps and crashes blended in with all of it to form the symphony of a brawl. And Mia knew her side wasn't winning.

This was payback.

She'd known it was coming but hadn't imagined Pickford and his crew would respond so quickly. Organizations like theirs didn't often react quickly, instead biding their time to watch and plan.

Unless....

He twisted her around and pinned her to the wall, squeezing her throat harder.

She felt her lungs start to tighten, begging for air.

Desperation kicked in, and she could think of only one other move.

Mia snapped her head forward, straight into Reggie's forehead.

The blow stunned him for a second, but he whipped his head sideways to shake off the haze.

She struck again, and this time felt his grip loosen.

Mia fell to the ground, landing on her feet but too weak to stand. She collapsed to her knees, catching herself with her palms against the wet pavement.

Reg tilted his head back and rubbed the skin just above the bridge of his nose, wincing in pain.

"You know what?" he snarled. "I was thinking about letting you live. Keeping you for myself."

She felt bile rise in her throat at the thought. The world spinning around her didn't help things. She clawed at the ground, trying to find enough balance to stand again.

"But now . . ." he continued. "Now I'm gonna kill ya." He took a step forward and delivered a kick to her abdomen.

Mia felt the air sucked out of her lungs. A whimper was all that escaped, like he'd kicked a stray dog.

"But I think I might have a little fun with you first," he said.

She coughed. Unable to keep herself upright any longer, she fell onto her side in the muck.

He took a menacing step toward her, his swollen eyes now full of twisted lust.

Mia coughed again, her chest burning for air. Finally, her diaphragm relaxed, and she breathed in huge gulps.

Reg reached down and grabbed her by the hair. He pulled hard, nearly ripping out a handful by the roots.

She yelped and found her feeble legs struggling to stand.

"Yeah," Reg said, looking her up and down. "I'm going to have a lot of fun with you."

"Let her go," a voice said from the other end of the alley.

Reg turned his head toward the source of the order, indignation now masking his beaten face.

"Get out of here. This ain't none of your business," Reg fired back.

"I'm making it my business."

Reg couldn't make out the features of the man's face. Only a pair of green eyes glowed in a sliver of streetlight reflected off a window.

"What you're doing is making a mistake, friend. Now move along before I make an example of you."

The man standing in the shadows didn't move. He simply stood there, his black leather jacket absorbing most of the shards of light. He wore faded blue jeans and a white Foo Fighters T-shirt.

All these details Reg accumulated in seconds. But the man's face remained in shadow, as if light itself feared him.

"I would prefer you try than beat up a helpless young woman," the American replied.

Reg sighed and shook his head. He looked back at Mia, then shoved her against the wall. She hit it hard, and her head smacked on the surface.

More fog filled her eyes. The world twisted again, and she felt herself slide to the ground.

Once she hit the pavement, she felt nausea sweep in and grab her stomach, but she didn't surrender and managed to keep from vomiting as the scene before her steadied.

She looked to the left, toward the man who'd interrupted her beating.

"You don't know who you're messin' with, mate," Reg blared, jabbing a meaty finger at the American as he took a threatening step toward the man.

"I'm not your friend. And I'm not your mate," the stranger corrected. "And if you want to eat a normal breakfast for the next six weeks, I highly suggest you leave right now. Looks like someone already worked you over pretty good. Maybe fighting isn't your thing."

"Oh, you think you're a funny one, yeah?" Reg sped up his pace, stalking toward the man as vengeful energy coursed through his body, sending his mind into a rage. "You're going to pay for that."

Reg reached out as if to grab the stranger, raising his fist at the same time.

Instead of getting a fistful of the man's shirt, the American grabbed his wrist and twisted, pressing into the thumb socket with his own thumb.

Reggie howled as the man wrenched his arm around behind his back and forced it up into position that pushed the shoulder joint to the brink of dislocation.

"Now..." the American said.

Reg struggled but couldn't break free.

"I think you owe that young lady an apology."

The suggestive reply came with an expletive.

"You know, I thought you might say something like that." The American kicked Reggie's knee out from under him, and he dropped to the pavement like a dumbbell. The fall came with another agonized shriek as the shoulder strained to free itself from the joint.

"I'm sorry. I'm sorry. Okay? Is that what you wanted to hear? I'm sorry."

Mia looked on from her position on the ground by the wall. Her vision had cleared, and things didn't spin around her anymore. She caught glimpses of the man's face, but every time the light tried to highlight it, he turned just enough to keep it at bay.

Mia wasn't sure if she'd been knocked senseless or not, but she heard her attacker whimpering like a wounded puppy. And he was apologizing.

She didn't for a second believe it was genuine, but it was a pleasant surprise.

"That's better," the American said. He shoved Reg down onto the ground, where his face splashed in a filthy puddle. "Oooh. No telling what was in that water, huh? I wonder if some of the patrons come back here when there's a line for the toilet."

Reg breathed hard, bracing himself on the ground as dirty liquid dropped from his nose and chin. *Who was this geezer?*

He started to get up but made a subtle move toward his pocket while his body shielded his actions from the interloper.

"I'm sorry," he repeated. Then abruptly, Reg sprang up and whirled around with a knife in his hand. "Sorry I didn't cut that bloody Savage to pieces before you got here. No worries, though. I'll be sure to do that the minute I'm done with her."

The American shook his head. His brown hair fluttered only slightly in a late-night breeze. But he noted the detail. The angry mobster had called her a Savage.

Spitting rain splattered tiny droplets on the ground, and in the many puddles littering the pavement. Dak watched as a single raindrop dripped from the thug's blade.

His eyes then locked on to Reg. "You should have left."

"And you shoulda minded your own business," Reg spewed.

He charged at the stranger, who deftly stepped to the side and swiped his hand down hard in a judo chop across Reg's back.

Mia slowly rose to her feet in the corner, watching as the unexpected savior toyed with her tormentor.

Reg slumped forward toward the street as the stranger turned slowly to face him again, putting his back to the pub's rear wall and the dumpster next to it.

"That's it!" Reg roared as he recovered and twisted around. "You're dead!"

He rushed forward, and again the American dodged the knife thrust, easily stepping aside. As Reg passed, the stranger kicked him on the tailbone and sent him sprawling forward toward the dumpster.

Reg tripped and turned his head sideways at the last second. A sickening crack shot through the air. His body collapsed instantly to the ground.

The American stared at him for several seconds, as if waiting for the man to get back up. But he didn't move.

Mia stepped forward from the shadows into a dim light from a building above. She stared in horror at the man on the ground.

"Oy," she said, stepping closer upon seeing him lying perfectly still. Her courage continued to swell until her toes were inches from his face. She kicked him gently, but he didn't respond.

The American moved closer and squatted down close to the

Houghton enforcer. He checked the unconscious man's neck, then wrist.

Nothing.

He turned to Mia, whose temporary relief had soured into abject fear that oozed from her eyes.

"He's dead," the stranger announced.

"What? How?"

The man leaned closer, turning Reg's head slightly until an indention appeared on his temple where the corner of the dumpster had hit his head. Upon further inspection, the American noticed the man's knife protruding from his right side, just below the ribs.

"Did he accidentally kill himself with his own knife?" Mia asked, worry building inside her like a tropical storm.

The stranger looked down at the dead man, assessing the situation in seconds. "No. There's nothing vital right there that could kill him so quickly."

A car drove by on the next street over. The sound startled Mia, and she started looking around.

The sounds of the fight inside the pub had faded to intermittent thumps, or glass breaking.

"We need to get you out of here," the American said.

"What?"

"It's not safe here, and the cops will come around at some point. You didn't do this, so you're in the clear."

She shook her head, looking at him, bewildered. "That's nice and all, except you have no idea who you just killed. Do you?"

"Technically, I didn't kill him. He killed himself. And from the brief glimpse of his manners I just got, I'm inclined to think the world is better off without him."

She couldn't disagree.

"You don't understand. His uncle runs a powerful mob in this part of London. When he finds out about this, it'll be bad."

The man turned to her, his face finally illuminating. "You have a place you can go?"

She nodded, blinking rapidly as she thought of her little brother. The last thing she wanted to do was endanger him.

"Okay, let's get you there. Is it far?"

"No. I walked here."

He flashed a look that suggested her close proximity wasn't ideal. "I'll walk you there."

"That's really... not necessary." She found it difficult to tear herself from his glowing emerald eyes.

"Not an offer. It's happening. What's your name?"

Without thinking, without hesitation, she said, "Mia."

She wouldn't have to most strangers. She didn't trust anyone in this world except her brother and herself. But she found herself trusting this guy, someone she'd known all of two minutes.

He *had* just saved her life, but she quickly threw up her defenses anyway. "I'll be fine," she added. "I can take care of myself."

"I'm sure you can. But it's late, and I won't be able to sleep if I don't know you made it home safe."

She rolled her eyes. "I said I'll be fine." She looked him up and down, assessing his athletic, lean figure. Mia stuck her finger at his chest. "But thanks for the offer. Very chivalrous of you."

He put up his hands in surrender. "Your call. I won't push anymore. Just want to make sure you're okay."

"I'll be all right." She nodded, feeling like she was back in control. "What's your name?"

The man grinned. It was a cool gesture, mostly cracking to the right side of his face. He had an old school look, something the James Dean types of the world could pull off, but very few others.

"Dak," he said. "You can call me Dak."

10

George Pickford watched the buildings along the street pass by without really noticing them. While his eyes were staring out the window, his mind was somewhere else—another time, another place.

And on a promise he'd made.

"You gonna be okay, George?"

Pickford's driver, Albert, had been with him for years—including during his rise to power in the London underworld. Albert was one of the few people Pickford trusted—as much as he could trust anyone.

Pickford knew early on in his career that he'd need lieutenants around him that were both competent and obedient. He'd marked Albert as one of those guys, and set about grooming him for when the time came.

Albert was one of the only members of the Houghton Mob that could call Pickford by his first name.

Pickford took a long breath through his nostrils and exhaled slowly. He thumbed his chin thoughtfully, memories of his dying sister filling his head. He never let anyone in his organization see his emotions. Not that he had many of those anymore.

He'd made it a priority to bury his feelings in a bomb shelter under a volcano, then smothered it with lava until no one could get to them.

No one except the ghost that haunted his imagination.

"I'm fine, Albert. Thanks for the concern." He meant it.

Pickford knew his man wouldn't overstep, and wouldn't insinuate weakness of any kind toward his employer. He also knew Albert understood how sensitive this was. The driver was the only person he'd shared anything with during his time in the Houghton Mob. Albert had seen Pickford's agony when his sister died so abruptly in the car crash. And he'd seen Pickford try to raise her son, Reginald, the best he could.

Reg had never really felt like a son to George. More like a bad rash that nothing could cure. And it came around nearly every day.

Despite the annoyance Reginald consistently heaped onto Pickford, he was still family. Beyond that was the promise.

George loved his sister. Agnes had been the only person he'd ever really cared about in this world. She'd basically raised him.

And it was Agnes who introduced him to the Houghton Mob.

She'd been seeing one of the guys close to the boss at the time, and he'd been willing to take a chance on young George.

It was an opportunity he made the most of.

In many ways, Pickford owed everything he had to his sister. And in that regard, he ached inside.

She'd asked him to only do one thing before she surrendered to her injuries. With tears in her eyes on a bloodstained hospital bed, she begged Pickford to take care of her son.

He knew what that meant.

It was time to make good on everything she'd ever done for him.

Agnes hadn't worded it that way. And she probably hadn't meant it that way. She'd never been the type to keep score.

Pickford had seen in her eyes only sincere concern about the well-being of her only child—a rough teenager who dipped in and out of trouble with school and the law.

When he swore to Agnes on her deathbed, Pickford hadn't taken that oath lightly. Reginald was a screwup, sure, but had he been so different when he was that age?

The car stopped at a red light even though there were no other cars at the intersection.

Albert sighed, frustrated.

Pickford stared at a fish-and-chips place he fancied. It was one of the few businesses he let slide now and then with their payments—because it had been his sister's favorite.

He'd taken Reginald there more times than he could remember throughout his teenage years. The petulant lad hadn't ever really expressed true gratitude, except once—the first time Pickford took him to that shop.

After that, however, Reg had turned into a feral cat. Feed the thing, and it never goes away, and loses its survival instincts.

Perhaps Reg didn't possess those instincts in the first place. He'd turned out to be worthless, a drag on his organization. In truth, Pickford resented the young man. Reginald had caused more problems than he was worth.

The light turned green, and Albert accelerated through the intersection with one last insulting profanity slung toward the traffic signal.

Pickford sighed and shook off the thought about his nephew.

It didn't matter if he liked the worthless sot. He was family. And the promise to Agnes was one of the few things Pickford held in high regard.

Now that was gone.

He'd failed.

A newspaper stand whooshed by, boarded up for the night.

A relic of another age, Pickford thought.

A similar thought had been nagging at him recently, but not about the stand.

He'd come into the organization and the criminal underworld as a young man. Now, the man who stared back at him in the mirror every day was older.

Was he a relic, too, soon to be replaced by the next best thing?

That crown always hung on him like a bag of sand.

No. He denied the thought with a grunt. He still had plenty of good years left in him.

With the death of his nephew, however, Pickford had lost any fragment of hope he'd ever clung to for a legacy.

Not that it mattered. Pickford couldn't have left leadership of the organization to Reginald. The empire would have crumbled in weeks. Maybe even days.

Pickford saw no sense in entertaining such thoughts. Houghton would continue as it had before, with someone new stepping in to run things. There might be a brief power struggle before things were consolidated, but that wouldn't be his concern. He'd be dead.

Just like Reg.

Albert stopped the car across the street from Winston's, checked the mirrors, then got out and opened the door for his boss.

Pickford straightened, always intent on looking professional and in command of the situation. No matter what.

He climbed out and flattened his navy-blue sport coat, wincing at splattering rain striking his head and face.

Without mention of the weather, Albert promptly produced a black umbrella and hoisted it over his employer's head. "Here you go, sir," the driver said, returning to the more formal way of speaking to Pickford now that they were out in open air again.

"Thank you, Albert."

The two walked across the street with little regard for any vehicles that might be coming their way. At this late hour, there'd been sparse few cars, and only a smattering of delivery trucks hauling their wares to local businesses.

Those trucks were one of the ways Pickford had elevated the Houghton Mob.

He'd started saving early on in his days working for the mob, putting money away in a sock drawer, under a pillow, and inside his mattress at Agnes' home.

Eventually, he'd put back enough cash for a down payment on a delivery truck. He leased it, with the help of Agnes' credit, and soon had guys from the mob working for him under the umbrella of the organization.

Albert had admired the move, and it was no small reason as to why he'd sided with Pickford in the early days.

Pickford, even as a young man, saw the value of owning all the assets to the empire—from production to shipping. Why pay someone else when you can have a closed loop?

Now, nearly every driver in this part of London was on Pickford's payroll. He considered expanding into other territories, but that would incite a war with the other families, and he wasn't interested in the kind of chaos that could cause.

Then again, that was the reason he was here—at Winston's.

The two men stopped at a police line, where two cops in rain gear stood looking like they wished they'd chosen a different career path in their youth.

Only a single police car sat in front of the pub, and its lights were off.

There were more squad cars along the street running to the back of the bar, but their lights, too, were out.

This crime scene was not meant to draw attention.

That had been Pickford's instructions to the cops he kept on the books.

The one on the right with a thick push broom mustache nodded at Pickford, stepped aside, and raised the tape.

"Thank you, Billy," Pickford said in a somber, resolute tone.

The cop only nodded curtly as the two men passed.

A plastic sheet draped across the entire alley behind the pub. It flapped in the breeze, glowing from the bright lights within.

Pickford had never seen a crime scene set up like that before. Then again, he'd never had to ask for additional discretion when involved with one.

Usually, it was understood. He'd had an arrangement for years with the local precinct. They knew what to do.

In this case, however, things were different. This was Pickford's nephew.

Whoever had committed this atrocious act was firing a shot across not only Pickford's bow, but the organization's as a whole.

Another cop pulled back the partition in the plastic drape and allowed the two men to enter without so much as a questioning look.

Once beyond the divide, Pickford saw the body first, sprawled out on the wet pavement.

No segue. No warning about what he might see once he went in. Just pull back the flap and see your dead nephew.

The head of the investigation stood in a corner, discussing something with one of the forensics team when he saw Pickford enter the scene.

He immediately left the conversation and hurried over in an attempt to soften the blow of the sight. "I'm sorry, sir," the cop said. "I meant to meet you out front and—"

"You don't need to prepare me for something like this, Inspector Newfeld. I've seen my share of bloodshed."

The pale, birdlike cop nodded. Dark circles hung under his eyes, and his skin draped from his jaws like tire flaps off an eighteen-wheeler.

"I just—"

"Thank you for keeping things as quiet as possible. I trust the Yard doesn't know anything about it?" Pickford dragged his eyes from the body and met Newfeld's nervous gaze.

"No. No, sir. Of course not."

"And none of your men here will make that call. Correct?"

Newfeld nodded his head.

"Then you have nothing to worry about. I want this kept hush-hush. If our enemies find out about it, then they'll start thinking we've gone soft. Better they not know."

"Understood."

Pickford returned his stare to the corpse on the ground. "At least you closed his eyes," he said, his voice as distant as his thoughts. He sighed, despondent. "Make sure there are no leaks on this one, Newfeld. If I hear one word on the street about Reginald, or anything making the slightest reference to this, I will hold you accountable."

"Yes, sir," Newfeld said, his voice full of tremors.

For several seconds, no one said a thing. The other investigators inside the sealed off area went about their business, doing their best not to listen to the conversation.

Pickford wasn't worried about them or their opinions. He paid them to keep quiet.

"This was my sister's boy," Pickford mused. "I promised her I would take care of him. Now I've failed."

Albert clenched his jaws, anger rippling through him.

"I'm sorry," Newfeld offered.

"Don't be," Pickford countered. "He was a lousy excuse of a human being. But I let my sister down. She was the only person I ever truly loved. And who ever loved me. Make no mistake, Newfeld," he turned to the cop, dark flames burning in his eyes, "whoever did this is going to pay."

The cop nodded. "We'll make every effort to stay out of the way, as usual."

"See that you do."

Pickford looked back to his nephew once more. "How did he die? I see the swollen cut on the side of his head."

"It appears, Mr. Pickford, that your nephew got into a disagreement with someone, and they struck him on the side of the head. We haven't found the weapon."

Weapon? What a joke.

Who cared if they found the weapon. It wasn't like that was going to change anything. Maybe they could track down the killer. Maybe. But Pickford wanted to handle this on his own.

"Where are the others?"

Newfeld's attention had wandered to a pretty brunette standing off to the side with a tablet in her hands. Her brown glasses accentuated the intelligent beauty in her eyes and on her face.

"I'm sorry?" Newfeld stuttered, suddenly realizing he was being addressed. "The others?"

"Yes," Pickford said, exasperated. "The rest of my crew. Where are they?"

"Oh. Right. They're just inside," the cop said, motioning to the back door. We held them for questioning, but we were waiting to release them... until you arrived. Didn't want them getting attacked on the street."

"I appreciate the concern, Inspector."

The cop couldn't tell if Pickford was being sincere or sarcastic.

Before Newfeld could agitate him further, Pickford moved toward the door. He pulled it open and stepped inside, leaving the cold, wet air outside for the warm, toasty embrace of the pub.

He'd been here many times in the past, but not recently. Still, there was something about the place that smacked him as different. It was colder than it used to be. He wondered if it was due to a lack of music, food cooking in the kitchen, or patrons lined up outside the door to get in.

Pickford walked through the corridor to the front of the building, where he found a single cop standing guard by the door. Four men sat at the counter, a beer tankard in front of each.

"I send you twats to do a job, my nephew gets killed, and all you four do is sit around drinking beer?"

His voice escalated with every syllable until it roared like a tornado. He swept his hand across the counter and knocked a beer over, cracking the glass along the rim.

"Sorry, boss," the one closest to them said.

Jerry stood farthest away and nodded. "We're not drinking to celebrate," he added. "We know what this means."

"You have no idea what this means!" Pickford raged, shaking the heads clinging to the rims of the beer glasses.

He exhaled, inhaled, and exhaled again in dramatic, painful fashion. "You have no idea," he repeated.

"It means war," Jerry offered. "I know that much."

"Yes," Pickford surrendered. His men didn't need to know about the personal toll this took on his mind, his heart. "It means war. A war with a piddling little gang."

"What do you want to do, boss?"

"I want? What do I want? I want to know what happened to my nephew!"

Jerry shrugged. "He wanted to come along with us. When we got here, he said he saw someone go around back."

"Did he say who?"

"No. And I didn't see anyone. I figured he just wanted to go back there and take a leak."

As much as it nagged Pickford to admit it, that was exactly the sort of thing Reg would have done. "So, he went around back, and someone killed him. And you three have no idea who."

"We were in here, doing like you asked."

"Yeah," one of the others added. He wore a black leather jacket over a plain white T-shirt. "We beat 'em up good, boss. Just like you wanted."

Pickford looked around the room, making a show of his search for the missing evidence. He put his hands out wide when he found nothing.

"I'm sorry. Where are the bodies? Huh? Because the body of my nephew is out back in the street!" He pointed toward the rear door as he yelled.

The guards sat still for a long ten seconds, letting the sound in the room evaporate to nothing but the coldest chill of silence.

Pickford walked around behind the bar. He ran his fingers along the tops of the mugs until he found one he liked, then picked it up and spun toward the row of taps.

He made a show of selecting a lager from the offerings and pulled the tap back. Golden beer flowed into the tankard. He expertly killed the stream at the right moment, allowing the foam to build up to a healthy, but minimal head.

Pickford looked at the beer and nodded. "To Agnes." He whispered so low the others in the room couldn't hear him. "I'm sorry, Sis."

He tipped back the drink and took a long, hard pull until half the mug was empty.

Then he slammed the container onto the counter and wiped his lips.

The men wore both fear and admiration on their faces.

"If they want a war, they can have one," Pickford said. "Fending off an upstart like this might prove advantageous for us as we look to expand our operations." He looked down at the beer, then back to Jerry. "I think it's time we make an example of these so-called Savages. We'll make sure this sort of thing never happens again."

"What about business, boss? Collecting and all that?"

"Keep things operating as usual. We don't want our enemies to think a bump like this will shut us down. Nothing stops. Understood?"

The men nodded.

"Start by getting my money from that old history professor. He owes me big."

"Dyer, sir?" Leather Jacket clarified.

"Yeah. James Dyer. He's been dodging me for weeks."

"Word is he skipped town," Jerry offered.

The information caused Pickford to tighten his jaw, but he suppressed his anger. "Then find him. He couldn't have gone far. It's not like the guy is sitting on a pile of money in the middle of a private island. He's gotta be here in the country."

"We'll find him," Jerry reassured.

"See that you do. And when you do locate him, I think it's time we take one of his fingers, just to make sure he never does anything like that again. Send a couple of the boys out to deliver our message once he's found."

"You don't want him dead?"

"Not yet. Dead men don't pay their debts."

11

Dak watched Mia enter her building from the shadows one street over. The second the door closed behind her, he felt a surge of relief fill him.

The apartment building was nothing fancy, but at least it was a home. She'd be safe there. Safer than on the streets.

Dak's bigger, more immediate concern revolved around the death of the assailant in the alley.

She'd talked like it was going to be a problem, but Dak didn't know about local turf wars—who was involved, where the boundaries fell, any of it. He knew that sort of thing went on. London was a big town. And big towns usually had big crime operations operating under the shiny veneer of renovated homes, shiny new high-rise condos, and the sense of "community" that the local real estate agents loved to crow about.

Turning to walk back down the sidewalk toward his hotel, Dak froze for a split second.

A silhouette lingered in the shadows just inside an alley across the street. The figure didn't move. Which either meant they were minding their own business, maybe on their phone or sparking up a smoke, or that they were watching him.

With no sign of the signature glow radiating from a phone screen, and no orange tip burning in the darkness, that left only one option.

And it raised a question.

Was the person following him or simply happened to be there at that exact moment... at that extraordinarily late hour?

Dak didn't believe in coincidences, but he also didn't want to poke the bear if the beast had no intention of attacking.

Instead, he started down the sidewalk, strolling in the general direction of his hotel several blocks away.

He'd been on his way back to the room when he heard the commotion in the alley outside the pub.

Luck, it seemed, was always a fickle friend.

Had he taken a different route to the hotel, or perhaps only been delayed a minute or two, he might not have stumbled into the situation with the young woman and her attacker.

It was lucky for her that he had, but now Dak was responsible for the death of a total stranger. And according to the girl, that stranger was connected to bad people.

He'd been unable to pry much information out of her, but as far as he was concerned, the dead told no tales, and there was no evidence that could pin the crime on him. Besides, he'd actually done nothing wrong.

Dak hadn't even assaulted the guy. On the other hand, the dead man had been going to town on Mia, and ended up accidentally killing himself when Dak interrupted.

It was the first time he could recall anything like that happening. And he'd been in more fights than he could ever remember.

Even if the cops figured out he was there, they'd have no evidence to charge him with anything. He'd merely stepped out of the way to dodge a clumsy attack.

His innocence didn't change the fact that Dak preferred to stay clear of the cops as much as possible. Plus, this wasn't his sandbox, and he didn't know who all the power players were making the rules.

He kept walking and stopped when he reached the next intersection. First, he looked to the right, down the street at the sparse traffic coming and going along the road. Then, he turned to the left and twisted his head a little more than normal to get a peripheral glance back toward the alley.

The figure had shifted to the near corner and appeared to be waiting.

So, the stranger *was* following him. *But why? And who was it?*

Dak didn't feel like sticking around to get the answers. He already had one manslaughter on his tab for the night. He didn't need any other bodies littering the streets of London. He'd been there less than twenty-four hours.

Best to keep his head down as much as possible.

He huffed at the thought and then crossed the road when the light changed.

This time, when he started moving, he did so at a trot. It was under the guise of being courteous to the few drivers waiting at the line, but really wanted to add one more test to the person tailing him.

Dak cut left the second his foot touched the other sidewalk, and he kept moving at a brisk pace—technically walking, but more akin to Olympic power walking.

He didn't look back again until he made it to the next intersection. Once there, he stopped again and looked back over his shoulder—blatantly this time.

Sure enough, the shadow had emerged from the alley to follow him.

"That answers that question," Dak muttered.

Now he had to make a decision—confront the tail or try to get away.

It was much too late to pick another fight. And jet lag was pulling on his eyelids like fifty-pound dumbbells.

Dak decided to go with the get-away route and hope that whoever was following him didn't already know where he was staying.

Then again, maybe there was another way.

He quickened his pace, pushing his step to a near trot. The hotel building was just ahead but still a few blocks away. To the right, a small park opened up—full of trees, benches, a pond, and surrounded by a wrought-iron fence with a six-foot-high brick base.

One of the entrances loomed to the right just ahead, and Dak decided this would be as good a spot as any to make his move.

When he reached the gate, he ducked to the right and through the entrance into the darkened park.

The tall brick base of the fence surrounding the property seemed to keep out some of the city light, only allowing the light of the lamps lining the walkways to pierce the darkness.

Dak found a large bush to his right, just beyond the brick archway.

He crouched down and hid between the bush and the fence, keeping low so the brick foundation kept him out of view from the street and sidewalk. Dak had used this method a few times when someone was following him. It hadn't worked out well for the tails.

At least here, in the relative darkness of the park, he could interrogate the suspicious character and find out who they were working for and what they wanted.

He listened intently, waiting for the imminent sound of footsteps on the concrete beyond the wall.

Seconds slogged by like they were stuck in sorghum.

Finally, he heard the sound of footsteps clicking nearby. They moved in a rapid staccato, signaling their hurried approach.

It was the tail. And whoever the guy was, he was trying not to lose his mark.

Dak steadied his breathing, waiting for the moment when the figure would appear around the corner.

Maybe the guy would look right immediately and see Dak crouching behind the bushes. Fortunately, he was close enough to the entrance that if the person did see him, the tail would have to be extremely fast to take Dak down before he attacked.

The thought caused Dak's muscles to tense. His blood pulsed with battle energy. More tactical thoughts filled his head.

Was the man armed? Was it a man at all, or was it a woman? He'd initially thought it looked like a male figure, but in the dark and from a distance, certain details could be blurred.

That didn't matter.

The armed thing, however, did.

Guns weren't permitted for citizens in the United Kingdom, but that didn't stop some criminals from getting them.

It was like some of Dak's friends back home used to always say, "Criminals don't care about gun laws."

Still, he knew that if the person watching him was armed, it would most likely be a knife of some kind, and probably nothing unusually long like the hunting knives he had back home.

He'd read about the knife violence in London in the past, but hadn't expected he'd ever encounter it.

And here he was, crouching behind a bush in the middle of the night without a weapon.

The footsteps hurried faster, and Dak knew it would be mere heartbeats before the menace appeared.

He readied himself to pounce, waiting with the utmost patience.

Then, a black trench coat flapped around the corner. It hung from narrow shoulders.

Dak risked moving an inch forward toward the threat.

The person didn't detect him.

Then, as the tail started to take another stride, Dak leaped from behind the shrubbery and grabbed them with one arm around the neck.

"Why are you following me?" Dak snarled.

"What? What are you doing? Let me go. Help!"

Dak squeezed the young man's throat a touch tighter, just in time to cut off the last word before it reached the canyons of streets surrounding the park.

"I said, why are you following me? Now, I'm going to loosen my grip, but if you scream, I'll squeeze even tighter. And the next time, I won't let you out. Understood?"

The terrified man nodded vigorously.

"Okay, good. Now, I'm going to ease up. Don't scream."

The captive nodded again.

Dak let off on his choke hold enough to let the man catch his breath. He nearly doubled over as he sucked in the air his lungs so desperately craved.

"Who sent you? What do you want?" Dak pressed the questions, barely giving the man time to regain his composure.

"I don't know what you're talking about," the man confessed in his English accent. "I'm supposed to meet my girlfriend here at the park right now. We were going to do a midnight picnic."

"What?" Dak asked, suddenly confused and feeling blood flush through his cheeks.

"A picnic. I know it's not midnight, but I got off work at the bar late."

Dak let go of the man, grabbed his shoulders, and spun him around.

The sallow face that looked back at him didn't remind him of a deadly bounty hunter or any kind of threat in the least.

And he held a small brown bag with a baguette and a bottle of wine jutting out of the top. The only thing missing was a charcuterie board and a bunch of fancy cheeses.

Dak's eyes lingered on the bag for several seconds. Then his head snapped around, and he searched the sidewalk and street for any sign of his pursuer.

"Picnic?" Dak asked, jerking the young guy closer. He didn't look more than twenty-two. And that was being generous.

"Y-yeah. I know. It's stupid."

"Yeah. It's pretty stupid at this time of night, kid. I could have killed you."

His lips trembled. "Are you going to mug me or something? I don't have much money."

Dak frowned. But the expression was a mixture of confusion and humor. He didn't crack a smile, though it took considerable effort.

"No. I'm not a mugger." He waved his right hand to shoo the guy away.

"What then? A secret agent or something?"

Dak's face darkened. "I can't tell you that."

A grin crept across the guy's face. "Or you'd have to kill me? That is so cool!"

"Okay." Dak rolled his eyes. "Move along now. Go meet your girlfriend for whatever all this is."

"Yes, and thank you. For whatever it is you do. Wink. Wink." The clumsy guy stumbled away down the walk and into the park, following the lamplight while looking back every other step.

Dak shook his head, and when the guy was gone, returned to the gate and looked down the street in both directions. There was no sign of the tail anywhere.

After waiting a good two minutes—inspecting every nook and cranny along the street—Dak decided to get moving.

If someone was going to attack him out in the open, they could go ahead and try. He needed sleep, though he had a bad feeling he'd get very little.

12

The smack across her face stung like a giant bee plunging stinger-first into her cheek.

"What happened, Mia? Huh? Did you do this? Did you set up the ambush?"

She reeled from the blow, the skin and sore tissue underneath still aching from the beating she'd taken the night before.

"Are you crazy?" Mia lashed back, shoving him away.

The others in the room stared in awe at her disregard for authority.

"I didn't do this. And don't you ever lay a hand on me again." She raised a threatening finger at him.

This wasn't the first time he'd hit her, but she was determined to make it the last. Miles had taken her in, albeit at a price. She'd pushed the resentment for her sacrifice deep down, but now it was coming out, and Mia was done with it.

"They jumped us. Okay?"

Miles glowered at her, but he didn't strike again. He breathed hard, listening while trying to think of something else to say to save face in front of the others.

They had all gathered in the gang safe house, an old tube

station that was no longer in use. The musty smell of the air combined with the rusting metal and dusty floors to evoke an earlier time when Brits had gathered down here to regroup amid another war. Mia had imagined this was what the 1940s smelled like.

"They jumped us," she repeated. "They hit us when we least expected it. Except I told you Pickford would retaliate."

He swallowed his pride with an ounce of pain.

"I knew they would try," Miles admitted. "I didn't think it would be so soon."

She cast him a glare of condescension. "What? Did you think they would sit around in their boardroom and plan out their revenge for a few months, allowing you to build up your resources so you could defend yourself? Of course they hit us immediately. We're lucky it wasn't worse."

She kept one significant detail to herself. Two details if you counted the American who had come to her rescue.

Mia wondered what the man was doing now, where he was. Had he skipped town for fear of being implicated in the death of Pickford's nephew? He didn't seem like the skittish type.

She found herself wishing he was here right now. The man named Dak seemed to have an air of common sense to him that felt lacking in this place, and in this gang.

He also didn't seem the gang type. Then again, neither was she.

It was a means to an end. And she constantly hoped that the end was near.

Miles nodded, but the look on his face wasn't one of agreement. "Yeah? Could have been worse? Well, guess what, Mia? It just got worse."

"What?"

"Pickford's nephew, Reggie? Someone killed him last night in the alley behind the bar."

"I haven't heard anything about it," she deflected, hoping he didn't know she'd been involved.

"And you won't. This isn't going to be on the news or on social media. They're keeping it quiet. My guess is so that Pickford doesn't look weak to some of his rivals."

Mia nodded. "That would make sense." She felt a relaxing gust wash over her skin. "Especially if a small-time operation like ours took out one of his own. Can't have that getting out."

"No. You certainly can't. My question is, which one of you did it?"

He took a menacing step toward her, his eyes locked on hers. He wore a long, leather duster over matching black pants and T-shirt.

Miles loved wearing stuff like that. She couldn't decide if he was trying to look like a Sith lord or prepping to dive into the Matrix. Maybe he was singlehandedly trying to bring back 1988.

He never took his eyes off her, and in that moment, Mia knew that he knew.

Miles took another step closer.

She could smell the body spray on him from four feet away. He used so much of that crap, she could detect it from anywhere in the room.

"The others were inside getting their teeth kicked in," he went on, jerking a thumb over his shoulder to roughly indicate everyone else in the room.

One of the guys at the bar grunted. His right eye was black and blue, and nearly swollen shut.

"Johnny over there has cracked ribs, or at least I'm sure that's the problem. Dill's face looks like it was used as a bowling ball." He raised his head, motioning to her. "You look like you took a pretty good beating yourself."

"Yeah, but she wasn't in there with us," Dill clarified. "She left when you did."

Miles could have taken offense at the comment. It almost sounded like Dill resented the fact that Miles had managed to skip out of the bar mere minutes before Pickford's crew showed up.

"I guess I was the only lucky one," Miles announced, knowing he needed to address that elephant in the room. He inched closer to Mia. "This wouldn't have happened if you'd just come home with me."

She ignored the suggestion. "Reg attacked me behind the pub. I'm pretty sure he had more on his mind than just beating me up." She'd been thinking about how to tell the story of the man who'd saved her, but decided to leave that part out. "Reggie's death was an accident. He was trying to corner me, lost his balance, and hit his head on the dumpster. I guess it struck him just right because the blow killed him instantly. I checked. He was gone."

Miles listened to the explanation with a critical stare in his eyes. He paused when she was finished, as if assessing the truth of it.

"You're telling me that Reg killed himself by running headlong into a dumpster?"

Mia nodded reluctantly. "Yeah. That's right."

"Wow. I mean, what are the odds?" He looked around the room, pretending to look for a response to the rhetorical question.

"I was lucky," she said.

"I'll say. And while I should probably be upset for the additional heat we're going to see from the Houghton Mob now, I have to say this turn of events could bring about some new opportunities for us."

He turned around and ambled over to a chair he liked to think of as his throne. He'd never said as much, at least not to Mia, but she knew that's exactly how he viewed the seat.

Ever since he'd claimed the lost crown of Llywelyn, Miles had seemed disconnected from reality. He had always been in a different world, but this was more so than usual.

The crown sat on an end table next to his high-back leather chair behind an old table they'd found somewhere. He eased into the chair and reached over with his right hand, grasping the crown with one hand. He placed it on his head and relaxed, as if wearing the thing took away all the worries of the world.

Mia knew it was very much the opposite.

"What do you think Pickford is going to do next?" Miles asked.

All eyes focused on Mia as everyone waited for her to answer.

"I don't know. Probably try to find our hideout. Which he can do, by the way. The man is connected to everyone in this part of the city, and in other areas, too. We won't be able to hide forever."

"Yes," Miles agreed. "And it's too much to hope that the vengeance he took earlier at the bar will suffice. His nephew is dead. Pickford will blame us for that. Whether we did it or not. Unless, of course, you're lying about how it happened."

"I don't lie," Mia defended with vitriol. "I never have."

"I know," Miles said. "That's the only reason I believe you right now, as silly as the story sounds." He exhaled through his nose and looked around the room. "We can either fortify this, or we can spread out and hope he doesn't find us."

Mia had another idea, and it served two purposes. "There's a third option," she suggested.

"Oh? And what's that?"

"We go on the offensive."

He allowed a curious smirk to cross his face. "Go on." Miles waved the fingers on his right hand as if he really were a king allowing his subject to do his bidding.

"We already hit them once," she continued. "Why not spread out and wait for his goons to come around again? They'll be collecting more payments this week. Cut them off. So, while he's trying to keep things running like normal, and trying to find us, he'll never think that we would be on the attack."

Miles considered the advice with a shrewd look on his face. "Pickford will have his men out hunting for us. And the rest of his enforcers will be collecting payments."

"Divide and conquer," Mia added.

"Yes," he said, elongating the word as he contemplated the idea.

She saw the gears turning in his mind. All Mia really wanted to do was cut his throat and let him bleed out right there on that "throne" of his.

He'd hit her—not just tonight, either. Since the first time it happened years ago, she'd been biding her time to get back at him.

Initially, her thoughts had been to take over the Savages, to become the boss. But she knew that was outrageous. Life in a gang was no life at all. It was just a stupid game, a temporary ride that always ended the same way—dead.

"I like it," Miles said. "Commence planning at once. We'll need all hands on deck for this. It's time we take our place at the table."

With his approval, Mia felt something flutter in her chest. If Miles and the rest of the Savages went after Pickford's goons, many would end up dead. And hopefully, Miles too.

She didn't care who won, but she had a feeling she knew it wouldn't be her crew. There were no emotional attachments here. She loathed almost everyone and had only stuck around this long for fear of what might happen if she tried to leave.

Now, however, there was a chance she didn't have to go anywhere.

13

Dak sipped his coffee as he steered the rental car down the narrow country road. He'd stopped in Cambridge to get a quick bite to eat and the cup of joe he now enjoyed.

For a tea country, there were a few spots in England to get a good cup of coffee, and he'd found one such café in the city that was better than almost anything he'd ever had. Aromi was a coffee shop recommended by a friend from the area but who was now living abroad.

Dak had sent a quick message to find out who had the best coffee in his hometown, and the one-word response "Aromi" had not disappointed.

The car hit a pothole and nearly caused him to drop the cup just as he took a sip, but Dak managed not to spill any on himself.

"Good one, Dak," he said, placing the drink in the nearest cup holder. "That would be something. Go to meet this guy with coffee all over your clothes."

He shook his head and focused on the road. According to the GPS on his phone, he was close to the farm and only needed to locate the entrance.

A simple enough task that he felt would go awry out here in the countryside. He'd passed a number of small farms with nondescript gates and driveways. Most of them had mailboxes with the address numbers on the side, so that helped, though there were some that didn't, and it was one of those Dak felt would be the place where the elusive Mr. Dyer was holed up.

He slowed down as he neared a place on the map where a pin marked the spot he was trying to find.

Dak steered the car around a curve where a rickety fence of stacked stones lined a field of tall, green grass.

On the left side, a driveway appeared where the road straightened, and Dak eased the car onto the gravel.

He stopped for a second to make sure he was in the right place, and after checking the pin along with his surroundings, he determined this had to be it. That, or he'd keep driving around in circles until nightfall.

Dak turned the wheel and followed the two grooves in the driveway up a gentle slope toward a stone house at the top of a knoll. The structure looked as if it had been built out of the same rocks as the wall surrounding the farm.

Gray smoke plumed from the chimney, and a white sedan sat off to the right between the house and a brown barn standing fifty yards away.

Dak admired the area. The many farms surrounding the city stretched out as far as the eye could see, only interrupted by the occasional forest or outcropping of trees and shrubs, or the walls and fences that seemed to be so common.

After stopping the car, Dak climbed out and looked out across the countryside one more time. There wasn't much high elevation in this region, but this one gave a spectacular 360-degree view of nearly everything.

In the distance, the spires of the famous King's College Chapel reached into the blue sky. It was then Dak realized that the gray clouds had subsided and he was getting to experience something most people in England rarely got to see—the sun.

He recalled reading an article about the sunniest city in England,

and that it only received a few hundred hours of sunlight every summer.

The amount came out to the equivalent of only a week or two of sunshine.

Being from Tennessee, Dak was accustomed to more sunny days than not, so being here in the UK presented some challenges. He found himself wondering how much the gloomy weather affected people here.

Dak parked the car and walked over to the front of the house, where the steps led up to a porch that spanned the front façade.

He smelled onions and beef cooking inside. There was another odor that blended with the fresh country air, but he didn't know what it was. Probably a vegetable of some kind.

He stopped at the door and knocked four times, hard enough to be heard anywhere in the small farmhouse but also soft enough not to sound demanding, like a cop serving a warrant.

Dak waited for a minute before he heard locks clicking. Then when the door opened, it was only a crack.

The professor's face appeared in the doorway through the narrow opening. Dak only recognized the man from his picture in the file Will had given him, but he knew right away it was Dyer.

"Who are you and what do you want?" Dyer asked.

Dak saw the shotgun muzzle around waist high. Most guns weren't permitted in the United Kingdom, but several makes of shotguns were exceptions.

This one looked to be the double-barrel variety.

"James Dyer?"

"Who wants to know?"

"My name is Dak Harper. I'm not here to hurt you."

"You sound like an American. I didn't realize Pickford was sending Yanks to come after his debtors now. You can tell old Georgie I'll have his money soon. I just need a little more time. Or I can shoot you now and let him figure it out."

Dak liked the guy's spunk, but there was no way the retired

history professor was going to stand a chance against a former Delta Force operator. Even when he was armed and Dak wasn't.

"Who's this Pickford?" Dak asked.

"Yeah, right. Like I'm going to fall for that."

Dak pouted his lower lip as if accepting defeat, and nodded. "Okay, James. Have it your way." He turned as if to leave, causing the man to lower his guard for just a second. Then Dak turned abruptly and kicked the door hard with his right foot.

The blow sent the door crunching into the man's shoulder and face, knocking him back onto the floor just beyond the threshold.

Dak stepped in and bent down, picking up the shotgun before the guy could raise it again.

"No! Please. I'll get Pickford the money. I swear it! Just don't kill me!"

Dak held the shotgun by the barrel and stared down at the cowering man. Moments before he'd been so brave, so brazen. Now he merely whimpered.

"Get up," Dak said. "I told you I'm not here to hurt you. I have a question for you about an artifact. An artifact that I believe was recently found after being lost for a few hundred years." He ejected the shells from the weapon and leaned it against the doorframe before closing the door.

Dyer rubbed his cheek where the door had smacked him in the face. "For someone who claims they aren't here to hurt me, you've sure done a great job of it."

"You didn't give me a choice. If you'd listened, your jaw wouldn't be in pain right now. You'll be fine, though. Give it a few minutes. I doubt it's broken or anything serious."

"What are you, a doctor?" Dyer looked up at him with tired, gray eyes. "You don't look like one."

Dyer bore the appearance of a man who'd spent most of his days in a sedentary desk job, researching, studying, learning. His hands looked as soft as cotton, and Dak knew the second he shook one of them he'd discover that observation to be true.

"No," Dak said. "But I've been in a few fights during my time. I know what's bad and what isn't. You're going to be fine. Won't even need an X-ray. Who is this Pickford?"

He had no way of knowing if that was true or not, but all he cared about at the moment was settling this guy down and getting as much information out of him as he could.

Dyer clambered to his feet and nearly fell over from standing up too fast. "You're serious? You don't know?"

Dak surveyed the room in more detail. Then he cast a cautionary glare at the man that demanded more answers.

"He's a crime boss in London. I... thought you were one of his collectors."

A humble kitchen with old appliances, wallpaper that could have been sixty years old, and a collection of rickety wooden chairs surrounding the table filled out the room.

Something cooked in the oven, and a pot of cabbage simmered on the stove. Those aromas added to the overall smell that poignantly reminded Dak of his grandmother's home growing up.

"I hope I didn't interrupt your lunch," Dak said.

"I don't eat much for breakfast, so I eat an early lunch," Dyer explained.

"Great. I don't care about your eating habits, Professor. I'm here to see if you know who might have this."

He took a photo out of his jacket and set it on the table.

Dyer frowned, taken aback by the sudden inquiry. "What is this?" he asked.

"The lost crown of Prince Llywelyn," Dak said. "I was led to believe you might know its whereabouts. Maybe I was led wrong."

Dyer's face paled. He looked at Dak with astonishment. "Yes. Of course. I recognize it now. The Welsh Crown. Disappeared centuries ago."

"Then why did you ask what it was?"

Flustered, Dyer cleared his throat. "I apologize if I'm a touch off. Getting hit in the face with a door and thinking a hit man for the mob was here to kill me sent me for a loop. And second, do you know how many crowns I have seen in my lifetime? I've lost count. Sooner or later, they all start looking the same. But yes, I recognize the so-called lost crown of Prince Llywelyn. Not that it matters."

"Why?"

"Why what?"

Dak sighed, choking down his exasperation. "Why did you add the last part? Where you said 'Not that it matters.'"

Dyer shrugged and wiped the back of his hand across his forehead. "What do you know about this crown?"

"Not much," Dak confessed. "Only that it disappeared a few centuries ago. The prince died in a military campaign. That pretty much sums it up."

Dyer peered at him from behind wire-frame glasses that perched on a thick nose. "Yes. Well, I'm afraid I don't know much more about it, either."

The former professor acted nervous. Dak knew the man was lying.

"That's interesting," Dak said.

Dyer shifted. A bead of sweat trickled down the side of his face. "Yes, well . . ." He cleared his throat and shuffled over to the door, pulling it open once more to show his uninvited guest that his visit was over. "I have much to do today, so if you don't mind."

He motioned to the door with his right hand.

Dak pressed his lips together and nodded. He walked over to the door, stopped in front of the man, and then faced him. "You know that if I can find you, so can Pickford's goons."

Dyer stared into Dak's bright, almost unnaturally green eyes.

For several seconds, the professor pondered the statement. Then he shoved the door closed again.

"I owed Pickford a lot of money," Dyer said.

"Owed?"

"Fine. Owe. Since I'm retired, and there's no chance of going back to the university; I had to take whatever money I could get." He sounded like he carried a bushel of regret on his head. "I was contacted by someone from another syndicate. They were a lower-level organization than the Houghton Mob."

"Houghton Mob?"

"Pickford's organization. I'll come back to that."

"Fair enough. Go on," Dak encouraged, not wanting the man to get distracted now that he was talking.

"The leader from another group, a guy named Don Shilton, approached me about analyzing something he'd found."

"The crown," Dak realized.

"Connected those dots yourself, did you?"

Dak chuckled at the barb.

"Anyway," Dyer continued, "he called me. No idea how he got my number, and I don't want to know. But I was desperate. He offered me ten thousand just to take a look at the thing. I can't imagine what he must have paid for it."

"Did he pay you in cash?"

"Of course. I don't want that kind of income burst raising red flags with the government."

"Smart."

"So, I took the job. I figured, what could it hurt? Either Shilton kills me, or Pickford does. At least doing a favor for Shilton got me a little closer to paying back Pickford. And my hope was that maybe I'd picked up an ally in the process."

"Did you?" Dak asked.

Dyer shook his head. "No. Some other crew took out Shilton and most of his lieutenants. We haven't seen an organized crime bloodbath like that in a long time in London."

"Pickford took out Shilton and his gang?"

"No. Rumor has it some upstart named Miles Tidmouth from a street gang pulled the job. They call themselves the Savages. I find it hard to believe they could succeed at that sort of an attempt. But I wasn't going to stick around town to find out. The second I heard the news, I left town and came out here. I know it's only a matter of time until Pickford finds me, but at least here I can see them coming, and maybe defend myself."

Dak made a mental note of the name, Miles Tidmouth. *Another lead,* he thought.

Dak was hung up on a detail from a minute before. "You said Shilton paid you ten grand. But that only got you part of the way to what you owe?"

Dyer's face reddened. "I'm not proud of it. Okay? It's a problem."

"How much?" Dak pressed.

"It's hard to say, you know with the juice running and all."

"How much?"

"You're not one to give up easily, are you?"

"No," Dak chirped.

Dyer turned away, still embarrassed. "Twenty-five," he said. "I owe him twenty-five grand."

Dak didn't blink. "So the ten you received from Shilton got you nearly halfway there."

"Nearly."

"Unless you thought you could double it on another bet. You didn't do that. Did you?"

Dyer lowered his head in shame.

"You have to be kidding me. Seriously? You dumped back the whole ten?" He couldn't believe it and turned away to let his eyes wander for a second so he didn't dole out too much judgment.

"Not the whole ten," Dyer added quickly. "Only half of it."

"Perfect," Dak said, nodding rapidly in disbelief. "So, you owe a mass murderer twenty thousand dollars."

"Pounds, actually. We use pounds."

"Even worse. So, now you owe him twenty." Dak briefly considered using some of his funds for this particular investigation to help the man out of his financial trench, but Dak knew what would happen. The guy would go right back to gambling and within two months find himself in the exact same situation he was in now.

No, handing out money wasn't going to solve the problem. On top of that, Dyer hadn't given him anything of real value yet.

"Let's get back to Shilton and the crown. What happened next?"

"To the crown?" Dyer clarified.

"Yes."

Dyer rolled his shoulders. "No clue. My guess is whoever killed him and his crew took the crown. If they did, I haven't heard anything about it. And no one else has called to have me look it over. Pretty sure that revenue stream is gone for good."

"And the only name you have for me is this Miles character?"

"You're starting to sound like a cop." He paused, waiting for Dak to defend the accusation. "Like I said, I don't think Tidmouth could pull it off. I've heard of him before. Big ambitions, but he's sloppy. Only a matter of time 'til the street eats him alive."

Dak knew better than to underestimate the high ambitions of a criminal.

"I'm not a cop, if that's what you're suggesting. I don't have a badge. What I do have is an employer who wants that crown. If it's in the hands of a criminal, I'll take it from them."

Dyer puzzled over the explanation. "That's a strange sort of career, isn't it? And it sounds dangerous. Do you always do this kind of thing, or do you have another job?"

"This is it right now. Unless you just happen to have seen a former United States Army colonel named Tucker hiding out somewhere."

The confused look deepened on the host's face.

"Never mind," Dak continued. "Yes, this is my gig. And it seems like it leads me to unsafe places most of the time."

"How often do you go out on a quest like this for your... employer?"

"Not often. This is my fourth. But I didn't come here to talk about what I do or why I do it. I'm going to get that crown. And it sounds like the guy who has it probably isn't on the city's Best Citizen List."

"Best Citizen List?" Dyer wondered.

"Don't worry about it." He turned toward the door.

"Wait. You're leaving? Where are you going?"

Dak looked back at him. "Two minutes ago, you didn't want me here. Five minutes ago, you were pointing a gun at me. Now you sound like you don't want me to go."

Even Dyer knew he was being ridiculous, or at least must have sounded that way to the visitor.

"No. It's not that. It's just—"

"Oh, I see," Dak realized. "You want me here because you think I can protect you. Is that the reason for your change of heart?"

Dyer blushed and lowered his gaze to the floor. "It's just that, well, they could be here any time, and I can't take them all on by myself. I won't last a minute."

"And you think I will?" Dak arched an eyebrow. "Pretty big assumption to make for a guy you just met and know almost nothing about."

"I have a good sense about things like this."

"I bet you do," Dak spat.

He knew the type. They were soft, living in a world of ultimate convenience. When it came down to it, if society collapsed, guys like Dyer would be the first to go.

"Please. Take me with you, then."

"Not gonna happen. The last place you need to go is back into the city. And besides, where I'm going probably isn't a good idea for a guy like you."

"What's that supposed to mean?"

"I have a contact in London. I'm going to meet them and ask them a few questions about this crown. I think bringing you along for the ride might cause them to wonder if I'm legit or not. You know, the way you thought maybe I was cop?"

"Oh. You think they might think I'm a cop?"

"You just stay here, keep your head down, and try not to get killed by Pickford's men. I'll be back after I pay my contact a visit."

Dak started to open the door, then heard a car door shut outside.

He froze at the entrance. "You expecting someone?"

Dyer shook his head slowly, fear trickling across his face.

Dak leaned down and peeled a thin cream-colored curtain away from the narrow window next to the door.

Two men walked toward the front porch, and neither of them looked like they were cops.

"Well," Dak sighed, resigned, "I guess I'll have to stick around a little longer than planned."

14

"Who are they?" Dyer asked, desperation now clinging to his words.

"You want to look outside and tell me?" Dak asked.

Dyer shook his head rapidly.

"I didn't think so. You got a place you can hide? Basement? Attic? Crawlspace?"

"There's a cellar here. I can hide down there. You don't think I should just ignore them?"

"They'll come in anyway," Dak whispered, aware that the men would be on the porch within seconds. From the one second he'd looked at them, he pegged them as the breaking-and-entering types. "Get to the cellar. I'll let you know when it's safe to come out."

"But—" Dyer started to protest, but Dak cut him off with a warning glare. "Okay. Okay."

The man turned and skittered down the narrow hallway, made a left, and disappeared through a door.

Dak heard his shoes clumsily clomping on the stairs leading down to the cellar. He rolled his eyes with every thump, irritated that the guy who was so afraid for his life had such little awareness of the noise he was making.

Within seconds of his disappearance, one of the men outside banged on the front door. A heartbeat after that, a man shouted. "Oy! Professor Dyer. Open up. We got some business to discuss with ya."

Dak made them wait. He also made himself wait. No one stood by their door all day waiting for unannounced company to show up. It would have been weird if he'd opened the door right away.

Instead, he slapped on a sleepy look, counted to ten, and then reached for the door. He pulled it open as one of the men standing at the threshold held up a fist, about to knock for a second time.

"Oh hello," Dak said lazily, rubbing his eyes as if he'd just woken up from a late-morning nap. "Can I help you guys?"

"Who are you?" The guy wore a beige jacket over a white T-shirt and black jeans. He had a shaved head like Jason Statham, and looked every bit as tough. The other one, a brown-haired guy wearing a black windbreaker and gray trousers, was slimmer and shorter but still looked like he'd been in more than a few brawls. He was what people would consider wiry, though Dak wasn't sure he'd ever described anyone that way.

"Eddie. Who are you?" Dak lied before throwing the question back at him.

"What are you doing here, Eddie? Where's Professor Dyer?"

"Who?"

The man scowled at Dak and Black Jacket took over. "James Dyer, you twat," he spat. "Where is he? We know he's hiding out here."

"James Dyer?" Dak looked up into the gray sky as if the clouds might share the answer with him. "Can't say I know anyone by that name. Although I heard someone bought the Dillon farm up the road. Could be over there."

The two guys looked at each other for a second. It was the kind of look that asked, *Is this guy kidding?*

"Do you know who we are?" Statham's doppelgänger asked.

Dak stood there with a blank look on his face, then widened his eyes as if hit by a twenty-six-ton epiphany.

"Wow!" Dak exclaimed. "Is it really you?"

The bald one scowled in confusion.

"You're the actor from the Guy Ritchie films, right? Oh, and *The Transporter*. So good. I didn't care for the sequel, but that's the way sequels go. Am I right?" Dak laughed. "I have to say, though, that my favorite was your role in *The Italian Job*. Wahlberg is cool, but I think you stole the show in that one."

The two interlopers glanced at each other again, with the same befuddled and annoyed look from before. Only more confused.

"Gosh," Dak kept going. "I cannot for the life of me remember your name. But if it's any consolation, I don't recall your character names, either."

"Shut up." Statham's twin snapped the word, and Dak started for effect. The truth was neither of these two morons worried him.

He'd already searched them for weapons. The one on the right had a knife tucked into the back of his belt, which Dak thought was an odd place to keep it. He didn't see a weapon on the other guy, but figured he had something, too. Maybe even a gun. Still, Dak remained unconcerned.

"Sorry," Dak whimpered.

"Where is James Dyer?"

"Yeah," Black Jacket chimed in. "We know he's here. We did a little digging. I don't know what game you're up to, but you better tell us where he is or else."

Dak's face darkened at the threat. "Or else what?" he rumbled.

The bald one took a step forward, raised his finger, and pointed at Dak. He nearly tapped him in the chest. "Or else things get ugly."

"Yeah. Ugly," the other one echoed and brandished his blade.

Dak regarded the knife the same way he might have a double-glazed donut in the hands of a 95-pound swimsuit model—curiously.

"Well," Dak said in a calm, sinister tone, "we wouldn't want things to get ugly. Would we?"

"That's right. Now, get out of the way, and tell us where he is."

The bald guy stepped toward the threshold, but that was as far as he went. Dak slid to the side, blocking the man's way in.

The intruder nearly bumped into Dak face-first. "What do you think you're doing?" the goon snarled.

"Sorry, but I can't let you in my home, sir. I mean, I know you look like—"

"You better get out of the way, or I will *put* you out of the way."

Dak didn't back up an inch. He may have even moved a few millimeters forward. "No. You won't. I'm sorry if you have the wrong house. But you can't come in here. There's such a thing as private property."

The bald guy started to raise his right hand, but Dak turned his head once. "A poker player I knew once said don't push anything at me you're not willing to lose. I'd put that hand down. You might not get it back."

"You're a cocky one, aren't you?" He threw a fist at Dak, trying to catch him off guard.

Dak's right hand shot up and caught the man's fist four inches in front of his face. The guy was strong. Dak had to give him that. The edge, however, went to Dak.

The American held firm, his face burning red with the exertion.

The guy with the knife could only stand there and watch, so mesmerized he didn't know what to do.

The bald one pushed as hard as he could, doing his best not to let up. While the mind was willing....

Dak felt his opponent losing the battle, his slightly inferior muscles giving up the fight despite their master's wishes.

Fear rippled through the guy's eyes. His partner saw what was happening and panicked.

"Come on. Get him. You can take him."

"Shut up, Teddy, and cut this guy."

Dak shook his head. The moment in time froze like an icy lake, reflecting three men in a doorway.

Black Jacket hesitated, which gave Dak enough time to kick the left knee out from under the guy he held. The cartilage and ligaments gave way with a pop, and the man howled. On his way to one knee,

Dak twisted the now considerably weaker wrist, and used it to absorb the stab from the knife held by the other guy.

The sharp tip jabbed through the bald one's wrist and exited through the top. The man screamed even louder from the fresh wound.

Dak frowned at his partner in confusion. "You just stabbed your own man," he said.

To his credit, Black Jacket let anger fuel his courage, which resulted in a sloppy charge with his right fist raised.

Dak considered toying with him but decided to end it with a simple broken wrist and send him on his way.

Black Jacket rushed forward, and Dak let him throw the pathetically slow roundhouse and caught his fist. Then he twisted hard toward the ground, leaned into the guy's midsection, and judo-flipped him over his back while still gripping the wrist.

The guy's bone snapped on his way to the ground, where he yelped in pain as he tried to roll away and down the porch steps.

The bald one was already retreating to the driveway, hobbling gingerly as he gently held his wrist with the knife still sticking out of it.

The two hurried back to their car as best they could with their wounds.

"I'm sorry you couldn't find your friend!" Dak shouted as they made their retreat. "Like I said, maybe check up the road at that other farm I suggested before. Or build a time machine and go back to the moment where you chose not to leave and suggest to yourselves maybe you should just go."

The men fired sneering glares back at Dak, but nothing else.

He knew they'd be back, which meant his new acquaintance would need to find somewhere else to hole up until all this was settled.

Problem was, he wasn't sure what to do next.

He watched the car spin out on the gravel driveway as the two men angrily left the farm. The back tires kicked rocks and debris out behind the rear bumper.

Dak knew the men were doing it out of anger as well as a healthy dose of fear. He'd just thwarted whatever plans they'd made before coming here, and they would need medical attention for their injuries as the price of their incompetence.

Dak wondered if all the men under the mob's employ would go down so easily, but he knew better than to even harbor that hope.

These two were just the tip of the iceberg.

When the car was out of sight, Dak closed the door and walked over to the entrance to the stairs.

"Professor?" he shouted down. "You can come up now."

No answer.

Dak frowned. "Professor?"

"Sorry!" the man called back. "I just wanted to make sure it was you."

Dak rolled his eyes. He sounded nothing like the two goons he'd just encountered. Not that he could really blame Dyer for being so paranoid. Two men had just come to his house to collect money he didn't have. And when someone couldn't pay a debt to a mob loan, well... things could get dicey.

As in they would literally dice him up. Dak guessed they'd start with fingers or toes. After all, killing Dyer wouldn't get them their money. But those criminal underworld types were big on getting things moving with physical torture.

Dyer appeared at the top of the stairs still looking nervous. He poked his head around the corner and looked out toward the front door. "Are they gone?"

"Yeah. They're gone," Dak said, almost laughing.

"Are you sure?"

"Would you get up here. Yes. Of course I'm sure. And they're both going to need a doctor."

Dyer looked up at him from the stairs below. He searched Dak's eyes for an explanation to that statement.

"A doctor?"

"Yeah," Dak laughed, unable to keep it in any longer. "They weren't so tough. Just a couple of thugs."

The man climbed the last few steps, still looking toward the front door as if the two enforcers might appear at any second.

"They're gone," Dak reassured him. "But they *will* come back."

Dyer snapped his attention back to the uninvited guest. "How soon?"

"Hard to say. Their boss will be angry about it, though. I can tell you that."

"What did you do to them?"

"Nothing they didn't to do themselves," Dak hedged. "They'll live. For now."

"Pickford will think I hired protection." He looked hopeful.

"Don't even think about it," Dak warned. "I don't do security detail."

Dyer snorted. "Not that I could pay you anyway. Not having any money is what got me into this."

Dak considered recommending he give up gambling, but that was a different conversation for a different day, and with someone more qualified than him.

"For now, do you have anywhere else you can go to lay low for a while? Any family somewhere? Friends?"

"Most of my friends are in the city. And my family has moved abroad."

Dak nodded. After what he'd just done, the mob would send more men to Dyer's house, but would also be on the lookout at train stations and airports. He couldn't cover them all, but he didn't have to. All Pickford had to do was keep Dyer in the country. That meant watching international train and airline departures. He could accomplish that with a small portion of his forces.

"There's no one?"

Dyer sighed. "My ex-wife lives in Newcastle. But I can't go there."

"You sure?"

"Things didn't end well."

"Maybe it's time to make amends," Dak suggested. "Your options are stay here and die or go there and deal with your ex-wife for a few days."

"You think it will only be a few days?" Dyer looked hopeful again.

"I have no idea. But the time frame doesn't matter. The mob doesn't have connections in Newcastle, do they?"

Dyer shook his head, thoughtful. "Not Houghton. Pickford's crew only operates in London. Other organizations are in that town."

"Then you'll be fine. You may get nagged a bit while you're there, or berated for all the things you did wrong in the marriage. Beats being dead."

"I suppose you're right," Dyer agreed. "Okay. I will go to Newcastle."

"Good idea, Professor."

"What are you going to do?"

Dak looked back toward the door. "I'm going to do what I came here to do—find the crown." *And with any luck, Colonel Tucker, too.*

"How are you going to do that?"

Dak had an answer for that, too. "I have a contact I can speak to."

15

Mia strolled down the sidewalk toward her apartment. She barely noticed the people she passed, the shops to her right, or the cars on the street.

All of it was just background noise and visuals.

Her mind spun with possibilities.

She'd been saving her money for years to finally leave London and move to America to attend college, but American colleges weren't free. They offered some incentives for foreigners, but those subsidies didn't cover everything. And school was expensive.

Still, she had her mind set on it. And once she set her mind to something, there was no turning back.

There was no chance for her to attend college in the United Kingdom unless Miles was dead.

Until the last twenty-four hours, it would have taken a miracle to make that happen. Now, however, she saw the light—a slim chance that maybe, just maybe, the man with the leash around her neck could be killed.

She rounded the corner and turned up the side street leading to her flat. Her brother was still in school, but he'd be getting out soon, and she had to be there to pick him up and bring him home.

Mia didn't mind it. She loved her little brother more than anything. She took joy in picking him up from school every day.

Their dad was at work at the moment, but even if he wasn't, she knew he'd be in no condition to show up at the school and get Adam.

He'd done that one time, and it had caused more harm than good. Her father had made an arse of himself, showing up to the school completely hammered. She was surprised he hadn't thrown up in the building.

Fortunately, the school's director had handled things professionally, but she'd also issued a stern warning.

"Nice day for a walk," a man's voice said from somewhere behind her.

She spun around and found the guy from the night before standing five feet away.

"I thought I recognized your voice. You out doing good deeds in the city today? Saving more damsels in distress?"

"Not yet," he said, twisting his head to look out toward the street. He made a show of searching the faces as if one of them might need his help. "But the day is young."

She chuckled. "That's a good dad joke."

"Is it?"

"I don't know. My dad doesn't tell jokes."

"What does your dad do?" Dak asked the question, wary he might be prying too much. But he needed to soften the conversation before asking about the crown. It would be awkward to just come out swinging with that. Then again, he wasn't sure there was a subtle way to get around to that question.

"Drinks, mostly," she said without an ounce of self-pity. "Factory worker when he's not doing that."

Dak nodded. "Sorry to hear that."

"Don't be. It could be worse. Could be better." The last phrase signaled a touch of pain. "How long you been standing there waiting for me?" she asked, steering the question away from the uncomfortable subject.

"Not too long," he lied. It had been three hours.

"Lucky you, then," Mia said dryly. "To what do I owe the pleasure, Dak?

"You like coffee?" he asked, ignoring her probe and instead looking around as though he didn't trust their surroundings.

Her eyebrows pinched together over her nose. "You're a bit old for me, aren't you?"

He blushed. "I'm not asking you out. I'm—"

"I was just messing about. Come on, Dak. I'll get a coffee with you. I know a good place right around the corner." She threw on a mischievous look. "You're buying, by the way."

"Works for me."

Dak followed her back down the street and around the corner to a coffee shop a block away. He'd seen the place before and wondered if it was any good, but had been so focused on the list of problems piling up in this investigation that he hadn't had a chance to swing by.

The hotel coffee made sure he didn't get a headache throughout the day, but it was barely more potable than gray water.

"This is a good place," Mia said as they stopped at the door. Dak opened it for her, and she thanked him for the courtesy. "Such a gentleman," she chimed.

"It's how I was raised."

"I don't meet many proper gentlemen. Most of the guys I know are lowlifes."

The scent of fresh-brewed coffee, espresso, and pastries smashed into Dak's senses as he followed her into the shop.

"I do love the smell of a coffee shop when you first walk in," he confessed.

"Yeah, me too," she agreed. "Too bad for the baristas you kind of go nose deaf to it eventually."

"I've heard that."

They walked to the counter, and Mia greeted the person taking the orders—a young woman probably in her early twenties with a nose ring, green hair, and tattoos of forest scenes on her forearms.

"I'll take a cappuccino," Mia said. "Double shot, please."

Dak nodded, pursing his lips to show he was impressed with the order of double the caffeine.

"Black coffee for me," he added.

The barista keyed in the order on the register, and Dak handed her a prepaid credit card.

Mia noticed the card but said nothing. Instead, she looked around the room for a seat. There were plenty available since it wasn't one of the rush hours.

"I'm going to go grab a table," she said and headed off to the front corner of the shop, where an empty table with two chairs sat next to huge windows.

Dak clenched his jaw, but there was no stopping her. He didn't like sitting in the front of a restaurant or café, any place of business. Especially one with so many clear windows. He could see the charm in it—a view of the street where a patron could watch the people walking by.

But sitting out front and in the open came with inherent risks that common people never considered. To their credit, they didn't need to. He assumed none of the people in this shop were being hunted by a lunatic former commanding officer.

And everywhere he went on one of these missions, Dak found himself in more trouble than when he started.

He took the receipt from the cashier and ambled over to the table where Mia had taken a seat facing the street. Which meant Dak was going to have to sit with his back to the window—the most uncomfortable place for him to be.

He stopped at the empty chair and looked over at her, still reluctant to take the seat.

She motioned with one hand to the chair in the corner. "You going to join me or just stand there?"

He pressed his lips together, fighting back the urge to ask her to move. "It's just that... I like to face the entrance, and the street."

"Yeah? So do I? I like to watch the people. It's fascinating to me, all the lives that walk by every day. Their problems. Their victories. We'll never know most of them."

"Um, yeah, that's not what I meant. I just... I prefer to—" He stopped himself and sat down, choking down his concerns. They'd only be in there a few minutes anyway. He angled his body sideways so he could at least keep an eye on the entrance, just in case.

"Why are you being weird?" she asked.

"You mean in general or just right now?"

"Why choose if you don't have to?"

He had to admit, she had a wit about her that he'd not seen in many people her age. "You're sitting in my seat," he answered plainly.

"Excuse me?" she protested, confused. "What are you talking about?"

"Whenever I go somewhere in public, I always face the door. Also, I almost never sit in the front of a place like this. Too close to the street. Too many variables to track."

"Variables?" She almost laughed.

"Yes. Danger. You know, threats?"

She scrunched her face to express utter confusion, then shook her head. "No, actually, I have no idea what you're talking about."

"You sit in a back corner if possible, and always face the door in case someone dangerous comes in the front."

Mia turned her head to the side and glanced over at the door. Then she surveyed the room and its occupants.

"No one in here seems particularly dangerous." She leaned in close, lowering her voice to a conspiratorial tone. "Are you worried one of them is onto us?"

"Now you're just toying with me again."

Mia laughed. "Yeah, I am a bit."

"Dak!" the barista shouted.

"Excuse me while I get the drinks," Dak said.

He stood up and walked fifteen feet to the edge of the counter, where he picked up their drinks and returned to the table.

After setting Mia's drink in front of her, he pulled his cup closer and popped off the lid to let the coffee cool.

"So, what did you want to talk to me about, stalker?" Mia asked.

His head drooped to the side in mock disappointment. He knew she was kidding. Or he thought he knew she was.

"I'm looking for an artifact," he said. "Something of historical value from Wales. I heard someone named Miles has it."

In mid-sip, Mia nearly spit her drink all over him but managed to hold it back with the most gargantuan of efforts.

"What?" he asked innocently.

"Sorry. Just down the wrong pipe.. That's all."

"Ah."

She looked around nervously, concern washing over her face and filling her eyes with fear.

"You shouldn't have come here," she whispered. "And if you're looking for Miles, you should stop."

"Why? Does he come in here often? I'd like to meet him if possible, ask him some questions."

Mia huffed at the notion. "You? Meet Miles?" She shook her head and looked down at her drink. She lifted her gaze again to meet his disarming jade eyes. "He doesn't take meetings. Not from people like you."

"People like me?"

"You look like a cop. You act like a cop. Although I will say"—she raised a finger—"you don't cover up a crime scene like a cop."

He didn't flinch at the reference. "Maybe you haven't met enough cops."

She snickered in a musing way and turned her head, looking out the window to her right at nothing in particular. "I've met plenty," she admitted. "And I don't care to meet more. Not on the side I'm currently on, anyway."

Dak allowed a slight grin. "I noticed you said currently."

"Yeah, well, we're all running from something. Aren't we?"

"I suppose so."

"Not smart to run around here using your real name like that, Dak." She emphasized his name then took another sip, staring at him over the top of her cup.

"I don't mind if people know I'm coming. It might make things easier on my end."

"Has it ever?"

Dak laughed, smiling wider as he did. "No. But hope springs eternal, right?"

"Not around here." She took a sip and looked out the window again, this time gazing longer at the people walking by.

"If your friend Miles won't take a meeting with me, maybe you could help me with what I'm looking for."

"Some kind of artifact, yeah? I'm sorry, I don't know much about history and all that. What are you looking for? A four-thousand-year-old tablet or something? Because I haven't seen anything like that."

Dak shook his head. "No. No. Nothing that old."

"How old?"

"Few hundred years." He reached into his pocket and took out the picture of the crown. "This was the last time it was seen. Pretty recent from what I understand. I learned that some mobster purchased it on the black market. But that guy ended up dead."

He slid the photo across the table and gauged her reaction, which was significant.

"Get out," she said, half in amazement and half in fear. "What do you know about this?"

"So you have seen it," Dak realized.

"Of course I have." Mia looked around the café again, making sure no one was eavesdropping. "Miles took it off that mob guy you were just talking about."

So Dyer's intel was good after all, Dak realized.

"How did he manage that?"

She sighed, wondering how much to tell this stranger. Her eyes stayed fixed on the window. When she spoke, her voice remained distant.

"We hit another mob organization. It was ambitious. I didn't agree with Miles on doing it. But once he has something in his mind there's no changing it." Mia turned and faced Dak again. "Miles wants a seat at the table."

"What table?"

"You don't know how it works around here, do you?"

"Nope," Dak said and raised his coffee to his lips. He let the steam fill his nose.

"Gangs like the one I'm in... We operate beneath the families, the bigger organizations."

"Like the remora."

She puzzled over the statement. "What?"

"The remora," he repeated. "It's a scavenger fish that swims along with a shark, usually very close to it. The shark kills its prey, and whatever bits float away, the remora eats."

"So, it eats the scraps."

"Yep. Pretty much."

"Wow." She bobbed her head slowly. "Yeah, I guess we are a lot like the remora. But Miles doesn't want to be that anymore. He wants to be a shark."

"And to become a shark in these waters, you have to kill the other sharks."

"Bingo, Ringo."

It was starting to make sense, at least on an elementary level, to Dak. Things worked similarly in the States as far as he understood, though he'd never spent much time around people who were in gangs or the mob, and certainly didn't study up on their common practices and operating procedures.

He doubted that manual was real anyway.

Dak didn't want to overstep, but he had to ask. "So, you're telling me that your boss, Miles, has this crown?"

"He's not my boss," she corrected. "He gives the orders, but I do my own thing."

Dak knew false bravado when he saw it. She was shoveling it in heaps, but that wasn't a hill he was willing to die on.

"Sorry," he offered. "But you're certain he has the crown?"

She nodded. "Yep. Same one."

He noticed the casual way she regarded the subject. "Do you know what this is?" he asked, tapping the photo with a finger.

"Some lost crown Miles stole from a guy when he killed him."

"Yes. But do you know where it came from? Who it belonged to?"

She raised one shoulder and dropped it. "No. Why should I care?"

Dak pulled the picture back to his side of the table and stuffed it into his pocket. "That crown is the lost crown of the Welsh kingdom. It belonged to a prince named Llywelyn. It went missing after he was killed during a military campaign. For a few hundred years, no one knew where it was."

Her eyes grew wider with every word out of his mouth.

"It's cliché to call things priceless. You hear it all the time about this priceless thing or that," Dak said. "But there are certain artifacts out there that really don't have a price tag. The value is whatever another person is willing to pay. And very often, for something like this, that price is extremely high."

"How high?" Mia asked before she could stop herself.

"Depends," Dak hedged. "But something like that crown? No clue what someone would pay for it. Millions. More than that, maybe. People are paying more for much less impressive stuff these days."

"Yeah, I suppose you're right." She paused for a second, thoughtfully sipping her cappuccino. "So, you want this crown why again?"

"I don't want it. My employer does. And when he wants something, he gets it."

She pretended to be impressed. "Oooh, it sounds like you spoil him."

"No. He has a reason behind sending me out to find these things. They're always in the hands of a bad person."

"Bad, huh?" She dug deeper. "What constitutes that? I wonder: Are you a bad person, Dak?"

He didn't hesitate. "No." He looked out the window and across the street at a window he'd been looking to off and on since he sat down. "I'm a terrible person. I've done things, awful things. Funny part is, when I was in the military, I believed that the orders I followed were for the greater good—no matter what I was told to do. It turns out some of it wasn't for good. Or it hasn't panned out that way yet. With this gig, I know every time that I go out, I'll find someone as terrible as me. If not worse. If the people who possessed these kinds of artifacts were decent, good folks, I'd never show up at their door."

Dak tilted his head to the side, noting a cut on her face he hadn't seen the night before. "Did Miles do that to your face?"

She'd been listening to his comments, not realizing that her breath quickened with every word.

This man across from her was far better than any man she'd ever had in her life, including her father. Especially her father.

"It's fine. It's nothing. Just a scratch."

Dak nodded, but a fire burned in his eyes. And he didn't attempt to smother it.

"That's what victims say. You don't strike me as a victim. Are you a victim, Mia?"

"Nah," she said, blowing off the question. But there was no fooling him.

"Don't make excuses for him. He's given you nothing. And he only takes. Sometimes in the form of hurting you. That will only get worse, by the way."

She sighed, resigned. "He's given me a chance to survive up to this point," Mia countered. "No one else helped me when I was at my most desperate moment. Miles did. For that, I owe him."

"I'd say your debt has been paid," Dak argued. "And now you have someone in your corner who asks for nothing from you."

16

George Pickford cracked the peanut shell and dumped the nutty treasure into his palm. He tossed the nuts into his mouth and chewed. Then he grabbed a pint of Pilsner sitting on a wooden shelf and took a drink.

Pickford's personal darts room occupied three hundred square feet in the back of his favorite pub, and no one was allowed to play in his room without his say-so.

He didn't own the joint—not in the legal sense of the word. But he did call the shots, and no one ever questioned his say.

"Where them boys at?" Pickford growled to one of the grunts standing next to him. The mountain of a man didn't say anything. He knew better. Despite the fact he could crush Pickford like a walnut.

The guy merely rubbed his thick, black beard in silent contemplation.

Jerry stood at the line, holding two darts in his left hand and one in his right. He looked over at the boss and snickered. Without taking his eyes off Pickford, Jerry threw the dart at the board.

He only missed the bull's eye by an inch.

"I don't know, boss," Jerry answered. "They should have been back an hour ago."

"Two hours ago," Pickford corrected. "And why haven't they called to check in? It isn't like them. Everyone knows to check in."

"I know, boss. You want me to send out two of the other boys to track them down?"

"No. They'll show up eventually."

Jerry looked at the board and threw another dart. This one struck dead center.

"Just irritates me when guys don't do the simple things I ask."

"You want me to work them over when they get here?" Jerry almost sounded hopeful about the proposition.

"Nah. Nah. Nothing like that. We need every able-bodied man we can get."

One of the women who worked for him sat off to the side near a stained-glass window. The curly brunette hair hung down past her bare shoulders, partially covering the tattoos adorning her pale skin.

"Able-bodied man?" she asked.

"Sorry, my dear," Pickford apologized awkwardly, insincerely. "You know what I meant. You're my best, after all."

She grinned back at him as though she accepted the compliment. He even halfway meant it.

Natalia was one of his best—a former Russian operative who washed up on the banks of the Thames looking for work and a way to stay hidden from high-up Russian government officials. He'd never asked specifically, but Pickford figured it could go as high up as the president of the Russian Federation.

She took a swig of beer and went back to playing cards with one of the other hired guns.

Jerry wound up to toss another dart. In the middle of his throw, a loud banging on the back door interrupted his motion, and he sent the dart flying into the wooden panel below and to the right of the target.

"What the—" Jerry swore angrily.

"Go see what that's about," Pickford ordered. "We're not due for another delivery until the end of the week."

The pub had been a conduit for moving drugs throughout Pickford's turf. This place was the hub where all their wares could be distributed to the street peddlers who got unsuspecting, desperate citizens hooked.

People looking for an escape from pain, stress, or boredom could find whatever they wanted from Pickford's low-level dealers.

Jerry ducked around the corner separating the dart room from the back entrance to the bar.

Pickford heard him slide the viewing window open. Then he heard a few expletives from Jerry's mouth.

Curious, Pickford left his seat and stepped around the corner as Jerry opened the back door.

The two guys they'd sent out to find Dyer limped into the narrow corridor, both with significant injuries.

"What happened to you two?" Pickford blurted.

Jerry helped one of them into a seat close to a table near a window.

Natalia and the other members of the crew watched the men stagger in.

"Jerry," Pickford said, urgency lacing his voice, "get the doctor."

"Yes, sir." Jerry didn't hesitate. He instantly set into motion, taking out his phone and stepping out the back door to call the mob physician.

The doctor had been employed by the Houghton Mob since before Pickford took over. The man was in his late sixties now but still did good work. And he knew how to keep his mouth shut, which was the most important detail of all. That, and he did good work for cash. Everything was off the books, the way it had to be.

The two men looked like they'd seen a ghost. They were both drenched in sweat, and their skin had turned ashen.

"What happened?" Pickford demanded. "Did Dyer do this?"

The one on the left shook his shaved head, grimacing in anguish. "No. He hired someone," the guy managed. He looked down at the knife sticking through his wrist. "I... wasn't sure if I should take it out."

The one in the black jacket held his broken wrist gingerly in the fingers of his uninjured hand. "He was American," he offered. While in significant discomfort, he appeared to have gotten off easier than his partner, who both had a bad limp and a knife sticking out of his forearm.

"American?" Pickford asked. "How does Dyer have the money to hire private security when he can't afford to pay me what he owes?"

"Not sure, sir," Black Jacket groaned. "But he's definitely a professional."

Pickford nodded. *Yes. And apparently, you two are not.* He kept the thought to himself but fumed on the inside at their incompetence.

The problems were piling up faster than he could count them. His nephew was dead. His enterprise was under attack from an upstart street gang. And now one of the people who owed him money had hired some kind of private bodyguard to watch over him.

Everything felt like it was coming unraveled.

While he'd been in charge, nothing like this had ever happened before. Pickford had never been challenged in this way. And for the first time in his reign, he wasn't sure what to do.

He had to compartmentalize things. And the first order of business was finding out who this brigand was that had injured two of his collectors.

"This American...," Pickford said calmly, "what did he look like?"

The bald one leaned his head back against the wall to rest. "Brown hair. Strong. About my height. He had kind of a Southern accent. I think."

It took all the man's energy just to get those words out. He closed his eyes and took a shallow breath, swallowing hard.

"Get these boys some water, would you?" Pickford barked at two men sitting at a table across the room.

The two hopped into action and disappeared around the corner toward the front of the pub.

"Did this American say anything?" Pickford pressed, hoping the interrogation would provide something of use that could lead them to Dyer's protector.

"Not really. I mean, nothing except threats. He moved like

someone who's trained, though, boss. Probably former military. Hard to say. But he's definitely been taught how to fight."

"Great." Pickford stood up straight and stretched his back until it cracked a couple of times. "So, we have some former soldier working for a guy who owes me money." He knew his "men," save for Jerry and Natalia, were useful when it came to bullying the people in their part of town. But when it came to combat, they were more brawlers than anything else. Their techniques, while effective, were often clumsy and brutish. Most used their size and strength to their advantage. The weaker ones always had weapons to use as a crutch when it came to fights.

Based on the look of things, that hadn't worked out too well for these two.

"He tried to tell us that we were at the wrong place," Black Jacket went on. "He said we should check the next farm over."

"And did you?"

"No, sir. He was lying. That was the place. I know it." He winced as a fresh surge of pain ripped through his arm from his broken wrist.

One of the two men fetching drinks appeared at the end of the hall holding two glasses of water. He stepped over to the men and handed one glass to Black Jacket. The other guy watched as he stood back with his arms crossed.

The bald guy slowly cracked his eyes open and leaned forward to take the glass with his good hand.

"Drink," Pickford ordered. "You're probably in a state of shock right now. Don't want that getting worse."

"The doctor will be here in ten minutes," Jerry announced as he returned from outside.

"Good," Pickford said. He looked back to the two wounded. "We'll have you lads patched up soon."

Black Jacket nodded and finished his glass of water.

"You two stay here," he said, then rounded on the guy in the hall with his arms crossed. "Take watch. I don't want Dyer's bodyguard deciding to go on the offensive. But if he does, we need to be ready."

"What about the Savages?" Jerry asked.

"We'll handle them, too."

"They will likely hit us again, sir. This time, closer to home. Especially after our retaliation. It's unlikely their leader will see it as a warning. More like an invitation to fight."

Pickford nodded. He knew his lieutenant was correct.

"Natalia." He spoke the name with respect, but also a touch of hesitation.

"Yeah?" She looked over at him again from her table, where she'd been the entire time.

He motioned with his right hand for her to come over.

She begrudgingly did as requested and sashayed over to the table where the two injured men sat. She held a shot glass in her hand, full of clear liquid.

"Go get Dyer for me. And kill his bodyguard."

She nodded. "As you wish, m'lord." She tossed the vodka into her mouth and swallowed. Then she curtsied. "Consider it done."

She spun on her heels and walked out of the room. The back door slammed shut after she left.

Jerry looked at his boss with questions in his eyes. "I could have handled it, boss," he grumbled.

"I know you could," Pickford said. "Which is all the more reason I need you here. Natalia is ruthless. She'll be fine."

He actually didn't care. She'd been a potential thorn since the moment he brought her into the organization. Natalia had never betrayed him, but Pickford didn't fully trust her. Perhaps it was the nature of where she'd come from.

"You got something on your mind, boss?" Jerry asked, interrupting Pickford's thoughts.

"Yes. It seems we're fighting a war on two fronts now. And if the other families find out about it, they may sense blood in the water. Make sure security at my house is tighter than usual. I doubt any of the Savages know where I live, but I would rather not take the chance."

"You think she'll be able to handle the American and Dyer?"

"If they're still at the farmhouse, then Natalia will take care of it."

"If?"

Pickford nodded. "I doubt they hung around. It would be stupid to do so, honestly. I wouldn't if I were him."

"So, you think Dyer skipped town, too?"

"That's why I sent her. Natalia is a useful ally, but allies can be bought or sold. If the American and Dyer did skip town, Dyer—at least—will be back. They always come back sooner or later. Those types of degenerates can't get away from what made them and who they really are. We haven't seen the last of James Dyer."

Jerry knew his boss was right about that. For some reason, these people always had a bad habit of coming back to the city. He'd seen it during his entire career with the mob. They couldn't help themselves.

"And the American?" Jerry pressed.

"I doubt we'll have to worry with him anymore. More than likely, he doesn't want the kind of trouble we can bring. If Dyer left the farmhouse, I'm sure the American went to bully someone else in the world for a few quid before he moves on to the next green pasture. But if he's still around, Natalia is more than capable of handling him."

She certainly was capable. And ruthless. Jerry had seen her do things to people that turned even his hardened stomach. But she came from a different culture, and a different kind of upbringing that bred darkness into a person's soul.

That breeding was difficult to undo.

Fortunately for Pickford, she was on his side. For now, anyway. He also knew that could change in the blink of an eye and was always prepared for that to happen.

"What about the Savages?" Jerry asked. "What's your plan to take care of that problem?"

"The Savages," Pickford said, "are like a species of wasp a farmer brings in to root out other insects that damage the crops. Eventually, the wasps become more of a nuisance than the insects they were brought in to kill."

"So, what should we do about these... wasps, boss?"

Pickford's face turned dark, resolute. "The same thing you always have to do with them. You take out the nest, the queen, their entire system. Only then will you be rid of them."

"What do you have in mind?"

Pickford's lips parted. "Nothing yet. Let's wait and see if our retaliation did enough to put them back in their place. A little spanking like that can go a long way sometimes."

"And what if it didn't? What if they come back and in greater numbers, start hitting some of our clients next?"

"Then," Pickford said with an evil grin, "we do what our clients pay us to do. We take care of the problem. For good."

17

"How can I get to him?" Dak asked.

"To Miles?" Mia laughed. "You got a death wish or something?"

"I'm not afraid of some two-bit thug."

"No. I imagine you aren't." She took a sip of her cappuccino and considered his request. "You can't get to Miles. I don't know what your deal is with the crown, but he ain't gonna let it go. He's always surrounded by four or five of his toughest guys."

"How tough can they be?" he mused.

Her face turned stone cold. "They'll kill you. They've killed people before. These aren't just some bullies on a school yard. They're legit gang members. To be in the Savages, you have to be savage."

"They sound nasty," Dak said, unconcerned.

"I wouldn't blow it off. On top of his personal bodyguards, Miles is crazy. He'll do things that no one else will. Because he's not afraid to die."

"Why's that?"

She shrugged and took another drink. "I don't know." Mia looked at the cup in her hand, regarding it like she would a crystal ball. "Maybe he had a messed-up childhood."

"Did you?"

"Did I what?" Her eyes narrowed.

"What was your childhood like?" He pressed. Dak knew he was walking on thin ice, but he wanted to know. Strangely, he didn't know why.

For a second, she looked confused. He wondered if that confusion would turn to anger, but it didn't.

Instead, she blew it off. "Nothing interesting. Mum died a few years ago. Dad drinks too much and works too little. I had to take care of my little brother, Adam. He's all that matters to me."

"And you think joining a gang was the right way to take care of him?"

She snorted her derision. "I took a job for a little while. But that didn't pay enough. And then there was the issue of keeping Adam safe. Miles offered us protection. Anyone messes with me or Adam; they get punished."

"But it's okay for Miles to hit you."

When she didn't respond, Dak knew he'd hit the mark.

Her expression soured, and for a second, he thought she might get up and leave. Instead, Mia swallowed her pride. "No. It isn't. But he's a means to an end. I won't put up with it forever."

Dak considered his next words carefully. An ordinary person might have looked around the room, worried that someone would hear. He already had—with only a flick of his eyes to the left and right.

"I suppose killing him is out of the question."

Mia pulled her head back at the insinuation. "You mean you?"

"I meant you."

She chuffed. "Maybe you didn't hear anything I said before. There's no way to get to him without getting past his goons."

"The guy has to sleep sometime," Dak said coolly. He picked up his cup and stared across the top of it at her.

She stared back, gauging whether or not he was serious. Mia didn't find a joke anywhere on his face.

"Too risky." She looked out the window, tearing her gaze from his eyes. "And besides, I'm no killer. I don't think I could do it. Much less handle it after the fact." She faced him again. "Something tells me you've killed before."

"I was in the military. It's part of the job."

"Is it part of your new job?" she hedged.

Dak only hesitated for a blink. "No. That's extra."

Mia waited. Then laughed, shaking her head. "You're funny." She pointed a finger at him, bobbing her head. "I like that."

Dak shrugged. "I try."

"No, but seriously. This job of yours. Seems like it must put you in trouble."

He turned his head and looked out the window across the street. The flow of pedestrians continued, seemingly in perpetuity.

"Trouble is something I can't avoid right now, no matter what line of work I'm in."

She puzzled over the statement as she looked at him. "What's that supposed to mean?"

"Nothing," he said, bringing his focus back to her. "I need that crown. And I'm going to do whatever it takes to get it."

"Even if that means killing me?"

The question caught him off guard, and this time he couldn't conceal it. "No."

"You didn't sound sure about that."

"No. I wouldn't kill you. In fact, I don't really want to kill anyone. I would prefer it if your boss would just give me the crown and let me be on my way."

Mia snickered at the insinuation. "Yeah, I don't think that's going to happen. But it's a lovely idea."

"It doesn't belong to him," Dak insisted.

"Yeah, but it don't belong to you, either, now does it."

From her side of the table, it was a good point.

"Nope. You're right. It isn't mine. Or my employer's. Which is why he tries to return the things I collect to the proper owners, or to museums that can study the artifacts and gain new insights into history."

Mia twisted her head to the side and lowered her chin. "Look at you. I'm impressed. That was a really noble statement. But you don't work for free."

"No."

"So you're doing it for the money. Just like the rest of us. You can paint it with all that nobility, but in the end, you're just trying to make a few quid."

Way more than a few quid, he thought but kept it to himself.

"A man's gotta eat," he deflected. "Besides that, I need to stay on the move. I don't like to be in one place too long."

She studied him for several seconds. "You're running from something. Aren't you?"

"Pretty obvious. Which is all the more reason I need to sit in that seat." He indicated her chair with a nod.

She rolled her eyes and shook her head. "You're not going to let that go, are you?"

"Only when I walk out of here." He looked out the window and then stood up.

"You leaving?" she asked.

"Nah. Just going to the loo. I'll be right back."

The bathroom was a small space with a single toilet that looked as old as the city. He looked in the mirror as he washed his hands and sighed.

He didn't know what to think of Mia. She was strong-willed but bordered on arrogance. And arrogance could get you killed. Especially in the sandbox where she played.

He'd sat in his seat as long as he could stand, but Dak couldn't shake the feeling that he had a target on his back.

Dak turned off the faucet and dried his hands before pulling the door open and stepping back into the narrow hallway at the back of the shop.

He looked back to the corner where Mia sat and noticed she'd moved to his seat. Gang member or not, she was a good person, Dak thought. Just thrown into an unmanageable situation.

Life had dealt her a tough hand from the sound of it, and he found himself spinning another plate in his mind—one that involved helping her get out from under the boulder weighing down on her.

He sauntered toward the table.

She watched him with amusement until he sat down. "Happy?"

"Happier," he replied. "Thank you."

She took a long breath through her nose and exhaled slowly. "I wrote down an address on that napkin." Her eyes dropped for a split second to a folded paper napkin on the table. Dak saw black ink bleeding through ever so slightly.

"An address?"

She nodded. "Yeah. If you want to commit suicide, you should show up at that address tonight at eleven."

"Tonight at eleven," he repeated.

"Right. I won't be there to help you," she added. "So don't expect me to be."

"I'd prefer it."

She raised both eyebrows. "Oh really?"

"Safer that way. Wouldn't want you to get hurt by accident."

Her eyes narrowed again as she assessed him. "Why do I feel like accidents tend to happen often around you?"

Dak rolled his shoulders. "Sometimes they do."

"Well, just be aware that you'll have your hands full with that crew."

"Thanks for the tip. I'll try the diplomatic approach first."

She looked at him like he was crazy. "Good luck with that." Mia laughed and leaned back in her chair. The second she did, Dak noticed the figure across the street.

"Stay here. I have to go."

She frowned and watched as Dak abruptly stood up and stormed toward the door.

Dak didn't look back at her. His focus remained on the figure across the road. It was a man, and Dak believed it to be the same person who had been following him before.

He slipped by a patron who opened the door and stepped into the coffee shop, smiling at the woman as politely as he could while trying to squeeze through.

Once on the sidewalk, he redirected his attention back to the opposite side.

The man was on the move. His long black coat trailed behind him in the breeze.

Dak saw the man's face this time, but barely. The guy wore sunglasses and a black baseball cap. The two items did more than enough to conceal any details that might reveal the man's identity.

Dak hurried to the sidewalk, hoping he could slip between oncoming cars, but traffic was too heavy, and he knew he'd never get across the busy intersection.

He rushed to the end of the block and waited with several other people for the light to change. His eyes remained on the man in the black coat, but with every passing second it got more and more difficult to track the guy amid the seething mob.

Finally, the light changed, and the signal for pedestrians to walk lit up.

Dak barged past the cluster of people standing on the edge of the street and trotted through the crosswalk until he reached the other side, where he was forced to slow to a brisk walk.

He looked in the direction the man had gone, but the guy had disappeared.

Dak cursed himself for losing the tail. He couldn't have gone far.

Picking his way through the crowd, Dak risked jumping up and down a few times to see if he could catch a glimpse of the man.

His heart pulsed faster as he continued trying to twist and weave his way around all the people. It felt like for every step forward he took, he was being pushed two steps back.

Finally, he reached a break in the mob and broke into a jog again. The sidewalk ahead, however, gave him no hope of finding the mysterious man. His head turned left to right. He checked the nearest alley to see if the guy had escaped through there.

No sign of him.

Dak's shoulders slumped.

That was the second time he'd lost the tail.

He wondered why the guy hadn't taken a shot at him. If he was an assassin, there'd been more than one opportunity.

Like five minutes ago when Dak had his back to the street.

Maybe the man didn't have a gun. Or perhaps he wasn't an assassin at all. On the fringes of Dak's theories, the guy could have been some sort of weird stalker who'd stumbled on Dak at the airport and decided he'd be a fun one to follow.

Dak shook that one off. It was silly at best.

He sighed, standing in the middle of the sidewalk with people walking around him on all sides. Some of them wore annoyed looks on their faces as they passed by, irritated at the guy standing in their way.

He turned around in a circle, eyes scanning the faces, the masses, for any sign of the man.

Nothing.

Resigned, Dak slogged back to the intersection, then crossed again to the coffee shop, where he found the table empty—except for the napkin.

He saw one of the busboys walking toward the table with a plastic bin. The kid would unwittingly throw away Dak's only way of getting to Miles and the Savages.

Unless he found Mia again, but he didn't want to keep pestering the young woman. He felt like he'd overstepped by a few miles already.

He pulled the door open and nearly tripped over a boy holding some kind of frozen beverage. The kid's mother flashed an angry *Watch where you're going* glare that Dak shed with an apologetic, but hurried, smile.

The busboy was nearly to the table—only steps away. Dak was still halfway across the shop from it, and with a cluster of people hovering around in front of the counter either waiting on their orders or standing in line to place one.

Dak shuffled quickly by a mother holding two daughters by the hand. Then did a spin move to get around a guy in a business suit.

"Wait," he snapped at the busboy, probably a little louder than he should have.

The young man with the bin had just set the plastic tub down on the table, and he'd begun putting silverware, plates, and cups into it.

The napkin with the ink on it still sat there, folded up where he'd left it. He cursed himself for not taking a peek at the address. He could have memorized it or come close enough that he could figure out the missing details if necessary.

The busboy started at the sudden command and turned toward the oncoming American with newfound fear in his eyes.

Dak skidded to a stop at the edge of the table, out of breath and looking like a crazy person. He picked up the napkin and held it aloft. "Sorry. Forgot my napkin."

The busboy simply stared back at him with bewildered confusion written in his expression.

Dak then realized how insane he looked for making such a commotion about a napkin.

"Sorry," he said to everyone in the shop staring at him. "Really important note on this. Very important." He pursed his lips together and nodded, accepting the scrutiny of the onlookers. Dak then slunk out of the coffeehouse, doing his best not to draw more undue attention to himself.

Once back out on the street, he looked around hoping he might find Mia. But just like the man watching him, she was gone.

Right now, that didn't matter. He had what he needed.

Dak had a reservation with Miles and the Savages tonight. If all went well, he could be out of London by tomorrow morning. Then again, if Tucker was still here, this might be the only chance Dak had to take him out.

After tonight, he'd be at a crossroads without much time to make up his mind.

Dak sighed and unfolded the napkin. He needed to commit the place to memory in case he lost the note or it got wet, which was entirely possible with the way the weather misbehaved around here.

He stared at the scribbling for several seconds.

Mia had written down an address. And a name.

Dak lifted his gaze from the paper and searched the throngs of people. She was nowhere to be found.

He returned his attention to the napkin and stared at it, imprinting the details in his memory.

Dak had no idea why Mia had written down a name with the address.

He read it out loud one time. "Dylan," he said. "I wonder what surprises this guy has in store."

He folded the napkin and stuffed it into his pocket.

He'd find out who this Dylan character was later. Before that, Dak had one other place he needed to visit.

And questions that needed answers.

18

The sun set in the west beyond the London skyline, casting a net of orange, pink, and purple across the sky.

Dak walked along the street, passing fewer and fewer people the farther away from the city center he went.

He'd heard about this part of the city. It was one of the rougher boroughs in London where knife and gun crime was higher than everywhere else.

For someone like Dak, he felt comfort in knowing what to expect, and that he could handle pretty much anything some street rat could throw at him.

He passed several nice-looking brick homes—all with matching steps that climbed to a landing beneath two-story, cookie cutter architecture that stretched down the length of the street as far as he could see.

At the next intersection, Dak stopped and waited for the light to change, then crossed and turned left down a side street littered with pubs, night clubs, and pawn shops.

He found the sign he was looking for hanging over a black door near the middle of the alley.

The black wrought-iron sign displayed a picture of a bird of prey with wings outstretched, staring down at those who dared pass under as if it might swoop down and rip flesh from bone with its sharp, realistic talons.

"Not much for subtlety," he muttered. But Dak knew this place was subtle enough. There were no words, no markings to insinuate what this place really was. To any casual observer or passerby, they would think it merely another pub. But this one didn't have windows, and looked like it was set in the back of another business.

It had all the makings of a speakeasy, with the exception of the red phone booth posing as the entrance.

Dak had been to a few of these places in other cities. They always had the same sign hanging over the entrance, and only members of the guild could get in, or even know the locations.

They never bothered moving from one place to another because the people that were inside were some of the most dangerous in the world. The cops, not even the government, would mess with them. And in some cases, as Dak had learned, occasionally government officials contracted through a place like this.

Dak stepped up to the door and looked into the fisheye camera lens hanging above the entrance.

He rapped on the door three times and waited for a response.

"Name?" a female voice said through a speaker by the doorframe.

"Dak Harper," he said.

He waited, wondering what the sound of his name had done beyond the door. Had it caused the woman to spin into a frenzy, prepping everyone else for a fight? Or was she merely looking it up on the global database of mercenaries?

Dak had never worked as a merc before. And he had no plans to do so. But he'd learned of these mercenary nests years ago from his friend Will, who just so happened to have access to the database—which was one of the most secure in the world.

Fortunately for Will, he didn't have to be a hacker to get into the system. He only had to be the smooth operator he was with a particular female in one of the secret locations, and the rest was history.

Dak's name on the roster meant that for another merc to take a contract on him, the price had to be double that of a usual contract. This was to discourage hitters from taking each other out and thus literally killing the business model.

The network of mercenary nests was big money, and it benefited no one for the killers to eliminate each other.

Something buzzed inside the door, and then Dak heard three clicks before it swung open automatically.

Inside, the smell of cigars and cigarettes and weed filled the air, wafting out beyond him to evaporate into the city.

He stepped in and looked around. There were no bouncers waiting there to escort him. Dak turned and watched as the door closed itself. The locks against the solid concrete wall buzzed again and repositioned the bolts in their housing, securing the place once more.

With security like that, he figured they didn't need to pay someone to watch the door.

Dak stared down the dark hallway that stretched thirty feet to the next wall, where the corridor turned right. He heard men's voices and laughter coming from around the corner.

Dak walked to the other end of the hall and turned into the next room, where a window with bars over it was set in the wall.

A guard stood at a door in the back-left corner of the little room. His muscular arms remained crossed as he watched the newcomer with analytical eyes.

A man inside the cage with a shaved head and a black beard stood at the counter. Dak noticed the weapons behind him, all tagged with names of the people who'd left them.

"Remove all your weapons, and place them on the counter, please," the bald man groused.

He wore a white tank-top undershirt and gray trousers. An odd outfit that Dak thought might be more at home in the ditch outside a liquor store.

Dak shrugged. "I don't have any on me."

The man looked at him like he was trying to drink a glass of water straight from the Thames.

"No weapons, huh?" He turned to the bouncer. "Brutus. Swipe this guy for me. Says he has no weapons."

The bouncer uncrossed his arms and walked across the room to a spot on the wall where a metal detector hung from the wall. He plucked the wand from the nail and stepped close to Dak.

Few people looked down at the American. This guy was one of them. He was a good three inches taller than Dak, which put him around six feet four.

The man's broad, hardened face didn't crack. He stared back at Dak with cold blue eyes under a scruffy blond head of hair.

"Arms out," he said in a sharp English accent.

Dak did as ordered and raised his arms like a bird. He also spread his feet shoulder width apart.

The guard waved the wand over one arm, then the other, then down the left leg and the right before he stood up and nodded to the guy in the cage. "He's clean," the bouncer announced.

"Wow," Tank Top said. "You really were telling the truth, weren't ya?"

"I always do," Dak said.

"Yeah, right. I never met a merc in this joint that always tells the truth. Although"—he said, looking down at the counter and to the right for a second—"come to think of it, I don't know many mercs who ever tell the truth." He burst out laughing.

The bouncer chuckled for a few seconds and then returned to the door opposite the cage.

The guard opened the door and held it for Dak to pass through.

"Thanks, gents," he said as he quickly made his way to the portal.

That's what it really was—a portal into another world, a place few normal citizens would ever venture. And if they did happen to be in that place, Dak doubted it was for a job or information.

Information was what he was here to collect. Not money or a contract.

Before him, the sound of American blues music filled the air. Tables occupied floor space from one end of the room to the other, and nearly each one was taken by some of the toughest-looking people Dak had ever seen.

Being former Delta Force, that was saying something.

The door closed behind him without fanfare, and a few eyes darted in his direction.

Dak didn't stand there long. He didn't want anyone in the bar to think he was soft or confused. Any form of weakness here would be devoured. Sure, fighting in a mercenary nest was forbidden, but he knew it happened from time to time, and he prayed that today wasn't one of those times.

He sauntered around the corner of the bar and found an empty stool on the end. After he eased onto the seat, Dak looked over the offerings of the liquor shelves behind the counter. The bartender wore a leather apron with black straps the way hipsters imagined they did back in the 1800s. He also sported a mustache from the same era, with the tips curled up on each end.

He's half right, Dak thought with an inner chuckle.

He didn't care. He actually thought he might want an apron like that for his place back in Tennessee. Something like that would be useful in his workshop, or when he was out by the grill cooking.

The bartender saw Dak and let him know he'd been noticed with a simple upward tilt of his head as he poured a draft beer for another... patron.

Dak wasn't sure that was the right word.

Sure, these people paid for their food and drink. From what he'd seen and heard, the menus were always stellar, though Dak had never actually eaten at a nest.

A lot of money flowed through these places. Hunters worked for big-money contracts. Anyone who was a guild member—and you had to be to get into these places—carried a minimum ten-thousand-dollar retainer. That deposit was never returned whether the job was completed or not. But as far as Dak knew, that didn't happen often—if at all.

Fees were always negotiated between a bounty hunter and a

client. Those fees were tacked on to the minimum ten grand. Most contracts exceeded twenty thousand anyway, and everyone looking in one of the nests for a hitter knew better than to come cheap.

The barkeep finished pouring the other patron's drink, wiped off his right hand with a rag hanging from his belt, and hobbled over.

The guy looked like former military, but Dak wasn't sure which country. The hobble told Dak the bartender had likely been injured, either during combat or after. He knew a few guys who got wounded in the service, then forged a security career after. Mercenary work operated in a similar fashion.

"What'll you have?" the barkeep asked. His voice was gruff and very Scottish. "Bourbon," Dak answered. "Neat."

"Preference?"

"Whatever your best is."

The bartender gave a nod accompanied with an impressed expression. "That's a hundred a shot."

"Make it a double then," Dak said coolly. He'd been staring straight ahead, and only turned to make eye contact with the bartender when the man hesitated, waiting to see if this American was serious.

"Yes, sir," the man said. He turned and shifted a small stepladder over to the right so he could reach up to the top shelf where the most expensive liquors sat.

Dak had no plans on getting drunk. That wasn't his thing. He enjoyed a good drink, but he didn't usually enjoy it too much. This was a social visit, merely to get information.

He leaned back, watching the bartender as he took down a bottle from the shelf and returned to the counter with it and an empty glass.

Dak took the opportunity to twist his head around and take in the room's occupants, making a quick observation before bringing his attention back to the barkeep.

He noted every person in the room. But one caught his attention over all the others. Of course, Dak knew better than to let his gaze remain on the person for too long.

The man sat sideways in a booth along the far wall. He stared at his cell phone. From the looks of it, he was drinking either gin or water. Or maybe vodka.

Dak took out his phone and opened up his crypto app. He kept a percentage of his money in cryptocurrency so he could always have access to it, and in case he needed to visit a place like this.

The nests preferred crypto, but they also took dollars, pounds sterling, and euros. Money in other denominations had to be exchanged.

"Here you go," the bartender said and slid the glass carefully toward Dak.

"Thanks," Dak replied. He held up his phone so the barkeep could see the code on the screen.

The man nodded, retrieved a device that looked like a retail price gun, then scanned the code.

Dak hit the blue confirm transaction button, and the purchase was made instantly.

"Let me know if you need anything else," the bartender said, impressed with the generous tip Dak included in the transfer.

"I will."

Dak nodded and stood up. He knew if he asked the bartender anything about the mysterious man in the corner booth, that the barkeep wouldn't give up much. It was policy. Guild mercenaries preferred to keep their anonymity, and their business, to themselves.

Dak took his drink and ambled over to the booth where the man sat with phone in hand, busily typing a message to someone.

"That looks important," Dak blurted, stopping short of the table.

The man flipped his phone over to conceal the message. He fired an irritated, threatening look at Dak that immediately melted the second he realized who'd said it.

"I knew you'd come here," the man said, looking up into Dak's eyes for the first time. His skin was slightly tanned, and brown hair trickled down just above his ears. The haircut reminded Dak of the one he used to get when he was nine.

"I know," Dak said. That confidence reflected in his voice, unlike the other guy.

He sidled to the other bench and slid into it, helping himself to the seat. "I'd ask if you mind if I sit down, but I don't care if you mind or not. House rules mean we can't beat each other to death in here, so I figured we'd have a little chat."

The man tilted his head sideways. He stared back at Dak with eyes that mirrored his irritation, but also seemed devoid of emotion.

Dak knew right away that this guy was a stone-cold killer—one of those sociopath types who could kill innocent people without thinking twice.

Seemed like he'd gone into the right line of work.

Dak took a sip of his bourbon and set the glass down.

"What do you want?" the guy asked. His accent sounded Spanish.

Dak stuck out his lower lip and shook his head. "Nothing. Just wanted to know what you looked like. You're the one who's been following me."

"And you're not supposed to be in here. One word to the bartender, and they'll take you out back and cut you to pieces."

The protocols each of these merc nests operated by were different in every part of the world, but Dak had a rough knowledge of what they did to those who snuck in—which didn't happen often.

Their security was good enough that only someone on the roster in the database could gain entry. Dak figured a hacker might get in once in a while, but not often. And when they were discovered, Dak knew it wasn't a pretty ending for the sneak.

"Go right ahead," Dak groused. "They won't be kicking me out. That much I can tell you."

"You're not a member of the network," the guy insisted.

"Looks like someone hasn't done their research. Can't be lazy in this line of work, son. That'll get you killed."

Dak picked up the glass and drew another drink through his lips. He swallowed and clicked his teeth together in approval. "Good stuff," he said. "It better be for what they charge."

"It would be unwise to get drunk," the assassin cautioned.

"Why?" Dak leaned forward as if about to share a secret. He lowered his voice. "Because you were hired to kill me?"

The man cocked his head to the side. "Yes."

"Oh, well then, maybe you're right. I guess I should have only ordered a single. Meh." He shrugged and took another drink, nearly emptying the glass this time.

"Foolish, Dak. Very foolish."

"I could say the same about you, kid," Dak mused. "You should have picked an easier target."

"And that's how I know you're lying," the other said. "It's forbidden, according to the guild rules, to put out a contract on a current member. So, if you really did belong here and your name was in the database, your contract wouldn't have gone through."

Dak nodded, appreciating the fact. "Yes. That is true. And I haven't quite sorted that one out yet."

"How you got in here?"

"No. How they put out a contract on me. Maybe the rules have changed."

"Not that I've heard." He took a drink from his glass and set it back down.

Dak watched with tepid interest.

"Yes. Well, that isn't for me to figure out. My job is to kill you. And I will."

With a nod, Dak said, "Maybe. I doubt it. But maybe. You could just walk away, kid. No reason for you to die. You look young, and healthy enough. Go to college. Get a job doing something less dangerous. What are you, twenty-four?"

"My age doesn't matter. What matters is my skills. And I'm very skilled."

Dak nodded. "I'm sure you are, kid. You don't get to be a member of this network if you aren't. But take a look around. You don't see a lot of old bounty hunters in this place. You won't. That's because sooner or later, you lose a step, then you get sloppy. Then you get dead."

The younger man looked into Dak's eyes without flinching. "You know, my client said you'd gone soft. I wasn't sure I believed him, but now I see it. Just look at yourself, Dak. Sitting there drinking your bourbon like a wannabe aficionado while trying to convince the guy who's been hired to kill you not to do it. It's kind of pathetic, honestly. I expected more from you."

The mention of Tucker caused Dak's heart to skip a beat, but he didn't let on.

"You should lower your expectations," Dak replied in a cool tone.

"Perhaps. For now, I'm content to simply watch and wait."

"That's not creepy at all."

The bounty hunter merely offered a short, amused hum. "Jokes won't save you, Dak."

"I wasn't joking. But I will say something."

"Are you going to beg for your life? Or perhaps you're going to try to offer me money to not kill you."

Dak laughed. "No, nothing like that. I don't beg. And while I probably do have the money to cover whatever Tucker paid you, I wouldn't give it to you. I don't have to bribe my way out of trouble."

Another hum.

"What I was going to say, before you interrupted me, was that you should return Tucker's money to him. Or you can keep it and run to whatever emo hole you crawled out of. But if you stick around here, and you try to take me out... I'll kill you."

"So much bravado from a mark. I have to admit that is highly unusual, Dak. But it won't save you."

"Maybe not," Dak said, downing the last of the whiskey. He stood up and looked down at the younger man. "But you can't say I didn't warn you."

He turned and walked to the door, giving a nod to the bartender as he passed. "Thanks for the drink," he said.

The man replied with a nod of his own.

A couple of minutes later, Dak stood on the sidewalk.

He hadn't caught the bounty hunter's name, but he didn't need it.

And he knew the guy wasn't going to back off his job. That almost never happened from what he understood.

Once a hitter took a job, they finished it or died trying.

Dak knew this could only end one way.

Problem was, he found himself in a war on three fronts.

19

Dak stared up at the illuminated blue-and-white sign hanging over the sidewalk.

"Little Med," Dak said out loud, reading the sign to himself.

The shop reminded him of sandwich joints back home that remained open during the late hours to catch drunken revelers and offer them a hangover-preventative meal before they stumbled home to their flats or hotel rooms.

This place offered Mediterranean fare, from Greek to Middle Eastern.

Dak figured they must go through more pita bread in a day than most people saw in a year.

The line inside was small, only a few patrons waiting to place their orders and one standing in the pickup line.

Dak also took note of the people working behind the counter, making gyros, shawarma, and other handheld food. The young guy in the pickup line received his white bag of food and turned for the door.

He left the building and walked by Dak, paying no attention to the American standing there staring.

Dak caught the door before it swung closed, and stepped into the takeout restaurant.

The smells of chicken, lamb, and beef filled the air, along with onions, garlic, and fresh-baked bread.

He doubted the bread was baked here, but they sure did a good job of making it smell that way.

The air was warm, and he only realized how chilly it was outside the second the door closed behind him.

He walked to the back of the line and waited, looking up at the glowing menu that hung over the counter and stretched from one wall to the other.

Three workers behind the counter operated like a machine. One took the orders at the register, while the other two prepared the food.

Dak continued to look at the menu but stole a glance at the name tag of the guy taking orders when the young man wasn't looking.

He was skinny, with tattoos on his pale neck. The blue hat he wore as part of the Little Med uniform was twisted at an angle on his head.

Dak read the name on tag.

Dylan.

He looked like he might be nineteen years old, but he could have been older—perhaps in his early twenties.

While Dylan looked like he could be in a gang, the fact he was working here at a pita place caused questions to arise in Dak's mind, questions that he would hopefully find the answers to soon.

The person in front of Dak placed their order, paid, and slid to the side—watching while the other workers made a couple of shawarma wraps.

"What can I get for you?" Dylan asked as Dak stepped to the counter.

He sounded tired.

"At the end of your shift?" Dak asked.

"Yeah," Dylan said without thinking. "Done in a few minutes."

"Shop closing soon?"

"Nah. We're open until two in the morning."

"That's pretty late."

"People get pretty drunk. Then they get pretty hungry."

Dak liked the smart-aleck response, and showed it with a slight grin.

"What can I get you?" Dylan pressed his company line again.

"I'll take a chicken shawarma wrap, please," Dak said. He pushed a ten-pound note across the table.

"Okay, one shawarma, chicken. Anything else?"

Dak slipped another bill across the counter. "This one is for you," he said, lowering his voice.

Dylan looked down at the money with confused draw on his face. His eyes widened at the sight of the hundred.

"What do you mean?"

Dak lowered his voice and leaned closer. The other two workers and the two patrons didn't seem to care what was going on at the register. "Mia sent me. She said you might be able to help out with something I'm working on."

"Something you're working on?" Dylan looked around the room, concern showing on his face.

Dak only nodded.

Dylan took the ten first, rang up the order, and gave Dak his change. The hundred still sat on the counter.

"I'd take that before someone else does," Dak advised.

Dylan's eyes darted to the right, probably to make sure the other two weren't paying attention. Then he put his fingers on the bill, pulled it toward him, then stuffed it in his pocket.

"I get done working in ten minutes," he said in a conspiratorial tone. "Meet me out back."

Dak nodded, took his change, and stepped to the side to wait on his order.

He watched the other two employees make the food for the other people before they started on his.

He stood patiently, still observing as the two sandwich makers stuffed the ingredients into the thick wrap before encasing it in foil and stuffing it into the bag.

"Here you go," the guy said, handing him the food. Dak smiled back at the young man. He looked Turkish, and Dak would know having spent a fair amount of time in Istanbul and the surrounding area.

He thanked the young guy and left the restaurant with his bag.

Outside, Dak turned right and walked to the corner, where he stopped and leaned against the building to eat his food.

He made quick work of the shawarma, and when he was done, balled up the foil and stuffed it and the paper bag in a nearby trash bin.

Checking his watch, he noted that it was nearly quitting time for Dylan.

Dak looked down the alley. He assumed this was what Dylan meant when he said to meet him out back. The narrow street ran all the way through to another street on the other side.

He watched the alley with casual interest, counting the seconds tick by. Finally, a blue door swung open about a third of the way down the street.

Dylan emerged in the dim glow of an orange light hanging on the opposite wall. He reached in his pocket and retrieved a pack of cigarettes, then a lighter from the other pocket.

He planted a cigarette in his mouth and lit it. The glowing orange flame looked like a signal to Dak.

He left his corner and strode into the alley to meet Dylan.

The young man puffed on his cigarette, blowing out huge puffs of smoke.

He raised his head as Dak approached. "Oy, what's all this about?" Dylan asked, sounding like he was paranoid.

"Mia said you could help me."

"Yeah. We already established that. Not too bright, are you?"

"I never professed to be."

"What kind of problem would Mia send you to me for? I don't deal drugs if that's what you're looking for."

Dak shook his head. "Nothing like that. I'm trying to find Miles."

Dylan's face twitched with concern. He took a drag of the cigarette, causing the tip to glow bright orange in the darkened corridor.

"Yeah? You a cop or something?"

"Not a cop," Dak said. "Though, it seems I'm asked that question with growing frequency."

Dylan stared blankly back at him.

"No. I'm not a cop," Dak reiterated. "Miles has something that doesn't belong to him. It's my job to get it back."

"What's that? A car or something?"

Dak shook his head. "No. I hunt down missing artifacts." He watched, gauging Dylan's reaction to the confession.

"Like some kind of Indiana Jones or something?"

"No. But I do know a couple of guys like that. My job is slightly different. I track down items that have been stolen, or went missing sometime in the past. Miles has one of these items. I heard you could help me find him."

Dylan chuffed and blew out a puff of smoke. The bluish-gray haze swirled and plumed into the sky, evaporating into the night air. It was his turn to gauge the American.

"You got a name?" he asked.

"Dak. Let's leave it at that. I'd rather keep a low profile"

"That's smart, Dak. Looking for Miles Tidmouth on the other hand, not so much. I have to wonder why Mia sent you to me. She could have pointed you to him."

"I asked myself that same question," Dak mused. "Could have saved both of us some time. I figured she must have a reason for me to come see you first."

Dylan considered Dak's statement. "I'm not sure. Unless...."

"Unless what?"

A cryptic smile crept across Dylan's face. "Unless she thought I could use you."

"Use me?" Dak felt red flags springing up inside his brain. "For what?" He also didn't like the way Dylan appeared to be sizing him up like he was picking out a steak.

"Yeah. You'll do nicely."

"I'll do what nicely?"

Dylan only replied with a broad, cryptic smile.

20

Natalia stopped outside the farmhouse and killed the engine before she was too close, keeping the sedan on the edge of the parking area, both to keep from alerting anyone inside and to block the exit in case someone had the idea to try to escape.

The moon peeked out from behind the thick clouds overhead just long enough to give her a good view of her surroundings.

No cars sat in front of the house, and only a solitary light burned inside, somewhere in the center of the house—a common trick used by people who went out of town to make potential thieves think someone might be home.

She didn't know a thief alive who fell for that. And she knew many.

The fact no cars were present already told her most of what she already thought—that Dyer and his bodyguard left town, maybe together. Maybe separately. It didn't matter to Natalia. She was there to recon and report. Unless she found one of the men still at the house, in which case she would take care of the problem herself and reap the rewards from her boss.

She walked ahead, her black leggings and matching leather jacket shielding her skin from the cool night breeze.

She approached the front porch and paused, looking at each corner before ascending the steps, where she stopped at one of the windows by the door.

There, Natalia leaned over and peeked through the glass. "Doesn't look like anyone's home," she said to herself, willing to cast caution to the wind at the sight of a vacant house.

Still, she knew better than to just look through a window and assume everyone was gone.

There'd been one instance similar to this one when she'd been sent to collect a debt from a particularly dirty scumbag. He'd been ducking Pickford for months, and the boss had finally decided to take the loss.

Which meant the debtor would take the ultimate loss.

When Natalia went to the man's house out in the country, he'd pretended not to be there. No cars were present. The lights were off. And nothing stirred in the house.

She decided to investigate anyway, and she soon discovered the debtor hiding out in his basement with a shotgun pointed at the stairwell.

After he'd discharged both of the shells in his double-barreled weapon, she made sure he didn't have time to reload.

Natalia flew down the stairs as the man desperately fumbled with new shells, clumsily trying to load them into the chambers.

The police didn't find the body for days.

His throat had been slit, and the debtor left right where he'd been sitting with the shotgun still in his cold, dead hands.

Natalia hadn't left a trace of evidence at the scene. She'd honed that skill to near perfection over the years, and she was, in her estimation, Pickford's best assassin.

The others could kill. She knew Jerry to be particularly ruthless. But his methods were sloppy at times, and she knew him being caught was an inevitable eventuality if he didn't change his ways.

Not that she cared.

Natalia held no affections for Jerry or anyone else in the organization. She was a tool, just like the rest of them. The best she could do was prove herself necessary, valuable, indispensable.

She'd done that and more.

Natalia knew that most of the men in the organization only viewed her as a pretty face with an athletic figure. She'd caught them looking since day one, and their gawking never ceased.

That didn't bother her. If her appearance distracted some of the men from doing their jobs, that just meant she'd climb the ladder that much faster.

She hadn't mentioned it to anyone, but she'd been angling for Pickford's position since the day she joined Houghton. It would be hers someday. She just had to keep her head down, do her job, and be patient.

The opportunity would come if she waited.

For now, Natalia needed to make sure Dyer was truly gone, and if he wasn't—she'd make him wish he was.

She checked the front door but found it locked—as suspected. She sighed and looked out over the property. Out here, away from the city, things were peaceful, serene almost. The stars twinkled brighter here. And it was so much quieter.

Natalia hated it.

She wasn't comfortable outside the city. Sure, she remained on constant alert there with millions of faces passing by all the time. But out here, it was impossible to know where the knife to stab you in the back might come from.

The upside of being out here was that if someone were to approach her, she'd detect it much easier than in the noisy city of London. But if someone were crouching in a field with a sniper rifle —ready to pick her off—there'd be no way to know.

The thought sent her head twisting in both directions as she scanned the immediate area for what must have been the fifteenth time in two minutes.

Her head was always on a swivel, continuously looking for trouble.

Nothing moved except tall strands of grain in a nearby field and some leaves on an oak tree in the yard, both teased by the late-night breeze.

Natalia glided across the porch to the right corner and looked around the side. Then she vaulted over the railing and landed on her feet with a thud. She drew a knife from a sheath on her hip and held the curved blade in front of her as she'd been trained long ago.

The curved metal looked like an eight-inch scimitar. It was a unique weapon unlike any other.

Natalia stalked down the length of the house until she reached the back corner, then paused to lean around it, making sure no threat waited to ambush her.

Nothing but an old barn sat behind the farmhouse. The wooden loft window hung loosely open and the breeze pushed it gently back and forth, causing it to creak on rusty hinges.

She acknowledged it and kept moving, skirting along the back wall until she reached another porch—this one smaller than the one out front. The deck didn't have a roof over it like the other porch.

It was an insignificant detail to her. Natalia only cared about getting in the house at this point, though with every squeak of the barn window hinges she felt compelled to check that building too if the house proved fruitless.

Dyer was desperate, and desperation led people to do some unusual things. Like hiding in a hay loft.

She climbed the steps to the top of the deck then tiptoed to the back door. She reached out and grabbed the doorknob, hesitated, then turned it.

Instead of the resistance she'd met at the front entrance, this door opened easily.

As the crack between the frame and the door widened, she hesitated again—fully aware she could be walking into a trap. She eased the door open, silently hoping that it didn't make even half the noise of the hay loft window.

Thankfully, the hinges on the door appeared to be well oiled, and it didn't make a sound as she pushed it wider and slipped through.

Once inside, Natalia eased the door shut again and surveyed the room. A lamp glowed on a nightstand, casting a yellowish hue across the room. It was the light she'd seen from outside.

Standing perfectly still, she didn't hear anything except the ticking of a clock somewhere in the house—in the kitchen, unless she missed her guess.

Natalia crept across the floor, passing an old, upholstered couch with hideous floral patterns splashed across the fabric covering the cushions.

She avoided the coffee table and continued ahead toward the kitchen, noting a hallway to the right. The first door in the corridor was closed, and from the looks of it, led down to a basement.

Great, she thought. *Another basement.*

Visions of the guy with the shotgun danced in her head, but she didn't let it distract her or keep her from doing her job. She was better than that.

Rookies might have been concerned about such a thing, but not Natalia. If her quarry was hiding down in the basement, she'd deal with it the same way she'd done the last one.

She left the hallway behind and entered the kitchen through an archway. Natalia realized Dyer must have left in a hurry. A loaf of bread sat on the counter with the plastic folded under it. Dirty dishes sat in the sink, and the chairs hadn't been pushed back underneath the table—though she realized that could just be the way Dyer kept them.

She read the scene as she would a book, following the clues that told the story of what had happened here.

Another long room extended from the kitchen toward the back of the house. She padded over to it and looked inside, only finding a washer/dryer combination and a hamper full of dirty clothes.

Dyer definitely left here in a hurry, she surmised.

She turned around and headed back into the kitchen, then into the living room once more.

Natalia considered checking the bedrooms first but decided to go downstairs into the basement instead, thinking that was the most logical place for Dyer to hide.

She gently pulled the door open and found the darkened stairwell beyond.

She reached out a finger to flip on the light, then heard a noise from behind. The floor creaked, signaling that someone was approaching.

Her heart skipped a beat as she spun around to face the threat, knife extended in a defensive position.

It did no good.

A dark figure loomed only two feet away. She couldn't see the man's face in the darkness, but she detected the movement of his foot as he extended his leg and kicked her in the abdomen.

Natalia felt the wind sucked out of her lungs as she fell backward into the stairwell. The sickening feeling of nothing behind her overwhelmed her mind with panic and desperation, hoping to land safely on something but knowing that wasn't in the cards.

Finally, after what felt like a full minute, her tailbone struck a step, and she tumbled head over heels down the stairs to the basement floor.

She breathed heavily, fortunately able to take air into her chest after only a moment, but pain ripped through her nerves from her lower back to her neck to her head. One of her legs was bent at an awkward angle, and she knew the bone, or bones, were broken.

Natalia saw the dark figure in the stairwell now, standing there staring into the darkness.

She could see little else in the nearly pitch-black basement.

Her fingers searched the floor but found no purchase of the knife she'd wielded so confidently only moments before.

Natalia grimaced in agony as she tried to pull herself along the concrete floor. A thud on the top step drew her attention back to the stairwell, and she saw the silhouette descending toward her in a deliberate, methodical cadence.

Her hands continued to scour the floor for any sign of her blade. Desperation swelled in her chest with every passing second the man drew closer.

He moved with the kind of speed a serial killer in a movie would, never in a hurry yet always catching up.

Except he had nothing to catch up to. She'd broken her right leg, and on top of that, she felt dizzy from hitting her head in the tumble.

He reached the bottom of the stairs and nearly drowned out what little light spilled into the basement through the stairwell door.

The man stopped a few feet short of Natalia. She continued to feel around for the missing knife but couldn't located it.

Then she saw him raise something into the light. A knife of his own.

"Who do you work for?" she demanded. If this guy was going to kill her, she wanted to know who was behind it. Perhaps because she thought there might be a chance for revenge in the next life. Or maybe she was merely curious.

The man sighed. "That's none of your concern. I wasn't waiting for you. But now that you're here, well...."

He bent over at the hips, as if to lean down and snatch her up.

With a last, frantic effort, she jerked the phone out of her pocket and slid her finger down from the top, then pressed the button.

The flashlight blazed to life, shining directly into the assassin's eyes.

In the abject darkness, the white light seared his vision, and he stumbled backward amid a series of profanities in both English and Spanish.

Natalia swept the floor one last time for her knife, but she couldn't find it.

As the killer staggered off to the side with hands over his eyes, she clawed at the floor in an attempt to reach the stairs.

If she could get to the top, she could lock him down here, call for reinforcements, and maybe, just maybe, find a firearm somewhere in the house and blast this guy back to whatever pit he crawled out of.

She pushed hard with her good leg, pressing her foot against the concrete as she pulled herself closer to the first step.

Natalia reached it and felt a surge of adrenaline pump through her, fueling her muscles to keep going.

Her left hand hit the second step. The right hit the third. She was making progress, dragging her broken limb along as she ascended the stairs like some drunken frat boy trying to make it back to his bedroom after a six-hour kegger.

Halfway up, she felt the temptation to look back, but that wouldn't help. She had to keep going.

One step. Then another. She was moving faster now, getting the hang of whatever kind of movement this could be called.

Two steps from the top, she felt a rush of relief wash over her. She was nearly there.

Then a hand slapped down onto her broken leg, and her nerves screamed out in pain again. He twisted the leg, and she screamed. With her last ounce of energy, Natalia kicked her good leg downward, driving her foot into the man's face.

He fell back, catching himself on the railing with his right hand before he fell to the floor.

Natalia pulled at the top step with her fingernails, planting her healthy foot against a step to almost jump from her awkward, sprawled position.

Her right hand smacked against the tile of the main floor. *Almost... there....*

She stood up on her good leg, balancing herself by holding onto the doorframe.

Using the railing as a crutch, she pushed down hard with her right hand and raised up her foot toward the main floor.

It was an inch from touching down when she felt a sudden, painful tug on her hair.

She yelped, but the sound didn't last long before she felt the razor-sharp edge of a knife drag across her throat as the assassin pulled her head back.

Natalia tried to scream. Tried to shout the word *no*. But nothing came out except a sickening series of gurgles.

She felt warmth splashing over her chest and heard the blood hitting the floor at her feet.

Within seconds, she fell to her knees, painfully, but barely noticed as her life spilled from the gash.

As she lost consciousness and the world around her blurred into a haze, she stared into the killer's vapid eyes for her final few seconds before she surrendered to the darkness.

21

Dak had felt trepidation hundreds of times in his life. Most often, it had happened during a mission back when he was with the military.

Sometimes intel was bad, and that led to less than-ideal-circumstances for operators like him. Then again, he and his team were trained to perform in exactly those kinds of scenarios.

Since leaving the service, most of the trepidation he felt surrounded other people—innocent bystanders who just wanted to live their lives. Dak did everything he could to protect those folks, and keep them from getting hurt.

In this instance, the trepidation was more like the old feelings he used to get in Delta Force. Like the last mission before he and the rest of his team went into that cave in the Middle East.

"What is this place?" Dak asked, staring at the stairwell leading down to the London Underground.

Dylan looked at him like the answer should have been obvious. "Seriously? It's the tube, mate. Well, one of the old tube stations. No trains go through this section anymore."

"Right. So, what are we doing here again?"

Dylan's reply was the same coy smile Dak saw earlier.

"You'll see." He motioned with his hand and headed down the stairs.

Dak hesitated. "Sorry, this feels a little like a setup to me. I follow you down the stairs into the dark, abandoned subway tunnel where you and your buddies roll me."

Dylan stopped halfway down the stairs and looked back up at him. "You're a paranoid one, aren't you? I'm not going to mug you, mate. That's not my thing. I'm not one of the Savages, if that's what you're thinking."

"I wasn't thinking that."

"Okay then. And do you have any money on you?"

"Few hundred. Not worth dying over."

"You or me?" Dylan asked. He only waited a second before he added, "I'm kidding. No one is going to kill you. Well, I hope not."

Dak started to ask what that was supposed to mean, but he figured Dylan was going to keep some of the mystery for himself until the big reveal. Whatever that was.

He took a few steps down the stairs then stopped again. "You gotta give me something here, kid. What am I walking into?"

"Number one rule of this place is you don't talk about this place," Dylan replied.

"Seems like I've heard that somewhere before."

"Come on. Do you want to get to Miles or not?"

Dylan had him on that one. Notwithstanding a trip back across town to Mia's place, this was going to be Dak's best and fastest bet to locate Miles.

"Fine. But I'm former Delta Force. In case you were thinking of some kind of ambush. It won't work out well for you or your friends."

Dylan snorted with a nod. "Perfect. I was hoping you were former military. And Special Ops, no less. This will be easier than I thought."

He turned and marched the rest of the way down to the bottom of the stairs, where a red metal door blocked the way.

Dak watched as Dylan knocked on the door and then waited.

"You coming?" Dylan asked, looking up over his shoulder. "Last chance."

"Why do I feel like I'm going to regret this," Dak said as he descended the stairs.

"That's the attitude. Positive thinking, yeah?"

"You are way too chipper for someone who just got off a long shift at this hour of the night. You know that?"

Dylan laughed. "Yeah, I'm a bit of a night owl I suppose."

A slide in the top third of the door opened, and two bloodshot eyes stared back out.

"Oh, it's you," a gruff voice said from behind the door.

"That doesn't sound like a friendly greeting," Dak muttered.

"It's fine," Dylan reassured. Then he turned back to the door. "Mick. Come on, mate. You owe me for that time I helped out your sister."

The eyes behind the slot narrowed. "The guy you hooked her up with ended up leaving her for someone else, you twat."

Dak winced at the response. "Good one."

"Not helping," Dylan said. "Mick, you can't expect me to see into the future. How was I supposed to know that would happen? And besides, do you want your sister in a long-term relationship with someone like that? I know I wouldn't."

Dak could see the conflict stirring in Mick's eyes. *There's no way he's buying this BS, is there?*

Then again, he'd followed Dylan this far. Maybe Mia's friend was a master con artist.

"I guess not," Mick surrendered.

Both of Dak's eyebrows shot up in utter astonishment. *Is this guy really going to buy—*

A creaking sound followed by a click answered his question.

The man inside opened the door and stepped aside to let the two visitors pass. Once they were in, Mick closed the door and slid the bar lock back into place.

He stood three inches shorter than Dak, with twenty more pounds of weight unevenly distributed under an old button-up shirt with blue stripes over white. The jeans he wore looked like they hadn't been washed in months.

Thankfully, any smell the man's lack of hygiene might have produced was drowned out by the overpowering scent of stale cigarette smoke, with a hint of cigar.

Dak heard the sound of voices shouting from somewhere. But it wasn't a dispute or an argument. It sounded like they were cheering something, like fans at a sporting event.

A quick look to the right told him where both the sounds and smells were coming from. A stairway led down into the tube station, presumably where an old platform occupied a large chunk of subterranean London.

Dak had heard about these places, many of them used in World War II as bunkers and command centers, particularly during the Battle of Britain. He started to ask if the cops knew about this place but decided against it. Dak got the feeling that bringing up the police wasn't a great idea.

"So," Mick said, still looking Dak up and down, "what's the story with you?"

Dak looked at Dylan, expecting an answer. He sure wasn't going to tell this guy about his past. That would only make him suspicious.

"He's a former Special Ops soldier from the States," Dylan blurted.

Dak rolled his eyes. *So much for secrets between new acquaintances.*

"Oh, is that so?" Mick asked in a snide tone. "Like the one you brought in who was a trained assassin? Or the time you brought the so-called world's strongest man? Or perhaps this one is more like the Marine you brought in."

"Okay, first of all, he really was a Marine."

"He was drunk when it was his turn to fight!"

Dak scowled upon hearing that last part. "What did you just say?"

"Nothing, Dak. Don't—"

"It sounded like you said fight," Dak continued, ignoring Dylan.

"So?" Mick asked, sticking his hands out by his sides. "Or did your new friend here not tell you what he's getting you into?"

Dak turned his stern expression to Dylan, who did his best to look innocent, turning his palms up and lifting his shoulders. It didn't work.

"What kind of fight, Dylan?"

Mick only laughed, rubbing his hands together as he enjoyed the free drama.

Dylan shrugged. "Just, you know, a sort of Fight Club kind of thing. Underground style."

Dak tried to process exactly what in the world was going on, but he couldn't for the life of him grab a logical explanation. So, he tried to work his way through it with slow, methodical speech. "Dylan? Why would you bring me to an underground fight club? And how is that going to help me get what I want?"

Dylan scratched the back of his neck.

"Well, I owe some money to Miles. Borrowed it to fix my mom's car when it broke down. She needs it for her job. Travels all over. But he was running some sick juice on the loan, man. I mean, it has to be sixty percent or something."

Mick huffed and crossed his arms. "You're an idiot."

"I needed the money. All right? I didn't have any choice. She was broke, and so was I."

"Yeah? Maybe you shoulda gone to a proper bank," Mick suggested.

Dak was thinking the same thing.

"I did that. They wouldn't lend me the money. Or her. She's already overextended on credit as it is. Hospital bills from when Dad was sick."

Dak felt a tug on his chest. He didn't have to ask what happened to Dylan's dad. The look on his face told the story. It could have been any number of illnesses. Which one didn't matter now. Only the result.

Now Dak felt guilty, though he still didn't appreciate being pushed around like some pawn. "And how is this fight club supposed to help you?" Dak asked.

"The challenger who beats the champion takes all the prize money. We split it, fifty-fifty."

Dak didn't ease up on the frown. "So, I do all the work. Possibly get the crap beat out of me. And my reward if I succeed is only half?"

Dylan leaned his head to the side. "Finder's fee?"

Dak shook his head. "You could have at least mentioned this to me on the way here."

"I thought you would have said no."

"You were correct to think that."

"I don't mean to be rude," Mick said, clearly not concerned with that. "But if you're going to challenge the champion, you'd better head down. No one has yet, but I heard he's leaving in thirty minutes if no one steps up."

"All undercards then so far?" Dylan clarified.

"Yep."

"Okay." Dylan looked to Dak, pleading in his eyes. "If you don't want to help. I understand. I'll still give you Miles' address. I shouldn't have tricked you."

Dak swallowed his anger and set his jaw. "Who's the champion?"

Dylan looked up from the floor, a sliver of hope in his eyes. "You serious?"

"Don't get excited, kid. I haven't won yet."

22

Dak surveyed the scene in the tube station, still not believing what he was seeing.

The bizarre scene featured dozens of men and a smattering of women, all hovering around a spot on the platform where two fighters duked it out with bare knuckles.

The two fighters in the middle of the living ring squared off, dancing around in circles as they tried to assess the best avenue of attack.

They were lightweights, and shorter than Dak, but the men's agility and quickness were absolutely lethal.

Dak could tell immediately that these two knew what they were doing in a fight. He wondered how many in this underground fight club could boast the same.

From the looks of some of the spectators, he doubted they had much experience and were probably only there for the betting portion of the program.

There were some, though, who looked like an international who's who of Interpol's most wanted.

Most of them had multiple tattoos on their skin, some all the way up the neck to their jawline.

The fighters watched the battles differently than the pure spectators. They were easy to pick out, too, with their eyes locked on technique instead of simply enjoying the violence. Each of the guys paying close attention was sizing up the competition, or absorbing a few things they might incorporate into their own style.

One of the guys in the ring, wearing blue shorts, charged ahead, sensing an opening, and lashed out with a series of wild punches.

The opponent in red shorts blocked most of them, only taking a few glancing blows off the cheek before retaliating with an impressive roundhouse straight to the jaw.

Blue Shorts' head snapped to the side, and his eyes went vacant between the time he took the shot and when he hit the floor.

He rolled over, but it was too late. The guy in red pounced on him, straddling his chest while he pummeled the opponent with hammer fists until a man in a black T-shirt and sweatpants stepped from the crowd and pulled the winner off the dazed man.

Blood stains decorated the floor around the loser, who still hadn't regained his balance or his faculties. Dak doubted the guy knew where he was. He'd been knocked nearly unconscious once. Took a concussion from it. Dak remembered being dizzy for several hours until his equilibrium adjusted and brought things back to normal.

A couple of people from the crowd stepped out into the ring and helped up what appeared to be their friend.

They dragged the guy out of the way to the roar of the mob.

"No mercy for the damned, hey, Dylan?" Dak said to his tour guide.

Dylan stood close. He hadn't taken his eyes off the fight the entire time, watching it with a sort of disturbing grin on his face.

"Not here. The only one who gives mercy is the referee."

Dak's eyebrows knit together in doubt. "Captain Sweatpants over there?" He pointed to the thick man who'd stopped the fight. He looked strong, but the belly hanging over his waistline didn't give Dak a ton of confidence that the guy was in good enough shape to stop a public execution if that's what was happening.

"Anyone ever die?" Dak asked, not sure he wanted the answer.

"A few times," Dylan admitted as if it was no consequence. "They know what they're getting into."

"Must be nice seeing how I had no clue what I was getting into before we arrived here."

He looked over at his host with a scathing glare.

"Hey, you needed help. I needed help. We're helping each other. Okay?"

"Yeah, but you're not the one going out there to potentially get the crap beat out of you."

Dylan nodded. "I wouldn't last five seconds out there. I'm not a fighter."

"Lover not a fighter?" Dak joked.

"Not really. I don't have much experience with either."

Before Dak could ask any other questions, a guy in a black T-shirt and acid-washed jeans so skinny they could have been painted on, stepped out into the middle of the ring.

"Ladies and gentlemen!" he shouted to the crowd. He waved his hands over his head to demand silence.

The mob simmered into a quieter version of disorder.

"Thank you. Thank you. What a night of fights it's been, but it's not over yet. I hope." He looked around, darting his eyes from one section of the crowd to another. "There's still one fighter left to go for the night... The champion, Bruuuuuutus!"

The people roared as the one named Brutus stepped from their midst, marching out into the middle.

Dak didn't need to take much time to size the guy up. He was an absolute monster, standing a couple of inches taller than Dak and carrying at least thirty more pounds with dense muscle packed under his bulk. The man's thick dark hair was done up in a man bun, and the matching beard hung down to the middle of his neck in three braids.

Dak turned to Dylan, who deliberately kept his eyes focused on the champion to avoid the scathing fury spewing from Dak's eyes.

"That... is the champion?" Dak clarified, pointing at the mountain of a man.

"Yep. That's the champion."

Dak shook his head. "Why... why would you think I can beat a guy like that?"

"Mia believes in you," Dylan answered with a shrug. "She wouldn't have sent you to me if she didn't."

"So, she sent me to help you out of your predicament, and in exchange you would help me with mine. And yet, somehow, I feel like I'm the one coming out of this on the short end."

Brutus roared as he turned slowly, looking into the terrified and mesmerized crowd—as if seeking the prey he might feast upon.

"And his name is Brutus," Dak added. "Seems about right for a guy that size."

"He's slow," Dylan said in a hushed tone. "Don't get close to him, or he'll grab you and won't let go."

"Thanks for the tip. Any other sage advice, Mick?"

Dylan frowned at the reference. "Mick? Who's Mick? I'm not Irish."

Dak shook his head. "I figured you were too young to have seen the Rocky movies. That'll be your assignment for the weekend. If I get out of here alive."

"You'll be fine. You're strong and you're trained. Brutus is nothing but a bully, a brawler. Stick to that military training of yours, and it'll all be okay."

"You don't know anything about me or my training. For all you know, Mia could have sent you a busboy from a pub."

Dylan looked Dak up and down for one second. His lips cracked in a smile again. "Nah, mate. You ain't no busboy."

"Busboys can't look like this?" Dak held out his palms.

"Sure. But you ain't one of them. Nah, man. You're a killer. I can tell."

Dak didn't press the issue, wondering how in the world a kid working at a gyro place could possibly assess the history or talent of someone he'd only met that night.

Instead, he kept his eyes locked on the behemoth standing in the middle of the crowd. He'd fought men that big before. Bigger once. But he didn't enjoy it.

The one advantage Dak could always count on when it came to taking on larger opponents was that they were usually slower. Dak wasn't the fastest fighter, but he figured he could duck and weave long enough to wear this guy down.

He hoped.

"You ready?" Dylan asked.

"Just like that, huh?"

"Yeah, pretty much."

"Fine. Let's get this over with. But if I get killed, I'm taking it out on you."

Dylan laughed but stopped when he saw the dead-serious look on Dak's face.

"Right then." He raised his hand. "Oy! We have a challenger!"

For a second, the entire room fell into a hushed silence. Every eye in the room, including Brutus', stared at Dylan.

Then, the champion burst out laughing. Half a beat later, the rest of the room exploded into laughter.

Dylan looked around the room, confused at the response. "What?" He tried to shout over the cacophony of the crowd, but no one seemed to hear. "What's so funny?"

Finally, Brutus shook his head and pointed at Dylan. "You should keep your mouth shut, boy. No reason for you to die here tonight."

When the realization hit Dylan, he nodded dramatically. "Oh, I see. Yeah. You think I'm the challenger. Not me." He jerked his thumb at Dak. "Him."

Brutus redirected his attention to Dak, but the sardonic smirk remained. "What's your name?" he demanded.

"Why?" Dak asked. "You're not going to remember it in the morning."

"Oy?" Brutus looked around at the mob in disbelief. "What did you just say to me?"

"I said you're not going to remember it in the morning." Dak paused. "You know. Because I'm going to beat the crap out of you?"

The grin melted from Brutus' face. A furious scowl replaced it. His face reddened, and his eyes narrowed.

"I don't need to know your name," he growled. His voice echoed through the stunned London underbelly. "Only one who needs to know that is the undertaker."

A collective "Ooooh" rolled through the station.

Dak nodded. "I guess we'll see." He had no intention of taking the trash talk further.

In his experience, the best thing you could do was get your opponent riled up—get them thinking about how much they want to kill you instead of *how* they could do it.

From the looks of it, this bear didn't need any more poking. His face burned red, and the muscles in his arms rippled.

Still, Dak decided he hadn't poked this bear enough. "You okay?" He pointed at the man's neck. "Looks like you have a few veins popping up. That's usually a sign someone is pissed off."

Brutus said nothing. But Dak saw the comment had the desired effect.

The champion methodically removed his shirt and tossed it onto the floor close to the front row of fans encircling the ring.

"Wow," Dylan said, mouth hanging open wide like a whale scooping krill. "You really are a madman, aren't you?"

Dak faced him, the stern look covering his face and filling his eyes never wavered. "That was the plan."

"What? Seriously? Are you mental?" He extended his arm toward the monster without looking at him. "Look at him."

"What?" Dak asked, taking off his shirt. He hung it on Dylan's hand before he could retract it. "I thought you had faith in me."

"That was before you went and poked the bull."

"Bear."

"What?"

"You poke a bear. No idiot would poke a bull. Have you seen those horns?"

Dylan was lost for words. For half a second. "Horns? Are you out of your mind?"

"Probably. Don't drop my shirt," Dak said, pointing at the clothing still hanging from an extended hand. Then he looked down at his jeans. "I guess these pants are a lost cause. Definitely going to get some blood on them."

Dak turned around and faced the mountain across from him. He smiled as he thought of the verse from the Bible talking about moving mountains. "Time to put that to the test," he muttered.

Dak took a step forward. He put out his hands like he'd done each time he'd sparred with someone. There was always a fist bump between fighters. It was like that on the pro circuits, too. Dak had seen it a hundred times while watching MMA fights.

As Brutus stormed toward him, Dak realized there wasn't going to be any of that kind of sportsmanship. Not that he really expected it. But playing the role of the patsy who'd just walked into something bigger than he realized was all part of the plan.

The champion charged forward, cutting the distance by a yard with every step.

He yelled something unintelligible but terrifying as he raised a meaty right fist over his shoulder.

Yep. I pissed him off.

Brutus showed his hand before Dak had even done anything. The huge man was trying to end this in one blow, after which he would probably stomp the unconscious Dak into oblivion. With as much rage as Brutus displayed, Dak figured the guy could probably pulverize him into an unrecognizable hamburger patty.

But he'd have to catch Dak first.

Dak waited until the last second, holding the line as if Mel Gibson was shouting at him while adorned with blue face paint and a kilt.

Then, as Brutus drove his fist forward, Dak sidestepped and stuck out his right foot.

The hulking adversary didn't have a chance to slow down. His left foot hit Dak's shin, and the man immediately went tumbling down. He hit the floor hard but managed to roll to his feet and into a kneeling position—ready to defend a counterattack.

None came.

Instead, Dak simply took a few steps back as he observed the champion.

Brutus now wore an even angrier, but also humiliated, look on his face. His nostrils flared, swelling and retracting with every furious breath. The champion pushed himself up off the ground as the hush that had fallen over the crowd began to rise to encouraging shouts and cheers.

They really want this guy to kick the crap out of me, Dak realized. *Whatever happened to rooting for the underdog?* He smiled. "They *are* rooting for the underdog," he said to himself.

Brutus stalked toward Dak now, apparently having learned his lesson from the first, reckless attack. This approach was more methodical, deliberate.

"Sorry about that," Dak stabbed. "You okay? Looks like you took quite the tumble."

"I'll kill you," Brutus snarled.

He picked up his speed again and rushed Dak—this time with his arms in front of him as if to tackle the American.

Dak nearly rolled his eyes but managed to hold that back as the lumbering man charged.

Again, Dak stepped to the side, this time to the left, and stuck out his foot.

Brutus corrected on this approach, slowing enough to make the subsequent fall less painful.

Nonetheless, it still looked painful when he lost his balance and stumbled to the floor. Especially the part where his shoulder struck the hard concrete.

Brutus grunted and snapped his head around.

Dak was surprised that the guy could look even madder than he did before.

Brutus picked himself up again, slower than the first time. He cracked his neck to both sides—more posturing. Dak had seen other guys do this before getting their teeth kicked in.

This time, when the champion approached, he did so with his fists in a boxing position. And he didn't charge or appear like he was going to go on the offensive at all. He merely eased closer to Dak as he would a wild animal in the forest.

"I am really sorry, Brutus. I didn't mean—"

Brutus didn't let Dak finish. He took a step forward, jabbing with his left hand. Dak retreated a step, allowing the fist to miss his nose and the enemy to overextend. He could have countered, but Dak knew better.

He knew Brutus was faking it this time based on the way he held the right fist and the way his body was still cocked, ready to deliver a devastating roundhouse.

Instead of stepping inside the danger zone to offer a jab of his own, Dak simply danced sideways, forcing the big man to adjust and twist his body quickly before his exposed flank took a blow.

Dak had no intention of going on the attack yet. He remained content to let Brutus throw more jabs, a roundhouse, even a clumsy kick that Dak embellished with a dive roll.

With every missed attempt, the big man exhausted his muscles. Within ninety seconds, he was gasping for air—chest swelling and falling as he breathed.

There was no bell ringer to save him and send the two of them off to their separate corners for a water break.

Brutus clomped at Dak again, this time swinging his arms wildly on a plane.

"Swing and a miss," Dak goaded.

Another fist whooshed by his face. "Juuust a bit outside," Dak continued.

The fatigued champion clenched his jaw in agitation and summoned one last burst of energy.

Dak knew he couldn't let the man get close to him. Do that, and he might not be able to get away.

A vision of a sweaty, gross bear hug from Brutus passed through Dak's mind. It ended with his back breaking and the champion dropping him to the floor like a dishrag.

Brutus kicked out with his right leg, extending it toward Dak's torso.

Dak spun out of the way, grabbed the man's foot, and jerked him closer for a half second before whipping the champion's leg away. In the same movement, Dak took one step forward, raised his other foot, and drove his heel into the outside of Brutus' other knee.

A loud crack echoed through the crowd.

Brutus roared in pain as the joint collapsed under his weight, the ligaments destroyed. From the grotesque angle of the man's leg, Dak knew he'd dislocated the knee.

With a smack, Brutus fell to the ground, grasping the wounded joint with both hands.

Dak sauntered over to the fallen champion and hovered over him for a few seconds. The once-raucous crowd now watched in stunned silence as Dak rolled the writhing man over and sat down on his back.

The movement sent more pain through Brutus' leg, and he let out a pathetic yelp.

"Help me!" he shouted. But no one moved.

"Somebody! Please! Help me!"

The referee in sweatpants merely stood by with his arms folded. In this ring, no fight was ever called, never ended with a technical knockout.

It ended when one fighter was unconscious, or dead.

Dak had no doubts what Brutus would do if their roles were reversed. The champion would have killed Dak in an instant.

Sitting on the giant man's back, Dak held on to his head while he bucked and tried to roll. But Dak wasn't going anywhere, and he slipped his hands around Brutus' jaw, gripping one side with his left hand and the opposite temple with his right.

"No! Please! No! Someone! Anyone!"

"You would have killed me, Brutus!" Dak said for all to hear. "You would have shown me no mercy!"

"No! I would. I would. Please!"

Now everyone in the room saw him for what he was—a big bully.

"No mercy for you, Brutus. It's time to get what you deserve."

"No! Please!"

Dak tightened his grip, pulling the man's head back so everyone on that side of the room could see the terror in his eyes. His neck stretched as Dak pulled, exposing the bulging veins around his throat.

Brutus' voice cut off from the tension, and he could barely struggle against Dak's strength.

Then, Dak turned the man's head to one side. "Don't worry, champ," Dak said in a menacing tone. "It only hurts for a second."

Everyone in the room knew what was coming. The challenger was going to snap the other's neck. A few turned away, unwilling to witness the gruesome execution.

Dak grunted. Then he let out a loud yell that could have raised the dead.

He shoved the man's head forward and stood up. "Mercy is for the strongest," Dak said. "I hope you remember that going forward."

Dak turned toward Dylan.

The younger man's mouth hung so low it nearly touched the tops of his shoes. Dylan didn't say anything. He just stared in utter astonishment.

Dak started walking back toward him, and then Dylan snapped out of it and rushed forward—still holding Dak's shirt in the same hand.

"You really are mental!" Dylan shouted, barely able to contain the grin.

The crowd started chanting for Dak's name. They wanted to know who this new king was who could topple the greatest of champions.

In reality, Dak knew Brutus was hardly a king. He was just big. Something most opponents would let intimidate them.

"That was incredible," Dylan went on. "I mean, you finished him in less than three minutes."

"Were you timing it?" Dak asked, taking his shirt from Dylan's hand.

"No. But it felt like less than three minutes."

Dak looked back over at the fallen champion. Brutus breathed like an ox that had just sprinted a mile. He'd stopped screaming and now sat on his haunches, holding the dislocated knee while a few people attended to him.

"I guess there's not an athletic trainer or orthopedist here, huh?" Dak joked.

Dylan shook his head. "No," he said, completely missing the sarcasm.

Dak rolled his eyes. "Come on. Let's collect your winnings."

Dylan's eyes lit up. He nodded determinedly. "You mean our winnings."

Dak shook his head. "Nah. I'm good on money, and this guy wasn't so tough. You make sure you take care of your mom."

"I can't do that, Dak. You know that, right?"

The American nodded. "I figured you'd say that. Go get the money, and I'll meet you back here."

Dylan turned to go, but Dak grabbed him by the shoulder and spun him back around. "Where is Miles Tidmouth? How do I get to him?"

"Right. I almost forgot." Dylan reached into a pocket and produced a folded piece of paper. "Here you go. I'll be back in a second."

Dak nodded as Dylan disappeared into the mob of people standing around. Some were making their way out of the old station. Others remained, whispering as they pointed and stared in Dak's direction.

Yep. I definitely need to get out of here.

He had no intention of splitting the money with Dylan. Not after the story about his parents. Maybe he was lying. Didn't matter to Dak as long as the kid gave him what he wanted.

Dak unfolded the piece of paper and read the address and name written on it. He bobbed his head, annoyed. "Why do I get the feeling this is another Good Samaritan gig?"

It didn't matter. This was the next place he needed to go. And he wasn't going to stick around any longer. Every second he remained, his face imprinted deeper into the memories of everyone still there.

Dak folded the paper and stuffed it in his pocket, then made his way quickly to the stairs and disappeared above.

23

George Pickford cracked his eyes open against the piercing rays of sunlight stabbing through the curtains at his window.

One of the perks in his career was picking the days he could sleep in. He believed in getting up early when it was a workday, but on his days off he liked to sleep a few extra hours.

Sleep was important. It kept a person young. And for someone in a line of work as stressful as his, Pickford needed all the compensation he could get.

He sighed and rolled over, unwilling to get up just yet. There were no pressing issues—nothing that couldn't wait until tomorrow. He always had responsibilities, but none were more important than others.

He closed his eyes again, pushing his face deeper into the soft pillow.

No more than ten seconds passed before he heard his phone vibrating on the nightstand. He took a deep breath and exhaled, hoping it was a wrong number or that someone had accidentally called.

No such luck.

The thing kept buzzing incessantly.

Pickford rolled over and sat up. He took the phone off the nightstand and looked at the screen. Not that he needed to. It had been on Do Not Disturb all night. And only one person in his life had been cleared to allow the call to go through no matter what.

Jerry.

Pickford rubbed his eyes and hit the answer button. "What is it, Jerry? I hope it's important."

"You know I wouldn't call you if it weren't, sir."

Concern bubbled in Pickford's gut. "What happened?"

"It would be better for you to come down and see for yourself."

"You're here? At the house?"

That *was* unusual. Jerry wasn't due to pick him up today, not until later in the afternoon. The fact he was here now didn't bode well.

Then it hit him.

"Natalia," he realized. "I'll be right down."

Jerry didn't have to say anything else.

Pickford had sent his assassin to scope out Dyer's farm, and kill him and the American protecting him if they were still there.

The fact Jerry was calling and not her, could only mean one thing —she didn't come back.

Pickford threw his legs over the edge of the bed and planted his feet on the floor, getting his bearings for a second before standing.

He grunted at the soreness in his lower back and the stiffness in his legs. Getting out of bed wasn't as easy as when he was ten years younger—something he now realized he'd always taken for granted.

Normally, he would have ambled into the wardrobe to pick out something comfortable to wear for the day, but based on the way Jerry sounded and the message being about Natalia gave cause for rapidity.

He slipped into a dark crimson smoking jacket and a pair of trousers, shoved his feet into some black slippers, and stepped out of the bedroom and into the hall.

He heard some of his men downstairs on the landing at the front door. The walls muted their voices, but Pickford could tell they were concerned.

After making his way down the stairs, he opened the front door and found Jerry and three other guys standing there. Jerry and two of the others were Pickford's best men, and he knew they would have his back no matter what. But the fourth one he'd never seen before.

The guy looked younger than the others, and was dressed in black with a long coat that looked like something between a trench coat and a duster. His short, messy hair barely moved in the morning breeze. He said nothing, but his blue eyes could have frozen a volcano.

Pickford looked down the street in both directions, then held the door wide so the men could enter. "Better we discuss this inside, yeah?"

A solemn and angry look stretched across Jerry's face as he nodded.

The three walked by Pickford, each bowing their head in reverent greeting as they passed.

Pickford shut the door and led the three into the kitchen. "You boys had coffee yet?" he asked. His tone was deep, aggravated—despite the cordial offering.

"No, boss," Jerry said.

"Well, we might as well all have a cup while you tell me what's going on." He looked at the new guy. "What's your name? I don't think I've seen you before."

"Oliver," the younger man said.

"Oliver?" Pickford repeated, glancing at Jerry for confirmation. "You sound like a Spaniard."

"I am."

"Oh." Pickford turned to the coffee maker and pressed the Brew button. He preferred to prep the machine at night and usually had it set to a timer on most days. Today he did it manually, and typically much later than usual.

"He... uh...." Jerry stumbled trying to find the words.

Pickford faced him again and puzzled over his lieutenant's sudden loss for words. "Well, what is it?"

"He brought us something, sir," Jerry informed.

At that cue, Oliver tossed a sandwich baggie on the counter. Everyone's eyes fell to it, but Pickford's were the most surprised. And they accompanied a burst of profanity.

"What is that?"

Jerry took a deep breath before he answered for the visitor. "Natalia's trigger finger."

Pickford looked up, meeting the eyes of the Spaniard. "What did you do?" Then he turned to Jerry. "And why did you bring this guy here?"

"Your assassin is dead," Oliver answered before Jerry could mumble something incoherent. "I assume you sent her to find the American, along with the man who lives in that home—a James Dyer, I believe."

Pickford shifted nervously. It was something Jerry had never ever seen out of his boss.

This young killer was cooler than the other side of the pillow—in an unnerving way.

Pickford recovered quickly, though, and went on the offensive. "What do you want, Oliver? If that's even your real name. I should have my men kill you where you stand. It was stupid of you to come here alone."

Oliver shrugged. "Perhaps. I like to think of it as an act of good faith."

"And why would you do that?" Pickford remained on his guard, easing his right hand toward a snub-nose revolver he kept tucked in his belt. Sure, guns were illegal, but so was everything else his organization did.

"Because you and I have a common problem."

Pickford puzzled over the response. He looked to Jerry as if his second-in-command would have the answer. Jerry merely shrugged.

"And what, might I ask, is this common problem you and I have?"

Oliver stepped to his right and inspected a painting hanging from the wall above a decorative wrought-iron table with an oaken top. The painting depicted an angel with a flaming sword standing watch over a gate surrounded by lush, green vines.

"The archangel protecting the way into Eden," Oliver said. "A fantastic work. And a stark reminder that we are powerless against the greater forces of the universe."

Pickford frowned. "I never thought about it like that, but you didn't come here to talk about art."

Oliver paused, thoughtful for a moment, and then turned his head and gazed vacantly at the unwilling host. "No. I did not. But one should always appreciate art. It is the window into the soul of entire civilizations, cultures, people . . . and individuals."

Pickford remained silent, hoping this intruder would hurry up and get to the point of his visit so Pickford could have his men kill him.

"The American who troubled you before is Dak Harper." Oliver reached into his pocket, a move that sent Pickford's men reaching for weapons.

Jerry produced a pistol and pointed it straight at the assassin's head.

"You're not supposed to have those," Oliver said coolly. "But I assure you, I am unarmed." He cocked his head to the side as if staring at an ape sucking its toes. "Or did you forget checking me for weapons a few minutes ago."

Jerry nodded slowly, recalling the frisking he'd given. "Right. Sorry. Force of habit."

"No apology needed for insisting caution. Better safe than sorry, they say." He withdrew a folder from his jacket and handed it to Pickford, who took it reluctantly.

Suspicion oozed from his eyes as he opened the folder and looked over Harper's dossier.

Then he swore.

Concern melted across his face. "This guy? This is the one Dyer hired?" He looked at the Spaniard over the black rim of his glasses.

"He is the one you should be concerned about. But Dyer didn't hire him."

Pickford didn't understand.

"What do you mean, Dyer didn't hire him? He beat up two of my men. Seriously injured them both. He was there protecting Dyer."

"He wasn't protecting him. Other than in that instance. He was looking for something, something Dyer must know about."

"What would that be?"

"The lost Welsh Crown of Prince Llywelyn."

Neither Pickford nor his men had a clue what the guy was talking about.

"The what?"

"Harper is hunting for the crown, though I'm not sure why. My contacts tell me he's been asking questions, looking around town for it."

"How do they know that?"

"As good as Harper is at keeping a low profile, I'm a better investigator. The crown is in the hands of one of your enemies, the leader of the gang known as the Savages."

Pickford's eyes lit up. "What did you just say?"

"You heard me. Miles Tidmouth possesses this crown. Its worth is incalculable, though some have tried. You cannot put a price on such an important, valuable piece of lost history. But I'm sure it would be fun to try."

"Tidmouth," Pickford spat as if trying to expel a foul taste from his mouth. "What's a punk like him doing with a priceless relic like that?"

"I'm sure I don't know. But I know he has it."

"And how did you come by that information?" Jerry cut in.

Oliver swiveled his head to face him. "I have many resources at my disposal."

"Oy," Pickford said, bringing the focus back to him. "You said this American is looking for the crown?"

"Yes. I've heard he's been involved with a few other hunts of this nature. It seems he's trying to accumulate black-market artifacts."

"And why would he be doing that?"

"My guess is he needs money—illicit, untraceable money. Harper has been on the run for a few years now, ever since he left the military."

"Sounds like he did something bad if he's trying to lay low and scoop a pile of cash from the black market," Jerry offered.

"Desperate is more like it," Pickford corrected.

"Yes, he is desperate. So desperate that he dared approach me for a face-to-face conversation."

"Wait a second," Pickford said, holding up a hand. "This Harper guy approached you, and you didn't kill him?"

Oliver snorted in derision. "There are rules of engagement we both must follow."

"Rules? I make the rules around here."

"True. On the streets of London. But in the underworld where I operate, the rules must not be broken."

Pickford tried to process what he'd heard, but without context, he felt lost. "Underworld?"

"I feel certain you can put the pieces together, Mr. Pickford. You're a smart man."

It only took the boss a couple of seconds to figure it out. "So, you're a contractor." It wasn't a question.

"Yes. And the bounty on Dak Harper is one that I don't want to lose."

"What are you proposing?" Pickford hedged.

"An alliance of sorts," Oliver answered. "We both want Harper dead. And you want Tidmouth dead."

"How do you know that?"

Oliver sighed. This man was testing his patience. He loathed people like Pickford—heads of a large and profitable organization but with the brains of a cat. "Word gets around. Let's leave it at that."

Pickford didn't want to, but he let it go.

"Fine. Yes, I want Tidmouth dead. He jumped some of my boys. Likewise, I should kill you for what you did to Natalia."

"Fair enough," Oliver said, putting out his hands wide. "Go right ahead. But what I offer is far more valuable than revenge for the death of the woman you sent to kill Harper and Dyer."

Pickford assessed the man. The Spaniard didn't seem to care one way or another what the mob boss did. It was foolish, or perhaps it was shrewd. Strange how often those two crossed paths.

"You got plums, I'll tell you that. Or you're insane. Either way, anyone brave enough to come here into my home—unarmed—is either an idiot, or they have something they know I'll want." He thumbed his nose. "What do you want?"

"My payment is assured once Harper is dead. I don't need anything else, from you or anyone."

"Your contract must be a big one then. Who did this Harper piss off?" Pickford asked.

"As I'm sure you must figure, I'm not allowed to reveal the identity of my employer. As to what's in it for you, when Tidmouth is dead you can have the crown of Llywelyn. Do whatever you want with it. Sell it. Keep it. I don't care. I'm not here for an artifact. And I certainly have no interest drawing attention to myself in an attempt to sell it."

Pickford's eyes peered at the Spaniard through narrow slits. "And you think I can move it?"

Oliver shrugged. "I honestly don't care if you can or not. That's your problem. But a resourceful man like you shouldn't have any trouble."

Pickford considered it, taking a split second to glance at Jerry. Not for approval but just to buy himself a tick of extra time.

"I may know a guy who can move something like that for me," Pickford said after his momentary contemplation.

He stuck out his hand.

Oliver let his hands drop and then extended his right.

As they shook on the deal, Pickford kept his eyes firmly locked on Oliver's sky-blue orbs.

"You have yourself a deal," Pickford added. "Now, how do we eliminate these... problems?"

24

When Mia woke up, her father was already gone.

Just like most days, he got up early and went to work. It was the one thing she could depend on from him.

Mia crawled out of her bed—if it could be called that. It was nothing but a mattress on the floor next to her brother's. As she stood, she looked down at Adam, who still slept as the first light of day glowed through the window.

She didn't always get up so early. Typically a night owl, she often slept until the late hours of the morning. Something had awoken her, though. Was it a sound? Someone hitting the buzzer downstairs? Or was it just a touch of insomnia that roused her at such an unpleasant hour?

Mia didn't know, but she was up, and she was certain falling asleep again wasn't an option.

She walked to the kitchen and turned on the coffee pot she'd prepared the night before. Within seconds, the thing gurgled and steamed. Less than a minute later it was dripping fresh coffee into the carafe.

She liked tea, too, like any respectable English person should. But coffee had its place too. And right now was that place.

A loud buzz shook her from the slog of lingering slumber. She turned toward the door. *So someone had woken me,* she realized.

"Great," she muttered. "What is it now?"

She walked over to the intercom and pressed the button on the left with the speaker icon printed below it.

"Yeah?"

"Mia?"

"Dak? What are you doing here?"

"We need to talk."

"Do you have any idea what time it is? You woke me up?"

"I know. And I'm sorry."

She wasn't accustomed to a guy making an apology. Miles never did that, which was on brand for him. He wasn't the type to say he was sorry. Miles did what he wanted, and didn't care about the consequences. But Dak seemed to genuinely care.

That didn't chase away her irritation.

"What do you want, Dak? My brother is still asleep."

There was a pause, and she pulled away from the intercom for a second, staring at the panel.

"I did what you asked me to. I helped your friend out of his predicament."

"Oh. That. Good then. Glad it all worked out."

"He sent me back to you. Said you're the one to get me in with Miles."

Now it was her turn to remain silent while she tried to collect an explanation. Dak wasn't the kind of guy she wanted to upset, but she'd wanted to help her friend Dylan, and he seemed like the right guy for the job.

"You sent me to an underground fight club," Dak continued. "I don't like being used or jerked around, Mia. I'm sure you can appreciate that."

She pressed her lips together, fully aware that he was right.

She nodded. "Yeah. I can. And I'm sorry. I didn't want to, but I knew you could help him."

"You could have told me."

"I didn't think you would do it."

"You're probably right. I wouldn't have." He stopped for a second. "Look, as enchanting as it is talking to you through this box, I would prefer in person."

A trickle of fear snaked through her. She wondered if it was a good idea, but remembered if he'd wanted to hurt her or have his way with her, he'd already had ample opportunities for that.

The coffee pot beeped in the background, signaling the machine had finished its task.

"You want to come up for a cup of coffee? I take it you didn't sleep last night."

"Not yet. I'll steal a nap later. Coffee sounds good, though."

She hesitated for another second then pressed the button to unlock the downstairs door.

"You know which flat, yeah?" she asked.

"The number's on the box," he groused.

"Right."

Rolling her eyes and shaking her head, she turned and walked over to the coffee pot, took out two mugs from the cabinet overhead, and set them on the counter.

In her head, she visualized where Dak might be in the stairwell. *First landing. Second floor. Next landing....*

She poured coffee into both mugs, glad she'd actually made enough for more than one cup. Though she usually made enough for four anyway. Her caffeine addiction and ridiculously late nights demanded it of her in the mornings.

Should be arriving on my floor now.

She picked up the mugs and walked over to the little table in the nook next to the kitchen, set a mug down in front of the chair facing the door, and then walked to the entrance.

Last thing she wanted was Dak to wake up her brother, so she unlocked the door and opened it a crack.

Quiet footsteps echoed down the hall, accompanied by a quiet whooshing sound.

She waited until he was close before opening the door wide.

Dak stopped at the entrance and smiled while raising one eyebrow.

"That for me?"

"No," she said and took a long sip. Then she flicked her head toward the table just inside. "Yours is in there."

She wore a cocky grin despite feeling annoyed that he was here. At least so soon.

"I don't like being toyed with, Mia," Dak said.

"I'm not toying with you. I poured you a cup. It's right there."

He looked beyond her shoulder at the mug sitting on the edge of the table. Then he brought his eyes back to hers. "I'm not talking about the coffee. Although, thank you."

"You're welcome. I even—"

"Put it where I can face the door. I appreciate that. Although probably not as big of an issue in someone's home. Or maybe it is," he said the last part as he looked around, checking both ends of the hall.

"Come in," she ordered. "Don't like to keep the door hanging open like this."

He obeyed and stepped into the little apartment. There wasn't much to look at—a small, narrow kitchen with an old fridge and a stove that looked like it could have been the refrigerator's grandpa.

Beyond the tiny living room to the left, a bathroom stood between two bedrooms. Dak saw the young boy sleeping on a floor mattress in the room to the left.

"Are we going to wake him?" Dak asked, sincere concern on his face.

"Nah," she said. "He could sleep through the Battle of Britain."

"Good reference." He looked over at the mug. "Coffee smells good."

She closed the door and wheeled around. "Thank you," she said, taking another sip. "I can't splurge on much. But I try to take good care of my little brother, and I buy good coffee once a month. It's the luxury I give myself."

"You have to give yourself a treat now and then. Otherwise, you're not really living. Just surviving."

A surprised smile creased her lips. "I like that. Did you make it up?"

"I don't know. Maybe." He walked by her to the proffered chair and sat down, lifting the mug to his lips. Dak held it there for a few seconds, letting the aromas soak into his senses. Then he drank and let the hot, roasted goodness roll down his throat. Even though the caffeine wasn't in his system yet, he still felt a rush of energy course through him at the mere taste.

"I'm still mad at you, by the way," Dak said after tasting the coffee. "You could have just asked me to help your friend."

"Would you have said yes?"

"Probably not."

She laughed. He joined her with a snicker of his own.

"Which is why I had to do it the way I did. Look, I would have sent you to Miles straightaway, but then you would have left." Sadness seeped into her words. "Good people are hard to find in this world, let alone this part of London. Every day all I see and interact with are hardened criminals or people who want to be." Her voice grew more distant. "I just want out."

He remembered her saying something about that before. Or maybe it was his imagination. Being sleep deprived messed with anyone's memory. Even someone like Dak.

"Dylan's mother will be taken care of. He won't have to worry about her bills anymore. Now, I need to know where I can find Miles." He put on a stern mask to match his request.

"And I'll tell you how to get to him. A deal's a deal, yeah?"

"I would hope so." Dak took another sip.

"He keeps a hideout over on the—"

The buzzer on the wall interrupted her.

Mia snapped her head around to see who was ringing but instantly remembered those panels didn't have caller ID like a phone.

Dak looked at her, surprised and a little concerned.

"Expecting someone?"

"No," Mia said. "Not at this hour. I haven't even showered yet."

The buzzer sounded again.

She rolled her eyes and took a deep breath, sighed, and stood up. "It's probably just some delivery person bringing us a parcel."

"You get a lot of deliveries at this time of day?"

Mia caught his meaning and shook her head, narrowing her eyelids. "No. We don't."

"Then why would you—"

The thing buzzed again, and she walked over to it if for no other reason than to silence the obnoxious intercom.

She pressed the receive call button and leaned close. "Yeah?"

Mia twisted her head slightly to look over into the bedroom where her brother still slept. Fortunately, all the noise hadn't roused him. But even Adam had limits.

"Hello, my dear," the familiar voice said through the speaker.

She released the button and looked over at Dak with abject terror splashed across her face.

"Who is it?" he asked.

"It's Miles."

25

"What?" Dak asked. "Here? Now?"

"Yes. And I can't not let him in."

"Why not?"

She fired him a scathing glare that told him everything he needed to know.

"Okay," Dak said. "Point taken. But this makes things simple. He comes up, I handle him, and you're free to do whatever you want."

"He won't have the crown with him, Dak."

The buzzer sounded again.

She exhaled in a gasp then pressed the button. "I'm ringing you in. Just had to put on jim-jams."

"You don't have to do that," he said playfully.

"Oh, leave it out, Miles. You know that's never going to happen. And my brother is here, so be quiet when you come in."

"He won't hear a peep."

She pressed the button to unlock the downstairs door then turned to Dak. "You need to go."

"Not a chance, kid. This guy has what my employer wants. And he sounds like a bad egg. You should let me take out the trash."

"Then you won't get that crown your boss wants so much. Miles won't tell you where it is. He's stubborn like that."

Dak allowed a cryptic grin to reach across the right side of his cheek. "I know how to deal with stubborn dirtbags."

"I'm sure you do. But I already told you, not here. Not now. You have to go to him. Don't you bring your wars into my home."

He retreated visually. Dak nodded assent. "What do you want me to do?"

"Hide in there," she said, pointing to her father's bedroom. To say it was cluttered would have been a severe injustice to the word. She didn't know how often, or if ever, he cleaned it. Her thought was if Miles checked in there, he might decide to turn back once he caught sight or smell of the room and its "contents."

"You sure?"

"Go," she said with a nod. "He'll be here any minute."

Dak sighed. Reluctance filled the exhale, but he knew there was no getting around this. As far as he knew, Miles wasn't aware of who Dak was. But if Mia felt the need to keep his presence a secret, she must have suspected something. She knew the guy better than he did.

He turned abruptly and walked over to the bedroom door, paused for a second to look back, then disappeared inside. Once in, he eased the door shut. He didn't close it all the way, leaving a crack between the door and frame so as not to arouse further suspicion.

Dak looked around the messy room. Shoes scattered across the floor along with clothes—dirty or clean, he didn't want to know.

Magazines, including a few dirty ones, festooned the ill-kept dresser against the wall to the left.

Dak wondered at the example of awful parenting. *This guy really is a piece of work,* he thought with disgust.

Now I just need a place to hide in all this.

MIA WATCHED Dak disappear into her father's room and close the door most of the way. She hoped Miles wouldn't think about looking in there. *But why would he?*

She padded over to her room and closed the door so Adam could continue sleeping, though her hopes that he could get another hour in were probably in vain.

Within seconds of shutting the door, loud knocking came from the entrance.

She rolled her eyes and exhaled through her nose, hoping the sound hadn't roused her brother.

Mia hurried over to the door on her tiptoes. When she opened it, she wore an annoyed scowl on her face.

"What do you want, Miles," she hissed. "Do you have any idea how early it is?"

He snorted with a shrug. "Of course I know what time it is. I haven't gone to bed yet." He looked past her to the coffee mugs on the table.

"Don't look like I woke you, though. Already having your morning coffee, I see."

She looked back over her shoulder and felt a thread of fear crawl through her. It felt like a centipede slithering across her spine.

Within a second, she composed herself enough to face him again. "I'm talking about my brother. He's still asleep, and he needs to rest. He had a long week at school. "

Another snort. Miles shook his head. "School? Still on that, are you?"

"Adam has a chance to get his education, Miles. Doesn't matter what you think about it."

He raised both eyebrows and pretended to be hurt. "Oh, look at the morning sass on you." He pushed her aside and entered the apartment without an invitation.

"Please, Miles. At least stay quiet. This is one of the few days in the week he gets to sleep in. And he stayed up way too late last night."

Miles looked around the kitchen and humble eating area with casual disdain. "Been a while since I was in here," he said, completely ignoring her request.

"Yes. I know." Mia eased the door shut and returned to her chair and coffee. She figured going back to what she'd been doing before might keep him from being suspicious.

"Nice of you to make a cup for me," Miles said, looking down at the cup. Then he frowned. "Why is it half empty?"

"Maybe it's half full," she retorted.

He snickered. "Always the hopeful one, aren't you. Always thinking things are going to be better just around the corner."

"Better than going through life thinking you have to take what you want."

"My luxury flat would disagree with that, but you do you." He picked up the cup and took a sip.

On the inside, two emotions battled for Mia's attention. One was laughing hysterically about Miles drinking out of Dak's cup. The other, however, was terrified that he'd realize someone else was here.

He swallowed the drink and nodded. "Good coffee."

"Thanks," she muttered and buried her nose in her mug. She took in the smell of the coffee before taking a sip again.

"You don't have to live like this, you know."

"Not this again, Miles."

"I'm just saying, if you want to live a better life, come live with me."

"So I can be one of your harem? I don't think so."

Miles chuckled. "Suit yourself. Beats being in this dump."

She clenched her jaw, refusing to let him push her buttons.

He eased into the chair and leaned back lackadaisically. His eyes wandered, absently surveying the little apartment.

She tried to be cool, to not look like she was hiding something from him, but it was one of her weaknesses. Miles always made her nervous. She could usually blow through that anxiety with a dash of attitude. But those times she wasn't harboring someone who fully intended to rob him of something extremely valuable.

"We're going to make our move on the Houghton Mob tonight." He blurted out the sentence and then went back to drinking the coffee as if he'd merely commented on the weather.

"What?" Now she was the one being too loud. Immediately, she lowered her tone and sat back down in her chair. "Are you crazy?"

"Now is the time to strike," he said. "We hit them. They hit back. It's our turn again. But this time, we're going to finish the job. We're going to take down Georgie Pickford, and when we do, his turf will become mine."

She shook her head. "That's suicide, Miles."

"Glad to hear you care," he mused.

Mia wanted to say she didn't, but that wasn't the truth. One of the best scenarios she'd imagined before bed most nights was watching Miles being shot or thrown off a building or dumped in the Channel.

As yet, none of those manifestations had entered her reality.

"What's good for you is good for me," Mia said. The callous statement seemed to surprise him.

"You truly are a Savage. But you're not wrong. That's why I need all hands on deck tonight for the hit."

She didn't like where this was going. "All hands?"

"Yes. That includes you. I've received word that Pickford and his crew are having a meeting tonight down at the docks. His drugs run through there, probably a few other products, too. Word is he's expecting a big shipment tonight. And Pickford himself is going to be there to oversee things."

"Why would he get involved in low-level stuff like that? Doesn't he have better things to do?"

"If it's as valuable as I heard, then I would do the same thing. Can't be too careful."

"Sounds like you don't trust the people you have working for you."

He huffed. "I don't."

"That must be exhausting."

Miles shrugged. "Comes with the job."

She sighed at the cliché. "Miles, I don't want any part of that. You know Pickford's men are going to be armed."

"So will we."

"And you think you and the crew can take them out? Pickford has more men."

"True. But we have the element of surprise. They'll never know what hit 'em."

"Unless it's a trap." She arched her right eyebrow.

He snorted and made sure she caught the derision. "I highly doubt that. Pickford can't see past his own belly."

"You're on his radar now, Miles. That little stunt you pulled, beating up his guys, put you right in his crosshairs."

"Maybe. But I didn't kill his nephew."

She shifted uncomfortably. "Yeah, well, I don't think it's a good idea."

"Don't matter what you think. You'll be there." He leaned in across the table and sneered. "Or else."

Mia focused on keeping her breath even.

"Don't threaten me, Miles. You don't scare me."

"Yes I do," he snapped.

Something fell in one of the bedrooms, and Mia felt a chill slither across her skin.

"What was that?" he asked, his voice matching the suspicion written on his face.

"I told you to keep quiet," she deflected. "You probably woke Adam."

"He needs to wake up anyway. Sun is coming up. Can't sleep all day."

"I have things I need to do, Miles. It's exponentially harder if I can't get them done while he sleeps in."

He puzzled over her statement, shook his head, and stood up.

"If I didn't know any better, I'd say you're hiding something from me."

Miles took a step toward the two doors.

"Miles. I swear. If you wake up my brother—"

"You'll what?" he snarled. "You going to kill me, Mia? Is that it? You think you can take me down? You want to run the Savages as their queen?"

He'd gone off the rails again, just like she'd seen him do before. His eyes filled with that distant, crazed look.

She shook her head, and knew there was no hiding the fear on her face.

"Please," she pleaded. "Miles, don't wake Adam up. He really needs his sleep. And I have things to do."

She knew deep down that he wasn't buying it. The light of day was already radiating through the windows. If her brother wasn't awake yet, he would be soon.

Now, it had more to do with Miles not finding the American hiding in her dad's room.

He stalked toward the door on the left. She couldn't stop him and knew trying to would only make things worse.

Miles halted at the door and paused, then turned the knob and pushed it open. Mia held her breath and watched.

Through the open door, she saw her brother still sleeping on his floor mattress, his body facing the window.

Miles shook his head and eased the door shut—a considerate act she didn't know he had in him.

"Well," Miles said. "I guess it wasn't your brother."

She sighed a breath of relief, but it was short-lived.

"Guess that means it came from the other room."

"No. Miles, you can't go in there. That's my dad's room. If he catches you in there—"

"He'll do what?" Miles produced a switchblade and whipped the weapon around in a show of machismo before stopping with it in his right hand. A menacing look spread across his face. "You know what I think, Mia?" His eyes darkened.

She shook her head. "There's no telling."

"I think you're hiding something, or someone, here in your flat. The only question is, why? Why would you be hiding someone from me unless it was one of my enemies?"

Mia saw the paranoia in his eyes now, and there was no turning back.

"There is no one else here, Miles," she lied. Despite her best efforts, Mia felt like he knew she was lying. In this instance, dishonesty felt like the best policy, but if he went into the room and found Dak in there, she wasn't sure what would happen next.

"Are you the mole, Mia?"

"What?" The effort to contain the falsehood vanished in an instant of sincere confusion. "No. A mole for who?"

"Pickford. I've been wondering if someone was feeding him information. Like how he found us the other night."

"You mean how he found your guys. I noticed you seemed to get away just in the nick of time."

"So did you," he countered. "Are you insinuating I set up my own men?"

She wanted to say he'd done crazier things than that but kept it to herself.

With another warning glare, he turned and made for her father's room.

There was no stopping him now. He was going in. He'd find Dak, and the American might well kill him. Unless Dak thought he could force the gang leader to tell him where the crown was located.

Miles stopped at the door and shoved it wide open, holding the knife out ahead of him in case someone lay in wait just inside.

He swept the blade from left to right, matching his searching eyes. All he found was a cluttered room of empty beer cans, dirty plates, clothes lying around all over the floor, and a litany of other junk that made moving around in tiny bedroom nearly impossible.

He waded farther into the room and looked down by the bed on the other side. Then he returned to the interior wall and opened the closet door. More junk piled up inside under a few haphazardly hung clothes.

Miles shook his head and walked back to the door. "I can see why you keep the window open in there." He jerked his thumb at the single window on the far wall. It was cracked open, and air from outside whistled through. "That room is disgusting. I'm no clean freak, but what is wrong with your father?"

"More things than I can count," Mia said. "Why you think I want out of here so bad?"

He shrugged. "I offered you a way out."

Her face hardened. "My answer to that one is still no, Miles."

"You're a stubborn one. I'll give you that."

"I'm going to make it my way. Not someone else's."

"I am sure that's an admirable quality to someone. Best of luck finding them. He walked over to the door, folded the knife, and slipped it back into his pocket.

"Meet us at Hopkins' down by the pier at eight o'clock tonight. We'll go over everything before we hit Pickford and his crew."

She knew there was no point in telling him she wouldn't be there. Mia wanted nothing to do with their little turf war, but there was nothing she could do. He really would kill her if she refused to join them. And Mia wasn't sure how long Dak was going to stick around.

"Okay, Miles," she surrendered. "I'll see you there."

"Good girl," he said through his teeth. He stood by the door and looked over at the table again. "Thanks for the coffee," he said. "Good stuff."

The temptation to laugh was squelched by the knowledge that she'd be going into a fight tonight. Fear gripped her, but she forced herself to smile. "You're welcome."

Then his eyes wandered around the room again, disgusted by what he saw. Without fanfare, Miles opened the door and walked out, closing it loudly behind him.

She let out a long sigh with her hands on her hips. Her head dropped, nearly touching her chin to the top of her chest.

How had he not seen Dak? She pondered the question, but as she glided across the room to her father's room, Mia realized Miles had hinted at the answer without knowing it.

She looked through the bedroom at the window in the corner. It hadn't been open before. Her father almost never kept it open because he didn't like the noise of the city pounding at his ears while he tried to fall into a drunken coma.

Mia picked her way through the mess on the floor and pulled the window open wide. She stuck her head out and looked to the right. Immediately, her eyes widened at the sight of Dak standing there on a ledge no more than six inches wide, holding a vertical pipe with both hands.

"He gone?" Dak asked. He sounded as if he could hang out there for a few more hours without concern.

"Get inside," she snapped. "You're going to get yourself killed."

"Glad to know you care," he replied. Then he shifted his feet toward the window and stuck one inside. Then, still holding on to the pipe with his left hand, lowered himself down until he straddled the windowsill.

When he planted both feet on the floor, she stared at him in disbelief.

"You're insane," she said.

"You said he couldn't know I'm here."

"Well, I thought maybe you would hide under the bed or something."

Dak turned his attention to the bed and slapped on a look of disgust. He raised a finger and pointed at it. "Have you seen what's under there? The window ledge with the chance of falling to an ugly death seemed like the better choice."

"Point taken."

Dak looked past her at the door to the apartment. "I just let my best chance at recovering that crown walk right out that door."

She shook her head, wearing a coy smile. Maybe she could tip the odds in his favor with the plan for the evening.

"No, you didn't. I can tell you exactly where he's going to be tonight, and when."

The grim expression on his face softened. "Yeah?"

She nodded. "He wants all of our gang down at the docks tonight at eight. Said we're going to hit Pickford hard. I think he's underestimating that old man's cleverness. He hasn't been the king of his turf for as long as he has without being smart."

Dak drew in a breath through his nostrils and exhaled. It was what he often did when contemplating something serious.

"If Miles is at the docks, the crown won't be with him."

"No. I guess not."

He crossed his arms while he thought. "If Miles is killed tonight, then the crown is lost."

"Maybe not. I've seen the safe where he keeps it."

"You have?"

She nodded. "Yes, but without the combination, I don't know how we can get into it."

"Yeah, that is a problem." Dak pondered it for another few seconds before his face eased into a contented look. "I may have a solution."

Mia felt her heart sink at the statement. She'd hoped he could be convinced to come help out with the battle at the docks, but that had been a pipe dream.

"I need the location, Mia. Where is your gang's hideout—the place he keeps the crown?"

She nodded and walked over to the corner of the kitchen. A notepad and pen sat on the surface. She picked up the pen and quickly scribbled down the address.

"Here," she said. "Eight o'clock would be the perfect time to do whatever it is you're planning. No one will be there."

"Okay," Dak said. He eyed her suspiciously. She didn't sound like she meant what she said, as though she were disappointed. "You all right?"

"Yeah," she said too quickly, bobbing her head emphatically.

He knew she was lying, but he had a job to do. He'd check on her after he had the crown in hand.

"Thanks again," he said, holding up the paper.

"You're welcome."

Dak walked over to the door and stepped outside. Closing it behind him, he paused in thought. It was clear she'd wanted something else from him, but what it could have been he had no idea.

He let out a deep exhale and continued down the hallway, staring at the address on the paper to commit it to memory.

26

Dak sat in the back corner of the coffeehouse, staring toward the front door as he sipped his drink. The hot coffee startled his senses, waking him up a little more. Not that he needed that. Standing on a ledge several stories up on a building had snapped any groggy threads of slumber still clinging to his mind.

Caffeine would keep the alertness going into the afternoon, or at least a little while longer.

He'd sent a text message after placing his order at the counter. It could have been sent the second he left Mia's apartment, but that would have been risky.

Miles could have left and been lurking in the shadows, ready to ambush him with a couple of his guys.

Or perhaps the assassin he'd met at the guild nest might have been waiting for him to come by at just the right moment to make the kill.

So, he kept his eyes peeled as he hiked from Mia's flat to the high street, then on to the coffee shop ten blocks away.

He wanted to keep his distance from her in case the place was being watched, or if he was being followed. The last thing Dak wanted to do was bring more trouble into the poor young woman's life.

Everywhere he went, trouble followed. And it was usually the kind that could get a person killed. He wouldn't be able to live with himself if that happened. Especially considering how that would directly impact the well-being of her little brother.

Dak glanced at his phone. No response yet.

He took another sip, and as he drank, the phone started vibrating on the table.

He slapped his hand down on it and muted the call before picking it up and pressing it to his ear.

"Took you long enough," Dak grumbled into the phone.

"What? I called you back in less than four minutes."

Dak smiled with mischief. "Make it three next time."

Will let out a "Pfft" on the other end. "I think I know what your problem is."

"Oh, yeah?"

"You're spoiled. I've made things too easy for you."

Dak laughed. It was an easy, comfortable sound that Will always seemed to bring out of him.

"Maybe I am," Dak said. "But I've got something for you that won't be easy for either one of us."

"Really now?" Will sounded curious. Dak knew how to lure his friend in. The promise of a challenge was something that always tempted Will. Dak figured it was because his friend lived a pretty easy life—when he chose to. But Will only liked things easy for a while before he got bored—which is how he found himself tied up in gun running for freedom fighters in various parts of the world. "What do you have for me? Wow. It's so weird to ask that question. Usually you're the one asking me what I can do for you."

"This is both, actually," Dak said. "I did say *us* earlier."

"Hmm." Dak recognized that sound. It was the sound that his friend was remembering back to the past, and that might not have been such a good thing. "Seems like the last time we did something together, I ended up with a bomb strapped under my butt."

Dak recalled the wild scenario where he'd rolled his friend out of the apartment in Nazaré and down to the beach where he then had to drag the chair through the sand and into the water before he could get Will free of the explosive device.

The witnesses standing around on the beach must have thought it was the craziest thing they'd ever seen.

"Good times," Dak said.

He imagined the aghast look on his friend's face.

"Not good times. Not at all," Will blared.

Dak could only laugh and had to force himself to keep his voice down.

"Yeah, I'm sorry about that one, pal. But I think I've already apologized before."

"It's not enough," Will countered.

"Fine. But this time, we won't have a bomb strapped to you."

"How do you know?"

Dak shook his head. "So untrusting. Have I gotten you killed yet?"

"You're funny. You know that, right?"

"I try."

Will sighed audibly. "What's the job, Dak?"

"You're a man of useful skills," Dak answered. "One of which happens to be cracking safes."

"Oh no. I am not robbing a bank with you, Dak."

"The guy who smuggles guns is worried about breaking the law?"

"Actually, yeah. I am. With my business, I'm in control. No cameras. I make the drop-off points. I set the times. I choose the movers."

"You call them movers?"

"Why not? They move stuff, don't they?"

"Okay. I didn't call to talk about what you call your assistants. I need to get in this safe. Can you help me or not?"

"That all depends," Will said.

"On?"

"Where you are, first of all. If you're in the States, I probably can't get there."

"I'm in London."

"Oh, that's not far then. I'm in Paris right now."

"Then you can be here before supper," Dak said.

"You buying me dinner, too?" Will joked.

"I didn't say I was buying."

Will laughed. "Oh, you're buying. Dragging me away from all this fine Parisian food and drink to come help you crack a safe in London. What's the weather like over there right now?"

Dak continued looking out the window. A spitting rain had started for what seemed like the tenth time that day.

"Sunny and warm," Dak lied.

"You're so full of it. I know better than that."

"I'll give you ten thousand just for showing up. Even if you can't get the safe open."

"Wow. Big spender. And no refund? I have to say, you're tickling my interest, Dak. Care to make it fifteen?"

"Not really. That's why I said ten."

"Well, I guess I can manage."

Dak chuffed. "Yeah, you'll suffer through it. We'll be in and out of there in less than ten minutes if I remember your abilities correctly."

"I don't know, Dak. Been a long time since I did anything like that."

"You were the best in the military from what I hear," Dak countered. "Only person I've ever heard of that was given B-and-R missions."

"Hey, sometimes the enemy keeps their secrets in safes, safes that someone needs to know how to crack."

"We're not dealing with a foreign adversary this time. It's a gang hideout."

"Gang hideout? What are you doing messing with a London gang, Dak? I know you're good, but you can still die."

"I'm well aware," Dak said. He leaned forward and propped himself up with an elbow on his left knee. "But there won't be anyone home."

"How do you know that?"

"I have someone on the inside."

"A London gang member? How did you forge that friendship? No. You know what? I don't want to know."

Dak chuckled.

The espresso machine steamed and gurgled as the barista making the specialty drinks swirled a carafe of milk around under a metal tube.

"Are you in a coffee shop?" Will asked.

"Yes. But listen, this girl isn't my friend. She's just a connection. And I met her by accident."

"Her?" Will sounded surprised, but Dak knew he was mocking.

"Yes. But you know me better than that."

"I thought I did, but...."

"Stop," Dak said with a laugh. "Look, I have plans to make, so are you in or out?"

Will exhaled through his lips. The flapping noise sounded like a small boat motor through the device. "Well, things have been a little slow lately. I'm convinced something is building right now. Not sure what, but I got this feeling."

"Feeling?"

"Yeah. Like something is about to happen. An invasion. An attack. I don't know. Been real quiet. Too quiet."

"Business is slow?"

"Slower than normal. Still good, but not like it has been." Will only took another two seconds to add, "Count me in. I could use a little injection of cash right now, and this gig sounds like a fun challenge."

Will was the only person Dak knew who thought going into a potentially dangerous situation was fun.

"How soon can you get here?"

"I'll have to get transportation, but that shouldn't be an issue. Give me four hours, and I should be there. Where do you want me to meet you?"

Dak relayed the details of his hotel and room number. "Oh," Dak said, tacking on another bit of information. "One last thing."

"Why do I have the feeling you're about to give me the bad news?"

"Because I am."

"I should have known."

Dak shrugged. "It may be a nonissue. But there's someone from the mercenary guild on my tail."

"A hitter?"

"Yeah."

"Do you know who he is?"

"Only by face. I talked to him at the local merc nest."

Silence permeated the speaker for a few seconds. "Wait. You talked to him?"

"Can't attack me at one of those safe houses. You know that. It was a low-risk move."

"Yeah, but you let him know that you know he's on contract."

Dak knew that. He'd considered every angle of his move before he made it. He knew it was risky, and it blew any chance he had at the element of surprise.

"I needed to feel him out."

"I hope it was worth it," Will conceded. "He working for Tucker?"

"Yes. He didn't say it, but I know he is."

"Well, that definitely changes things. Does he know what you're up to?"

"No. He just knows I'm in London. But if he keeps track of me like he has been, it's only a matter of time until he figures something out. But with the gang out of the way for a few hours, I'll be able to focus on keeping a lookout while you break into the safe."

Will drew in a long breath so loud, Dak heard it easily through the phone. "Okay, man. I'll let you know when I'm on my way."

"See you in a few hours."

Dak ended the call and set the phone back on the table. Across the street, he saw the assassin standing next to a bookstore, leaning against the corner as he smoked a cigarette. His eyes never left the café, specifically Dak.

Dak shook his head. Then he picked up his cup of coffee raised it in a mocking toast, then took a sip.

Deep down, he knew either he or the assassin would be dead by the end of the week.

27

Mia stood with her arms crossed at the edge of one of the warehouses down on the docks. A huge crane sat next to the building on the front corner. The churning charcoal sky above would have been foreboding if that hadn't been the norm.

She didn't want to be here, didn't want to have anything to do with this turf war and Miles Tidmouth's ridiculous ambitions.

But she didn't have a choice. The sad part was that she knew if anything happened to her, Adam wouldn't have a choice either. He'd be left to essentially raise himself—a fate she desperately wanted to avoid, more for his sake than her own.

Miles stood among fifteen other members of the Savages.

"This is our time," he was saying, but Mia tried to ignore his little pep talk. "Now is our chance to strike a blow to all the families who kept people like us down for so long. We don't have to be their lackeys anymore. We're nobody's whipping boys from now on. We make our own path. And we share in the spoils."

Everyone nodded, staring intensely at him as though they were English Premier League football players standing in the tunnel ready to explode onto the field.

Mia rolled her eyes. She knew exactly how Miles shared, and money wasn't one of those things he split evenly with anyone else.

He viewed himself as a pirate captain, and the captain always took the biggest percentage.

Miles handed out orders to each of the men, dividing them into teams of three.

To his credit, the plan was solid. He understood that they needed to surround the enemy, essentially putting them squarely in a kill box.

Pickford's men would have the advantage of cover inside the building, but eventually Miles and his teams would move in closer until they squeezed Pickford to death.

Miles stepped over to the back of his car. He lifted the trunk lid and motioned inside.

"I brought you all a little surprise that should give us a strong advantage over Pickford's crew."

Inside the trunk were more than a dozen pistols and a couple of shotguns.

"Whoa," one of the men with a tattoo across his throat exclaimed. "You got guns? How'd you manage that?"

"Yeah, Miles. How *did* you manage that?"

He responded with a smirk first. "I have connections, my dear. You know that. I'm a resourceful guy."

She rolled her eyes again.

"Help yourselves, lads. Everybody load up. Tonight, we're going to take what's ours."

The men each grabbed a weapon. A few chose shotguns. Most preferred the pistols.

Mia wanted to know if his plan was going to remain the same if Pickford had likewise armed his group.

But she kept that part to herself. The last thing she wanted to do right now was question him in front of the others. He hated that. And he would spare no amount of wrath to express his displeasure.

He looked at her as she stood rigid, hesitant to take a weapon.

"You should arm yourself, Mia," he offered.

"I am armed," she replied coolly.

He frowned. "With what?"

She took out a knife from her back pocket. The thing wasn't more than four inches long.

He scoffed at her. "I guess you've never heard the saying 'Don't bring a knife to a gunfight'?"

"I don't want a gun," she said.

Miles ignored her and turned to the trunk, picked up a pistol, and extended it to her. "Take it," he ordered. "It's not a request."

She'd protested as much as she knew she could. Anything further would look like dissent and could invoke Miles' rage. With him holding a pistol, she decided it wasn't the best time to do that.

Mia reluctantly took the gun, checked the chamber, magazine, and trigger, then stuffed it into the back of her belt.

Miles watched her go through the motions, and must have wondered for a moment where she'd learned to do that with a gun. If he did, he didn't mention it.

He turned to the rest of the group, who were also checking their weapons. He quickly and concisely finished laying out the plan, telling each team of three where they would take their positions to surround the building.

Once he was done, he looked back to Mia. "You're with me," he said.

She didn't want to go with him. He was Pickford's biggest target, and being anywhere near him, in any capacity, made her the second-biggest by default.

But Mia knew it was useless to resist. It was Miles' way for now.

The teams split up and spread out, making their way along the row of warehouses that stretched from one end of the waterfront to the other.

Miles led the way down the main thoroughfare until they reached the building next to the one Pickford was supposedly using. He stopped at the neighboring warehouse and looked down the alley between the two buildings. There was no sign of any guards standing watch by the doors. But there was also no sign of life inside the building.

No sounds of men talking, machines lifting heavy crates, and no lights on.

"You sure this is the right place?" Mia asked, secretly hoping it wasn't. She would be so relieved if Miles had gotten the wrong night or time or warehouse number.

She didn't dare to believe she was that lucky.

"Yes, I'm sure. My contact told me this was the place and time."

His contact. That's where Mia was still confused about all of this. *Who was this mysterious mole who'd penetrated Pickford's organization?*

Mia wasn't aware of such a person. Miles didn't tell her everything. She knew that. But she was clever, and it was strange that this little detail had slipped by her.

"Maybe your contact got it wrong," Mia suggested as meekly as she could.

He turned to her with a scathing glare. "The intel is good," he countered. "No more talk about it. Okay? Think you can handle that?"

Her eyes widened at his rudeness, but she agreed with a nod.

"Good. Now, watch my back. I don't want someone sneaking up on us."

"I thought you said they'd all be in the warehouse."

"They should be, but Pickford is smart enough to post some guards outside."

Which we don't see, she thought.

"Come on," Miles said. "Head to those containers over there next to the building. Move fast. Don't want to get caught out in the open."

He didn't know anything about military tactics, but he was right about that. There were more than a few open spaces out here on the docks, and while cover was plentiful, getting to that cover could prove problematic if they got caught out in the open.

Miles took off at a sprint and skidded to a stop next to the stack of two containers. Mia stayed close behind and took a position against the warehouse wall.

"What now?" Mia asked.

"Shut up," Miles snapped. He touched a radio earpiece in his right ear, then spoke. "Team One, check in."

"Team One checking in."

"You in position?"

"Yes, sir," the guy replied.

He went through the list of teams in his head until he'd confirmed all of them were where they should be and ready to attack. The last group to check in was Team Five, but they had the farthest to go to reach the front southwest corner of the building.

They would loop around, taking a wide track until they reached cover behind a stack of crates in front of the next building over.

"Any sign of Pickford?"

Team One was the first to respond. "No sign of him, sir. And there aren't any cars out front here." Miles frowned.

Mia sensed that he was worried, that maybe her suggestion of the mole not being accurate with their information could actually be correct.

But she didn't dare mention it.

"Team Five, any sign of them?"

"Not yet, Miles."

"No lorries or anything?"

"No, sir."

Miles sighed in frustration. When he spoke, it was to himself and Mia, but more the former. "They were supposed to be here at eight. It's eight now."

"Maybe they're running a little late. They're the mob, Miles. Not a Swiss train company."

He considered her words then nodded. "Yeah. You're right. Probably just running a few minutes late. No worries." He tapped the button on his radio again. "Stay in position. They're just running a few minutes late. Be ready."

Miles returned his gaze to her and grinned. It looked like the devil himself was smiling at her. It was a distorted, ugly expression not dissimilar to the one a prowling tiger might give its prey.

"Shouldn't be long now, Mia. When we leave here, we'll be in control of all the Houghton Mob's turf. Then we'll live like kings."

Mia didn't want to be a king, or a queen. She just wanted a normal life—whatever that was.

Just then, one of his men interrupted, and he held up his hand to stop her from speaking, which she had no intention of doing.

"Looks like they're here, Miles," Team Two's leader said.

"How many?"

"Two moving vans and a couple of Land Rovers."

Miles' eyebrows crowded the tops of his eyelids. When he spoke, it wasn't through the radio. "Only two vans and two SUVs?"

"What's wrong?" Mia asked.

He shook off the question. "I thought they would have more firepower with them. I guess Pickford isn't as smart as I thought."

Mia wasn't so sure. "Miles, I have a bad feeling about this."

"Don't start that, Mia. Not now."

She pressed her lips together at the warning.

"This is going to be easier than I thought."

"Stay in position, teams," he ordered through the radio. "Wait until they're inside. Whatever is in there is probably locked up. Once they're inside, close in on the building. Then, when I give the word, we go in from every entry."

There were six doors in and out of the warehouse, one on each end, and two on each side.

Mia had to give him credit, Miles had done at least a little rudimentary reconnaissance before setting up his plan. It still had flaws, but for someone with no experience in this sort of thing, he was proving to be a pretty good general. Except for his underestimation of the enemy.

"Come on," Miles said, motioning for her to follow as he hurried over to the nearby door.

She felt exposed standing there on the edge of the thoroughfare and the alley between buildings.

They stood by the door for what felt like twenty minutes. They heard the sound of the heavy rolling doors opening on the other end of the building. The wheels protested with loud squeaks and groans.

Miles swallowed, holding the pistol up close to his face—ready to go in with the muzzle blazing.

Mia wondered if he'd ever fired a gun before in his life, but he seemed to be handling it with a small degree of experience.

Then the sound of the moving vans' engines echoed through the warehouse.

"Here we go," Miles said to her.

"Vans are going into the building," Team One's leader said.

"Wait for it," Miles ordered. "Wait until both lorries are inside."

The sound of the motors grew louder. Then the engines cut off.

That was the signal Miles had been waiting for.

"Do it. Now. Light 'em up."

He expected to hear the sound of gunfire as his team of gunmen tore apart Pickford's small contingent.

Instead, another sound came through his radio.

"What the—" Then a gurgle.

28

Dak and Will stood on the edge of the sidewalk in front of the tall building where Miles supposedly kept his most precious possession.

Standing ten stories high, it looked like it had been constructed recently. The metallic walls and huge windows were more of a modern trend than something from previous decades when concrete framed tiny windows—except for the penthouses and executive offices.

"A gangster lives in this place?" Will asked, the disbelief evident in his voice.

"That's what I was told," Dak answered. He clearly found it shocking as well.

"Man, I didn't know many dudes in gangs back in the States. Maybe one or two, and I'm not even sure about them. But I know this: They were not living in a place like that. Most of them were in bad parts of town."

"Apparently, things are different here in London," Dak joked.

"Yeah, you can say that again."

"Not only that; our guy's apartment is on the top floor."

Will cast a sidelong, befuddled glance at his friend. "Seriously? That's the most expensive one, yeah?"

"I would think so. It would seem things have been going well for our friend Miles."

"No kidding. I thought we were breaking into some underground hideout. You know, like in a warehouse or a secret basement in a pub."

"Nope. Not this one."

Will looked to the front door and noted the camera hanging in the corner. His eyes dropped to the key panel next to the double glass doors.

"Looks like they have video surveillance," he said.

"That a problem?" Dak asked.

"Nothing a couple of hats covering our faces won't fix. The bigger issue is going to be the key panel. You either enter a code—probably four digits—or you use a card key to get in."

"RFID?"

"Most likely. Could be UWB or infrared RTLS. But RFID is still the most common. And, in my opinion, the one to use."

"I'm not even going to get into the weeds as to why you think that. Let's skip to the part where we get in. How are we going to do that?"

Will fixed his gaze on the building for a few more seconds before slowly turning to face his friend again. "It's a highly technical process."

"Yeah? You going to bypass the system? Hot-wire it somehow? Or can you hack it remotely?"

Will chuckled. "Nah, man. We're going to follow one of the residents in."

Dak blushed, which his friend barely noticed in the dark of night. "Oh. Yeah, I guess we could do it that way."

A steady stream of people walking on the sidewalk in front of them gave plausibility to Will's plan. People coming home from late dinners wouldn't think twice about holding the door for another resident.

"Okay," Dak said. "So, we just wait here like a couple of weirdos, loitering on the side of the street?"

"Pretty much. We shouldn't have to wait long. Everyone's coming home from the pubs or having a bite to eat or maybe staying late at work."

"I hope you're—"

Before Dak could get the last word out, they saw a woman with shoulder-length blonde hair in a black business suit walk up to the key panel. She held a fabric supermarket bag with two bottles of wine in it.

A black leather clutch dangled from her wrist, and she had to set the bag down at her feet to open the clasp.

"This is our chance," Dak said. "Play it cool."

"Once we're inside, we need to get on the elevator with her."

"Why?"

"Because," Will explained, "it could be one of those elevators that requires a key to go up. You've stayed in those hotels that use those, right?"

"Oh yeah. I didn't think about that."

"And you usually think of everything."

Dak snorted. "It's been a long week."

"Come on," Will urged. "Be cool."

Dak shook his shoulders as if he were about to enter the ring against a heavyweight fighter.

The two twisted and weaved through the flow of pedestrians until they reached the entrance to the apartment building.

The woman had the card in her hand and held it against the black plastic façade next to the keypad.

A green light blinked on the panel.

She continued holding the card as she picked up the bag of wine and moved to grab the doorhandles.

"May I?" Will asked in his most polite voice. He extended his hand and wrapped his fingers around the handle before the woman could say no.

She looked at him—surprised at first—then she smiled at his

easy grin. "Why, thank you so much."

"No problem." He held the door wide for her and allowed her to enter while Dak followed, the look on his face leaving no doubt to how impressed he was.

Will merely shrugged and followed them both inside the lobby.

A glass wall framed in steel to the left housed the leasing office. Computer monitors displayed various screen savers at empty, neatly organized desks.

The entire place looked as clean as anything Dak had ever seen, which he figured was intentional to reflect the desired appearance of the building itself.

The matte-white ceiling hovered twelve feet over the gray, hardwood floor. To the right, the entire wall was composed of black mailboxes with golden latches.

Fortunately, the blonde woman wasn't interested in checking the mail. With her hands full, she strode across the lobby to one of the two elevators on the left.

Again, Will offered to help, and pressed the button for her.

"Thanks again," she said, almost flirtatiously.

Dak rolled his eyes but said nothing.

Within seconds, the doors opened, and the woman stepped into the lift with Dak and Will in tow.

She scanned her card without thinking and pressed the button for the seventh floor.

Dak pressed the button with a ten on it and stepped back.

The young woman flicked her right eyebrow up. "You two live on the tenth floor?"

"Not yet," Will answered coolly. "We have a friend on ten. He's trying to convince us to move here, though."

"You're Americans," she said, her tone indicating she approved.

"Yes."

"How long are you in town?"

The numbers couldn't go by fast enough on the digital readout over the doors.

"Just a few days," Will said honestly. "Going to see how we like it, then it's back home to figure out the next move."

Mercifully, the elevator slowed to a stop. Right after an electronic ding, the brushed metal doors opened.

"Very nice to meet you," the woman said as she stepped off. "I hope you'll consider our building for your move."

Will nodded. "Me too."

He waved as the doors closed.

Dak let out a sigh of relief. "Going to see how we like it?" he asked.

"Hey, I had to play it cool. Look at you, all clammy and nervous. I can't believe a guy who's stared down more gun barrels than anyone I know can get thrown off by a pretty young blonde."

"It wasn't her appearance that got me. I'm just not a good liar. Not usually. I mean, not to innocent people."

The elevator continued up three more floors to the top.

When the doors opened, the two men stepped out, both keeping their eyes peeled for trouble.

The elevator alcove was empty.

"What's the number of his apartment?" Will asked.

"Ten seventy-five."

They turned and looked at the wall in the corridor. A placard designated which direction the apartment numbers were located. They saw that the one pointing left was where 1075 fell.

"Looks like it's that way," Will stated.

"Figure that one out by yourself?"

"You know, one of these days I'm not going to be your friend anymore if you keep running that mouth of yours."

Dak stopped his friend short of the hallway and held him back.

"What? I was kidding."

"No, I know. But I just want to make sure there are no guards at Miles' door."

Dak didn't say another word. He stuck his head around the corner just far enough that his right eye could see all the way down both ends.

The vacant corridor offered no immediate threat.

"We're good for now," Dak said. "But we need to hurry. Who knows if or when he'll be back. And I would rather not be here when Miles returns."

They emerged from the alcove and walked down the hall.

"You spooked by this guy?" Will asked. "That doesn't seem like you."

"No. Not spooked. Just being careful."

They continued to the end of the hall until they reached the door with the number *1075* hanging next to it.

Will quickly produced a lockpicking set from his pocket, opened the little case, and found the tool he was looking for.

As he knelt down to start, Dak turned around to watch his back. Suspicious wouldn't begin to describe how the two looked with Will on his knees picking the lock and Dak standing there over him.

A click sounded from the door.

Dak looked back at his friend. "That was fast."

"That was only the door lock. I still have to do the deadbolt."

A needle of disappointment stung Dak, but he knew his friend could handle it. Will was one of the best, or so Dak had heard Will say on numerous occasions.

He'd once joked about a plan for if his life went downhill. Will decided if he was at rock bottom, he'd start robbing banks, and talked about how he would do it. He'd even assessed the types of vaults several banks used, and how to get into them.

Of course, everything was always much simpler in theory than practice, and Dak doubted his friend would ever attempt such a thing. While Will wasn't always a rule follower, he didn't stray far beyond the gray.

Will kept the first tool in his hands while he removed another one from the case. Then he set to work on the second lock. Dak crossed his arms and watched the corridor, silently praying no one would step out of the elevator alcove or any of the other doors that lined the hall.

"Almost got it," Will announced quietly.

No sooner had he said the words, a door a third of the way down the hall opened.

"Will," Dak said.

"Yep."

Will didn't have to be told twice. He pocketed the tools and stood up just as an older woman in a red dress stepped out of her apartment.

Dak only took a second to notice her before turning around and knocking on the door.

He didn't dare look back at the older woman.

Will also faced the door and took a step back so it didn't look like they were desperate to get in.

"You think he's home?" Dak asked, loud enough for the woman down the hall to hear. If she was still there, he hoped the question would set aside any concerns that might have arisen.

"I hope so," Will replied. Then he risked a look over his shoulder.

The woman was nearly to the elevators. The second she turned into the alcove, Will got back to work on the lock.

He made quick work of it on the second try, and opened the door as soon as he removed his tools from the keyhole.

"Nice," Dak said, allowing his friend to enter the flat first.

"It's a useful skill," Will said.

Once inside, Dak closed the door behind them and locked it again.

Then he turned and looked around.

The lavish apartment sat nearly empty, devoid of most of the usual kinds of furniture one would expect to find in such a high-end home.

There were no expensive seats or sofas. No art adorned the walls.

The modern kitchen displayed a clean look, despite the empty pizza boxes on the end of the counter and several beer glasses gathered around the full sink.

"He's a slob," Will realized out loud.

"Yeah. So it would seem." Dak motioned toward a door in the far wall. Beyond it, an unmade king-size bed sat inside. The white sheet and gray blanket were piled up in the center, where Miles had apparently rolled out of bed, tossing the covers away from him.

"I mean, I don't make my bed in the morning. But the rest of this place needs a maid's attention."

"Isn't the worst bedroom I've been in this week," Dak quipped.

"Oh?"

"I don't want to talk about it. Let's just find the safe."

The two crossed through the huge living room where a 72-inch flatscreen television sat on top of a glass entertainment center behind a couple of game consoles. Beyond the television, huge windows made up the wall allowing the occupants to see out into the city. It wasn't the tallest building in the area, but it did give a good view of the neighborhood, and of a few skyscrapers in the distance.

Dak walked close to the windows and inspected the thick glass supported by a brushed steel frame.

The two entered the bedroom and looked around. A pair of sneakers lay haphazardly in the corner. Another television sat atop a black dresser that matched the bed frame.

"Where's the safe?" Will asked.

Dak felt like he already had the answer before his friend asked the question. He pointed to a tall painting leaning up against the wall on the floor in the back-right corner of the room.

"You don't think he's that lazy, do you?" Will wondered.

"I dunno," Dak admitted. "Look around. Seems like it's on brand for this guy."

"Fair point."

"Come on."

Dak picked his way through a few clothes lying on the floor and three more pairs of shoes. He stopped at the painting and picked it up. He set it down on the bed and looked at the wall where the artwork had been.

"Well. Look at you," Will said.

The two stared at the tall safe with intense interest.

"You think you can crack that?" Dak asked.

"I don't know," Will said. "I didn't expect it to have a digital keypad."

"What? Were you thinking it would be one of those old jobs where you turn the dial and listen for the click inside?"

Will threw up his hands. "I mean, that's what I'm accustomed to. Yeah."

Dak couldn't believe it. "Okay. So, what now?"

"I have something for this kind of thing."

He reached into a pocket and removed a small velvet pouch.

"Wow. Is that a coin purse?"

"Very funny. I carry a special powder in this thing for just such an occasion."

Will stepped close to the keypad while Dak looked back over his shoulder. If someone came in, it was unlikely he wouldn't hear, but there were other rooms down the adjacent hall, and he hadn't bothered to check them.

Will dipped his fingers into the bag and produced a gray powder, which he piled onto his palm. Then he gently blew the dust onto the panel and watched as it stuck to four of the numbers.

"What is that?" Dak asked.

"It sticks to the oils left by human fingerprints," Will explained. "Doesn't give me the exact code, but it cuts down the time it'll take for this bad boy to hack it." He dipped his hand into the black satchel he had slung over one shoulder and removed an electronic device that was slightly larger than the keypad.

"This fits over the panel and will hack the signal within the mechanism. Then it will cycle through all the possible combinations until it finds the right one."

"We can't just cut our way through?"

Will chuckled. "Nah, man. This safe has multiple locking bars, each one made out of solid steel. Even if I had a circular saw with the right attachment, it would burn the saw up before it got halfway through. Would take a lot of hours to get through all of them. If you got through at all."

"Okay," Dak said, putting his hands up. "You do your thing. I'm going to check out the rest of the apartment and make sure we're alone."

"Good idea," Will said, realizing they hadn't bothered to go through the place yet.

Dak left his friend to the task and exited the room. He turned right and strolled down the hall to the first door. It was cracked open, so he pushed it all the way back. The room contained a twin bed mattress lying on the floor. Dak stepped into the room and faced the closet set along the wall to his right. He pulled open the doors and found it empty.

He returned to the hall and continued to the next doors, one on each side of the corridor. Dak poked the door on the right first and found another similar bedroom. The door to the left opened into an empty bathroom.

He moved into the bedroom and surveyed it in one pass, then checked the closet and found it empty like the last.

"What a waste of a great apartment," Dak muttered.

"Hey, Dak!" Will shouted from the other room. "Anyone here?"

"No," Dak answered. "But thank you for announcing our presence if someone was."

"Yeah, well, you might want to come have a look in here."

Dak didn't like the sound of his friend's tone. He quickly turned and left the room and hurried down the hall.

"What is it?" Dak asked as he stepped into the master bedroom once more. He saw Will standing by the safe with the metal door wide open. "Wow. You *are* good, my friend. I have to say, I didn't think you'd be able to get it open so quickly. I thought it might take twenty minutes or so."

"Don't get excited yet, buddy," Will said. He stepped to the side, revealing the inside of the safe.

Dak found himself staring into a hollow space.

The crown wasn't there.

29

"I said light them up. Open fire."

More strange sounds pierced the radio in his ear.

Mia saw the concern drain his face of all color in an instant.

Another gurgle filled his ears. The voice of Team Two's leader followed next. Amid the grunts and sounds of a struggle, Miles heard him swearing. Then a single gunshot echoed through the night.

For a second, Miles felt relieved that one of his men had finally started shooting.

"Team Two, what's going on?"

No response.

"Team Two, can you hear me?"

Nothing.

"Team Three?"

Gunshots rang out from the near corner of the building.

"It's a trap!" Team Three's leader shouted through the crackling radio. A second later, more gunshots popped from the same vicinity.

"A trap?" Miles realized. "That's impossible."

"Miles, you need to get your guys out of here. We need to get out of here. Pickford knows."

"That's not possible," he said, his eyes betraying the state of denial in his mind.

"Miles. Listen to me. We have to get out of here."

One of his men screamed in the distance. The noise was cut off in an instant.

"Team Five. Do you hear me?" Miles persisted.

"We're here, but we're pinned down. They're attacking us from behind. We don't have much cover."

More pops blasted through the earpiece.

Miles breathed hard. "There's no way they could have known."

"Miles, listen to me. We either have to retreat... or try to help them."

He nodded. "You're right." He pressed the button again. "Coming to you, Team One."

He took off running down the corridor between the two buildings and caught sight of one of Pickford's men creeping along the wall toward where Miles and Mia had been waiting.

Miles raised his pistol and fired four shots at the man. Only one of them hit the target, but it was enough to drop the man. He fell to the ground with a bullet hole in his chest and a full pistol in his hand.

Mia turned around, aware they'd left their backs exposed, and caught another man by surprise. She raised the gun and fired two shots. One struck him in the shoulder, spinning him to the right. The other went through his right temple and out the other side.

The man was dead before he hit the damp asphalt.

Miles heard the gunfire from behind and spun around. Relieved it was someone on his side, he continued forward, toward the sounds of the battle.

He hadn't bothered to give his teams more than two magazines each, and from the sounds of it, the ones who were still alive were probably getting dangerously close to the bottom of the first mags.

Miles saw four attackers, two behind the nearest team's position and two approaching them from behind a row of steel barrels.

He crouched behind two wooden crates, propped his elbows on the top of one, and fired at one of the enemies.

His shots were devastatingly inaccurate, but he managed to catch one of the men in the leg.

The other turned toward him and raised a pistol of his own, but before he could open fire on Miles' position, Mia slid to a stop next to him and squeezed her trigger four times.

Two rounds to the torso felled the man where he stood. He didn't die as quickly, and based on where those bullets ended up, she knew he would suffer for several minutes.

More gunfire echoed from seemingly everywhere.

The leader of Team Three appeared to the right of Team One's lone remaining fighter. Together, the two Savages gunned down two of Pickford's men, taking a wide angle at both to cut down their cover.

Mia crouched behind one of the wooden crates, her heart pulsing and her mind racing.

Anger boiled inside her. She'd told Miles it was too easy, that this was probably a trap. But he hadn't listened. In his arrogant stubbornness, he'd gotten them all killed.

Miles stood up and emptied his magazine at another gunman hiding behind a shipping container. The bullets pinged off the steel, easily missing the target.

Miles dropped back down to his knees and clumsily ejected the magazine. He fumbled for another one, shoved it into the mag well backward at first, then turned it around when he realized it couldn't go in that way.

"We need to get out of here, Miles," Mia said. She looked across the shipping yard and saw two more Land Rovers charging toward them. "They have more reinforcements. We need to get our people out of here."

She looked in his eyes and saw panic. More than that, she saw a frightened child who'd gotten caught with his hand in the cookie jar. Indecision covered his face in a shroud of panic and fear.

"Miles!" Mia grabbed his left shoulder and shook him, trying to get him to snap out of it. "We have to do something!"

A bullet zipped just over their heads and ricocheted off the building wall.

Miles was clearly useless now. He'd charged into this battle thinking it would be an execution more than a fight.

He shook his head, his eyes distant. "I don't know what to do," he kept muttering, holding his pistol in quivering hands.

She glowered at him. "Give me that," she said and yanked the gun from his hands.

He looked up at her in confusion. Then he watched as Mia stepped out from cover, raised both weapons, and fired.

The gunman behind the steel container poked his head around the corner just in time to catch a round through the chin. He fell out of sight, screaming in utter agony.

Then she turned to the approaching SUVs and unleashed every round in her magazines.

The vehicles were still a good distance away, but she managed to hit one of them in the grill and send another round through the windshield. It wasn't much, but it was enough to force the drivers to take evasive action, jerking the steering wheels one way and the other to avoid the barrage.

The SUVs split off in either direction, both screeching to a stop behind three-high stacks of shipping containers.

Mia ejected the magazine from the gun in her right hand and dropped the other pistol as she charged toward Miles' two men hiding behind the containers. Just before she reached their position, she shouted, "Oy, you two all right?"

She knew the two would have itchy trigger fingers, so letting them know it was her coming would, hopefully, keep them from reacting too quickly as she rounded the corner.

Mia's boots scuffed on the pavement as she halted and ducked down just before a gunman opened fire from inside the warehouse. Until then, she hadn't seen who or what was in there. Now, though, she knew they were done for.

The two moving vans hadn't contained anything of value. They'd carried Pickford's troops.

Then she noticed George Pickford himself standing with his arms crossed at the back of the building atop a landing connected to metal steps. He stood there watching like a field marshal overseeing a rout, a smug expression on his face.

More bullets thumped against their shield.

"Are there any others left?" she asked.

One of the men simply shook his head, terror filling his eyes.

The other's expression remained blank.

"You two are useless." She looked over at the team leader lying dead on the ground, reached over, and took the radio from his ear. "Team leaders, check in. I repeat, check in."

Nothing but cackling static filled the radio.

She threw the thing down in frustration. Once more, she risked a peek over the top of the crate and saw at least a dozen more men fanning out. They had only minutes before the remaining three Savages were surrounded.

Mia saw something else just before she ducked down—Miles Tidmouth sprinting toward the gates, disappearing into the darkness.

"Coward," she spat. "Some king you are."

"What do we do, Mia?" the one closest to her asked.

She searched the docks between her and the water, then down toward the east side. Two of Pickford's men lay dead on the ground, and she realized they were the only ones covering that flank. That would change in seconds.

Her decision made, she turned back to the two.

"We have to make a run for it," she said. "It's the only way. We're outnumbered, outgunned, and I only have one magazine left."

"I'm out," one said. The other nodded the same.

"Then we run. Try to reach those shipping containers over there by the water. If they chase after us, we might still be able to disappear in the water."

"The water?"

She knew it would be frigid, but it was also dark, and amid the churning sea she knew they at least had a chance of disappearing.

Mia looked back over the crate and saw the men drawing closer. "We have to go now. Move!"

They stared at her with a *You first* expression in their eyes.

She didn't wait any longer. Mia took off at a sprint, immediately drawing the gunmen's fire.

The other two Savages hesitated for two heartbeats, then darted after her.

Mia didn't dare look back. She heard the rounds snapping the air around her and bouncing off the pavement, but looking would only slow her down.

The run to the containers by the water was nearly fifty yards. Not a gargantuan distance, but with so many guns pointed her way, it might as well have been a marathon. It certainly felt like a gauntlet.

She juked to the right, hoping that would throw off the men firing directly behind her. Mia found herself in a deadly crossfire, and the only thing saving her was the distance she put between herself and the shooters.

Every step felt like her feet were in sand. That sensation only grew worse as she got closer to her goal.

Twenty yards to go. Ten. Five.

She made it to the container amid a flurry of bullets sparking off the steel walls. Mia only slowed down enough to look back from behind the safety of cover.

The other two weren't there.

She frowned and peeked around the corner. One of the other Savages was already lying prostrate on the ground. He'd only made it ten yards before being gunned down.

The other was limping, clutching his hamstring where a bullet had torn through the muscle.

He didn't limp for long. Only twenty yards from the temporary safety of the containers, Pickford's men sent a storm of bullets into his back, dropping him in a puddle on the asphalt.

Mia ducked back behind the container. Shuddering for a second, she knew she was the only one left.

She had to keep going.

Her brother's face filled her vision, and she felt a renewed sense of purpose pulse through her.

"I have to survive for Adam," she muttered.

Then she turned, ready to keep running. Once more, Mia pumped her legs, running along the length of two shipping containers set end to end. The water lapped against the moorings to her right. Men's shouts from behind her muddled the air.

As she reached the corner of the second container, Mia felt convinced she was putting distance between her and her pursuers.

Suddenly, something moved toward her. It happened so fast, she didn't realize it was an arm until after she hit the ground.

Her head smacked against the pavement, sending her spinning into a dizzy world where the earth dipped and turned.

She closed her eyes to attempt righting her balance, but it didn't work, and she felt a wave of nausea wash over her.

When she was able to peel her eyes open, she found a tall man standing over her, pointing a gun at her face.

"Hello, my pretty," the man sneered.

Footsteps rattled the ground nearby, and within seconds more of the men surrounded her, everyone pointing their firearms at the girl.

She absently felt around the ground for her pistol, but it was nowhere to be found.

The man who clotheslined her bent down and picked up the pistol that lay four feet away from her.

"Looking for this?" he taunted.

Mia swallowed but said nothing. This was it. She'd failed. She was going to die here on the docks, and Adam would be left to fend for himself.

She wouldn't close her eyes, though, no matter how much she wanted to. She wouldn't give these jackasses the pleasure.

"Go ahead," she spat. "Kill me."

The man hovering over her puzzled at the request. "You're a brave one, aren't you? The boss might have use for you." He turned to two of the other men. "Take her to the boss. See what he wants to do with her."

Mia scowled. She kicked and jerked her arms as they pulled her up by the armpits. "Don't struggle, my dear. It hurts worse when you do that."

She stared at him, keeping her eyes locked on his as the men dragged her back toward the warehouse.

Part of her wished they'd shot her right there. For a girl like her, there were far worse fates than death.

MILES WATCHED in rapt horror from the safety of his hiding spot. Everyone was dead. Mia had been taken. If he'd cared about her or any of the others, he might have entertained the fantasy of charging in with guns blazing in hopes of rescuing her and avenging the others.

But he didn't.

Miles had learned long ago the only person he had to look out for was himself. They'd made their decision. It was their own fault they'd been killed. If his team had been worth their salt, they wouldn't be dead now. And Mia... what did he care? She'd blown him off more times than he could count.

"Get what you deserve, whelp," he spat. Then turned and disappeared into the shadows.

30

Dak blinked. Slowly at first. Then rapidly as if he could somehow will the crown to be there. He kept his breathing steady and ran through the possibilities in his head, trying to figure out what piece he was missing.

"You sure this is the right safe?" Will asked as he stood up and straightened his back.

"Yeah. There aren't any others in the apartment."

"Did you look thoroughly?"

Dak lowered his head to the side as if to say he obviously did. "Most of the rooms are basically empty. But yeah, I checked the closets. I didn't see anything unusual that made me think there could be a safe hidden in there somewhere."

"Okay," Will said.

Dak saw the gears turning.

"Maybe we're at the wrong apartment?"

Dak shook his head. "No. This is the place. This is exactly the kind of expensive, poorly furnished flat I would expect from a gangster like Miles. And it's the correct address and apartment number."

Will looked around the room and then back to his friend. "You think he hid it somewhere else?"

"I don't know. It's possible. But why would he do that unless...." Dak's voice faltered.

"Unless what?"

"Unless he knew we were coming."

It didn't take Will more than two seconds to put together what Dak was saying. "You think she sold us out?"

"No," Dak rejected the notion, shaking his head as he spoke. "She wouldn't do that."

"She's a member of a gang, Dak. You can't trust her."

"Some might say I can't trust a gun smuggler, either."

Will bobbed his head and pressed his lips together. "Touché."

"I don't think she sold us out. Miles must have done it on his own. It's possible he's not as stupid as I thought."

"Okay. So, if he were to move this crown to another location, where would it be?"

Dak didn't want to admit it, but he had no idea.

"I'll have to check with my source again. Maybe she'll know of a secondary place he might keep it."

"Yeah, but look how her intel has worked out so far."

"We can trust her, Will. I have a sense about people. She's not lying to us."

"You know where she is right now?" Will asked.

"Hopefully at her apartment. We can—" Dak cut himself off in midsentence.

Will was about to ask why he stopped, but Dak held up a finger, commanding total silence.

The look on his face also told Will that something wasn't right.

"Get down!" As Dak barked the order, he shoved his friend down to the floor just as a stream of bullets zipped through the open bedroom doorway.

Dak dropped down and rolled to the near wall, lying against it with his back pressed into the surface.

He drew the 9mm Will had provided before they entered the building. Both his and Will's weapons were equipped with suppressors. Apparently, the assassin also had a silencer on his gun.

"Daaaaak?" The familiar Spanish voice drifted through the doorway. "I know you're in there, Dak."

Dak said nothing as he looked over to his friend by the bed. Will had rolled over onto his stomach and now propped himself up on his elbows with the pistol pointed toward the doorway.

"Come on, Dak. We both know I didn't hit you with any of those rounds. Or did I?"

Dak briefly considered letting out an agonized groan or a grunt, something to bait the killer into entering the bedroom. The hit man wouldn't buy it. He wasn't that stupid.

"What do you want?" Dak asked.

"You know what I want, Dak. I have one job."

"Yeah. Maybe you should pick another job. Go on about your business and take a different contract."

The Spaniard laughed. "We both know it doesn't work that way, Dak. You have to die so I can get paid."

"Tell you what," Dak interrupted. "You tell me where Tucker is, and I'll let you live. Deal?"

"Even now, so desperate," the gunman taunted. "Pinned down and alone. Well, not alone. You have a friend in there, too. I suppose he'll have to die as well."

Will popped up and opened fire, blasting rounds through the wall and the open door. He kept squeezing the trigger until the weapon clicked. Then he dropped back down to the floor and searched his belt for another magazine.

More laughter echoed through the apartment.

"So desperate, Dak. That's so unlike you, at least from what I've heard. You're usually so calm, decisive."

"I've had a bad week," Dak retorted. "And you're not making it any better."

"Why don't you come out and face me, Dak. Put down your gun, and let's settle this the old-fashioned way."

Dak looked over at his friend. Will's head twisted back and forth as he mouthed, "Don't do it."

"I'm sure you'd like that," Dak answered. "I put my gun down, come out, and you blast me into oblivion so you can collect your prize."

"No honor among thieves, eh, Dak? Or killers, as it were."

"I'm not a killer. Not like you."

"It's all the same, Dak. Innocent. Guilty. Killing is killing. And I am well paid to kill."

"That's cute," Dak spat. "But none of that is going to cause me to trust you."

"Have it your way then. We'll just wait here until the Savages come back. If they come back."

Dak's immediate instinct was to ask what he meant by that, but he was smarter than that. He knew to keep things close to the vest.

"I'm going to put down my gun, Dak. In a show of good faith."

"Convenient since I can't risk taking a look around the corner to see if you're telling the truth or not."

"Surely there's some kind of mirror in there. Use it to look out."

"So you can shoot me in the back through the wall? I don't think so."

A sigh came from the other room. "So untrusting. And this from the man who approached me in the guild nest."

"The nests have rules. We're not in one of those last I checked."

"True. But your options are stay in there and wait out the stalemate until the Savages return, or come face me now. If you choose the former, you will be outnumbered, and I assure you the leader of the Savages will take no prisoners. He will sacrifice any number of his own men to kill you."

Dak knew he was right. Everyone Miles controlled was expendable. Even Mia.

If Miles decided to use her as a human shield, there'd be no way to guarantee her safety.

I'm getting real tired of always being between a rock and a hard place, he thought.

Dak looked over at the tall mirror next to the closet. A bullet had grazed the edge and broken off a shard about the size of his palm.

"What are you doing?" Will mouthed.

"I don't know," Dak whispered back.

Then he picked up the broken mirror from the floor and reached it around the corner until he could see the Spaniard standing there with his hands raised and a pistol at his feet.

Dak tried to recount how many rounds the man had fired, but he couldn't be sure he was counting accurately.

"Keep your hands right there," Dak said as he stood up and stepped around the corner into the doorway.

"What happened to trust?"

"There never was any," Dak replied coldly.

"No honor, indeed," the killer countered.

"You're so honorable. You tried to kill us."

"If I was truly trying, you'd both be dead right now."

"Why?" Dak asked as he pressed closer to the man, his pistol raised.

"Because I want to kill you in a fair fight. But if you want to murder an unarmed man, by all means. I have no fear of death. You know as well as anyone this line of work requires such a mindset."

Will had crawled out from his hiding spot. He kept his pistol extended toward the interloper and stopped several feet behind Dak.

"Don't listen to him, Dak. Kill this fool right now. He's an assassin. No cold blood here."

Dak didn't answer, which didn't sit well with his friend.

"You're not actually considering this," Will continued. "Tell me you're not considering it."

"What's your name?" Dak asked. He didn't see Will roll his eyes behind him.

"What does that matter?" the Spaniard wondered.

"I like to put a name with the corpse," Dak said, his voice cold like the Green Bay tundra in January.

"Oliver," the killer said. "My name is Oliver."

"All right, Oliver," Dak said. He set his weapon down on the floor and slid it back to Will with a kick of his heel. "We'll do things your way. My friend will referee."

"How do I know your friend here won't kill me when I beat you?"

"He won't. Ain't that right, Will?"

Will spat a profanity. "No way, Dak. I'll ice this fool."

"No you won't, Will. If he beats me. You let him go. Understood?"

"No, Dak. I—"

Dak turned and faced his friend. "It's not a request, Will."

Will clenched his jaw and finally nodded once. "Fine. But this is stupid."

Dak frowned a confused expression at Will. "Thanks for the vote of confidence."

Then he turned to face Oliver. "Okay, kid. Let's see what you got."

31

Dak stood his ground, watching the Spaniard simply stand there with his arms at his sides. If he was still armed, the weapons were concealed. Dak figured the younger man had at least one more firearm and probably a knife hidden somewhere in his black clothing, but there was no point in asking him to frisk himself before things came to blows.

Dak was just going to have to trust that Will would prevent any shenanigans.

Oliver stood perfectly still, unwilling to make the first move.

Likewise, Dak wasn't willing to show his hand yet. Instead, he assessed the surroundings without ever taking his eyes fully off the enemy.

The living room was big enough to hold an actual MMA octagon, but with the big sofa, chairs, glass coffee table, entertainment system, and every other design feature built into the apartment, there wasn't going to be much room to maneuver.

Dak knew this was going to play out more like a bar brawl than a tactical battle of the sweet science.

Still, he hoped it could. Aside from his training in hand-to-hand combat, Dak was an excellent boxer—some had called him a natural in the military.

Will watched from the doorway, keeping his weapon ready in case the adversary tried anything sketchy—like pulling a gun from his belt.

"What's the plan here, Oliver?" Dak asked as he inched closer to the man. "You going to beat me to death with your fists?"

The Spaniard shook his head. "No. I'm going to break your neck, or choke the life from your chest. Perhaps I'll throw you through that window over there." He indicated the glass with the slightest twitch of the head.

Dak snorted. "Pretty sure that glass is too thick to send anyone through it."

"Well, I guess you'll die trying."

Dak grinned. "Good one. That's a good one."

Then he charged.

It was a calculated move, a blitzkrieg he hoped would catch the younger combatant off guard.

Channeling Mike Tyson in his twenties, Dak rushed the assassin with fists cocked and ready to launch.

Oliver stood his ground until the last second.

Dak was a single step away when he launched his first attack.

The jab missed, Oliver easily ducking to the right. Dak had assumed he'd do that, and set him up for the maneuver with a quick hook to the jaw.

Oliver's head snapped to the side, and Dak thought he might have knocked him out in one blow. But the killer didn't fall. He absorbed the shot to his face and swept his right leg under Dak, clipping his shin just as he tried to reset his balance.

The force from the move flipped Dak over and onto the floor, where he crashed hard with his right shoulder.

He grimaced and started to get up, but Oliver pounced, wrapping his arms around Dak's throat, just as he'd promised.

"There. There. It will be okay. Let the darkness take you." He squeezed Dak's throat, keeping the air from flowing through.

Dak felt him moving his right hand around his face to find a grip on his jaw. He knew what would come next—a quick jerk with a sudden pop.

Will stood there, holding his pistol at arm's length. Even if he wanted to take a shot, Dak was a human shield now. The risk was too great.

Dak struggled. He'd only thrown one punch, and this punk had flipped the tables on him.

No, he thought. *I'm not going out throwing one punch.*

He grimaced, his lungs burning for air. The Spaniard was strong, his grip unrelenting.

In desperation, Dak jabbed his fingers back toward where he thought Oliver's face was, but the assassin only leaned back, putting more pressure on Dak's throat.

The apartment around him started to blur. He felt the call of the darkness, heard it in his ears.

"No!" he shouted. With every ounce of strength he could muster, Dak leaned forward, putting more pressure on his throat, but forcing the Spaniard off balance.

Dak was slightly heavier and used leverage to pick the younger man up off the ground. Will watched as Dak lifted the attacker's feet higher off the ground and in an incredible feat of strength, managed to flip both himself and the adversary onto the coffee table.

Glass shattered in a loud crash.

Both men grunted.

Dak rolled off to the side, gasping as he clutched at his throat, hoping to ease the tension and let the precious air in.

Oliver groaned and rolled to the side—glass crunching under his weight. As he stood, he clutched his side where blood stained his dark shirt.

"Clever," the Spaniard managed. The right side of his face twitched as he tried to fight off the pain.

Dak regained his posture and noticed the blood on his enemy's clothes. "Break a rib there?" he taunted with a casual glance at the destroyed coffee table. The support for the glass surface was wrought iron. "Guess you must have hit the metal pretty hard. You should probably get that looked at."

Oliver sneered. Letting his anger get the better of him, he lunged forward in a flurry of punches and kicks.

Dak deflected most of them, but absorbed a fist to the abs once, then a second time. The blows nearly knocked the wind out of him, but he kept his composure, letting the opponent wear himself out with the desperate attack.

The Spaniard was in obvious pain. His face never eased from the contorted look of intense focus—a defense mechanism Dak himself had used on occasion when in considerable discomfort.

When Dak felt like he'd allowed enough, he blocked an elbow with his palm, drove Oliver's arm up and clear, then plowed his own elbow into the man's ribs—right where it hurt the most.

The Spaniard let out a loud howl and doubled back. At least he tried to.

Dak didn't let him retreat far, instead pursuing him toward the front door as Oliver stepped back to reset.

Grabbing his shirt, Dak yanked him closer, this time snapping the assassin's nose directly into Dak's forearm.

A waterfall of blood followed the audible crunch as the delicate cartilage of the nose cracked and shattered. Blinded by the broken appendage, Oliver swung wildly now, almost entirely out of control.

He whipped his arms around like an Okinawan ceremonial drum, but there was nothing left behind the attacks. No power remained. Only flaccid desperation.

Dak snatched the man's left arm first and gripped the wrist tight. Oliver fired his other fist forward, only seeing a blurry target before him. Dak caught that fist, too, and holding both weakened arms by the wrists, twisted them up.

The Spaniard screamed as the tendons and ligaments strained.

Dak turned the man to the left, forcing his back toward the window.

"Will," Dak said, "you mind letting in a little air?"

"With pleasure," Will said.

He turned the pistol in his hands toward the window and fired six rounds through the glass. Cracks spread out like spiderwebs from the punctures in the surface.

Oliver kicked out his feet one at a time, hoping he might buy himself a second or two to recover. But it was no use.

"I gave you the chance to walk away," Dak said. "You should have taken it."

Oliver shook his head, looking through glassy, tear-stained eyes. The lower half of his face was covered in blood. "You're a fool, Harper." His voice cracked as he spoke the words. "He won't stop."

The man's words gave Dak pause. Normally, he wouldn't let an enemy monologue his way out of trouble, but at the mention of his nemesis, he felt compelled to change course—or at least to delay it.

"Tucker. Where is he, Oliver? Where is the colonel?"

The assassin's lips parted, showing off a bloody, toothy grin. "You'll never find him, Harper. He'll just keep sending more of us until you're dead."

Dak still hadn't been able to wrap his mind around where his former CO, Colonel Tucker, was getting the money to pay for these mercenaries.

Two-bit hitters could be had on the street for a grand, maybe less in some cases. But bounty hunters like this one were expensive. The guild rates were the highest in the seedy underworld of contract killing.

Like anything else in life, you got what you paid for.

"Where is he getting his money, Oliver? I know it's not from his pension."

"You don't know?" The Spaniard's wicked grin widened, knowing he held the secret over Dak's head. Then he laughed, a sickly, disturbing sound that would have made a serial killer's skin crawl.

Dak shook him, sending fresh surges of pain through the man's arms. "I need a name, Oliver. There are a whole lot of ways I can hurt you before you die."

More disturbing laughs escaped the man's bloody lips. "Do you think I fear pain?"

"I don't think you enjoy it. But let's see."

Dak let go of the man's left arm, raised the right, and slammed his elbow into the enemy's forearm.

The bone snapped with a loud crack. Oliver chased it with a haunting, shrill scream. He tried to drop to his knees, but Dak forced him to stay upright, now focusing on the other, relatively healthy appendage.

The broken arm hung limp at Oliver's side, mangled and useless.

The Spaniard breathed heavily, the color draining from his face as shock started to take over.

"You see?" he spat. "You're no different than the rest of us, Harper. Just a monster like me."

"I may be a monster," Dak snarled, "but I'm nothing like you. I fight for good. Not for men like Tucker."

"What is good, huh? What is evil? We're all just pawns in someone's game. We take sides, and for what? In the end, what does it matter? Might as well get paid."

Dak's patience ran thinner than turpentine. "I'm going to give you one last chance to tell me where Tucker is getting all this money."

"You really are that stupid, aren't you?"

Dak pushed him across the room, keeping the right arm still in his grasp as he shoved the man toward the cracked window. He stopped there, pressing the assassin's back against the brittle glass.

"Give. Me. A name," Dak ordered.

"I don't fear death, Harper."

"Everyone fears death. Otherwise, you'd already be dead."

For a second, the words caught Oliver's attention, and he paused with uncertainty. He took a breath through his nostrils.

"You can die quickly," Dak said. "Or I can make it hurt." He glanced down at the broken arm. "More. Much more."

Oliver licked his lips, and Dak knew he'd called the killer's bluff.

"The German," Oliver surrendered.

"What?" Dak searched the man's face for more. "What German?"

The sickening smile returned to the Spaniard's face. "Don't you know who paid all your friends for the treasures they pulled from that cave? Let's just say your old boss is working with him now."

Dak needed more.

"Who is he? Who is this German?"

Oliver summoned the last of his strength for one last attack. He kicked his right leg out and caught Dak by surprise. The shoe struck him in the gut, simultaneously sucking the air out of his lungs and loosening the grip he held on Oliver's arm.

The force, however, sent Oliver backward into the window.

For a second, the assassin wore a pleased expression—happy he'd caught Dak off guard. Then, in the instant the glass caved behind him, his face washed in utter fear as he fell through amid a downpour of jagged shards.

Dak grimaced, clutching at his abdomen as he staggered forward to the edge. Will rushed across the room, lowering his weapon en route to the window. He joined Dak in time to see the assassin hit the sidewalk below.

Fortunately, the concrete was empty at that late hour. And only a few cars crawled along the street up the block.

No one had seen.

Will put his arm around Dak's shoulder to help him stay up. "You okay, man?"

Dak nodded weakly. "Yeah." He exhaled, finally able to control his lungs again. "Yeah. Just... knocked the wind out of me."

He took a few more breaths before straightening his back. Then Dak looked at his friend. "You know what he's talking about?"

Will thought for a heartbeat. Then another as he looked out the window.

Wind blew through the opening, spitting tiny droplets of rain into the apartment.

"The German?" Will clarified. Then he shook his head once. "Can't say that I do right off the top of my head. But it's a big country."

"If what our dead friend down there said is true, this German is helping fund Tucker's little revenge game with me."

"Why would this German care?"

Dak shrugged. "I don't know. Maybe he thought I was flirting with his daughter in a *bierhaus* years ago."

"Were you?"

"I doubt it. I've only been to Germany a couple of times, and I don't recall that ever happening. I was always with Nicole."

"Is... Nicole—"

"No, she's not German, Will. You know that."

"I know," Will laughed.

"Still, I need to figure out who this guy is."

"How you going to do that?"

Dak stared at his friend for a long, awkward moment.

Will immediately realized what the look meant. "Fine," he relented. "I'll ask around. See what I can find out."

Suddenly, something ripped Will's attention away from Dak, and he snapped the pistol up in an instant. "Stop right there!" he barked.

Dak whipped his head around and found the apartment's resident standing in the open doorway.

Dazed and confused, Miles stared blankly in utter disbelief at the destruction. "What did you do to my flat?"

32

"Close the door," Dak ordered.

Miles didn't move right away. All he could do was stare through lifeless, bewildered eyes as though someone had taken the last cookie from his jar.

"Miles," Dak said, hoping the name would wake the guy from his semi-coma. "Close. The door. I don't want my friend here to have to shoot you."

Will's eyes flicked a sideways question at Dak, but said nothing and took the cue. "Yeah, don't make me kill you, too."

"Too?"

"Miles. Close the door. Don't make me say it again."

The gang leader nodded absently and pushed the door closed.

"Lock it."

Miles turned the deadbolt and faced the two intruders.

"What's going on here?" he asked. "What are you doing in my flat?"

"The crown, Miles. Where is it?"

The mention of the precious artifact roused Miles a little. "Oh. That's why you're here? To steal my crown?" he snorted. "Do you really think I would be stupid enough to leave it here for any of my underlings to yank out from under me?"

"Crossed my mind," Dak quipped.

"Well, I'm not. I assure you, it's in a very safe place."

Dak called his bluff. He could tell from the quiver in Miles' voice that he was lying.

"Where?"

"Why would I tell you?"

Dak lowered his eyebrows, slightly confused. "Because if you don't, he's going to put five or six rounds in your torso. That's why."

"What does it matter? I've lost everything. Even my flat." His eyes scanned the destruction again.

He stumbled into the living room and plopped down on the sofa.

Dak wasn't sure what to make of the spectacle, and from the look on Will's face, his friend was equally confused.

"Rough night?" Dak pressed.

Miles stared at the shattered remains of his once-garish coffee table. "They ambushed us." His voice was distant.

"What? Who ambushed you?" Dak held up his hand in a show that he wasn't going to have Will fill him with bullets just yet.

"Pickford. The Houghton Mob. I had everything planned out so perfectly."

"What happened, Miles?"

The Savages leader shook his head, his thoughts miles away. "We got word of a shipment. We were going to hijack it. Someone lied to me. The mole lied to me."

"Mole?" Dak wasn't getting anywhere with this guy.

"Turns out the mole was in my organization." He laughed the way a crazy person would just before an injection of Haldol.

Dak moved closer and stopped a foot away from where Miles sat. "What happened, Miles? Where is Mia? You didn't get her involved with this, did you?"

He didn't respond directly. Miles was still clearly somewhere else in his head. "There were so many of them. My plan was flawless. I had all the flanks covered. Every inch of that building. We had it completely surrounded."

"Miles. Where is Mia?"

"There were supposed to be two lorries. We were going to hit them, take the shipments, and kill Pickford and his men. I heard Pickford was going to be there himself. This was our chance to take our place, to rise to the top of the food chain." He looked up at Dak. "But they tricked us."

Dak's frustration swelled, but he decided to quell it for the moment and let Miles keep babbling through what happened.

"We got to the warehouse down at the docks," Miles went on. "Every angle covered." He was repeating himself like one of those crackpots on the street corners going on and on about the end of the world. "Just as we were about to attack, Pickford's men came out of nowhere. Way more than I ever thought possible. They ambushed us. Killed everyone."

"Everyone?" Dak felt a needle stick through his heart.

"It was a massacre. Most of my men were killed in minutes. Maybe some survived. But I don't think so. I barely escaped."

"Yeah, I couldn't help but notice you seem to be unscathed."

"Sounds to me like someone ran away before they could get hurt," Will added.

"Sure does," Dak agreed. "Just like a coward."

Miles ignored the barbs—partially. He winced slightly but didn't acknowledge the comments verbally.

"When I saw what was happening, I ran. I had to get out. There were too many of them. We never had a chance."

"So you tucked tail and ran," Dak offered. "And you let all your people die."

Miles nodded, but the look on his face seemed as though the statement hadn't fully registered.

"Where is Mia? What happened to her, Miles? Did you let her die?" Dak reached down and grabbed the gang leader by the neck. His fingers wrapped around the man's pasty throat and squeezed.

Finally, Miles snapped out of his haze.

"No. No. She isn't dead. Not last I saw."

"What's that supposed to mean? You better talk, or I am going to start breaking things."

"And he's already been breaking things tonight," Will added. "Just so you know."

Miles looked into Dak's eyes, then over at the blown-out window. "What happened?"

Dak let him go. "Take a look for yourself."

Will frowned, uncertain that was the smart thing to do, but he kept his pistol trained on the Savage's head.

Miles didn't obey immediately but slowly stood up from the sofa and gingerly moved over to the window's edge.

Dak found himself torn between hopes—that Miles would jump and that he wouldn't jump. But he leaned toward the latter, for Mia's sake.

"You killed him?" Miles asked, pointing down to the street below where someone in a black jacket was on their cell phone, probably calling the police.

"He chose his fate," Dak clarified. "Where is Mia?"

Miles nodded. "Who was he?"

"Contract killer."

"In my flat?"

"Don't get distracted," Dak warned. "He's dead. You're not. Not yet, anyway. Focus, Miles. Where is Mia?"

The beleaguered gang leader's head twisted back and forth like a ragged branch in the breeze. "I don't know."

"What do you mean, you don't know?" Dak snapped and grabbed Miles by the shoulders. He spun him around.

"I don't know where they took her, man. All right? I barely escaped myself."

"Yeah," Will said. "You seem to be doing just fine."

"I need you to focus, Miles," Dak cut in again. "Where did they take her? Where is Pickford's hideout?"

"Pickford?" The name seemed to jar the man from his fog. "Yeah.

Right. Pickford. He has... Um, there are a couple of places he uses—from what I know. But there could be more."

"Here's a thought. You tell me where I should start looking, and I don't throw you out this window right now."

"He runs a couple of pubs on this side of town. One he owns direct. The other is owned by someone else, but the owner pays Pickford protection money. You might have better luck with the second one."

"Why is that?"

"Because the owner is soft."

Dak was tempted to say "like you," but he kept it to himself.

"You seem like the kind of guy who knows how to... get information out of people," Miles said. "Maybe you can get him to talk."

"I need a name, Miles."

"His name is Jeffrey Watkins. If you're lucky, Pickford will be there when you arrive. Or unlucky."

"The only misfortune regarding Pickford is that he crossed my path," Dak said in a menacing voice.

Sirens echoed through the brick and concrete canyons of the city.

"Cops will be here soon, brother," Will said with urgency.

Dak didn't need to be told. He could hear them, too.

"What pub?" Dak demanded.

"The Dancing Turtle."

"Good boy," Dak teased. "Now, one more thing."

"What?" Worry stretched across Miles' face. "I told you what you wanted."

"Not all of it. Where is the crown?"

Miles sighed. "I told you. It's somewhere safe. Bloody Americans." He mumbled the last part.

Dak saw it now. He'd thought he noticed it before, but now he was certain. Miles didn't know the crown was gone.

"Come with me," he said and grabbed Miles by the shoulder.

"What? Let go of me." He resisted but with total futility.

"Dak? You sure we got time for this?" Will asked.

"Oh, there's time."

He dragged Miles into the bedroom and shoved him through the open door. When the gang leader stumbled to a stop, he regained his balance and looked back at the Americans.

"What is your problem, mate?"

"I'm not your mate. And it would appear that we have the same problem."

Dak waited until Miles realized where Dak was looking, then followed the gaze to the exposed safe in the corner.

"Hold on. What did you do with it?" Miles asked.

This time, Dak didn't see a trace of dishonesty in the man's eyes.

"We didn't do anything with it," Will answered.

"Where did you hide it, Miles? I'm only going to ask this one last time."

Miles swallowed and looked back at the safe, confusion filling his eyes. "I swear. It was right here. If you two didn't take it… then that means—"

The realization darkened Dak's face.

"Pickford beat us to it."

Now the mob boss had two things Dak had to rescue. Both priceless. But one far more valuable than the other.

33

Will stopped the car outside the Dancing Turtle and shifted the transmission into park.

"I noticed you didn't go with the stick shift," Dak said as he looked down at the shifter between the seats, then switched his gaze to the pub and the sign hanging over the front entrance.

"Have you ever tried driving one of these things from the other side of the car?" Will retorted. "It's nearly impossible."

"The Brits seem to do fine with it."

"They were raised on it like that. We grew up driving on the other side. Our whole country is right-handed when it comes to driving."

"Makes you wonder, doesn't it?"

"Wonder what?"

"I don't know. They use the letter *S* where we use a *Z*. And they're way too liberal with the vowel U in words like favorite."

Will chuckled. "Yeah, it's almost like a different language sometimes." He looked over at the pub. "What are you going to do?"

Dak sucked in a breath. "I'm going to go talk to Jeffrey Watkins. See if I can use my 'universal translator'"—he looked down at his clenched fist—"and see if he knows where our boy Pickford might be."

"And what if Pickford is in there right now?"

"Doubtful."

"What makes you say that?"

"Call it a hunch. Sounds like he was involved in a pretty big battle earlier. I imagine some of his men were injured in spite of Miles' ineptitude."

"What do you want me to do?"

"Wait here. Keep the engine running."

"I was hoping you'd say that. All this shooting and fighting stuff, man. I left that life a long time ago."

Dak eyed him as he would have a suspicious-looking piece of cheese. "You're a gunrunner, Will. Not a daycare worker."

Will laughed. "True."

Dak climbed out of the car and looked back inside before closing the door. "If I'm not back in ten minutes, come get me." He paused and then added, "Or run. You know. Whichever."

"I'm not Miles. If you're not back in ten, I'll be busting down the door."

With an appreciative grin, Dak stepped away from the car and walked to the pub entrance. The lights still burned through the windows. The hour wasn't late yet, but he got the impression that this was the kind of place that stayed open into the wee hours of the morning.

He pulled the door open and stepped inside. A warm, stale air wrapped around him as the door closed itself behind him.

The second the door clicked behind him, Dak wished Will had come into the pub, too.

Instead of the usual group of degenerates hovering over pints of beer, talking smack about their favorite football teams, Dak found five guys sitting on stools at the bar. And every one of them glowered at him with the *You don't belong here* look written all over their faces.

None of them were smaller than Dak, which wouldn't have been an issue if there were only two or three of them. But five? That could be problematic.

But Dak wasn't about to back down. The stakes were too high. At this point, Dak didn't care about the crown. Mia was his only concern.

"Evening, gents," Dak said to no one in particular. He waved a hand in greeting, but it did nothing to dispel the looming sense of anger in the room.

The men at the bar didn't say anything back; instead, they merely stared at him like he was a beef tenderloin.

"Any of y'all go by the name of Jeffrey Watkins?" Dak continued, undeterred.

"Who's asking?" the barkeeper questioned. He wore a black apron tied around his bulging midsection. His face was red like he'd been sprinting a mile before stepping behind the bar. But he was in no condition to do that. Dak doubted the guy could run full speed for more than ten seconds. His meaty fingers rested on the counter as he leaned forward with an irritated look on his face.

"Well, uh, I am," Dak said. "I guess that means you're Jeffrey."

"What if I am? What's it to you?"

"Oh, nothing major. I'm just looking for a friend of yours."

One of the guys at the end of the bar stood up and started drifting toward the row of booths to Dak's left. But Dak knew what the guy was doing. He was going to try to flank him. Fortunately, the door at Dak's back wouldn't allow anyone to attack him from behind—not with Will watching the entrance. If someone wanted to get to Dak that way, they'd have to go through Will first.

"Is that right? And what friend might that be?"

Dak watched the guy who'd left his seat continue to circle around until he was standing six feet away to the left.

"George Pickford. I heard you two have some kind of arrangement or something. Was hoping you could point me to him."

The bartender chuckled. Two more men stood up from the bar and ambled toward Dak.

"Yeah," the barkeep said, "we do have an arrangement, if you want to call it that. And it just so happens that he told me you might be coming around. He also said he'd pay a lot of money for your head. Seems you've been causing problems around here."

"Me?" Dak feigned innocence. "I think you have the wrong guy. I'm just trying to get something back from George that doesn't belong to him."

"No one calls Mr. Pickford by his first name, son," the barkeeper cautioned. "Not that it matters. You're going to be a stain soon enough."

Less than a second after the man finished his sentence, the guy to Dak's left lunged at him with a tightly balled, thick fist.

Dak dropped a step backward and stuck out the other foot. The assailant tripped and stumbled headlong into the wall to Dak's right.

It was hard to say what made the sharp snapping sound. The man's neck? His skull? Perhaps his nose? Maybe it was his spine. Whatever the cause, he fell like a boulder to the floor, shaking it underfoot with a thud.

With their comrade down for the count—perhaps permanently—the other four guys at the bar circled the wagons—or the American, in this case. Rallying to their fallen, the four closed in on four sides.

"Okay, guys," Dak tried to explain. "That... was... an accident."

The four didn't stop bearing down on him.

"I mean, he attacked me. I didn't even do anything." Dak pointed at the guy with an open hand. "He basically tripped himself. Am I wrong, Jeffrey?"

Dak peered between the broad shoulders of the encroaching men, as if the bartender would give him a crumb of validation.

"Fine," Dak said, backing up until his heels touched the door. "But I'll have you know, I'm giving this place a one-star review on Yelp."

The four men were so close, Dak could smell the stale, cheap cologne they'd bathed in earlier that morning.

He twitched his nose in response to the overwhelming, pungent odor.

"Do you four all share the same loo? Because I gotta be honest: It's a little weird you all use the same teenager body spray."

The two on either side of Dak reached out to grab his arms. From there, they would have proceeded to hold him down—either against the wall or on the floor—while the other two went to work beating him to a pulp.

They *would have* had they been able to snag the slippery American.

Instead, they grasped at air as Dak dropped to the floor, splitting his legs out wide from front to back. He simultaneously fired both fists out into the men's groins, instantly doubling them over in a wave of pain and nausea.

The two guys directly in front of Dak reacted rapidly.

The one on the right shouted an obscenity and tried to kick Dak in the face. The American rolled quickly to the left, pulling his legs up under him to stand, now positioned to the right of the man on his left.

The guy turned to throw a roundhouse punch, but he caught a jab in the nose instead a mere second before Dak's other fist sank deep into his throat—crushing his larynx.

While he stumbled backward into a high-top table and then onto the floor, the only uninjured guy left standing took his chance by charging at Dak like a pro linebacker.

The man's right shoulder slammed into Dak, jarring him off balance. Thick arms wrapped around him as the attacker continued driving Dak toward the floor.

They hit the hardwood with a dull thud. Dak's shoulder erupted in a fiery pain. He'd taken the brunt of the fall with a guy easily fifty pounds heavier landing on top of him.

The huge man straightened his back and tried to straddle Dak, raising a fist to hammer Dak's face into yet another permanent stain on the floor.

Dak had enough presence of mind to prevent that.

Most people would have tried to wriggle free or put up their arms and fists to block the imminent attack. Instead, he leaned into it.

Clenching his abs, he raised up off the floor and jammed his palm into the man's throat and squeezed hard.

The thick neck caved like a stress ball. The attacker's eyes bulged for a second. He changed tactics, grasping for Dak's wrist to free himself of the choking grip.

Dak thrust his left fist into the guy's abdomen, just below the rib cage. He felt the throat tighten in his other hand, and the man's body instantly weakened.

He bent over to the right, consciousness abandoning him.

Dak knew it was a horrible thing to have the wind knocked out of you. But while being choked, it felt like a heart attack.

The American rolled with the attacker and stayed on top of him until he felt the man go limp underneath him.

When the guy's arms dropped to the floor, Dak knew he was out.

The floor creaked behind him, and Dak spotted the shadow stretch across to his left.

He dove to the right and rolled out of the way just as the other two men tried to rush to their ally's aid.

They'd recovered from the shot to their crown jewels and now were hell-bent on making the American pay for what he'd done.

They both lunged, each taking a side.

Again, Dak didn't retreat but went on the offensive. He stepped forward, twisted, and jammed his elbows into the men's midsections as they tried to nab him.

They both doubled over for the second time as Dak pressed the backs of their skulls with his palms, jumped into the air, and used his weight to drive both men's faces into the hard floor.

He felt them go limp within a second of the sickening crunching sound.

Then Dak turned his attention to the bartender, who now wore a look of absolute terror.

"Now," Dak said, flattening his T-shirt, "I think you were about to tell me where I can find George Pickford."

The bartender's lips parted as if about to speak. Then the man turned and darted toward the door in the back.

"Great," Dak complained to himself. He checked his watch. "Still six more minutes." He then took a step, vaulted over the bar, and landed with his feet still moving. He ran through the doorway and into the adjacent hall.

No sign of Watkins except for an open door to the left at the end of the hall. Another door straight ahead provided the building's rear exit, but Dak would have heard that door slam shut the moment Watkins left.

That meant the man was still inside.

Dak figured the bar owner wouldn't abandon the place if there was a considerable sum of cash hidden... in, say, his office. But after the display Watkins had just witnessed, he'd have had to be either an idiot or greedy to stick around.

Probably both.

Dak crept down the corridor and slowed to a stop when he neared the open door.

"Jeffrey? Are you in there?"

A loud blast shook the hallway. A section of the wall a few inches from Dak's left arm exploded from bird shot of a 12-gauge shotgun.

Dak retreated a step, grateful to have been so lucky.

"Is that a yes?" Dak prodded.

"Get out of here!" Watkins demanded. "Or I'll blast you back into whatever hole you crawled out of."

"Now, Jeffrey. That isn't very nice. Wasn't I nice when I first arrived? I asked a very simple question in a nonthreatening tone. And then your goons tried to hurt me. Bad form, Jeffrey. Bad form."

"Shut up! I'll kill you!"

Dak nodded as if the man could somehow see him through the wall.

"Again with the threats. By the way," Dak looked down at the hole in the wall, "is that a double-barreled shotgun? I love those things."

"Why don't you step into my office and find out?"

Dak heard the man's question, but he was halfway down the hall and steering into the kitchen he'd spotted a minute before.

He found two useful items hanging from a rack over the stove. One was a stainless-steel frying pan. The other a cast-iron skillet. Dak unhooked the two items and stalked back through the door into the hall, then down to the doorway again.

He held the stainless-steel pan at an angle so that his face displayed a mutated reflection in the bottom. Then he lowered the pan toward the hole in the wall.

"Jeffrey? You still—"

The gun thundered again. The bird shot blasted into the pan, ripping it from Dak's grip.

He stepped around the corner and peeked through the door at the bar owner standing in front of his desk with a double-barreled shotgun in his hands. Smoke poured from the muzzles, dancing into the air before it evaporated.

Dak stormed into the office as Watkins fumbled with two more shells and desperately flipped down the barrels to eject the spent ones.

Before he could even get the first of the fresh rounds into the chamber, Dak whipped the skillet around and hit the man's forearm with the edge. Dak felt the bone snap before he heard the crack.

The gun fell to the floor amid a hurricane of anguish-fueled profanity. He received no pity from Dak.

The American dropped the pan onto the man's right foot, which sent a new surge of pain through his leg and into his consciousness.

Dak grabbed Watkins by the throat and slammed him back onto his desk.

"Now," Dak said, "I believe you were about to tell me where I can find George Pickford."

He stared into the man's eyes with the devil's own fire.

Watkins swallowed hard, measuring which path he should choose—the one that lead to his death by Pickford's hand? Or the hand around his throat at that very moment?

"They're still at the docks," Watkins spewed, taking the second path. "At Pickford's warehouse."

His lips quivered, glistening with spittle.

"Which one?" Dak growled.

"Number 42. Warehouse 42."

"That's better," Dak said. Then he raised the man up before shoving his head back into the desk surface.

Watkins' eyes rolled, and then his head lolled to the side as he gave way to unconsciousness.

Dak walked out of the office and back down the hall. He scanned the bodies of the wounded as he approached the exit. When he opened the door, he found Will standing there with his hand extended.

Dak frowned at him and checked his watch. "You're early."

"You said ten minutes," Will protested.

"It's been nine."

"Are you really complaining about one minute?"

Will looked through the open door and saw a leg on the floor, an arm in another spot, and realized everyone in there was either dead or unconscious. He wasn't going to ask for clarification.

"Yeah, well, I guess you're good," Will added. "Did you get what you needed?"

"Pickford is still at the docks. According to the bar owner, anyway."

"You believe him?"

Dak shrugged. "I broke his forearm. Intense pain has a way of bringing out the truth in people."

Will snorted. "Did you just make that up?"

"Yeah, but I feel like I'm stealing it from a movie."

"*Robocop*?"

Dak laughed. "No. Come on. We need to get to the docks. And I don't want to stick around for these guys to wake up."

34

Mia tried to open her eyes. She may as well have attempted to lift fifty kilos with her eyelids.

A dim light peeked through the cracks, but it was blurry, undefined.

Her other senses, though dulled, picked up the slack. Wherever she was felt cold and damp. As the seconds passed, she felt the tank top she'd put on before heading out to meet....

Mia's memory jarred her.

The gunfight outside the warehouse.

That was the last thing she remembered. The haze parted as the weight on her eyelids weakened. She still had trouble focusing on anything, but sounds and smells came through without difficulty.

She heard a couple of guys talking in another room. Their muted voices didn't fill in many details for her.

The smell, though, told her enough.

The odor of the water—fish and salt—filled her nostrils, combined with something she could only figure was grease.

The docks. She realized. She was still at the docks.

Bells rang somewhere in the distance, confirming her suspicion.

Mia shook her head to loosen the cobwebs, but it didn't help much. In fact, it caused her head to swim in a dizzy vortex of hazy gray.

She blinked rapidly to readjust and finally started to make out the room where she was being kept. That last little part shook her almost as much as her initial waking. She was a prisoner.

Now, more sensations caught up to the others. Mia felt plastic bands cutting into her wrists so tight her fingers tingled from the lack of circulation. The hard metal chair underneath her offered little comfort.

But at least she still had her clothes on. Recalling the last few moments before she'd been knocked out, it could have been a different story. Unfortunately, still captive to Pickford and his crew, that disturbing fate was still within reach.

She struggled against the bonds, but found she couldn't move her hands more than a few inches. A tight restraint against her shins also kept her from moving her feet. Now that she could see clearer, she realized her ankles had been duct-taped to the chair legs.

Mia grunted and strained, but her shackles wouldn't loosen.

A grim realization started to set in: Pickford was holding her prisoner, and no one was coming to save her.

The events of the battle streaked by in her mind's eyes. One memory, in particular, stuck out above all others—Miles running away. "Coward," she spat.

He'd held high ambitions, hoping to dethrone George Pickford and wrest his stranglehold from the mobster's firm grip. But Miles had underestimated Pickford. He'd underestimated everything and everyone up to this point.

He couldn't help himself. Miles had always tried to find shortcuts, always willing to sacrifice details for quicker results.

That recipe had resulted in the ultimate failure, at least for Mia and the rest of the Savages he'd brought to the execution on the docks.

That's what it had been. An execution.

Miles thought he was so clever. "Idiot," she muttered.

Pickford had been a step ahead of him the entire time. And now the Savages were all but extinct.

She didn't mind that so much. Mia hadn't been tied to anyone in the gang. It was a means to an end. Nothing more. And the means had ceased being useful to her long ago. Getting out was all she could think of, along with keeping her brother safe.

Now there was nothing to get out of.

Any surviving members of the gang wouldn't think twice about her. In a strange sort of way, she owed Pickford at least that much. Literal or metaphorical, it all felt the same to her.

The voices laughed in the other room, rousing her from the thoughts haunting her mind.

She looked around the room—a nondescript old storage room with no windows and only one door in and out. A few boxes were stacked in one corner. An empty soda sat bent in half on the floor near the opposite corner.

The room appeared to have been unused for a while—except as a holding cell.

More laughter erupted from the next room. A few seconds after, she heard footsteps approaching.

"Let's check on the girl," one of them said.

She recognized the sound but couldn't put a face to it. Not until the door opened.

The knob twisted, and the hinges squeaked a piercing protest as the man who'd caught her stepped into the room. Two other guys followed him. They were big but not as muscular as the leader. Their rounder faces and abdomens betrayed their addiction to overconsumption in all its forms. Still, thick muscles under a soft exterior meant they weren't to be taken lightly. In a brawl, guys like that were just as dangerous as anyone else.

"Well, well, look what we have here. Our little birdie is awake."

"Yeah," one of the henchmen said. "You going to chirp, little birdie?" He licked his lips and turned her stomach in the process.

"Looks like you picked the wrong side of the fight, princess," the leader said. The sterile fluorescent light above reflected dimly on his shiny head.

"I didn't pick anything," she countered. "I didn't want to be here."

"And yet here you are," he said, throwing his hands out wide.

"Yeah," the second henchman echoed. "Here you are, princess."

"What are we gonna do with her?" the first asked.

"Nothing yet. The boss has to decide."

"He won't care if we have a bit of fun with her now," the guy insisted.

"No," the leader said with more authority. "No one does nothing until Mr. Pickford says so. You got that?"

"Yeah, fine," the first said. The second one agreed in a series of unintelligible complaints.

"Good." The one in charge crossed his arms. "She'll fetch a fine price from one of Mr. Pickford's clients, I can tell you that. And I doubt they'd want to buy if they knew the likes of one of you two had sullied the product."

The two henchmen looked at each other, both wondering if they should be offended or not.

"Yeah," the leader went on. "I bet he makes a good amount on you."

Mia didn't respond. She wouldn't let him see what she was feeling, how afraid she was of everything he said. She'd heard of this sort of thing before—girls being sold to wealthy elites with a penchant for utter debauchery. She'd seen it in movies, too, but never thought she'd be the one for sale.

Most gangs didn't deal in such things—not typically. Their goods and services centered around drugs and the occasional hit to eliminate a rival. But sex trafficking wasn't much on the radar.

"I bet you would fetch a pretty price, too," Mia offered. "You have a pretty mouth," she jabbed at henchman number one.

"What did you just say?"

The leader laughed. "She's right about that, Phil. You do."

"What?"

The man covered his lips with fleshy, stubby fingers.

The second henchman giggled.

"Not sure what you're laughing at, Pillsbury. I bet some tycoon would love how soft you must feel."

"Hey," the guy snapped back. He pointed at her and started toward her, but the leader stuck out his arm like a parking lot gate, blocking him from going any farther.

"She can't talk like that," he protested amid a string of obscenities directed at her virtue.

The leader chuckled. "Easy, lads. Don't get mad just because she's got you figured. Won't matter what she says once Mr. Pickford decides what to do with her."

"It's already been decided," another voice joined the conversation from the next room.

The three men turned around. The two henchmen looked afraid. Their leader remained cool.

"Found a buyer, already?"

"Yes, Jerry. His representative will be here in the morning." Pickford cast a glare at the henchman on the left, then to the one on the right. "And no funny business from any of you. Our client would prefer to keep this one the way we found her."

Mia fought back the temptation to struggle against the zip ties around her wrists and the tape on her legs. She feared for herself in that moment, but the greater worry rested with her brother. What would happen to Adam if she was out of the picture?

He'd wonder where she was. That much Mia knew.

And he would never get an answer. She, like so many others, would vanish without a trace.

Pickford stepped between the two henchmen, who parted eagerly to get out of the boss's way.

When the one named Jerry moved aside, Mia saw Pickford holding something she'd not noticed when he was behind the other men.

"Where did you get that?" Mia blurted without thinking.

"This?" Pickford asked innocently, holding up the Welsh Crown as he might a stick of chewing gum. "Oh, I had someone pay a little visit to your leader's hideout. He broke in before your American friend arrived. Once the crown was in my hands, I allowed him to go back. It seems he had a job to do, something about killing the American. What was his name again? Oh yes. Dak Harper."

Mia's jaw tightened, indenting her cheeks on both sides. She couldn't resist any longer, and strained against her bonds once more—this time in a fiery rage. "No!" she shouted. "Leave him out of this!"

Pickford tilted his head to the side, observing her reaction with curiosity.

"Testy, aren't we?" Pickford took a step forward, still holding the crown in both hands. "He's a bit old for you, isn't he?"

"It's not like that. He's a good man. Unlike any of you."

Pickford's head retreated an inch. He splashed an offended look on his face. "Well, that isn't very nice. Why can't we be good men?"

"You're monsters. All of you."

"Oh, your friend is, too. I can assure you of that. Why do you think a bounty hunter was after him?"

"Bounty hunter?" She said the words before she could keep them from slipping through her lips.

"Yes. But not to worry. I'm sure he's dead now. The assassin was one of the best. And the man he worked for was paying a king's ransom to have Harper eliminated."

Tears formed in the corners of Mia's eyes. "No," she said, shaking her head. "You're wrong. Dak isn't dead."

"I'm quite certain he is," Pickford sneered. "But who knows? Maybe you're right. Perhaps your American friend is on his way here right now to rescue you."

The boss stared at her with a sort of pity in his eyes, two breaths before he burst out laughing.

The rest of the men in the room joined in, roaring at her delusion.

"You're wrong," she mumbled, only loud enough for herself to barely hear.

The men turned and walked out of the room with Pickford leading the way. "Jerry," he said in the middle of a guffaw, "please make sure all the men are on high alert for a single American headed our way."

The henchmen's laughter renewed as they left the storage room and closed the door behind them.

Mia was left alone with her thoughts and fears, the biggest of which centered around her brother.

But now another worry vied for her focus. She felt it in her chest—that Dak wasn't dead. Pickford was wrong about him. He had to be. And if he was wrong, Mia had to hope Dak Harper would find a way to get her out of this, no matter how improbable it seemed.

35

"This won't be easy," Will said, looking through a pair of night-vision goggles. "I count twelve guys. And that's just on the outside of the building. We have no idea how many are inside."

The two men stood behind stacks of pallets lined up against the fence near the docks. The gate was about a hundred yards away to the left, but Dak had no intention of using it. He'd already spotted two of Pickford's men standing watch at the entrance. The second they saw him and Will, they'd sound the alarm.

Dak knew his abilities better than anyone. He'd used stealth to take out guards like those two before, but with both men standing in a well-lit area, he didn't see an angle of approach that could keep him concealed long enough to take out one guard then the other.

"Safer to assume at least that many," Dak added casually. He peered at the building through his own goggles.

"Yeah. At least. Maybe more."

"It's possible, but I don't see much activity right now."

"You think the shipment thing was just a ruse to lure Miles and his gang here?"

"Maybe," Dak hedged. "Or it could be real. If there wasn't something showing up later, or already here, then why would Pickford and so many of his guys stay here?"

"You think Pickford is in there?"

"If he's not, we're going to have to go back to the Dancing Turtle."

Will grinned at the thought of going back and having a little fun with the owner. "I get to do the interrogation next time."

Dak scowled at him, lowering his goggles. "This is my gig. I make the calls."

"Yeah, but you need my help."

Dak rolled his eyes. "Yeah, okay. If we have to go back to the pub, you get to ask the questions. Let's just hope it doesn't come to that."

"I'm kind of hoping it does."

"If it does, that means Mia isn't here, and I don't want to know what that means."

"Okay. Okay. I get it." Will looked through the goggles again. "What are you thinking as far as plan of attack?"

"Did you bring the drone?"

Will faced his friend. His long face gave the real answer. "Yes, I brought it. But I don't think you realize how expensive those things are, Dak?"

"Few hundred bucks?"

"Yes. A few hundred. More like four hundred for the best ones."

"That's not so bad. Especially considering what I'm paying you." Dak didn't take his eyes off the building while he spoke.

"Fine," Will surrendered. "But it's coming out of your cut."

"Whatever. I need you to fly that thing as a diversion."

"Diversion?"

"Yes. Do a few flybys. Try not to hit any of them."

"Oh, okay. A little Maverick maneuver."

"Yep. Just buzz them. Once I take out the first two, we move to the next group."

"You'll have to move fast. These batteries are only good for about ten minutes."

Dak frowned. That was less than optimal, but he knew the limits of FPV drones. They could travel at incredible speeds, but the sacrifice for that was a shorter battery life.

He looked down at the rucksack Will brought for him. "What else do I have in the goodie bag?"

"Couple of nine millimeters. Four spare magazines. Oh, and I threw in two smoke grenades."

"No flashers?"

"Nah, not this time."

"Really?" Dak sounded sincerely surprised.

"Supply chain shortage," Will said with a shrug. "What are you gonna do?"

"Didn't realize that would hit the underground arms market."

Will snorted. "Yeah, well, it hits all of us sooner or later."

"I guess so." Dak bent down and unzipped the main compartment. He found the two pistols along with holsters, the four magazines, and the two smoke bombs. "This'll do, though, Will. I appreciate it."

"That's what friends are for."

"Oh, so you're doing this pro bono?" Dak asked with a coy grin.

"You're funny. How about I take my toys and go home?"

"You know I'm messing with you."

Dak holstered the pistols, one on each side, then clipped in the magazines to the belt, finishing with the smoke grenades—one for each shoulder.

Will took a pair of bolt cutters to the fence. He worked meticulously until a hole big enough for him to fit through fell open in the barrier.

"You ready?" he asked Dak when he was done.

"Yeah," Dak said.

"Get the drone prepped. You lead. We'll take the guys on the left corner first."

"You got it."

Will set the bolt cutters down and unzipped his own gear bag. He carefully removed a small drone built on a five-inch chassis with a camera fitted to the front. Then he took out a pair of goggles and strapped them to his forehead. Last, he removed the radio control from the bag and switched it on. Then he turned on the drone and waited until a pair of red and green lights cycled through each of the four motors.

"All set," Will said after running through his international checklist. "Ready when you are, Dak."

"Okay. Let's do it."

Dak slipped through the hole in the fence. Will pulled the goggles down over his eyes. If someone were to have snuck up on him at that point, he would never have known it.

The only thing he could see was through the lens attached to the racing drone.

Dak waited on the other side of the fence behind a collection of old steel drums.

Ten seconds after taking his position, Dak heard the loud buzz of the racing drone. The four motors were anything but quiet. They sounded like five hundred bees flying in a tight formation.

"You hear me?" Dak asked, talking into the radio he'd fitted to his neck and ear.

"Loud and clear, boss. I'm going to do a little drop-in move on these guys. Should scare the crap out of them."

"Whatever you think."

"Just keep an eye on them. You'll know when to make your move."

Dak checked the suppressors on both pistols at his side, making sure they were on tight.

No reason for the men inside the warehouse to hear the mayhem outside.

Dak crouched in the dark, fifty yards from warehouse 42. He listened as the drone screamed into the air and looked up to see the silhouette disappear into the gray sky overhead. A little rewiring kept the lights from continually blinking, giving a visual element of surprise even if the enemy could hear the thing coming.

"Moving into position," Will announced.

Dak said nothing but crept forward to the front barrel in line, cutting the distance to forty-five yards to the first targets.

He prayed in his mind that Mia was okay, but he feared the worst. It took every ounce of will he could muster to keep from thinking about what could be happening to her at that very moment. *Focus, Dak,* he thought. *One step at a time.*

"I'm in position for the drop," Will said. "Commencing attack now."

Dak inched closer to the warehouse, watching the men standing around under the corner light as they talked and joked.

Then, out of the sky, a black object dove into view.

The drone sped toward the men at incredible speed.

When the aircraft was a hundred feet above them, the men started to look around, and then up to find the source of the sound.

Dak rushed ahead, bending his run slightly so the men guarding the right-hand corner wouldn't be able to see him as easily.

The three men jumped and dove. One swatted at the air with his pistol like some kind of overzealous wasp hunter.

Dak pumped his legs as hard as he could. Halfway across the thoroughfare, he drew the pistols at his side and raised them.

The drone weaved back and forth, hovering then diving at one man then another.

The three guards surrounded the flying machine on all sides. Two of the men held pistols pointed at the drone, while the third gripped a cricket bat over his shoulders.

That's one I haven't seen before, Dak thought as he sprinted toward the guards.

When he was twenty yards away—nearly within range—all of a sudden one of the men with a pistol fired.

The drone shot up fifty feet in an instant. The other gunmen reacted to the first thug's shot, firing straight through the cricket batter's head before the bullet of the first shooter was done burrowing through his own chest.

"What the—" Dak breathed as he neared the bizarre Mexican standoff.

At least the gunmen's weapons were silenced, too.

With two of the men down, Dak only had one gunman to deal

with. And he was busy taking aim on the drone that had disappeared into the sky again.

The guard searched the heavens, aiming down his sights as if that would help locate the annoying aircraft. He never found it.

When Dak was only ten yards away, he lowered the gun in his left hand and focused on the pistol in his right—lining up the target on the fly.

Dak's trigger finger twitched three times. Two of the rounds met the guard in the chest before he even realized what happened.

Dak slid to a stop at the corner and waited for a second to catch his breath and reassess the situation.

He didn't have long.

The men at the back-right corner had seen him running across the pavement and were now charging his way.

Dak raised his pistol and fired. Too far to be dependably accurate, the round scared the men enough to cause them to dive out of the way. With his quarry on the ground, Dak ran at them, emptying the magazine in a flurry of shots.

On the ground and in the open, Pickford's guards were easy pickings, even at a full sprint.

Only one of the men was able to get off a wild shot before a bullet struck him in the head and put him on the ground for good.

"Heading to the south corner," Dak said between panting breaths. "See if you can cover me a little more."

"Roger that," Will said.

Dak heard the drone shoot up into the sky again, then loop around behind him. Within seconds, the machine flew past him and zoomed toward the three men at the far corner.

He ducked behind a dumpster just before the men looked his way.

Behind cover, Dak released the magazine and shoved a full one into the well. When he heard the swearing of the men as they tried to fight off the drone, he took that as his cue.

Dak jumped out from behind the dumpster and rushed forward with both pistols raised. The first guy to receive his dose of metal didn't even manage to turn around before rounds drilled through his back. The other two were facing Dak and quickly turned their attention from the drone to the man racing toward them with guns blazing.

They opened fire, but their aim was far from accurate. Dak's wasn't much better. Every jarring step caused his hands to shake and wobble, but he managed to keep his sights locked in long enough to put a round in one guy's gut and another through a thigh.

Both men fell to the ground, dropping their weapons as they clutched at their wounds.

"Don't get up!" Dak shouted as he passed the two fallen men and scooped up their weapons on the fly. He tucked them in his belt as he rounded the front corner.

Then Dak skidded to a stop.

The three guards from the other corner were only fifteen yards away and heading toward him with pistols raised.

"Oy! You! Stop right there!"

Dak was caught by surprise, and his weapons weren't in a firing position.

"Keep your hands right there, son," one of the guys shouted. The men slowed down, staying within arm's reach of each other—each one aiming carefully at the American interloper. "I'm sure Mr. Pickford would like to have a word with you."

"Will?" Dak said.

"What's that?" the guard who spoke before asked.

"I see them," Will said through the radio. "Battery is nearly dead. But this drone has one more little punch to it. You might want to close your eyes."

"Put the guns down nice and slow," the guard ordered.

"Okay, Will. Anytime," Dak urged.

"Are your eyes closed?"

Dak hesitated, then closed his eyes tight.

"Yes."

"Good. When you see the flash, count to two, then open them."

The moment seemed to last an eternity. Then Dak heard the racing drone diving from above.

"Another four hundred down the drain," Will said.

"I thought you said you didn't have any flash-bangs," Dak said.

"I don't."

The drone smashed into the ground right in the middle of the three men. Then a bright light scorched the night air. The heat from the explosion was the next thing Dak felt. But no concussion knocked him back.

He dared to open his eyes when the screaming commenced, and saw the three men consumed in a ball of fire.

"What in the world?"

"It's not napalm if that's what you're asking," Will said.

"No? Well it's a pretty good substitute."

"Make it count. That's the only drone I had with me."

Dak put the men out of their misery, more to silence their screams than anything else.

Stalking toward the men, he popped a round into every one of them within seconds, then turned to the front door of the building.

"That will have gotten some attention," Dak said, more to himself than his partner. "Might as well make a show of it."

"What was that?" Pickford demanded. "What is going on out there?"

He saw the bright orange flash outside through the dingy windows over the door.

"I don't know, boss," Jerry confessed.

"Well don't just stand there. Get out there and see what's going on?"

"Yes, sir. On it."

Pickford stood by one of the delivery trucks inside the warehouse as Jerry headed for the hangar door at the front. He held a pistol over his shoulder and motioned for four other men to join him on either flank.

"You want us to go with them, boss?" a guard asked from just behind Pickford.

"No. You stay with me. Jerry will handle this."

Pickford didn't sound certain, though, and he knew it.

He glanced back over his shoulder at the other six men surrounding the truck. He had enough drugs in there to support his business for the next two years, but even more important was the crown he'd managed to kite from the leader of the Savages. That would be worth more than five truckloads of heroin.

Jerry and his team waited by the front door next to the huge bay doors. He and two others took up positions to the left while the other two men took the right.

Pickford watched intently, never taking his eyes off the men.

The sound of glass breaking tore his focus from the big door and he looked up in time to see a canister flying through the air on the downswing of its arc.

He watched it as if the thing sailed in slow motion, mesmerized by its trajectory and curious as to what it was.

Then, time sped up again, and the device hit the hard floor with a clank.

Pickford's eyes widened in fear, and he shielded his face with his forearm, fully expecting the thing to explode.

Instead, it popped.

He shuddered, then saw thick white smoke begin spewing out of the thing.

"Is that tear gas?" Pickford asked one of the men nearest him.

It was a guy he knew who had military experience—the sordid variety Pickford looked for when hiring people to do his bidding.

"No, sir. Smoke canister," the guy replied in a thick Scottish accent.

"Smoke grenade?" Pickford paraphrased.

The huge warehouse began to fill with smoke. While it wasn't as harsh on the lungs as smoke from an actual fire would be, it still didn't feel great to breathe it in. And every second that passed spilled more of the cloudy stuff into the air, with the only open window the one the canister had sailed through.

Suddenly, the lights blinked, then the entire warehouse descended into darkness.

"What now?" Pickford roared.

"Whoever it is out there cut the power, sir," the Scottish guard said.

Another window shattered. It was close to the first.

A second clank came from Pickford's left, farther back toward the rear of the building.

Then the same familiar sound of smoke spewing from a cylinder echoed off the block walls.

As his eyes adjusted, Pickford could barely make out the silhouettes of the men around him. The entire blacked-out warehouse was flooded with smoke.

No one dared move.

To a man, every single person in the building stood almost perfectly still, relying solely on their ears to detect the enemy's next move.

Then, after what seemed like an hour of tense waiting, the first sound any of them heard was a loud click.

36

The bullet took out the first of the rear guard covering the inside of the back entrance to the warehouse.

The man never saw it coming.

Dak figured none of Pickford's crew would have night vision. And he certainly didn't expect any of them to have the kind of gear that could switch to thermal view.

He aimed at the next red, orange, and yellow body in his vision and squeezed the trigger as the man spun around at the sound of the first shot.

He fell near the first.

Toward the front of the building, Dak made out multiple bodies.

It was impossible to tell which one was Pickford, but he spotted the group of four near the front entrance and figured that might be him.

There was also a cluster near the truck in the center of the room.

May as well take out all the trash while I'm here.

Dak moved like a ghost in the fog, circling around to another guard who stood on a catwalk overhead. Dak aimed and fired, drilling a hole in the man's chest.

He grunted, lost his balance, and fell over the railing. He hit the floor with a smack.

Everyone in the center of the room spun around to face the source of the sound.

"Dak Harper!" a voice shouted. "Is that you?"

Dak said nothing, instead moving to the next target. He maneuvered around a collection of boxes and crates stacked haphazardly near the wall, and stopped when he'd reached his next target.

Crouching low, Dak aimed and fired the next round through a guard's temple.

He retreated, doubling back the way he'd come as the glowing figures to his left all turned toward the sound of his suppressor's discharge.

"What are you all doing?" Pickford shouted. "Shoot him!"

Muted pops filled the room. Bullets ricocheted dangerously off the walls, with sparks dancing in the swirling smoke.

"Stop firing!" another voice ordered from the front of the warehouse. "Are you mad? You'll kill us all."

Dak found two more guards on the other side of the room and made short work of them, gifting each with a round to the back of the head as the men focused in the direction of the truck in the middle.

At the sounds, the remaining figures again turned in the direction they believed the threat to be.

"Harper! Why don't you show yourself and fight like a man? Huh?"

Suddenly, something bright showed up in his goggles near the front of the building. Dak winced at the light and turned his attention to the men on the left side of the truck. He fired several shots, but with the light impairing his vision with the goggles, he only hit two of the four targets.

Forced to retreat and rethink his tactics, Dak slipped behind a row of steel drums and removed the goggles.

Blinking rapidly to adjust his eyes, he saw the problem.

One of the men at the front had turned on his cell phone flashlight. Another did the same, and soon all of Pickford's reinforcements held phones in their hands, waving the lights around meticulously to find the enemy.

So much for that plan, Dak thought.

Then again, the men were still basically advertising their position.

Dak counted twelve left. Five at the front. Two by the truck nearest him, and five more on the other side.

He raised his pistol and fired into the smoke toward the first of the two lights twenty feet away.

One of the men grunted as the bullet hit him. Dak had no way to know where, but based on the shower of obscenities flowing from the guy's mouth, it had to be painful. Dak fired again as the other henchman turned toward his partner. He shrieked for a split second before the light fell into the churning smoke.

Then Dak saw the lights fanning out.

The men were getting wise to his tactics, but by keeping their lights on they may as well have been wearing red coats in broad daylight.

He worked his way back to the rear of the building, keeping low to stay hidden in the fog that seemed unable to escape the walls.

"Get those doors open!" one of the men shouted from the front.

Dak knew he had to move fast now. When the doors opened, his camouflage would be gone in seconds.

He hurried around the back-right end of the truck and found four more targets. Something wasn't right.

There'd been five before. Had the fifth guy run to the front to help with the doors?

Dak reached another conclusion.

Pickford had to be the fifth guy, the general in the midst of his soldiers. Instead of staying in the back of the lines, though, this commander simply didn't turn on his light.

Dak noted the formation of the four men, standing in a box shape.

Pickford would be in the center.

Maneuvering carefully through the fog, Dak lined up the sights of his pistol and tightened his trigger finger.

Loud squeaks screamed from the front of the building where Pickford's men rolled away the heavy doors.

Then Dak saw Pickford's head appear as the fog began to clear. He was standing exactly where Dak figured.

Making a slight adjustment, Dak took one more step toward the target and... tripped over something on the floor.

He stumbled forward and hit the ground hard, only able to slow the fall with his elbows.

The jarring landing caused his trigger finger to pulse once. The bullet shot wayward into the ceiling.

The men in the middle heard the crash and the silenced shot. They turned their attention to the spot where it came from and opened fire.

Dak rolled out of the way with a nanosecond to spare.

He stopped with his back against a steel drum. Dak knew the magazine in the right-hand gun was running low. The left one was still good, though.

"He's over here!" Pickford shouted.

"Well, that'll bring the rain down on me," Dak muttered. *But I still have the element of surprise.*

He dove to the right and rolled up between a wooden crate and a steel barrel. With the opening at the front sucking the smoke out into the fresh, dewy air, the targets were exposed—something Pickford and his men hadn't counted on.

Dak took out the first one between him and Pickford. Two shots dropped the guy in an instant.

Now nothing stood between Dak and Pickford.

He looked at the man without pity or mercy, lined up his chest as the mob boss turned around at the sight of one of his men going down.

Dak savored the look of panic on Pickford's face. This man who'd murdered countless people in his desperation for power now stared into the pool of his own mortality.

"Night-night," Dak said and squeezed the trigger.

The weapon clicked, but not from a discharge.

Dak winced for not switching to the other pistol. "Come on."

The one in his right hand was empty.

He took aim with the left, but now Pickford was on the move, retreating toward the open door.

Within two seconds, he was blocked by the cargo truck and his three remaining guards.

Dak twitched his right eye in frustration, then blasted two rounds into one of the other guards a second before they opened fire.

He rolled back to where he'd been before at the end of the steel drums. He raised up on one knee and quickly aimed as he'd done so many times, both in combat and in training. Two clicks. A pause. Then two more clicks.

Both men were dead before they hit the floor, each with a hole in their skulls.

More voices shouted, and footsteps clapped on the floor around the other side of the truck. The cacophony included a series of muted pops and clicks from suppressed weapons.

Bullets pinged off the barrels and sparked from the walls all around Dak. He was pinned down with no way to escape. The nearest door was twenty feet away, but the path to it was in the open. He'd have to be the best tango dancer in the world to dodge all the bullets to reach it.

He was just glad these steel drums at his back didn't have fuel in them.

Then Dak noticed a canister with faded black letters on it in all caps: PETROL.

"Oh great," he said. One stray bullet could turn him into a burned biscuit in seconds.

The truck's engine rumbled to life behind him. Dak sighed. This was his one chance to get to Pickford. He didn't even care about the crown right now. He needed to find Mia. She had to be somewhere nearby. He hoped.

The truck motor groaned, and Dak knew his opportunity was

getting away. He eyed the gas can again, and an extremely foolish idea popped into his mind.

Dak reached over and grabbed the fuel can by the handle. He pivoted and swung it like an Olympic hammer thrower.

As he released the handle, Dak spun around and extended his pistol toward the flying canister.

Four gunmen stood in the open with their pistols aimed in Dak's direction. In his periphery, Dak saw the truck lurch ahead toward the opening.

He fired a single shot and dropped to the floor as the bullet punctured the fuel can. A loud boom rocked the warehouse.

Dak felt a wave of heat wash over him, and then in an instant it was gone.

Men screamed from somewhere behind him. When he stood up again, he saw the gunmen in flames. Two were on the ground, unmoving, while the other two rolled around trying to douse the flames.

Dak ignored them and took off at a sprint after the cargo truck.

The vehicle bounced through the door and veered right as Dak caught up to it.

He stumbled and nearly fell to the ground, but managed to keep his balance. The gun in his hand, however, slipped out of his grip. He couldn't stop to get it, or the truck would get away.

Making up his mind, Dak leaped for the back of the truck and caught the next-to-last rung of the metal ladder with his right hand.

His fingers wrapped around it. The muscles and tendons in his forearm strained. Dak's feet bounced on the ground as he struggled to pull himself up. He swung his left hand up to the ladder and grabbed it next to the right and dragged himself up onto the ladder beside the mechanical lift.

Dak leaned around the edge of the truck and looked into the rearview mirror but couldn't see Pickford in the dark cab.

It didn't matter. He'd see him soon enough.

Dak flipped up the clasp that locked the cargo bay door in place and then raised the door.

Inside, he found crates, each full of cardboard boxes. One of the boxes had been opened, and Dak saw the plastic-wrap package.

"That... is a lot of heroin," Dak realized.

The truck hit a big pothole and Dak nearly fell out. He managed to adjust his feet enough to keep his balance and then stumbled forward to the front of the truck.

Dak didn't have a weapon, but a rack of rebar hung on the wall offered Dak a solution.

He couldn't see into the truck cab, but he had a rough idea of where the driver was.

He removed a rod from the rack and planted his feet wide on the floor. Then Dak thrust the hard metal through the front of the bay.

Just as he suspected, the walls were thin—mostly made of cheap material.

Dak drew back the rod, and before he could jam it through again, bullets tore through the wall and shot out the back of the truck.

He ducked back to the passenger side as the driver fired wildly. When the shooting stopped, Dak took his makeshift weapon and speared it through the wall again, this time at an angle.

The truck jerked to the left, and his weight threw him off balance, sending him stumbling into the wall.

His shoulder hit it hard, and a sharp pain climbed up through his neck.

Dak fought through it and stood up again, this time bracing himself on the front cargo bay wall. The driver weaved back and forth.

Dak picked up the rebar and steadied himself again. The truck swerved left to right and back again, but Dak kept his knees bent and flexed with every move.

He raised the rod with both hands, took aim again, and stabbed it through the wall.

The truck jerked a little, then Dak felt it accelerate.

He tumbled toward the back of the cargo bay, hit a crate of smack, then rolled up over it. Dak grasped at the boxes but only managed to grab two packages of heroin as the momentum of the truck surged forward.

Dak fell through the open door and into the air.

He yelled something unintelligible. Even he didn't know what word he said as his body tossed through the air toward the ground.

Instinctively, he tucked his arms under his chest a second before he hit the ground.

Dak rolled on the wet pavement amid a cloud of golden dust. His head hit a few times, but as he came to a stop, he didn't feel any dizzying wave of nausea knock him senseless.

He stood up fast, only feeling a slight pain from his shoulders and knees, and he looked back toward the truck. A trail of heroin stretched from where he landed to where he now stood, and Dak realized the bags had cushioned his fall and maybe saved him from a couple of fractures.

The truck only traveled another two hundred feet before it barreled into a warehouse on the right.

The frail vehicle smashed into the corner wall and crumbled. Smoke instantly billowed out of the previously flat hood.

Dak ran toward the crash, now feeling a tightness in his knee that wasn't there a minute ago.

No time to worry about that. Pickford is no good to me dead. Not yet.

Dak stopped at the wreckage and cautiously looked up through the window on the driver's side. The man behind the wheel was slumped over to his side, but that didn't mean the guy wasn't faking.

Cautiously, Dak threw open the door and ducked back, fully expecting a series of gunshots.

None came.

As he caught his breath, Dak looked back into the cab and saw the rebar sticking through the guy's chest and into the dashboard.

Dak climbed up the step into the cab, hoping Pickford still had a few of his own breaths left.

"George? Where is she? Where is Mia?" Dak lifted the guy by the shoulder and then saw his face.

It wasn't George Pickford.

37

The sound of squealing tires stung Dak's heart almost more than any kind of disappointment or pain ever had.

He knew in that moment that Pickford was getting away. And at that distance, Dak could never catch him.

He let go of the rung on the side of the truck and dropped down to the ground, immediately looking back toward warehouse 42.

A maroon sedan sped away in the other direction.

"No," Dak said.

"What?" Will asked through the radio. "You okay, Dak?"

"Will?" Dak had forgotten about his partner during the radio silent attack.

"What?"

"Pickford. He's getting away. Dark red sedan. I don't know where Mia is, but he—"

"He's not getting away, Dak," Will corrected. "Only one way in and out of here right now. And I'm watching it."

Dak started running again. At first at a trot. Then a gallop.

The injured knee hurt with every step.

Dak cut to the left between two buildings and sprinted toward the fence. Fatigue gnawed at him. His legs felt like pudding, and his lungs burned.

"Be careful," Dak suggested. "Mia might be in the car with him."

Will didn't reply right away.

"Will? Do you copy? Mia might be in the vehicle."

Nothing.

Dak forced himself to run faster. He hadn't realized how far the truck had gone. The entrance was a good three hundred yards away.

His feet pounded the pavement with every step. But Dak felt like he was running in mud.

Then he saw headlight beams circle up ahead. Three seconds later, the sound of the car's engine revving echoed down the thoroughfare, paired with two headlights tilting hard to the right as the driver steered the car around the corner and into the lane.

"Will? Do you copy? Be advised. Mia could be in the car. I repeat Mia might be in that vehicle."

No response.

The sedan roared down the lane toward the entrance.

Dak had been slightly closer at first, but on foot there was no chance he could reach the gate before Pickford. Not that it mattered. Dak didn't have a weapon on him at the moment, but he knew Will did.

Unfortunately, by the time he reached his friend it would be too late. That put all the responsibility squarely on Will.

Trust your team, Dak, he heard the voice of Tucker in his head.

The commanding officer had a sit-down with Dak back when they were still on the same side—fighting in the Middle East.

Dak had always wanted to do things himself and not lean on others. It wasn't because of a sense of pride that Dak tried to do everything; he didn't like being a burden, and Dak had never felt comfortable about sending his men into a situation where all of them might not come out—unless he was in the mess with them.

He knew a guy who'd been in Vietnam—a former baseball player who'd been drafted into the army. That guy had three months left on his tour when his Jeep was hit by a Viet Cong rocket. He'd lost his eyesight from shrapnel, and one of his legs had been blown off.

And it hadn't even been his assignment. He'd been asked to send two vehicles through a particularly dangerous part of the jungle, and Dak's friend was unwilling to send someone on a mission like that without doing it himself.

So, he had fallen on the proverbial sword.

Dak had always done things that way, too, until Tucker had that talk with him.

It was one of the few things the commanding officer had ever contributed to Dak's life other than his current predicament. The man, evil as he might be, understood what it took to win battles.

In turn, Dak became a better leader as a result.

Trust your team, his mind echoed. *Trust Will.*

Dak hit the throttle on the last strips of energy he had left and kept sprinting.

His legs felt heavier with each step, as though they were being pulled down by the earth's core itself.

The speeding car lurched forward as Pickford stepped on the brakes. Then he yanked the vehicle to the right, driving through the gate with tires screeching on the pavement.

Dak was still a good sixty yards from the entrance to the docks. But he wouldn't give up. Despite another voice in his head telling him that all was lost, he couldn't stop running.

He had to try.

"Will? Come in. Do you copy?"

Dak felt a needle of worry stick through his gut. It injected cortisol into his abdomen and spiked his anxiety even more.

Something happened to Will, he thought.

Just as Dak reached the gate, he'd already prepared himself to find his friend with a knife in his back or a bullet hole in his head.

Five steps before he made it to the gate, Dak heard the car's tires squeal again. Then the engine roared loudly. He took a few more steps and turned the corner in time to see the red sedan zoom over the rise and disappear behind the other side of the hill.

A pause filled the air. Then a crash.

Dak had never felt such a pull of two conflicting emotions in his life: Relief that Pickford had wrecked the car battled with the overwhelming fear that Mia was in the car with him, and could have been seriously hurt—if not worse.

Dak summoned more energy than he thought he had left, and ran harder up the gentle slope.

"Dak? You there? I stopped the car."

"Will? You're okay?"

"Why wouldn't I be?"

"I've been calling you for the last few minutes."

"Sorry. I must have been sitting on the button."

"You were sitting down?" Dak asked

His friend appeared from the darkness just ahead. He stood up behind a row of crates, saw Dak, and joined his friend running up the hill.

"Did you hear the crash?" Will asked.

"Yes," Dak said, gasping. "You were sitting down?"

Will looked over at Dak with a smirk. "You seem hung up on that. Yes. I was sitting. Waiting to pounce like a coiled snake."

"Great... metaphor," Dak offered. "I hope you didn't hurt Mia."

"She's in the car?"

Dak clenched his jaw in frustration. "Maybe."

"I shot out the tires, so she should be okay."

"Let's hope so."

"You sound like you've been running a while," Will commented, barely feeling his heart rate tick up.

"Shut... up."

Will only laughed as they reached the top of the hill.

It didn't take more than a second for them both to see the wrecked car up ahead. Steam poured out of the crumpled hood where the grill had struck the corner of a brick building.

"Come on," Dak urged and found one last surge. The two rushed toward the car.

Suddenly, the driver's side door flew open, and Pickford fell out.

The man collected himself and stood again, then looked back and saw the two Americans running toward him.

Still a few hundred feet away, Dak knew the guy wasn't going to just surrender.

Sure enough, he took off running and disappeared around the corner into an alley.

"We got a runner," Will announced, his breath finally catching up to the cadence of Dak's.

"Check the car," Dak said, ignoring their quarry for the moment. He had a bigger worry.

"You have a gun?" Will asked, looking his friend over.

"Not... at... the moment."

They skidded to a stop, Dak by the passenger side back door, Will by the front. He aimed his gun inside but saw nothing. "It's empty."

"Open the trunk," Dak ordered and shifted his feet to position himself behind the vehicle's rear bumper.

"You sure?" Will asked.

"Do it."

Dak braced himself for anything—a gunman waiting in the trunk ready to blast him to oblivion, a pile of drugs or guns, or Mia.

The lid clicked.

Dak didn't hesitate. Reaching under the lip of the trunk lid, he pulled it up and found the young woman curled up inside in the fetal position.

She looked out into the dark night with fear in her wide eyes. That terror evaporated the second she saw Dak's green eyes.

He reached in and pulled her out, setting her on the bumper as Will stepped around the corner. "Are you okay?" Dak asked, brushing her hair back over her right ear.

She nodded, but the tears in her eyes told the truth.

"Will, can you cut her out of these?" Dak asked, pointing to the duct tape and the zip ties.

"Sure thing."

"Is he dead?" Mia asked. "Is Pickford dead?"

Dak turned to his friend. "Not yet. But he will be soon."

Will knew the look the second he saw it. He nodded and handed his pistol to Dak.

"Go get him."

"Be careful," Mia warned as Dak charged around the vehicle.

Will shook his head. "You don't know him very well, do you? Careful isn't really in his vocabulary."

Dak didn't hear the conversation as he sprinted into the alley.

Pickford could have been hiding anywhere in there. But the mob boss had made a fatal error.

He'd run into a dead-end street.

The walls closed in around Dak as he continued forward. At a dumpster, he stopped and waited, then burst around the corner with the gun in the lead as he checked behind the metal object.

He was about to check behind a pile of trash on the other side of the alley when he heard a scuffing sound from up ahead.

His eyes adjusted slowly due to the dim lights hanging along the walls over every business's back entrance. But where he heard the sound there were no lights. Only a dark wall standing twelve feet high blocked the way.

Dak heard a grunt, then the sound of shoes hitting the pavement.

"It's no use, Pickford," Dak said. "You're not getting over that wall."

Pickford's head snapped around. He raised a pistol and fired.

Dak dove out of the way, though the bullet didn't even come close to grazing him.

He rolled to a stop amid four more shots, then crouched behind a stack of pallets.

"I'll kill you, Harper!" Pickford shouted. "This isn't your fight! You don't belong here!"

"Not this sad story, George. You can do better than that."

The subsequent silence told Dak the man wasn't listening. He may have been reloading his weapon, though Dak doubted it. He didn't hear the usual sounds; quiet as they were, in this alley he could hear a mouse's heartbeat.

"That crown is priceless, Harper. Take it. It's yours. Sell it if you want to. Just don't kill me. Okay? You just walk back out of this alley, and we'll pretend none of this ever happened."

"Can't do that, George," Dak countered. "Your mistake is thinking this is all about the crown. That changed when you messed with Mia."

"The girl?" Pickford scoffed. "Fine. Take her, too. Do whatever you want with her."

"We already have her. But thanks for the offer. She's safe now. Which is more than I can say for you."

Dak noticed a beer bottle on the ground to his right. He picked it up and threw it across the street. The glass shattered against the wall and splashed onto the ground.

Immediately, Pickford opened fire at the place where the bottle hit. Bullets ricocheted off the wall and disappeared into the night.

Dak spun around the corner of his cover, lined up his sights, and fired one shot. The round snapped through the air and struck the target dead center.

Pickford howled. He dropped his weapon and clutched his right leg with both hands as dark crimson started leaking from just above his knee. He collapsed to the ground and rolled over onto his side, pulling the wounded appendage up toward his chest as he kept squeezing it amid a never-ending stream of profanity.

Dak approached the man with his pistol still drawn, pointed at Pickford's head.

The mob boss swore at Dak and everyone else for his misfortune.

Dak kicked his pistol away and stepped on the man's shoulder to keep him from rolling around.

Pickford grunted in protest. "Ah, my shoulder."

"I'd be more worried about your knee," Dak said. "But you do you."

"Don't be a fool, Harper. Take the crown and that little... whatever she is to you, and leave my city. The cops can't help you. Too many of them are on my team. And there's the matter of the assassin."

"Oh," Dak interrupted. "Yeah, I'm afraid that guy won't be chasing me any longer. He had an unfortunate accident at Miles' flat earlier."

Pickford frowned.

"Yeah," Dak went on. "You hitched your wagon to the wrong horse on that one."

Pickford swallowed, desperation filling his eyes. "Come to work for me," he offered. "I can pay you more than whatever you're getting right now. Just... get me to my doctor. He'll take care of all this. Then we can talk about what it would take to make you my new head of security."

Dak shook his head. "The lips of a desperate man always shake," he said. He couldn't recall where he'd heard that quote, but it seemed appropriate for this moment.

"And I don't need your cops," Dak added. "I have something better." He took out his phone, searched for a number while Pickford wriggled underfoot, then pressed the green Call button.

A woman's tired voice answered after two rings. "Which prison in which country are you in, Sean?"

Dak laughed. "I'm not in any prison. Not yet, Ms. Starks."

"Oh, Dak? New phone, I see."

"I have to bounce around. You know that."

"Yes, I do. Unfortunately, I haven't been able to locate Colonel Tucker for you. I hope that's not what this is about."

"It isn't. But I appreciate you trying."

"What can I do for you?"

Dak looked down at his prisoner and grinned like the devil in a hot tub. "I need a favor."

38

Dak sat at the end of the bar facing the exit, just like he always did.

The Cask & Crown pub only hosted a half dozen of patrons at this time of day, but the lunch crowd would come soon, and with it a bustling rush hour of food and booze before everyone headed back to work.

He sipped his lager slowly as he watched the local news play on the television over the bar.

A news anchor spoke in tight staccato notes about the arrest of George Pickford and his subsequent suicide two days later in custody.

Dak wasn't surprised.

He knew Pickford was a wanted man, not just by honest law enforcement but also—perhaps even more—by his rivals in the other mob families.

Dak didn't have to kill him. He knew eventually that would be taken care of by someone else.

Of course, whoever killed him had made it look like a suicide. Just like with so many people entwined with powerful political elites back home in the States and in Europe, or those with mob connections;

the one who got pinched always ended up taking a long swim in concrete boots.

"George Pickford was found dead in his prison cell earlier this morning, where he apparently hanged himself sometime during the night."

Dak heard the anchor's words but ignored her.

He knew the truth about those kinds of things. It was one of the reasons he was okay with letting the man be taken into custody—after Emily Starks from the Axis Agency had made a few calls—that is.

He knew he could trust her, and that anyone she sent to the scene could also be trusted.

Before Pickford could pull any strings, his known associates were alerted to the arrest. The man would never have seen a trial. Or prison time.

Dak's phone buzzed in his pocket. "Thank you," was all it said.

"You're welcome, James," Dak said.

Dyer had managed to escape Pickford's noose. But if he didn't clean up his act and get some help for his problems, he'd just end up right back at someone else's gallows.

A minute passed before he received another text.

"I put in a call to Mr. Schultz at the IAA, like you said," Dyer replied. "He said he'll give me a call next week. Said there may be some things I can help them with. I really appreciate it."

"Good," Dak responded. "You can trust Tommy. He's a good guy. Runs a good outfit there in Atlanta. They could use a knowledgeable guy like you, I'm sure. Best of luck going forward."

"Thanks, Dak. Same to you."

Dak slid the phone away from his nearly empty plate and picked up a chip. He chewed on it for a few seconds before his phone buzzed again.

He rolled his eyes, hoping it wasn't Dyer again. The man had already thanked him. Mission accomplished.

But it wasn't Dyer. It was from another area code, this time in the States.

Dak recognized the number *423* immediately.

He opened the message and read it.

"Call me."

Dak did as told and called the number. Boston picked up after the first ring.

"You're fast," the kid said.

"And you're demanding for a thirteen-year-old. You are thirteen now, right?"

Boston laughed. "Yeah. I just turned thirteen."

"Happy birthday."

"I mean, it was a few months ago, but thank you."

"Happy belated, then."

Boston giggled again. "Okay. Okay. Enough about birthdays. Great job on the crown. I knew you could do it."

"Yeah. Apparently, the guy who had it left it in his car when he crashed it and took off on foot. We found it in the backseat floorboard."

Dak recalled going back to the sedan and finding Will and Mia there with peculiar, secretive looks on their faces.

With the cops swarming around, they weren't about to pull the Welsh Crown out for all eyes to see, and instead had kept it hidden in one of Will's tactical bags until they were away from the authorities.

"We were lucky," Dak said.

"Yeah, right. You sure seem to be lucky a lot."

"Luck is my superpower."

Another laugh.

"I would love to have that power. Maybe not as much as flying, but it would be cool."

"You only call me when you have a reason, Boston. Don't tell me you already have another job for me."

"Well, if you don't want it, no problem. It can wait. Or I can give it to someone else."

Dak's eyebrows dove toward his eyelids with a frown. "Someone else? I thought I was the only one."

He knew the kid was messing with him but played along anyway.

"Okay. Okay. You are. But I gotta keep you on your toes."

"Good man. What's the gig?"

"What do you know about the Scythian Empire?"

Dak shrugged. He'd studied a good bit of history, but world history covered so many cultures, civilizations, and people that it was difficult to dive deeply into all of them. So, he'd sampled much of it like a buffet, learning a little bit about much, but not much about any specific thing other than United States history.

"Nomadic people, I think. Right? Lived on the steppes over in Russia, Ukraine, that area. How close am I?"

"You're dead on," Boston answered. "They were led by a nomadic warrior tribe of royals. And they occupied what is now Eastern Ukraine, Southern Russia, and parts of Kaz... Kaztck...."

"Kazakhstan?"

"That's the one. I can never say those Stan countries right."

"Some thirteen-year-old you are," Dak teased.

"Ha. Good one."

Nothing fazes this kid.

"What about the Scythians, Boston? Did someone take one of their prized artifacts or something?"

"You could say that."

Dak paused, wondering what the kid meant by that. It wasn't like him to be coy.

"Okay...."

"Well, I hesitate to even mention this one to you. It's really dangerous. And I don't know if it's possible or even worth it."

Dak stiffened his spine and looked around the room, making sure no one was looking at him. Not that they could hear what the kid was saying anyway.

"What's the job, Boston?"

"It's probably impossible. But it also sounds like an important gig. And it's five hundred."

"Thousand?"

"Yes."

"Um. I'm pretty sure I'll say yes no matter what the job is for that amount of money. Must be a pretty important artifact."

He didn't tell Boston that he'd given half of his cut to Will, plus a little extra he left in an account for Mia. When he'd told her goodbye earlier that morning, he left an account number and access codes in one of her jacket pockets—along with a note explaining how to get the funds, and some suggestions as to what to do with them.

She was going to be okay. And so was her brother. They would leave this town and never look back, forging their own path to a happier, more fulfilling life somewhere else in the world.

"Artifacts," Boston said.

"What's that?"

"Artifacts. Plural."

"What do you mean? Plural? How many artifacts are we talking about? And do you know who has them?"

A pause came through the phone before the kid spoke again. "Well, we don't know exactly where they are or who has them, which is usually where you come in anyway."

"How many, Boston?"

"Two hundred. Give or take two."

Dak's eyes widened. "What?"

"One hundred and ninety-eight, to be exact."

"That accounts for the two," Dak quipped. "What on earth are you talking about? That's a whole museum's worth of stuff."

"Exactly." Boston paused for effect.

Dak puzzled over the answer.

"A few weeks ago," Boston explained, "as you know, the Russian military invaded Ukraine."

"Hard to miss that one."

"Right? Well, turns out that the Russian president ordered the army to seize artifacts from a major museum in Ukraine. The museum director was captured and tortured, but she wouldn't give up the location of the artifacts, which she and other workers had hidden in boxes in a basement there. Eventually, the Russian-appointed 'curator' located them and extracted the priceless treasures back to Russia—I assume to Moscow."

Dak's face paled.

"Dak?" Boston asked after getting no response for nearly a minute. "You there?"

"Yeah. I'm here. I'm just trying to understand how I heard you wrong, because for a second there it sounded like you want me to go into Moscow and track down two hundred stolen artifacts that were taken by the Russian military and are probably sitting in the president's office at the Kremlin at this very moment."

"One hundred and ninety-eight."

Dak snorted. "You're right. This one does sound impossible."

"Yeah, I know. But I had to ask. It's a massive cultural loss for the region and for the nation of Ukraine. None of that stuff belongs to the Russians. It was a shot in the dark. I'll call you when I find you another job."

"Hold on," Dak said. "I didn't say I wouldn't do it. Nothing is impossible."

"Really?" Boston sounded like he was trying not to sound excited.

"Yeah. It'll take a lot more planning logistically, but I'll take a look at it. Let me get back to you. Okay?"

"Sounds good, Dak. You're the best."

"I know. That's why you pay me."

Boston laughed. Dak did, too.

"Take it easy, kid. I'll let you know soon."

"Okay. Thanks, Dak."

He ended the call, and Dak set the device down on the surface next to his plate. He lifted the glass to his lips as Will walked back into the bar from the bathroom down the hall to the left.

"What was that about?" Will asked, noting the phone call. He eased into his seat and knocked back the last quarter of beer left in his glass.

Dak eyed his glass curiously for a moment, then tilted it away from him, inspecting the bubbles as they drifted to the top of the golden liquid.

"I just got a call for a pretty challenging job," Dak said.

"Already? From the kid? Man, that's quick. You haven't even cooled off from this one."

"I never warmed up either."

Will chuckled. "Good one."

"It's in Russia."

Will's smile vanished. "What?"

"It's in Russia."

"I heard that."

"Then why did you say what?"

Will ignored the rhetorical question. "The same Russia that's in a war right now in Ukraine?"

"You heard of another?"

"Fine. What does the kid want this time? Did the Russian army take a golden goose statue or something?"

"More than that. And this gig pays way more."

"It better if you're going to have to go into Russia."

"You're coming with me." Dak kept his eyes on the beer.

"Yeah, thanks. But I like breathing. I'll pass."

"It pays a quarter mil each."

"When do we leave?" Will's tune changed instantly.

"It'll be dangerous, Will."

"Yeah, thanks. I got that when you said Russia."

Will looked around at the other people, making sure no one was listening. Just in case.

"They're so preoccupied with the war in Ukraine right now, they won't even notice us."

"You mean a couple of Americans walking around in their country? The country that is right now being told Americans are evil?"

"Yep. Should be easy."

"Nothing with you is ever easy," Will said, pointing a finger at his friend. "But for that amount of money, I'm willing to rough it a little while."

Dak smiled. "So, you're in?"

Will looked at his watch. "Nothing on my calendar is demanding my time right now."

"Good. I just need to make one call first."

"One call?"

"Yeah. To an acquaintance I met in Mumbai not too long ago. I think he might be able to help us navigate the Russian criminal underworld."

"Who is he?" Will wondered.

"Better you meet him before I tell you."

THANK YOU

I just wanted to say thank you for reading this story. You chose to spend your time and money on something I created, and that means more to me than you may know. But I appreciate it, and am truly honored.

Be sure to swing by ernestdempsey.net to grab free stories, and dive deeper into the universe I've created for you.

I hope you enjoyed the story, and will stick with this series as it continues through the years. Know that I'll be working hard to keep bringing you exciting new stories to help you escape from the real world.

Your friendly neighborhood author,
Ernest

OTHER BOOKS BY ERNEST DEMPSEY

Sean Wyatt Adventures:
- *The Secret of the Stones*
- *The Cleric's Vault*
- *The Last Chamber*
- *The Grecian Manifesto*
- *The Norse Directive*
- *Game of Shadows*
- *The Jerusalem Creed*
- *The Samurai Cipher*
- *The Cairo Vendetta*
- *The Uluru Code*
- *The Excalibur Key*
- *The Denali Deception*
- *The Sahara Legacy*
- *The Fourth Prophecy*
- *The Templar Curse*
- *The Forbidden Temple*
- *The Omega Project*
- *The Napoleon Affair*
- *The Second Sign*

Other Books by Ernest Dempsey

lestone Protocol
Horizons End

Adriana Villa Adventures:
War of Thieves Box Set
When Shadows Call
Shadows Rising
Shadow Hour

The Relic Runner - A Dak Harper Series:
— *The Relic Runner Origin Story*
— *The Courier*
— *Two Nights In Mumbai*
— *Country Roads*
— *Heavy Lies the Crown*
— *Moscow Sky*

The Adventure Guild (ALL AGES):
The Caesar Secret: Books 1-3
The Carolina Caper

Beta Force:
Operation Zulu
London Calling

Paranormal Archaeology Division:
Hell's Gate

Guardians of Earth:
Emergence: Gideon Wolf Book 1
Righteous Dawn: Gideon Wolf Book 2
Crimson Winter: Gideon Wolf Book 3

ACKNOWLEDGMENTS

As always, I would like to thank my terrific editors, Anne and Jason, for their hard work. What they do makes my stories so much better for readers all over the world. Anne Storer and Jason Whited are the best editorial team a writer could hope for and I appreciate everything they do.

I also want to thank Elena at Li Graphics for her tremendous work on my book covers and for always overdelivering. Elena definitely rocks.

A big thank you has to go out to my friend James Slater for his proofing work. James has added another layer of quality control to these stories, and I can't thank him enough.

Last but not least, I need to thank all my wonderful fans and especially the advance reader team. Their feedback and reviews are always so helpful and I can't say enough good things about all of them.

COPYRIGHT

Copyright © 2022 by Ernest Dempsey

All rights reserved.

No part of this book may be reproduced in any form or by any electronic or mechanical means, including information storage and retrieval systems, without written permission from the author, except for the use of brief quotations in a book review.

All names, places, and events in this story were fictional or were used in a fictional way. Any relation to real places, people, or events is coincidental.

Made in the USA
Las Vegas, NV
13 December 2022

62384597R00194